T0277573

Acclaim for

THE NIGHTINGALE TRILOGY

Realm Award: Fantasy & Book of the Year

Calor

"A fascinating magic system and a captivating dystopian backdrop."

— PUBLISHERS WEEKLY

"Amid adventures, battles, and healings, Sephone shows her many gifts in . . . The Nightingale Trilogy."

— BOOKLIST

"Even as I closed the last page of *Memoria*, the memories lingered. Memories of a beautiful, fallen shadow world so like our own. Of intense darkness pushed back by light, however weak and flickering. Of flawed, broken, deeply appealing characters. And of the assurance that 'This world is only a copy of what was—and what will be.' This hope that one day all will be put right is woven throughout every word of J. J. Fischer's powerful, heartrending stories. I cannot recommend The Nightingale Trilogy highly enough."

— SARA DAVISON, award-winning author of
Lost Down Deep and *Driven*

"*Memoria*, the conclusion of The Nightingale Trilogy, is the beautiful and creative ending readers have been waiting for. With vivid imagery and heart-wrenching scenes of courage and sacrifice, we are taught that our hope lies not in this world but through Christ alone. Though surprising twists abound, *Memoria*, and the entirety of The Nightingale Trilogy, will stay imprinted in your memories well beyond the last page."

— V. ROMAS BURTON, author of The Legacy Chapters

"*Memoria* gives a powerful conclusion to a powerful series. What makes this final installment of The Nightingale Trilogy so impacting is its deep messages about pain, individual suffering and universal suffering, and how broken people in a broken world respond to it—messages that every reader will know and understand. In this book Fischer concludes her masterful tale that portrays the world as it is while weaving in the promise of what the world can be, balancing the reality of our pain with the reality of our hope. I was touched and profoundly impacted, and I know readers will be too."

— MELISSA J. TROUTMAN, co-founder of *The Valley*
and author of *Trust & Deception*

"A tapestry of action and allegory, romance and redemption, *Memoria* is a well-woven conclusion to a masterful series. Fischer delivers a powerful tale that's as good for the heart as it is stimulating for the mind. The Nightingale Trilogy inspires readers to seek out the real in a world full of counterfeits."

— MEGAN SCHAULIS, author of *Protector*

"Fantasy lovers, stop what you're doing and read the first two installments of The Nightingale Trilogy, because you're not going to want to miss a second of *Memoria*. Fischer's pen is magic to the page. Each twist, reveal, and act of bravery is brilliantly crafted into an explosive final act that will leave you breathless. From its heart-pounding action to its butterfly-inducing romantic tension, *Memoria* pushes everything wonderful in this world into a beautifully satisfying conclusion. Get this series as soon as you can. You will not regret it."

— LYNDSEY LEWELLEN, author of *The Chaos Grid*

"Just wow. *Memoria* is the chef's kiss ending to this immersive and spellbinding tale of beauty, angst, and longing. This is the kind of series you place on your bookshelf and sigh, knowing you will be back to read it again . . . and again."

— S.D. GRIMM, author of the Children of the Blood Moon series
and *Phoenix Fire*

MEMORIA

Books by J. J. Fischer

The Darcentaria Duology
The Sword in His Hand
The Secret of Fire

The Soul Mark Duology
The Soul Mark
Carver of Souls

The Nightingale Trilogy
Calor
Lumen
Memoria

Regency & Regicide

MEMORIA

THE NIGHTINGALE TRILOGY | BOOK 3

J. J. FISCHER

For Dad, whose vivid bedtime tales first introduced me
to the thrill of creating worlds and stories,
And for Mum, whose excellent grasp of English and grammar
helped me in writing them down.

memoria
A Latin word meaning *memory*.

"You must always remain with me," said the emperor. "You shall sing only when it pleases you; and I will break the artificial bird into a thousand pieces."

"No; do not do that," replied the nightingale; "the bird did very well as long as it could. Keep it here still. I cannot live in the palace, and build my nest; but let me come when I like. I will sit on a bough outside your window, in the evening, and sing to you, so that you may be happy, and have thoughts full of joy. I will sing to you of those who are happy, and those who suffer; of the good and the evil, who are hidden around you. The little singing bird flies far from you and your court to the home of the fisherman and the peasant's cot. I love your heart better than your crown; and yet something holy lingers round that also."

— *THE NIGHTINGALE*
BY HANS CHRISTIAN ANDERSEN (1843)

"There are no beautiful surfaces without a terrible depth . . ."

— FRIEDRICH NIETZSCHE

PROLOGUE

DORIAN

Dorian Ashwood had spent half his life in dark alleys, and apparently tonight would not be any different. A bird shrieked somewhere in the gathering dusk, an ominous prelude to what he knew must happen next. A foul wind conjured up mischievous dervishes of dust and ash that made it difficult to inhale deeply. Shadows grated against the splashes of lanternlight, illuminating a scene so horrific he could gouge out his own eyes and he would still see it painted on the backs of his eyelids.

Painted in the blood of his wife and daughter, their bodies sprawled nearby.

A shadow fell over him.

"Draven."

"Lord Adamo." Draven looked down at the bodies. "Oh, I *am* sorry. This would never have happened if they had not come after you. The trap was meant for you alone, Dorian. I intended for them to live."

"You killed them, Draven, and for that, you will pay." Why did it feel like he was quoting lines he had said over and over again?

"Oh?" Draven sounded surprised. "And how will you make me pay if you are dead?" A pause. "Besides, are you quite sure that you have naught left to lose?"

The bodies were gone. Another woman lay there now. White-blond hair, pale, freckled skin, and tawny-brown eyes.

"Sephone!" He dropped to his knees beside her. "I've been looking for you for months. I've come to save you."

Her reply was so faint he could barely hear her. "That's impossible."

"She's right, you know," said Draven conversationally, his knife blade now glinting in his hand. "It *is* impossible."

Dorian glared at him. "If you're going to kill me, then get on with it."

"I don't need to kill you," came the easy reply. "Or her, for that matter. Your darkness will destroy you both."

"I don't know what you're talking about—" Dorian broke off as Sephone stiffened with a gasp. Black threads advanced from her chest toward her throat, a delicate pattern of vines that began no thicker than spider's silk and steadily grew in size until it seemed like a black-gloved fist encircled her neck.

She was wheezing now, each breath she took rattling in her rib cage, slowly strangling her lungs.

Wildly, Dorian looked around for the Reliquary, but only Draven stood there, his mocking gaze still trained on Dorian.

Dorian had to find an *altered healer* who could use the Reliquary to give Dorian's remaining years to Sephone, but Draven had gathered all the *alters* to himself.

Dorian's voice was thick. "It's too soon."

"I think you'll find that it's too late," Draven said, with a trace of venom.

Sephone's fingers scrabbled at her chest. "Dorian," she choked out as inky-black liquid leaked from the corner of her mouth. "I need to—"

"Don't speak," he said urgently. "Conserve your strength. Fight it, Sephone. You have to fight it! Don't let it get ahold of you."

But the poison already had a hold on her, and she no longer struggled against it. Every inch of visible skin was now streaked with black; even her hair looked as if it had been dipped in ink. Half-lidded, tawny eyes met Dorian's almost sleepily. He touched her hand, which was lifeless and cold.

He stroked her hair, wiping the poisonous ink from her lips even as more bubbled out. Another bird called, but this one's song was melodious and sweet. "Please. I won't watch you die. You cannot go."

She gasped for air and tried to reach for him. "But I . . . must." Suddenly, she sagged and her head lolled.

As his soul cried out in agony, something struggled to the surface of Dorian's mind. He lifted his head to Draven. "Tomorrow night, this will happen again. But it will be different. I'll save her."

"I think not, my lord. You do know what killed her, don't you?"

"All I know is that you did naught to help her." The words stung him more than they likely did Draven. He had done naught, either.

"Will you not admit it, Lord Adamo? Will you not claim ownership of the darkness that consumes everything and everyone you love?"

"Nay." He shook his head violently. "It was the poison. The poison killed her."

"I think we both know the truth, Dorian."

Dorian met Draven's eyes—his terrible, knowing eyes. Sapphire fire sparked in them like one of Asa Karthick's glowing spheres, and Dorian shuddered.

He jerked awake in the dawn light, gasping and streaming sweat, but he could still hear Draven's mocking voice, as clear as if the man were standing before him, declaring the awful truth Dorian had not accepted until this moment.

"It was *you*."

1

DORIAN

"So, let me get this straight."

Cass paced back and forth next to the fire, his arms gesturing wildly as sparks and smoke drifted toward the hole in the roof of the cavern. "We have no leads on Sephone's whereabouts—if we had any to begin with."

Cass pivoted abruptly on the spot, nearly tripping over Bear, who sat leaning against the cave wall with his long legs extended. At Dorian's subtle nod, he drew them closer to his chest, exchanging a mute glance with his twin brother, Bas.

The *lumen* didn't appear to notice as he went on. "No one has even caught a glimpse of Brinsley Winter in the three months that Sephone's been missing, which makes finding *him* impossible."

Thankfully, Cass didn't pause to recount the circumstances surrounding the disappearance of Sephone's brother: that Brinsley had used the Memosinian soldiers advancing on Nyx as a cover for his escape, and that none of them knew who had helped him. The guards assigned by Lady Xia to watch Brinsley had been struck on the back of the head. Neither man had seen their assailant, nor did they have any clues as to how Brinsley's rescuer had gotten through the locked door to creep up on them.

It was Silas Silvertongue and Thebe all over again.

"And without Brinsley," Cass continued, "we have almost no hope of finding Sephone." He paused in front of Dorian. "And now you tell us that Lady Xia wants us to keep looking. Where, I might ask? Does she think we're hiding Seph somewhere in these mountains?"

"I don't know what she thinks. But glaring at me won't help us to find Sephone any quicker."

"Perhaps," Cass shot back, "but it feels good to show you what I think of your leadership to date."

Dorian tossed the stick he'd been fidgeting with into the fire. "If you have any better ideas, Cass, feel free to share them. Don't hold your tongue."

"We wouldn't be in this predicament in the first place," Cass muttered darkly, "if you had just held *your* tongue."

Dorian flinched. Beside him, Jewel growled.

Next to her, Spartan held up a hand. "That's enough." His firm tone belied his youth. "Dorian has paid dearly for that mistake already."

"Nay. He's right." Dorian clambered to his feet and looked around at them: the Mardell brothers, whose devotion and loyalty to Dorian's family he had never forgotten; the acolyte, Spartan, whose previously shaven head now boasted a sheen of red-gold stubble; Cass, his blue-green eyes flashing behind a thin veneer of civility, likely close to running out of the liquor that suppressed his gift; and, finally, the wolf, Lady Jewel, who missed Sephone almost as intensely as Dorian did.

"Cass is correct," Dorian reiterated, absently rubbing his nose where the *lumen* had struck it, the same day Sephone was captured. It had healed over the past three months—mostly. He deserved no less a punishment for accidentally betraying her secret weakness to a man who had used it to steal her away.

Had she been injured that day? There had been signs of a struggle, and they had found blood at the scene, but Dorian still hoped it belonged to the guard who had died trying to save her. Even so, a greater danger awaited her now.

The Reliquary's power can only be accessed at a price. Whoever wields it must offer their lifeblood in exchange. Or the blood of another. Usually, the alter *whose power it enhances, but a substitute may also be used—a third person. Whatever the sacrifice, there must be blood . . .*

Even after all this time, Brinsley's words churned Dorian's insides. Sephone had been stolen for her gift—stolen for what she could do with the Reliquary. But her captor would be a fool to waste her life on one exchange, one sacrifice. He must be using substitutes.

Oh, Sephone. What horrors are you enduring?

Dorian shook himself. "We need a change of plan. If we are to have any hope of finding her, we have to rethink our strategy. Maybe we should go back to the beginning. To the start of the trail."

"Nyx was almost completely destroyed by Asa Karthick," said Bear, frowning. "There's no chance she's still being held there."

Sorrow stabbed at Dorian. He was glad Sephone hadn't had to witness the destruction of her birth city, for it was something Dorian wished he could forget. After Asa's unexpected display of mercy, Lord Grennor—the city's thane—had ordered Nyx's citizens to flee, leaving behind only the fighting men and some women, including Lady Xia. The ensuing battle had been fierce but brief. In the end, Asa had not needed the reinforcements from his father, for Asa's *alters* and the *altered* wolves known as Nightmares had overcome the city on their own.

When Lord Grennor fell in battle, Lady Xia had surrendered Nyx on his behalf. Before she could surrender herself, Dorian, Cass, Spartan, and the Mardell brothers had helped her and a small band of fugitives to escape. They included most of the remaining lords and ladies—some of whom were members of the old League—and Sephone's parents, who had refused to leave with the rest of Nyx's inhabitants. Together, they had sought refuge in the mountains named for Lord Grennor's ancestors, using the cover of the inhospitable peaks to evade the remaining Memosinian forces.

Asa Karthick had been furious that his prey had escaped him so easily. The rest of the people of Nyx had headed for Lethe's capital, Nephele, but they had not gone far when Asa's *alters* intercepted them. The *alters* had been ruthless, and from Lady Xia's reports, which came to Dorian and his friends a week later, barely a third of Nyx's people had made it to Nephele. That third had only survived because the Lethean army came out to meet them, driving the *alters* back.

"Our plan worked," Xia had announced with a sigh. "Nephele needed whatever time we could give them to finish the old-world weapons, and they had it. I only wish it did not come at such a great cost."

Once it was safe, Xia and the other members of the League had returned to her home city of Thebe to prepare for war, and at Dorian's request, she had taken Sephone's parents with her. Odiseas and Damae

Winter had become shells of their former selves after learning that their long-separated daughter had been betrayed by their only son—and that was saying something, for they had been nearly ghostlike before.

Dorian had reassured them as best he could. "We will find her," he had vowed to them the morning they departed. "*I* will find her. I promise."

Damae Winter had said naught, but her pale fingers had brushed Dorian's stubbled cheek in a consolatory gesture. She had lost weight in the week since Sephone had been kidnapped. Her husband had been the one to answer—a man who, Dorian was finding, had not lost his sharper faculties when he'd surrendered his memories.

"I suspect you *will* find her, Lord Adamo," Odiseas had said, "and we will thank you for it."

Fortunately, Lady Xia had agreed to Dorian's plan to remain in the Grennor Mountains to determine Sephone's whereabouts—though for her own, more politically expedient, reasons.

"Much hangs in the balance," she had confided in Dorian when they were alone. "Nephele's weapons will give us a tremendous advantage, but we are still greatly outnumbered. I fear that our people will suffer greatly if the war between Memosine and Lethe persists much longer."

Dorian had said naught as he'd studied her closely. Siaki Xia could be ruthless, but she was not heartless. He had often appealed to her compassion and sense of fair play.

"You were right, Lord Adamo. The only way to win this war, for either of our countries, is to end it before it begins in earnest. And Lord Draven—I refuse to call him King Draven—is the key to stopping the bloodshed."

"Then you—that is, the League—still plan to assassinate him."

"Aye. We think it is the best option. If Draven dies, Memosine may yet come to its senses."

"And what of his son, Asa?" Dorian had asked. "What if he chooses to fill the void his father's departure will create?"

Xia had cast a glance toward the mouth of the cave, where Spartan stood guard. She lowered her voice. "Perhaps his brother will know how best to stop him."

Dorian had frowned, for she'd evidently forgotten that the acolyte was chary of conflict. Not only that, but Dorian wasn't sure Spartan was completely on their side. "And how do you plan to eradicate Draven?"

She had raised clear eyes to his, and Dorian had blanched.

"Sephone," he said.

"She is still our best chance of infiltrating his defenses. We already know that his plans involve her and his son; we just need to arrange things so that *she* is the one making the plans."

"You're forgetting that Sephone has vanished from the face of the earth."

"Which is why I'm sending you to find her. You, the *lumen,* the acolyte, and your loyal men. Oh, don't look at me like that, Dorian. I know you would have remained to find her even if I forbade it. I'm not ignorant of the plans you've been making these past two days while we've sheltered in this cave."

Dorian's mouth had curved wryly. "I don't answer to you, Siaki."

"Aye, but you once answered to the League, and at the moment, I'm speaking for them." She had stepped forward to grip Dorian's hand. "Don't argue with me. This is what's best for Lethe *and* for Memosine. Find Sephone and the Reliquary, too."

"And the hooded man?"

She bit her lip. "We don't know that he isn't a friend—"

"He took Sephone against her will and killed the guard who tried to save her!"

"And he also saved your life in Idaea." Once more, she spoke quietly. "If this hooded man is truly an enemy of Draven, we may have found ourselves an ally. He may not have taken Sephone for a contrary purpose—in fact, we may even be working toward the same end. I know you care for her, Dorian, but think about it. More fates teeter on the edge of a knife than just hers. If Draven lives, Memosine and Lethe could destroy each other."

Dorian had bristled at Siaki's almost casual mention of his feelings for Sephone until he registered the latter part of her comment. "These weapons," he remarked just as casually. "You have said almost naught of what they do. And yet, just a few of them were enough to drive back Asa Karthick's *alters* to save the refugees from Nyx." Dorian stepped closer. "How did weapons, even ones based on old-world technology, repel *alters*?"

She had swallowed visibly. "I will tell you this as a show of confidence in our friendship, Dorian."

He'd waited.

"The weapons our scientists have been developing are based on technology from the world-that-was, aye. But they also rely on the magic of this world."

"What are you saying, Siaki?"

"Draven intends to breed *alters* to create a new class of humanity, and an unstoppable army. He is forcibly recruiting *alters* and killing or imprisoning any who dissent. You know this . . . it is why he wants Sephone. *Mems* will allow him to manipulate the memories of those who serve him and thereby alter history . . . and truth."

"As you say, I already know all this."

"We are up against *alters*, Dorian. *Alters* with powers we cannot defeat with ordinary weapons. It does not help that we have so few of our own *alters*—you and I both know that Lethe's vision of the future has never included gifted folk in the same way as Draven's. The new weapons, at least some of them, are intended specifically for *alters*. The science is somewhat difficult to explain, and the technology is both ancient and new, but they harness the lightning that targets gifted people."

Dorian had stared at her, dumbstruck. "And you're telling me this *now*?"

"Better now than later. Wouldn't you agree?"

"You're asking me . . ." Dorian had trailed off for a long moment, thinking of Sephone, Cass, Spartan, and any of the hundreds of *alters* he'd met. "How can you ask me to choose between the future of my kind and the future of my country?"

"Don't be so dramatic," she huffed. "I'm not talking about murdering Lethe's *alters*. You know me better than that. But if we are to face the army that Draven will send against us, we need to be prepared. Do whatever you can to find Sephone *and* the Reliquary—my network of spies and intelligence is at your disposal. And should this mysterious, hooded man be open for negotiation, then I want your word that you're willing to discuss an alliance. Whatever it means for Sephone."

"And now you're asking me to choose between my country and a woman I . . ." Dorian had stopped midsentence, uncomfortable beneath her piercing stare.

"I'm fully aware what I'm asking of you. But this is war. All of us stand to lose everything we love. You should know that better than anyone."

"Dorian. *Dorian*?"

The emphatic repetition of his name brought him back abruptly to the present, and Dorian looked into Bear's face, trying to recollect what had been said before he'd wandered into the past. *Again.*

But it was Cass who was speaking. "Thane?" The *lumen* scowled. "I hate to interrupt your daydreaming, but—"

"Aye, Nyx is destroyed," Dorian said to Bear. "But I doubt the hooded man would go far, especially with Asa Karthick's forces about." He used his boot to nudge an ember back into the fire. The blackened wood quickly flared to life. "I still believe he's somewhere in these mountains."

With a defeated sigh, Cass sank to the ground on the other side of Jewel. "It's been three months, Thane. She could be anywhere by now."

By the time you read this, I will be far away from here . . .

The words from Sephone's letter replayed in Dorian's mind, just as they had every night since her mother had given him the missive.

Asa Karthick visited me last night. He and his alters *are already here in Nyx. He has offered me a deal, and I accepted. If I go to him, he will leave Nyx alone and thousands of Letheans will live . . .*

Sephone had already done what Xia wanted—at least, she had planned to. She had sacrificed herself for her birth city, even though they had not accepted her. Given the choice, she would have done anything to save Lethe, and Memosine, too. Siaki knew that if she asked Sephone to kill Draven, Sephone would do it . . . no matter the cost. She had been brave and selfless since the beginning.

It was only Dorian who was the coward.

You have a powerful gift. I have always been so drawn to it, and to you, because in your presence I am not so afraid or so cold. And I mistook that for love. When I think back on it, I'm ashamed of how I acted and how I pushed you away. Forgive me, please?

Dorian's eyes burned at the remembering of those words, and he turned away from the others, lest they see his reaction. When he was once more master of himself, he addressed the *lumen*. "You said that Brinsley is the key to finding his sister. He said his part in the whole business was over, but I think—"

"He was lying," finished Cass.

"Aye. There's no way that an opportunistic man like Brinsley would distance himself from a lucrative venture. If he hasn't already, he will go after the hooded man."

"So, we double our efforts to find Sephone's brother," said Bear.

"And how do you suggest we do this, my lord?" asked Bas, who had barely spoken.

"The man is some kind of merchant. He had plenty of friends in Nyx, and there are many more towns in these mountains than the ones we've visited. Someone must have seen him or heard from him." Dorian glanced pointedly at the flask Cass was surreptitiously raising to his lips. "We will uncover the truth eventually. Though the more people we interview, the greater the risk of being sighted ourselves."

"I'm willing to take that chance," said Bas. Sephone's disappearance had shaken the guard more than Dorian had expected. It seemed that he'd grown fond of her in the time she'd travelled with them.

"Aye, me too," added Bear.

"Spartan?" Dorian asked, turning to look at the acolyte, who had said less than anyone over the past few weeks of searching the mountain caverns and towns. Was Spartan thinking of the man he and the rest of the Mysterium hoped would be the new king of Caldera? Or was it Asa Karthick, Spartan's warring half brother, who presently occupied his sober thoughts?

"Aye," he said, nodding. "I'm willing to keep searching."

Dorian smiled his thanks. "Something else has occurred to me. Brinsley claimed that the use of the Reliquary would require a substitute. If this hooded man is using Sephone for her gift, then he will need people. People who are less likely to be noticed when they go missing. Where else would he find them than in these remote parts?"

Cass leaned forward. "Then there'll be a trail of bodies to follow," he said pointedly.

Dorian nodded grimly and stood. "Get some sleep, all of you. We'll begin afresh tomorrow."

As they settled themselves on their bedrolls, Dorian turned to find Cass, and belatedly realized that he hadn't sought the *lumen*'s agreement before deciding their course of action. But he didn't seem angry—exactly the opposite.

"We haven't yet discussed, Thane," Cass said smoothly, "what we'll all do when we find her."

"What do you mean?"

"The Letheans are fighting back, with deadly results. If we find Sephone, will you return to the League, or make haste to Maera to defend your family? I, for one, have no desire to be caught up in this war."

"Then you'll go back to Marianthe?"

Cass gave a noncommittal shrug.

"Should the Karthicks defeat Lethe," Dorian warned, "they'll come for Marianthe next, you know. And you can't have forgotten you're a wanted man in your own country."

"Better a wanted man there than dead here." Cass's eyes narrowed. "As soon as we have her, I'm taking Sephone back with me."

"Against her will?" Dorian prodded, reminding him that the last time he'd asked her to go with him to Marianthe, she'd refused. "She's Lethean, Cass. She won't abandon her country or her family."

"Maybe the betrayal of her brother—a *Lethean*, you recall—will have changed her mind."

Dorian beckoned Cass away from the others to the mouth of the cavern where they'd sheltered for the past two days, recouping their strength and replenishing their supplies after months of constant searching. The night air was fresh and cool, but it carried the aroma of spring—a sweet scent that smelled uncomfortably like the snow blossoms that had first led Dorian to Sephone's family. His fingers strayed to the resin necklace around his throat, which had entwined itself with the chain that carried his and Lida's wedding bands.

Once outside, Dorian dropped his hand and lowered his voice.

"You said it yourself, Cass. It's been three months. Whatever Sephone's captor intends for her, and regardless of what Lady Xia says, it won't be pleasant."

"What does the lady thane say?"

"Xia believes the hooded man may be more friend than enemy. That he may be interested in allying with us against Draven."

Cass raised an eyebrow.

"I don't believe it, either. All I'm saying is, when we find her, Sephone may not be the same woman who left us."

Cass met Dorian's gaze. Even in the near darkness, Dorian felt his dislike. *The woman we both love,* Dorian meant, and he knew Cass registered his meaning. They had reluctantly formed a truce in order to find her, but Dorian was no more certain of Cass's allegiances than he was the hooded man's. The moment they found Sephone, Cass could betray them. Or even before, if it suited his purposes.

Dorian hadn't given Siaki his word to sacrifice Sephone for Caldera. He had his own plans for what he would do when they found her—and they didn't include sending her to her death. On the contrary, Dorian wanted her to live. He wanted her to have everything she had ever desired.

But he couldn't explain that to Cass. For one, he wouldn't believe Dorian.

"You didn't summon me out here to tell me that," Cass said at last, flatly. "And it's not as if the others are unused to our bickering."

"Nay," Dorian agreed, then hesitated. "I want you to promise that you'll let her decide."

"Between our countries?" The *lumen*'s mouth curved. "Or between us?" Cass patted his coat pocket, and Dorian heard the distinct crumple of paper. Judging by the scornful twist of Cass's lips and the smug light in his eyes, it was the letter Sephone had written him. Dorian had no idea what it said, just as Cass had no idea of the content of Dorian's letter. Both of them held their missive over the other; though Dorian was well aware that for him, at least, it was no advantage.

Sephone had been clear: she was saying goodbye to him forever. Had she said the same to Cass? Or had she been sorry to leave him? Had she realized, too late, that she loved him, but been forced to abandon him anyway?

We will probably never meet again in this world, but with all my heart, I hope that you will have a long and happy life . . .

"Whatever choice is necessary," Dorian replied—a vague but all-encompassing statement. His fingers once again drifted to the necklaces at his throat.

Cass's sharp eyes noticed the gesture and narrowed. "I'm not like you, Thane," he said, somewhat bitterly. "I always give people the choice to love me."

In your presence I am not so afraid or so cold. And I mistook that for love . . .

The *lumen's* words stung, more than Dorian cared to admit. "Neither of us can help our gifts," he said stiffly. "But I never coerced her."

"You never freed her, either."

The blow was fair. Three months was long enough to mull over all his actions, and he was heartily ashamed of them. If he could, he would do everything over. He would never try to cage Sephone . . . for in doing so, he'd lost her anyway.

Nay—he would set her free at the earliest opportunity. And when he did, he would face his greatest fear: that she would walk away from him. But, once again, he had no reason to explain all that to Cass.

When Dorian didn't answer his parry, Cass gave the faintest of scoffs. "Typical, Thane. But don't worry. When there's no longer any world to save, or people to rescue, or lost boys to love, she'll finally make the right choice."

He slipped past Dorian and returned to the cave.

Still smarting from Cass's rebuke, Dorian remained outside, inhaling the heady fullness of the breeze. Spring had come, and the Grennor Mountains, though rugged, were a place of unparalleled beauty. The sunrises in this part of the world were glorious, even through the gray. The world had never felt so alive, and yet Dorian had never felt so empty. More than anything, he wanted to close his eyes and enter a dreamless, emotionless void.

But every night, Sephone choked to death in his dreams, and he was barely clinging to hope. Hope that she was still alive and well and unchanged, even though the poison must surely be advancing through her veins—and rapidly if she was being forced to use her gift.

"I will free you," he whispered to the wind, praying it would carry his message to her and she would know he had not forgotten her. "I promise."

He missed her more than he could have ever thought possible—missed her, even though it had only been three months since he had admitted to himself that he loved her, and he still found himself, somewhat traitorously, grieving his wife.

But though he still loved Lida, his love for her felt more and more like a memory . . . more and more like it belonged to another life, another man. Even as he turned his face to the spring, it was winter that felt more vibrant, more vivid, more real. The woman in his arms had hair the color of ice rather than cornsilk, hair that silvered underneath a waxing moon rather than gleamed gold beneath the midday sun. She was the opposite of everything he'd ever thought he'd wanted in a woman, but somehow, she was everything he needed.

He remained outside for as long as he could, his senses straining for a hint of her on the breeze, searching his memories for any clue that might reveal where she'd been taken. Only much later, when he finally returned to the cavern and lay down on his bedroll, did he realize that Cass had done what Dorian had to Lady Xia. He hadn't answered Dorian's request to let Sephone decide.

And Dorian grimaced as he acknowledged that Cass had done it far more skillfully than he.

A light shone in my eyes. Was that real, or not?

Voices blurred above and around me, and a blotchy shape appeared in the corner of my vision. It came closer until I realized it was a face—a hooded, masked face, with only the eyes visible from within a swath the color of bleached bones. In contrast to the white, the eyes were blue and darkly lashed. A weaker blue than Lord Draven's, but no less dangerous.

I blinked sleep away and tried to focus.

"Come, Miss Winter," said a deep, rumbling voice as the light bobbed behind him. "Gather your strength. We are almost finished for the day."

All at once, I became aware of leaden arms and legs, a chest that carried the faintest of rattles when I inhaled, and a soul that ached.

"Soon, you can rest without interruption," crooned the voice, and a large hand rested on my shoulder. "Do what I say, just a little longer, and you will have a whole day tomorrow to sleep."

Sleep wasn't the inducement my captor believed it to be. Though I wasn't the one who bore the brunt of the memories, the use of the Reliquary, as I had learned, was not a perfectly seamless process, and things often leaked back through my connection to the others. I wondered if they felt my guilt, my shame at what I'd done. I hadn't slept through the night since I'd been abducted, however long ago that had been. Sometimes it felt like years.

"What do you want me to do this time?" I finally said, not bothering to disguise my weariness.

My early days of resisting the hooded man's commands were long over. I had learned, weeks ago, that more than one person would suffer if I struggled or refused to do what was demanded of me. Three fresh graves, somewhere beyond this foul prison, attested to that fact alone. I didn't know if the hooded man was an *alter*, but he liked to kill people in old-fashioned ways. The gorier, the better. He knew, of course, that I especially hated the sight of blood. He even knew about my fear of ice, though how he had discovered that, I had no idea.

The straw mattress beneath me dipped as the man perched on the side of my bed. He wasn't a large man, but he was tall and lean, and I'd learned, that first day when I'd tried to run away, that leanness did not equate to a lack of strength. But while he might be violent toward others, he had treated me well, almost like an honored guest. He had *tsked* over my broken wrist, instructed his masked minions to handle me carefully, and even when I'd initially refused to help him, he'd never once raised his voice. My room, though locked and guarded, was spotlessly clean and well-appointed.

In all my time as his captive, I hadn't missed a meal; though sometimes, if I had disobeyed him in some small way, a water ration would be delivered to me in the form of a bowl of ice shards.

"Now, Miss Winter," he said smoothly, and I raised myself to a sitting position, avoiding putting pressure on my still-tender wrist. Light strained to enter the room through the narrow window beside my bed. "I have one more task for you this afternoon."

I studied his face, trying as I had so many times before to ascertain his identity. His accent, slightly muffled through the fabric covering the lower half of his face, was neither Memosinian nor Lethean, and I didn't think it was Marianthean, either. His brows were pale like Brinsley's and my own, though Letheans didn't typically have blue eyes. No scars, moles, or other identifying features. His clothes appeared well-made, but they were plain and nondescript—some kind of shapeless robe, a continuation of the hood and mask concealing most of his face.

I was sure I didn't know him. But why would he hide himself from me, unless he feared recognition? Perhaps he covered himself for fear of my gift—but then, he didn't seem afraid of that, either.

He appeared to be waiting for my answer, so I nodded. By the slight creases next to his eyes, I guessed he smiled. "Very good, Miss Winter. Now, the task is simple. This afternoon's subject is a former member of Calliope's Council of Eight. One of the few, I'm told, who supported Lord Draven in his bid for kingship, and now a trusted advisor. This should be easy for you, given your loathing for Draven. I want you to discover whatever information you can from his mind. And then I want you to take his memories. All of them."

"All of them? For what purpose?"

The hooded man stood abruptly. "Have I ever explained myself to you before?" He snapped his gloved fingers. "Come."

My door creaked open, and two more men appeared, each of them masked but not hooded. One had dark hair, and the other's was fair, but the shadows leaking from the corridor beyond prevented me from discerning anything else about them. I had long since stopped looking for my brother; I hadn't seen Brinsley since the day he sold me to the hooded man and broke my wrist. It didn't stop me from wondering, night after night, why he had betrayed me. For money? An advantage of some kind? Or simply because he hated me?

As the dark-haired guard grabbed my gloved arm, I stood and allowed them to blindfold me. They only ever took me to one other room, but I imagined they wanted me to feel disoriented in case I ever got through the lock on my door. I always saw the same two guards, though there were others besides just the three of them. I'd woken twice on the overnight journey from Nyx to wherever we were now, and I'd seen at least half a dozen shadowy figures strewn around the campsite . . . and then there were the other prisoners, fodder for the hooded man's nefarious purposes. Judging by the thinness of the air and the frigid nights, we were now somewhere in the mountains.

I was propelled out into the corridor and steered along a drafty passageway. How, by the world-that-was, had they managed to capture one of Lord Draven's advisors? The other subjects to date had all been allies of Lord Draven, certainly, but their absence would not be immediately missed by him. They were mostly lowly guards or servants; the highest-ranking one had been a middling lord. The hooded man had only wanted information: about Lord Draven's whereabouts, about his plans for Lethe, even about Asa and Jerome and the other *alters*.

Once I had extracted everything of interest—and the hooded man always knew when I was holding something back—he would order me to wipe their memories. Usually only enough to erase any recall of their capture and subsequent interrogation; it would not do to alert Lord Draven to our presence or the possibility that the minds of his loyal subjects had been tampered with.

Dread coursed through me. Never before had the hooded man ordered me to wipe a mind completely. Such an action would destroy a person entirely, for what was someone without their memories?

Unbidden, Dorian entered my mind, and I grimaced. If he could only see what I had done—how the light ebbed from a person's eyes when I stole pieces of their past—he would never persist in his desire for such a thing to be done to him.

A door slammed shut behind me. The blindfold was tugged from my eyes; I immediately wished it had remained. This place would haunt me to the end of my days.

At the center of the room squatted a stone pillar, waist-high and hexagonal in shape. A heavy slab of stone covered its top, and on that slab rested the Reliquary, its petals unfurled and golden wires exposed. The central column of the relic glinted oddly in the lanternlight, the glass casting a greenish glow around the small room. I shivered, remembering how the poisonous black liquid had surged into the uppermost glass chamber of the hourglass from nowhere, slowly dripping into the lower chamber. At present, both chambers were empty.

Agonized groans punctured my observations, and I tore my gaze from the Reliquary. Arrayed around the pillar in a triangular shape were three long, narrow tables, each the approximate length and breadth of a human. Each table corresponded to one of the petals of the Reliquary, and two were already occupied. One held the groaning man, who was writhing against the leather straps that bound him to the table; the other bore a young woman, barely a year or two younger than I was. Fear clawed at my throat.

"Let us proceed," murmured the hooded man.

I yelped as the guards grabbed my arms. Paralyzed, I could only let them drag me over to the nearest table, where they forced me to lie on my back. Thick leather straps pinned my torso at the level of my armpits, my hips, and finally my ankles. My right wrist was similarly restrained beside me, while my other arm was extended above my head. The leather glove was tugged from my hand, and I felt the cool embrace of the wire glove; it immediately tightened around my fingers. I could no longer see either of the other captives, but I could feel the woman . . . then the man, as they likely forced his hand into the third glove. If I closed my eyes, I would be inside their minds.

I kept my eyes open.

"Remember," said the hooded man, leaning over me. "Information first, then a full mind-bleeding. I particularly want you to focus on Lord Draven's current whereabouts. He has long been eluding my spies."

"Why don't you just kill him?" I gasped as the wires bit into my skin, warming my flesh.

"The advisor, or Draven?"

"Both."

His eyebrows lifted. "It isn't so simple as that, Miss Winter. But I assure you, once you are finished with Draven's advisor, I have other plans for him."

"You want to capture Lord Draven alive," I said, suddenly understanding his ambitions. That was what all this had been leading to. He didn't just want to assassinate the new king of Memosine, he wanted to abduct him. But for what purpose?

He gave a tight nod. "I have plans for him, too." He patted my arm. "Now, be a good girl and close your eyes. We have work to do."

I should have been exhausted by the time I finished extracting all the information the hooded man wanted. My soul ached, aye. But it was the young woman connected to the Reliquary who bore the brunt of my exertions; it was her life force that allowed me to endure the extensive foray through someone else's mind, which would have been impossible on my own. I had never guessed that the Reliquary could be used in such a way, but it seemed that the presence of a third person allowed me to amplify my powers without becoming overly fatigued. And this was the most tiring interrogation yet.

It didn't help that I could feel every one of their fragile, spluttering breaths as if they were my own; every stab of pain as if it were me who had been tortured by the hooded man and not the advisor. The young woman's fear bled into mine, her frantic desperation eroding my composure. She had been taken from her home in the mountains by the hooded man's guards, and she knew naught of why. I tried to reassure her through the mental link that I would never hurt her, but I was no empath, and no *calor*. And I couldn't lend her courage I didn't possess myself.

"Very good," said the hooded man when there were no more secrets to learn. "You have done well, Miss Winter."

I recoiled at his praise, his silky tone. He might treat me well, and Lord Draven was my enemy, too—my sole consolation in assisting my captor—but the hooded man was no friend. No man of honorable intentions would kill innocent people to force me to do his will. I had concluded as much in my first week of captivity.

"Now," he mused, "you can perform the mind-bleeding."

The advisor's heart began racing, his breaths quickening. Through my connection to him, I registered a flurry of memories: his wife's laughing face, his son's first words, the day he was chosen as one of the Eight. Once again, I thought of Dorian. I had never known someone to cling to their memories with such desperation.

"*Now*, please, Miss Winter. I need not remind you of what will happen if you refuse."

I trembled, briefly retreating into my own memories. I could not help thinking of Lord Guerin and Traemore, forcing me to erase a past, over and over. But back then, I hadn't had the power of the Reliquary at my disposal. Now, I could do in one touch what I hadn't accomplished in many years of mind-bleedings. How many times had I longed for that kind of power? And now . . . it was nothing like I had imagined.

Returning to the advisor's mind, I showed him the memory I'd brought with me from my own: the hazy recollections of the three Letheans the hooded man had killed when I first resisted him. The youngest had been only a child, about the same age as the advisor's son.

This is what will happen if I don't do as he says, I told him. *I'm sorry, but I must obey him. I promise it won't hurt.*

That was the great advantage of being wounded by ice: you never felt a thing.

I felt his rising panic; he thrust the mental image of his son toward me, as if he still hoped to convince me to spare him. I winced at his desperation. He might be Lord Draven's man, but he was still another innocent—another man affected by the fear potions Lord Draven had used to take control of Calliope, then subsequently deluded by the lord's honeyed promises.

I'm sorry, I repeated. *He will know if I don't do it properly.* Warmth hummed through my fingertips, the glove burning hotter as it anticipated the release of power. In the advisor's mind, I knelt and touched my fingers to the dark, loamy earth of his consciousness. The ground hardened and solidified, ice streaking out from where I stood until it covered everything in sight. Nothing would ever grow there again.

The man's awareness changed; suddenly, he had no idea how he had gotten here. Who was he? What was he doing strapped to a table? Who was the stranger in his mind?

Chills needled my spine. Not long ago, I had visited a child's mind, but it was nothing like this. One was guilelessness and limitless potential; the other was a desolate wasteland of forgotten dreams.

He was nothing now. A wraith; a no-being. A ghost of future past.

Lifetaker, the old voices taunted me. But at least he had stopped groaning, probably forgetting the torture he had endured previously, though he would wonder how he'd come by the stripes on his back. I turned my attention to the young woman, glad the procedure was finally over and she could rest. The substitutes were always spent at the end of the mind-bleeding, but this one had been more extensive than the others. I hoped the hooded man would free her after today.

But there was naught. No flicker of consciousness, no memories, no gentle exhale of breath.

"I can't feel her mind," I said out loud, beginning to panic. Had she been disconnected from the Reliquary without my knowledge? The wires around my hand cooled and loosened, and my hand slid from the glove. The straps binding me to the table were undone, and I was half guided, half lifted from the table. The advisor still lay on his back, staring up at the ceiling, his eyes flicking vacantly back and forth.

I looked at the woman, and my throat constricted. She lay utterly still, her head tilted to one side, her eyes lidded. White-blond hair tumbled across her ashen forehead, shot through with thick streaks of black. Even from across the room, I could see the black marks veining her chest, her throat, her face, her arm. Her limp hand still rested in the metal glove, but the petal seemed to have wilted around her fingers. The Reliquary's hourglass was empty.

I tried to sink to my knees, but the two guards flanking me held me upright.

"Nay," I whispered. "I can't have—"

A hand slid over my shoulder; for the first time, it was ungloved. "It is a necessary cost, Miss Winter. Her loss is Caldera's gain, as you will soon see."

White-hot fury surged through my veins. He had done this. He had made me do this. I pivoted and grasped his hand in mine, reaching for my gift. But the Reliquary must have depleted me, too, for I felt naught but empty space where my power usually resided. I exhaled sharply; it was like a skilled orator suddenly losing the ability to speak.

The skin around his deep-set eyes crinkled. "Did you think I would make it so easy for you to overpower me? This troubles you, Miss Winter. But do you not see?" He indicated the dead woman. "It was either her . . . or you." He turned to his guards. "Take her back to her room. She deserves a rest." He released me and strode away.

Tears filled my eyes as I stared at the woman. Even when they blindfolded me, her image remained. I still had the few memories that had bled across our mental link, but not enough to know her name, who her family was, or anything of significance. They were small and well-cherished memories unique to her: a hand held in the dark by a loving mother after a terrible nightmare; a deep pleasure at the sight of her favorite spring flower after months of winter; the beginnings of a girlish crush on the son of a neighboring family.

All of that had died with her; now, it lived with me.

Back in my comfortable prison, words from a long-ago conversation with Asa Karthick floated into my consciousness, from the night he'd asked me to sacrifice myself for Nyx. I hadn't understood why he would willingly serve his father; why he hadn't rebelled against becoming the man Lord Draven had shaped him to be, as Spartan had.

You're a free man, Asa. Why would you let him make a monster out of you?

Because that is what I am, Sephone. And that is what you are. Do you really not understand that yet?

I had resisted it at the time, but I could deny it no longer. Asa had been right.

We were both alike.

3

SEPHONE

The hooded man didn't visit for another week. Perhaps he really wanted me to rest, although in truth I wasn't weary. At least, not bodily. The aching in my soul couldn't be relieved by sleep or anything else. If anything, it grew in the darkness, fed by loneliness, rage, and shame.

It was either her . . . or you.

If only it had been me. I'd had no idea that making the mind-bleeding permanent would cost another's life. The other innocents who had been attached to the Reliquary had lent me their strength, but never their lifeblood. If I had known the expenditure of my power would kill a person, I would have fought harder. I would not have given in.

And if he killed another to force your hand, Sephone? What of their *blood?*

My heart twisted. It was not so easy to decide. But in the end, I had destroyed two lives, not one. Lord Draven's advisor would live, but what kind of life could he have? He wouldn't remember his wife, his son. He wouldn't remember anything about his former self. While some might call that a boon or an opportunity, I had seen. I knew. It was a grievous loss.

The image of the dead woman was now burned onto my brain like a permanent brand. Whenever I closed my eyes, I saw the poison from the hourglass surging into her body, filtering through her veins. Sucking away the years of her life . . .

I choked on the memory. What if it was not the Reliquary's poison which had killed her, but mine? What if the webbing had been transferred? Had the other victims been similarly affected?

I scrambled off the bed and hurried to the vanity on the other side of the room, where a small mirror stood. A single lantern dangled from a hook on the wall next to it: just enough light to keep me from complete darkness, but not enough to prolong any illusions of day once the light from the window was spent. I sank onto the stool and peered into the mirror.

A stranger stared back at me. She was still young, but her eyes were older. Perhaps through the constant expenditure of my gift, my hair had grown longer at an unnatural rate, and it now brushed the tops of my shoulders. It was more blond than white, and wavy rather than curly. If not for my pale skin, I looked healthier than I'd been when Dorian rescued me from Nulla.

I loosened my shirt laces, trying not to think about the pendant that had once hung there, which I'd likely lost back in Nyx. A relieved sigh escaped my lips when I saw the webbing. It was still there—and I'd never been so pleased to discover that it had grown. It now broached the base of my collarbone, each mark wispy and delicate like calligraphy strokes, but thicker than they had been a week ago.

Turning away from the mirror, I closed my eyes. The hooded man had put this here to torture me with the webbing's progress, to tempt me with dreams of what could be. From the beginning, he had offered me incentives. If I helped him, he knew an *altered healer* who could erase the marks permanently. He didn't want me dead, or so he said. If I did as he asked, he would set me free when his work was done, and I could return to Dorian and Cass.

I hadn't accepted his offer, so he'd turned to crueler ways of getting me to do his bidding. After the second innocent was killed before my eyes—the boy—I'd finally given in. At first, I'd tried to withhold whatever information I could. I learned much from the minds of those he brought to me: Nyx had fallen, but most of the League had survived; Lady Xia, Lord Adamo, and their friends had fled into the mountains; Nephele had repelled Asa Karthick's *alters*, and Lethe was finally fighting back.

When he realized what I was doing, the hooded man had killed another innocent to make his point. After that, I no longer fought him. I told him everything I learned, even though every shared secret made me feel as if I was betraying my friends.

But what now? Weakness swept through my body, bringing me to my knees in the middle of my room. Before I'd been abducted, we'd been searching for a *healer* who could remove the poison. There had been hope. But now, I knew the truth: Any attempt to save me would cost the life of another. There was no way to live without someone else dying.

Had Dorian known that? Had Spartan? I doubted it. Neither of them would ever be so callous. I thought of the man from my dream, one of the enigmatic Three. The people who lived near the Mysterium said that he was a powerful *alter,* and I had sensed his kindness, his goodness. But he was also the rightful owner of the Reliquary, which Dorian had taken without the man's permission.

And I had helped him do it . . .

Returning to my bed, I buried my face in my pillow, wishing I could erase everything I'd done, along with the faces of those I missed so acutely. I wondered if Lady Xia still hid in the mountains, or if she'd returned to her treetop Thebe. Where were Bear and Bas? Had Spartan escaped the wrath of his brother?

Guilt stabbed at me. If I'd made it to Asa as I'd initially planned, Nyx would never have fallen. The blood of thousands was on my head . . . thousands of my people.

Lifetaker, indeed.

I recalled the look on Cass's face when I'd refused to flee with him to Marianthe. He had been more than disappointed, for I knew he loved me. I still wasn't sure whether I returned his feelings. But Dorian . . .

I clutched at my throat, but my fingers only closed around shirt laces. What had Dorian thought of my letter? Had he believed the things I'd written? It had seemed like the truth at the time. Still, perhaps my broken heart had spoken for me, had said those things in an attempt to salvage its shattered pride. I had wanted to hurt him deeply, the same way he'd hurt me—

"Miss Winter." The hooded man stood in the open doorway; I hadn't even heard the door. "You seem better rested today."

I scowled back at him. "What did you do with the advisor?"

He uttered a soft clucking sound. "What I did with him is none of your concern. I have another task for you."

"I won't let you kill again."

One of his pale eyebrows lifted condescendingly. "I think you will reconsider your stance once you have witnessed the alternative."

"The alternative? Every time I help you, I put someone else in danger." I stiffened my spine, drawing in a deep breath, ignoring the slight rattling of my chest. My cough had recently returned, though it was usually worse in the cold of the night.

The hooded man turned and barked an order. The same two guards filed into my room. When I didn't stand, they jerked me upright. My right wrist protested at the rough handling. Nevertheless, I stood still as they blindfolded me. No matter what they did to me, they couldn't make me use my gift again.

They would have to kill me first.

When the blindfold was removed, I once again stood in the room with the Reliquary. It was as cold as a tomb. This time, an older man had been strapped to one of the tables, his face turned away from me. Judging by the motionlessness of his body, they had sedated him. The second table bore a Memosinian soldier, but he was conscious. He must have struggled, for they'd gagged and blindfolded him. The leather straps strained as he wrenched his body from side to side. Both his wrists were bound firmly to the table.

One of the guards reached for my arm, and I jerked away from him, making for the still-open door. The second guard grabbed me from behind; I screamed and spun in his grasp, striking out at his chest, arms, and head. When I wrenched the fabric from his face, he looked briefly stunned, though his features weren't familiar. I tried to drag my glove from my good hand, but the guard had recovered quickly. Scooping me up, he pinned me against the wall, crushing me with the weight of his body while he pinioned both of my wrists. I struggled, but he was taller than me and far stronger.

"Now, Miss Winter," said the hooded man smoothly. "Didn't we discover early on what would happen if you tried to run away?"

"Kill me if you wish," I replied bitterly. "I'm done helping you."

The guard holding me looked expectantly at the hooded man, who nodded decisively. Grasping my right wrist, the guard twisted it sharply, and I screamed again, this time in agony.

"Devil," I gasped, tears coursing down my cheeks as pain splintered my entire arm, arrowing into my shoulder. He'd broken my wrist again.

The guard lifted me from the wall and spun me around, pinning my wrists behind my back. The hooded man loomed over me. "I didn't want to do that," he said sternly, "especially after it healed so well the last time. But you deliberately defied me. I had no choice."

"I still won't help you," I rasped, panting. "I will *not* be your monster."

"We will see."

Another pair of guards entered the room, dragging a young woman between them who was fighting even more fiercely than I had. She was about Cass's age, with golden-brown hair like Dorian's, though hers was long and ragged. As she passed me, I caught a glimpse of deeply tanned skin and iridescent topaz eyes, sharp and unsettling. An *alter.* Why had she been brought here?

"Get your hands off me," she hissed at her guards. "You *will* regret this." The hooded man came too near, and she spat in his face.

Despite my satisfaction at her treatment of him, I frowned. The *alter* spoke the common tongue, but her accent was unlike anything I'd ever heard. She had the look of a Memosinian, though I had never seen eyes of that color. They would be impossible to hide.

Was she perhaps . . . an outlander?

"Now, Miss Winter," said the hooded man pleasantly, turning to face me. Behind him, the *alter* continued to swear and hurl insults at her captors as they strapped her to the third table. "I think you'll find that rendering your assistance is infinitely preferable to the alternative."

He flicked his hand, and the first guard moved to the Memosinian soldier. The *alter* fought bitterly as they wrestled her hand into the metal glove; her resistance seemed to reinvigorate the soldier, who strained further against the straps.

One of the hooded man's eyes twitched, but they were cool and dispassionate as they settled on me. "I am well aware that hurting you is not enough to make you obey. But perhaps you will not be so defiant when others are forced to endure hardship in your place."

The woman suddenly went still, her face freezing as the golden wires crawled down her arm. She was fighting it, fighting the mental link. In response, the Reliquary was feeding on her energy, just as it had the first time I'd been connected to it.

My blood ran cold. For her to be here, strapped to the table in my place . . .

She must be a *mem*.

"Did you think you were the only *alter* in my possession?" the hooded man was saying. "Of course, Miss Vega's gift is not as strong as yours. But she will do for now."

"Nay," I whispered, forgetting the pain of my broken wrist. *"Nay."*

I had only met a few *mems* in my life, and none as strong as Cutter or me. I didn't know if the webbing—the curse—affected any of the others, but there was a good chance that it did. My weeks of being connected to the Reliquary had steadily advanced the poison. How could I let him torture her—poison her—in my place? Even if he let her live, I couldn't bear for another to endure what I had. She was innocent; I was practically a murderer. She was alive, and I was already dying.

The choice was simple.

"I will accomplish my ends with or without your assistance, Miss Winter," he continued. "But there is no need to waste another life. Do you not agree? Besides, I will not ask you to erase a mind again unless I absolutely have to. At this point in time, I only require information. Minor, cosmetic adjustments."

"Don't help him," gasped the *alter*. "I can bear it."

I hadn't realized she was still aware of what was going on around her. She must be stronger than the hooded man believed. But the golden wires were swarming her throat, and I remembered the woman from a week ago: her skin streaked with inky black, her ghostly pale face, her lifeless eyes.

"Stop. Please."

"Say the words, Miss Winter, and you can take her place."

"Nay!" the *alter* shouted, beginning to choke. "He is a liar! Don't listen to him!"

I remembered the face of the boy, the way he'd looked just before he died. How he'd begged and pleaded to be set free. So many dead, because of me.

The hooded man looked at me in silent challenge, and the blood surging through my veins slowed. I sagged in my captor's arms. "I'll do it."

At the hooded man's nod, the guard released me. I stumbled forward and grabbed the *alter*'s gloved arm.

"Don't fight it." I felt her start as she withdrew from the mental connection. The golden wires abruptly receded, and she opened her eyes. Vivid, yellow eyes, like an eagle's, stared back at me.

"You gave in," was all she said.

"I had no choice." Two guards came forward to free her from the table. She sat up, still staring at me, and I couldn't shake the sense that I'd somehow disappointed her. The man who'd broken my wrist secured me to the table in her place.

No longer struggling, she passed me with her guards flanking her, but not before she bent slightly and muttered something in my ear.

"There is *always* a choice, Miss Winter."

Expecting to be returned to my room, I was surprised when the guards undid my blindfold in a third, unfamiliar chamber . . . or rather, a cell. It was the kind of place I had imagined they would keep me from the beginning: A cold, drafty space, surrounded on three sides by bars, with the fourth wall constructed of heavy rock. There was one window, but it was high up and barred. The floor consisted of grimy stone and scattered straw, and though the low bed looked mostly clean, it was small and sagging deeply in the middle.

I turned to the guards. "Where have you taken me?"

They didn't reply as they pushed me into the cell, locked the door, and left. A single lantern lit the empty passageway outside my cell. Apparently, the hooded man had decided to make me pay for my earlier defiance.

Cradling my injured wrist, I sank down on the bed—more a pallet than an actual bed. The hooded man hadn't wanted anything besides information, and the old man had still been alive when they freed me.

Judging by what I'd learned from the Memosinian soldier's mind, Lord Draven was still ignorant of his enemy's interference . . . my interference.

"That looks painful."

I jumped at the low voice that came from the other side of my cell, shifting slightly to peer through the bars. A figure detached itself from the shadows and edged toward me. I started. The woman from before . . . the *mem.*

She nodded at my wrist. "You should splint that."

"With what?"

She reached behind her and rummaged in the darkness. When she turned back to me, she held a long, stout stick. "Will this do?"

I nodded.

"Put your arm through the bars and I'll wrap it." Before I could say anything else, she took her cloak and began tearing strips from the hem. A memory flashed unbidden across my mind: the rooftop in Ceto, and Cass knotting scraps of fabric into a rope to help us escape.

Hesitantly, I removed my glove and awkwardly extended my wrist, wincing as she took it carefully. It had healed well the first time; it was doubtful that it would do so again.

I studied her as she set about splinting my limb. Her dark eyebrows slanted down, making her face appear almost sorrowful, and though her lips were tightly pursed at present, she radiated the same compassion I'd seen in the Reliquary room. She wore gloves like me, but hers were made of a tough, reptilian leather.

"You're an outlander," I said.

She didn't pause in her work.

"A *mem.*"

She didn't give any indication that she had heard me.

"And a friend, I would think."

Now, she raised her head. "Aye. I am a friend."

To distract myself from the pain, I kept on talking. "Do you have the webbing, too?"

She frowned. "The webbing?"

"Marks on your chest, like black ink. Poison." Seeing her puzzled look, I shook my head. "Never mind."

Inwardly, I breathed a sigh of relief. Perhaps the curse didn't affect all *mems*. But if that were true, why had Cutter and I both been affected? Had Cutter lied?

"Why do you ask me about poison?" she said, tying off the last piece of cloth and leaning back. Gingerly, I withdrew my injured limb, which already felt less painful for being immobilized.

"Thank you." I nodded at my wrist, ignoring the question just as she'd ignored my earlier statements.

She inclined her own head gracefully.

"Is today the first time you saw the Reliquary?" I ventured.

"Aye, it is," she replied.

"Do you know what it does?"

This time, she shook her head. "I guessed it was some kind of torture machine."

I winced. "You could call it that."

"He said something about erasing minds." She studied me closely. "Was that what he asked of you?"

I nodded. "I didn't know he'd captured another *mem*."

"Only five days ago. I was foolish, really." She shrugged nonchalantly. "I should have been more careful." She tilted her head as she regarded me; the gesture was almost birdlike. "You gave in to save my life."

"The Reliquary probably wouldn't have killed y—"

"You shouldn't have."

Frowning, I shifted on the bed, trying to get comfortable. "I know you said I had a choice, but it's not that simple." Briefly, I explained how the Reliquary worked—and the sacrifice it demanded. Tears stung my eyes as I recounted how the woman had died lending me her life force for the mind-bleeding.

The newcomer was silent for a long moment. "I am sorry," she said eventually. "I see now what it has cost you."

"It was the logical decision." Seeing her confusion, I showed her the webbing on my chest.

She blanched, her eyes widening. *"Poison."*

"Aye. So you see, there's no point risking both our lives."

"And yet, you still could have let me die . . . but you didn't. I thank you—" She hesitated. "I don't even know your full name."

"Sephone Winter."

"Aleria Vega. Of the north, as you guessed earlier."

I leaned forward. "Then it's true?"

"Which part, Miss Winter? That the people who live beyond Caldera's borders are raiders who kill for sport? That we take your people as slaves? That we're savage and barbarian?"

I had to smile. "I meant that you exist."

"Of course we exist," she scoffed, throwing her head back, emphasizing a sharp, aquiline nose.

"Nay." I tried to explain. "Until recently, we didn't think anyone else had survived the world-that-was. That is, anyone besides the inhabitants of Caldera. At least, in this part of the world."

"A lie perpetuated by your leaders to conceal our existence."

"Until recently. Memosine is well aware of you now." I bit my lip. "Their king, a man by the name of Draven, has painted you all as invaders."

"We are not invaders. Why would we have need of your land when ours is twice as good?"

If she was telling the truth—and I believed she was—then most of Memosine believed a lie about the outlanders. Maybe no gray shrouded her country—maybe they had sunshine aplenty. Hadn't Dorian said as much about his home city, Maera?

"Do you know about Lord Draven . . . and his ally, Silvertongue?"

"What do you think I'm doing here in Lethe?" She smiled faintly. "It may come as a surprise to you, Miss Winter, that we outlanders are not so very different than Calderans. We have the gifts, same as you. We speak the common tongue. We share much of your culture and many of your traditions. We come from the same world, after all. The same ancestors."

"And you're a *mem*."

"My gift is not as strong as yours," she admitted. "But then, it is only my secondary gift."

She pursed her lips, and I tamped down the urge to ask her about her primary gift. I guessed she would share the truth when she was ready. "How did the hooded man know you were a *mem*?"

"Because I was foolish enough to try and use my gift on his men when they captured me." She shook her head. "It's nearly midnight, and you're injured. I'm not going anywhere. We should get some sleep."

Reluctantly, I lay down, trying to ignore my throbbing wrist. My head reeled with everything I'd learned.

What was an outlander doing in Lethe? Was Aleria Vega an enemy of Lord Draven and Silvertongue? Why had she told me that she wasn't going anywhere, as if it were within her power to leave?

Aleria settled into her own bed on the other side of the bars, and soon she was snoring softly. I remained awake, revisiting what she'd said. The outlanders, Silvertongue, the hooded man, Aleria Vega, even Lord Draven . . . none of them were what they seemed.

I had no one I could trust.

Be wary of your dreams, Regis had told me once. *The world may not be so kind in reality as it appears in your imagination.*

Little did my childhood friend know that I had long since abandoned any expectation of the world's kindness. I had abandoned it the day my brother betrayed me to the hooded man and callously stepped on my wrist. Only childish dreams had kept alive a hope that the world could ever be anything other than cruel, and I had left those dreams behind with Dorian.

Dorian, whose mind had once felt so different . . .

My eyelids finally grew heavy. A chill wind snuck in through the barred window, just as it once had in Nulla. I curled onto my side, wrapping the thin blanket around my shoulders as I looked up into the night, foolishly hoping for a glimpse of stars. Just before I closed my eyes, I saw a flash of bright white, almost like a bird wing. It was gone just as quickly as it had appeared. Had I imagined it? I sat up, straining my eyes in the gloom, for the lantern in the corridor had gone out, and the night was perfectly still.

There, again—it *was* a bird, hovering just beyond the bars of my high window. Some kind of dove, maybe, or a white raven. Both were rare in the mountains. Settling itself on the ledge, the bird opened its mouth and trilled a pleasant warble, like the patter of a brook over pebbles. I thought of the nightingale back in Nulla, whose sweet song had made my heart soar. A song of liberty was lovely to a slave; to a captive, it was a rare treasure, a long, fresh drink after days of aching thirst.

I settled back on my pallet, oddly comforted by the bird's presence. Even my soul felt a little lighter as I mentally replayed the notes of its song. Hopefully, the bird would stay, if only until I fell asleep. And then maybe, just maybe, it would still be there in my dreams.

DORIAN

For the fifth day in a row, they returned to their camp, empty-handed and bone weary. With Draven's army now on Lethe's doorstep—rumors abounded that they were regrouping somewhere on the moorland, not far from the River Lethe, and preparing to attack the capital, Nephele—the mountain folk were wary of strangers and none too willing to answer questions about missing people or pale-haired merchants. Eventually, Cass's truth-telling gift had become more of a hindrance than a help, and they were expelled from yet another village.

"We don't welcome *lumens* here," the man who'd turned them out had snarled, waving his arms at them. He spat in Dorian's direction. "Or whatever *you* are."

Thankfully, the man hadn't seen Jewel. Whenever they'd entered populated areas, the wolf had gone hunting in the mountains, ensuring that even if they uncovered nothing useful, at least they wouldn't go hungry. These mountains were different than the ones surrounding Dorian's home, though there was still plenty of game and numerous places to hide.

Fortunately for Sephone's captors, but unfortunately for Dorian.

On reaching their makeshift camp deep within an isolated gorge, Cass collapsed beside the empty fireplace in a cloud of travel dust, looking as desolate as Dorian felt. "Nothing," he declared. "Not even a trace."

"Perhaps I could go alone this time." Dorian bent to start the fire. "No offense, but the five of us stand out—three of us are *alters* and one is a giant. If they could hear me speaking their tongue, with their accent—"

Cass sat up and scowled. "You heard that man. 'Whatever you are,' he said. You're just as much an *alter* as the rest of us."

"A fact I could easily disguise."

"Good for you," he said sourly, and flung himself back onto the ground.

Spartan knelt beside Dorian. Not for the first time, Dorian welcomed the sense of peace that stole over him at the acolyte's presence. Some days, it was the only thing that kept him calm. Still, Dorian envied Spartan his serenity, for despite being a *calor*, Dorian had never once tasted the gift of courage for himself.

"Please tell me you have an idea for where to search next," Dorian said to him. "I feel like we've combed these mountains from top to bottom."

Spartan's bright blue eyes lifted. "Are you asking for my advice, Dorian?"

Dorian tried not to squirm. From the earliest days of their search, Spartan had counseled them to return to the Mysterium to consult the Three. They would know where to find her, he had assured Dorian. But what Spartan suggested was impossible. Return to the very place from which Dorian had fled with a stolen relic in his possession? The same relic he had now lost to their enemy?

And besides, no matter what Spartan believed, the Mountain was empty. There would be no Three to consult.

"New advice," Dorian countered.

"My advice remains unchanged."

Dorian frowned, still haunted by the youth's declaration from months ago.

A time will come very soon, Dorian, when you will face an enemy you cannot defeat. You will hold the lives of those dearest to you in your hand, but you will not be able to save them. In that hour, you will be given a choice between life and death . . .

Had Spartan been referring to their present predicament? For Sephone's life was in Dorian's hands, and he could do naught to save her. Just as he had been helpless to save his family.

"Courage, my friend," murmured Spartan, as if he'd sensed the change in Dorian's mood. "Hope is not lost."

"I wish I had your confidence." Dorian stared at his gloveless hands. "And your courage."

"Courage is a choice, Dorian, not a gift." Spartan straightened and moved away.

"Gifts," spat Cass, who had evidently heard his comment, and possibly their entire conversation. "Usually, gifts are something you can return if you don't want them."

Aware Cass was nearly out of liquor again, Dorian tried to keep his tone level. "And who would you return them to?"

"Whoever thought they would be a blessing and not a curse." Cass shifted. "I shouldn't complain, of course. My gift is a nuisance and a bother. But it's naught compared to Sephone's gift, which is literally killing her slowly."

It was the first time he'd spoken of the poison since the day he'd learned of the curse and punched Dorian for concealing it. "We'll find a cure."

"A pretty promise, Thane," Cass replied, grimacing. "Nevertheless, when we finally retrieve this Reliquary—"

"You'll what? Use it to rid yourself of your gift? You know the cost."

"I was going to say, we will use it to save her."

"Remember what Brinsley said. The relic demands a sacrifice. There must always be blood."

Did you never wonder why the Reliquary has room for three people? The words taunted Dorian.

"I remember, Thane," Cass said at last, more heavily. "I never forgot."

They exchanged a wordless look. Dorian hadn't told Cass about his conversation with Spartan following the revelation of the curse, about the plan that had formed in his head the moment Dorian had learned what it would take to save Sephone.

I was the one who betrayed her. I must be the one to bring her back.

And what then? Spartan had asked Dorian.

The Reliquary. Could she be healed through its power?

Spartan had nodded. *Aye, Dorian. But if Brinsley is telling the truth, and I believe he is, it would cost the life of another. One life surrendered freely so that another may be saved.*

I understand.

For the first time, Spartan's grim prophecy made sense. *In that hour, you will be given a choice between life and death . . .* Maybe that was what he meant: Dorian would be offered the chance to exchange his life for hers.

He'd made his choice. It was already decided. But he couldn't explain that to Cass, for multiple reasons.

"I'm sorry, Thane," Cass began, sidling closer, "that you are stuck remembering everything. Your wife and dau—"

"You will not speak of them," Dorian said through gritted teeth. "Not unless you want your nose to look like mine did." Apparently, he had absorbed some of Cass's foul temper.

Cass grinned, as if he felt better now that his poor mood had infected them both. "Even if it did, Sephone would still prefer my looks to yours."

Dorian's hands bunched into fists, but he was distracted by Bear's low exclamation—Jewel had returned carrying a motionless carcass.

"Saved by the deer," smirked Cass, and more than ever, Dorian wished he could plant his fist in the *lumen*'s smug face.

"The way I see it, my lord," said Bear a few days later, "there are few options available to us now."

Once again, they sat around the fire. Dorian had entered several mountain settlements alone, the iridescence in his hair disguised with dirt, but learned very little. People were indeed going missing, but there had been no pattern to the disappearances—one young woman had been taken from her family, another old man abducted from a village five miles away. Draven wouldn't be interested in taking inconsequential hostages, so it had to be the hooded man. But how could they ever cover an area of such magnitude, given that each mountain concealed hundreds of caves and hollows? Jewel was no ordinary wolf, but her enhanced abilities did not include sniffing out a woman who was probably being kept deep underground.

At least it meant that Sephone was still alive. If she hadn't been, there wouldn't have been any use for the missing people, none of whom had been *alters*.

"You said, my lord," Bear continued, "that there were no witnesses to any of the abductions, which occurred miles apart. Still, we know that Sephone must be here in the mountains, so we have no choice but to keep looking."

"I thought you said that we had several options," Cass remarked dryly.

"Not *several—few*. We can continue searching as one group, or split up into two smaller groups. We can even search individually. Then we can cover more ground more quickly."

"If we separate, we'll be vulnerable to attack," said Bas, frowning at his brother. "Draven's men are still looking for us, remember."

"And if we find Seph," added Cass, "how do you suppose we let the others know where she is? The hooded devil won't give her up without a fight. We might need all of us to rescue her."

Dorian hid a smile. What had it cost Cass to admit that?

"This camp is a central location," Bear replied. "We could meet here in five days' time. Then, if we've found nothing, five days after that— or whatever interval we decide on . . ." He glanced at Bas. "Besides, if Draven's men find us, what difference will five men make instead of three?"

"Depends on the men," Cass muttered.

"It's a good plan," Dorian said, ignoring the *lumen*'s comment. "And Jewel has always had a good sense of my presence. If she searches with the other group, and they find something, she may be able to track me down more easily."

Knowing the wolf probably understood everything he was saying, Dorian patted her head reassuringly. She hated being separated from him, but she also loved Sephone. She would understand.

One by one, the others nodded their assent to Bear's plan.

"So," Dorian ventured, "perhaps we can begin with two groups for now, and divide the area we haven't searched between us. If Bas and Spartan would come with me, Cass and Bear can go with Jewel."

"I don't know," said Cass. "What if you find her and decide to return to Maera without us?"

Dorian shot him an exasperated look. "Now isn't the time for petty divisions. If we're to find her, we have to work together."

"Then we stay together," Cass concluded smugly. "And Bas goes with Bear and Jewel."

"So you can spy on me?"

"Only if you do something suspicious, Thane."

Leaning back, Dorian relented. "Fine." The Mardell brothers would prefer to stay together anyway, and Jewel would protect them. Meanwhile, Dorian and Spartan could both keep an eye on Cass.

"We will resume searching in the morning," Dorian told the others, noting the tiniest of frowns forming between Bas's eyebrows. He didn't trust Cass—with good reason—and might still need to be persuaded that the *lumen* wouldn't thrust a knife between Dorian's shoulder blades at the earliest opportunity.

Come to think of it, Dorian himself might still need to be persuaded.

"Good," said Cass, and Dorian couldn't help wondering if maybe he'd intended them to divide their forces all along.

"This gorge goes on forever."

Dorian twisted in time to catch Cass covering a yawn, but when he saw Dorian looking, he successfully turned it into a scowl.

"Feel free to take the lead," Dorian said offhandedly, stepping over a small stream, "if you think it will bring the gorge to an end any faster."

"But you're doing such a good job, Thane." Cass glanced back at Spartan, whose steps were lagging. "Though our monkish friend is beginning to look tired."

Dorian paused. "You can admit fatigue, Cass. You're only mortal, and I'm exhausted, too."

"I thought we were *alters*, not mortals." He shoved past Dorian to take the lead, probably forgetting that in doing so, he presented his back.

Spartan caught up to Dorian. "He hasn't forgiven you, then," the acolyte mused between sips from his waterskin. Despite the cold nights, the days could still be uncomfortably warm.

Dorian watched the *lumen*'s receding outline. "I doubt he ever will. Still, we should catch up to him before he forgets we're traveling as one group, not three." He hefted his pack and started forward again.

The gorge had widened to allow two people to walk abreast, and Spartan travelled beside Dorian. The sun had long since slipped below the towering walls of rock on either side of them, and Dorian could feel Spartan's weariness . . . and his own. They had been up well before dawn for months now—earlier, even, since parting ways with Bas, Bear, and Jewel two days ago. But this was Dorian's quest, not Spartan's. Still, Dorian sensed that Spartan had liked Sephone, and he had been willing to follow Dorian, even when Dorian had ignored the acolyte's advice. What had Spartan said to him once?

From this point on, Dorian, my life is bound to your quest. I will not leave you now—not until the end . . .

Whatever end he had been referring to, Dorian was grateful for the acolyte's company. And for the fact that he'd volunteered to take up the rear as they travelled, which meant Dorian could keep an eye on Cass while he mapped out their route.

"Perhaps you should try to make amends with him," suggested Spartan, nodding at Cass's back.

Dorian looked askance at him. "Make amends? With a man who wishes me dead?"

"He is your ally now. And I don't believe he wishes you dead."

"Just out of his sight. And Sephone's, too."

Spartan inclined his head slightly, as if hesitating to agree.

"Even before he found out"—Dorian swallowed—"even before he realized I was his competition for Sephone's affections, he hated me. He has some bitter prejudice against the aristocracy."

What have I done to make you doubt my honor? Dorian had asked him in Thebe.

I simply doubt that any man is capable of giving up power once he is accustomed to its taste.

Yourself included?

Some men are never offered that choice.

Cass had shared his past with Sephone but not with Dorian. Dorian guessed that a lord had sold Cass into slavery, and that was why he'd despised Dorian from the very beginning. And then Sephone had expressed a preference for Dorian instead of Cass, when he doubted women usually denied Cass anything. Finally, to add insult to injury, she had told Dorian and not Cass that she was dying, suggesting a deeper intimacy had grown between them.

Dorian shifted uncomfortably. Whatever feelings had once been between them didn't exist anymore, at least on her part.

Cass didn't care that she had only told Dorian the truth because he had followed her to the *altered healer,* or that his betrayal of Sephone's weakness to Brinsley meant that nothing could ever come of their connection, even if he hadn't decided to give her his remaining years. It didn't matter that even if she hadn't chosen Cass, she hadn't chosen Dorian, either.

"You could show him the letter," said Spartan, breaking the uncomfortable silence. "The one she wrote you."

Dorian's boot sent a stone careening across the gorge. "I'd sooner pluck out my own eye with a toothpick."

"Because you're not willing to give her up yet?"

"She didn't pick either of us, Spartan. She *left.*"

"To save Nyx—and you."

"What are you suggesting?"

Spartan nodded in the direction Cass had gone. "He knows as well as you do that when you find Sephone, she won't belong to Asa Karthick. Maybe he needs to know that she won't belong to you, either."

Dorian stopped as Spartan continued on without him. Then, as realization dawned, he hurried to catch up with the acolyte. "You mean her freedom, of course. I was always going to set her free, you know."

Spartan faced Dorian. "I mean her heart." For a moment, Dorian forgot that it was a seventeen-year-old boy who was looking at him. "You don't know much about women, Dorian. But there are certain courtesies even I am aware of. If you don't intend to claim her, you should tell her. And you should tell Cass, too."

Shocked, Dorian stared at Spartan's back as he continued walking. He thought Dorian didn't know much about women? He'd been married for seven years, nearly eight. He would wager that he knew far more about women than Spartan did.

But he had to admit that Spartan was right in part. The chapter between Dorian and Sephone had to close. And when he found her, he would tell her so.

Telling Cass, on the other hand—

"Thane! Monk!" Their "names" echoed eerily through the gorge.

Dorian broke into a run, quickly catching up with Spartan. They passed through a narrow opening in the rock and came upon a wider clearing. Dorian grabbed his staff and snapped it to full length; Spartan extended his hands, probably preparing to summon one of his magical shields.

Cass knelt on the ground beside the river. He glanced up at Dorian and Spartan, raising a brow at Dorian's quarterstaff. "Nice to know you come quickly when called."

"What is it, Cass?"

"Good news and bad news." He held up a chunk of hair—matted but distinctly white-blond—and Dorian's heart lifted. Cass must have been cleaning it in the water.

"Is it hers?" Dorian said breathlessly.

"Looks like it. It's the same shade. Even has a bit of lingering iridescence, though there's not much light left to really tell."

Dorian crouched beside him, trying not to think about the kind of handling that might have resulted in Sephone losing a clump of hair. "Where did you find it?"

"On the far side of the gorge, near the wall. They must have passed through here."

"Or it could have been washed here by the river."

"I doubt it. There's been no heavy rain for weeks."

He was right. At least now they had a clue—the first real sign they'd had since she'd disappeared.

"And the bad news?"

Cass nodded toward the other side of the river. Even from this distance, Dorian could see the remains of a campfire and the imprints of several different-sized boots. Judging by the depth and shape of the prints, they were large men, probably soldiers. The hooded man, valuing stealth and secrecy, wouldn't have left such obvious signs of his presence; they had to belong to men who didn't care who came across their tracks.

Men who were hunters rather than the hunted.

Cass's face was grim. "It seems Asa may be close to finding her, too."

5

The hooded man hadn't sent for me in days—an unexpected blessing.

My gift had changed since the advisor's mind-bleeding and the young woman's death. It had always had the feel of wild magic, but now it seemed almost to have a mind of its own. Even when I wasn't using it, it had begun to replay memories against my will . . . memories so real and vivid that, at times, I wasn't sure if I was awake or asleep. They were memories from all the minds I'd ever visited, fragments of lives I had not disturbed in many years. Dorian and Cass featured in some, as did Brinsley and my parents.

None of them were pleasant recollections.

As dawn filtered in through the high window, I huddled on my bed, clutching my swollen wrist. My arm was a ghastly sight now with the rough splint and the hand-shaped burn one of Asa's *alters* had given me in Orphne. I craned my aching neck to look up at the window. The bird—a white raven—only visited under cover of darkness, but he had been there every night since my first in this cell. I couldn't put words to the sense of comfort he and his song gave me, but somehow, with both him and Aleria nearby, I didn't feel so alone. Not nearly as lonely as I had felt those months in my well-appointed room.

"He flew off a few hours ago." Aleria's voice drifted over from her bed.

I sat up, turning to face her. "You see the bird, too?" I had begun to believe I was imagining him.

"Of course."

"I didn't think there were white ravens in the Grennor Mountains. But I don't know these mountains very well."

"Nay, you're right. They're very rare. Even up north."

I leaned against the bars. "What do they think of *mems* in your country?"

She smiled. "Probably the same as they think of them here."

"But you're free?" I couldn't bear the thought of her being a slave, too.

Once again, she cocked her head in that strange, tilted gesture. "Aye. I'm free."

"I'm glad to hear it."

"But the nightmares . . . I have them also."

She must have heard me in the night.

"Among other things, I came here seeking a cure. Have you heard of the Mysterium, Miss Winter?"

"Sephone," I said quickly, and she nodded. "Aye, I stayed with them for a little while."

"You *stayed* with them?" she repeated.

"Aye. They're a good people, if a little reclusive. One of their number, Spartan, journeyed with us to Nyx." I hadn't told her about Dorian, Cass, or our quest for the Reliquary. I hurried on. "Spartan spoke of the Three, a trio whom the Mysterium serve. But I never met them."

I didn't mention the rest: that the Mysterium followed a man, the son of a powerful *alter*, and likely a powerful *alter* in his own right, who was the rightful king of Caldera. Not a king of land and wealth but a king of souls. Spartan had spoken about this man as if he were his brother . . . his friend. But to me . . .

I shook my head. Briefly, I remembered the vial Spartan had given me, the one I'd left behind in Nyx. Only now did I wish that I had sampled it . . . just once. Even if the Mountain proved to be empty, the Three a myth.

Aleria's eyes had gone wide. "I have heard of this Three. For a long time now, I've desired to meet them."

"They live far from here. First, we'd have to escape."

"You want to escape?"

"Don't you?"

Her gaze once again became veiled, and I had the uncomfortable feeling she wasn't telling me everything. I fidgeted with the loose end of one of my bandages. "Before, you said 'among other things.' Why else did you come to Lethe?"

"Because I may be free," she replied simply. "But my people are not."

"Then you're against Lord Draven?"

"He has threatened us for months. I plan to do everything in my power to stop him."

"So does the hooded man."

"Aye, but I do not like his methods." Aleria glanced pointedly at my wrist. "I was on my way to the Mysterium when I was captured. You know, I never expected to meet another *mem*, least of all here in the wilderness." She looked at me in earnest. "I sense you are important to my cause, Sephone, but more than that, I sense you are a friend. I promise I will do everything I can to free you."

I blinked. How could she free me when we were both imprisoned?

She went on, "The hooded man hides his face for a reason. I intend to discover why." Again, she spoke as if she didn't plan to stay for long.

"How did you hear about the Mysterium? The Three?" I hadn't thought their influence extended beyond Caldera.

"Like I said, Sephone. We outlanders are not unlike you, and we're from the same world, the same ancestors. One hears of the Three wherever they go."

Then she sealed her lips, and she would say no more.

Over the coming days, I came to depend on two things: Aleria's sharp and ofttimes witty conversation during the day, and my first glimpse of the white raven at night. He never accepted any food from my hand, no matter what choice morsels I saved for him, but he continued to hover outside the narrow bars, his white feathers gleaming despite the lack of moonlight.

Could the songbird be an *altered* creature like Jewel, with magically honed instincts and a closer relationship with humans than animals usually enjoyed? Sometimes I wished I could see him perching on the end of my bed, or even feel him sitting on my shoulder. His feathers looked so soft. But though he could squeeze between the bars easily, he remained where he was, never doing anything more than watching me or warbling a few pleasant notes.

Every passing day chipped away at my reticence. Piece by piece, I shared my past with my fellow prisoner, knowing I had little to lose if she betrayed me. She didn't seem to feel the weight of captivity as I did or be oppressed by the closeness of the walls. I'd had few friends besides Regis, Dorian, and Cass, and I sensed that Aleria understood not only what it was like to be an *alter*, but also what it was like to be a *mem*.

Cutter's voice frequently echoed through my memories, particularly the words he had said to me just before he died.

Understand this, girl. We are cursed, as cursed as we are gifted. Cursed to know the deepest secrets of mankind but to forever live in the shadows. That is the lot of a mem*, Persephone Winter. To always be alone. Even in the middle of a crowd . . .*

But I was beginning to doubt him. Unlike Cutter, *I* was not alone. I had people who loved me and cared for me deeply. Including Dorian. Even if he didn't return my feelings, he had always been there for me as my friend and protector. And then there was Cass and Aleria, Bas and Bear. Even Spartan.

As they always did, my thoughts strayed to the man from my dream, and the white horse who had carried me to him. If only I could escape with Aleria and return to the Mysterium . . . find out if the Mountain was truly empty. But the hooded man had never once let down his guard, and even if I escaped, there was still the matter of my deal with Asa Karthick. I had promised myself in exchange for Nyx.

But Nyx was destroyed, a voice reminded me. *That means you're free.*

At that, I would remember the poison, and despair would cloud my thoughts all over again. My parents didn't remember me, and my own brother had betrayed me. Dorian and Cass had no idea of my whereabouts—they probably believed I was with Asa. Even if they'd guessed who'd really abducted me, they wouldn't know where to look. But they were probably thinking of Lethe's war with Memosine, not me.

I was still alone.

Only Aleria's presence kept me from complete despair. As I shared my past, she shared hers. She had been born in the outlands, with very little knowledge of Caldera except that it was a land adjacent to her own, covered in thick patches of gray. When she was older, she had learned the truth: The Calderans and her own people came from the same ancestors, but her people had settled in Caldera first. When the world-that-was fell, the people who would eventually form the countries of Memosine, Lethe, and Marianthe had fled to Caldera, finding a world untouched by the destruction.

And a people who already claimed the land as their own.

"There was a war," said Aleria thickly, averting her face. "The newcomers killed many, and when they were victorious, they banished the survivors. My people were scattered, but eventually we found each other. We regrouped. We recovered our strength."

They had fled to the outlands—at that time, a land almost as barren as the one they had left behind. But then came the Greening, which had spread to the outlands. They soon found themselves the sole custodians of a rich and fertile land unaffected by the gray. Their numbers, which had been diminished by the warring, grew steadily. Sixty-two years later, they were numerous enough to present a challenge to Lord Draven and Memosine.

I gazed at Aleria, trying to digest all she'd told me. "I thought you said you weren't invaders."

"We're not. But Draven's warmongering has reopened the old wounds, and some of our people . . . well, some are convinced that we have been given the opportunity to take Memosine for ourselves, to avenge our ancestors for what was stolen from them." She gave a slight shrug. "I never said my people were completely noble hearted."

"But I have visited many minds . . . *older* minds. The only war I ever saw was the one between Memosine and Lethe."

Even as I said it, I questioned myself. I had seen many memories of a terrible war. I had assumed they belonged to the war between Memosine and Lethe, but what if they were echoes of a different conflict entirely? What if Lord Guerin . . . the people he and his soldiers had killed . . . had been outlanders?

"You may not have known what you saw. And you were not there. But you have felt the guilt, have you not?" Her yellow eyes were piercing.

I nodded. Even as a child, I had been crushed by the weight of those memories, the terrible stain of what those men had done. Yet almost everyone in those recollections was dead, and only Lord Guerin had remained, the last remnant of a past it seemed all of Caldera was determined to forget.

"If what you say is true," I stated, "then Memosine will soon be fighting a war on two fronts."

"Aye, they will. That is the other reason why I'm here, Sephone. Most of my people do not want war, but if it comes to that, they will do whatever is necessary." She bowed her head. "We cannot allow Caldera to be torn apart by fighting."

The door to the passageway suddenly opened, and several men filed through it. On her pallet, Aleria straightened. It was near dark—the raven would appear soon.

"Ah, Miss Winter," declared the hooded man in a congenial voice, studying me through the bars. "It *has* been a while since we last spoke."

I remained where I was, glaring at him.

"I have another task for you. I hope you will be more compliant this time—" He broke off abruptly as two men appeared from the other end of the passageway, another man struggling between them.

"Unhand me! Can't you see I'm a friend, you thickheaded fools?" Filthy white-blond hair peeked from beneath a brown hood, and I glimpsed a thin, grubby face.

I stood shakily, clutching my wrist. *"Brinsley?"*

He lifted his head and intercepted my gaze. A slow grin slid over his face. "Sephone, dear *sister.*" He glanced at my splinted wrist. "I would've thought that had healed by now."

Pain sliced at my heart. All these months, I had looked for him, trying to formulate the words to ask him how he could betray me. Now he was here, and no explanation resided in his eyes, not even the faintest hint of attachment or regret.

The hooded man was now glaring at Brinsley, who had been forced to his knees by the guards. "Explain your presence here, Winter."

My brother executed a low, mocking bow—all the more pathetic since he knelt on the floor. "I came to warn you, my lord. Asa Karthick is close. Too close." Brinsley jabbed a thumb at me. "He's probably coming after her."

"Idiot," muttered the hooded man, his dark eyes flashing. "You've led them straight to us."

"I know how to cover my tracks," Brinsley retorted. "I've done this before, remember?"

Done *what* before? I stared at my brother, wondering how I had ever believed he would accept me as his family.

The hooded man paced restlessly. "We have to move from here." He stopped and looked at his guards. "We depart tonight. Leave the other prisoners; there will be more where we are going. Miss Winter can erase their most recent memories." He gestured toward me and Aleria. "They'll need to be drugged, but only enough to suppress the gifts. We don't have time to carry them. As soon as you've made the necessary preparations, come back here and administer the mixture. You know what to do."

The guards nodded and departed. As Brinsley was getting to his feet, the hooded man cursed and cuffed him across the head.

"*Ow.* That's the thanks I get for coming to warn you?"

"You were meant to stay out of sight," the hooded man snapped. "Now go, before I have your sister wipe all *your* memories."

Oddly enough, Brinsley shuddered at the threat and did as he asked without another glance in my direction. The hooded man turned on his heel and left, too.

I looked up at the windowsill, struck with a sudden sense of loss. The white raven. Would it follow me, wherever we were going? How would it know how to find me?

"Listen," Aleria said from behind me, and I turned, surprised to find deep determination written on her features. "I haven't told you everything."

Dread churned my stomach. Would she betray me, too?

"I should probably just show you. You'll be quite shocked either way, really."

I stared at her. Or rather, I stared at the place where she'd been standing, for she was suddenly shrinking, her matted brown hair growing longer, her flesh melting away to be replaced by feathers,

the bones in her face re-forming into a sharp profile and a curved
nose . . . nay, a beak. When the transformation was finished, intelligent
topaz eyes flickered in the lanternlight.

"You're a . . . you're a . . ."

I remembered the bear who'd attacked us before we reached the
Mysterium. It had turned out to be a woman, and while I knew that
some *alters* could assume the shapes of animals, it had never occurred
to me that Aleria Vega might be one of them.

The eagle bobbed its head, then it was changing again, becoming
the woman I knew. Or had thought I knew.

I gaped at her, seeing her with new understanding. The feathery
hair; the aquiline nose; the sharp, yellow eyes. The birdlike movements
of her head and arms.

"So *that's* your primary gift."

She offered me an apologetic smile. "I'm sorry, Sephone. Like I said,
there's really no way to prepare someone."

"That's why you spoke like you could escape any time you wanted.
You *can* escape. Tonight, even." I looked at her window. It would be
tight, but the bars were not as narrow as my own window, and she
could probably squeeze through them in her eagle form.

The smile vanished. "I never intended to leave you behind."

"Was that why you stayed?"

"It's why I let myself be captured in the first place. That, and I
wanted to learn the identity of the hooded man before we escaped."
She made an exasperated sound and clutched the bars with her gloved
hand. "I didn't expect to have to formulate a plan by *tonight*."

The pieces were still falling together. "That's why you were using
your gift on the hooded man's guards. To find out who he was."

"I'm sorry I didn't tell you the whole truth. You had enough to
worry about, and I didn't want to give you false hope. He is still a
formidable enemy."

I stepped closer to the bars. "Who sent you to find me?"

She hesitated. "Siaki Xia."

I reared back. "Xia?" And then I remembered—Xia had an *altered*
eagle. A bird who had once delivered Dorian a message. "The eagle . . .
that was you."

"Aye, we've met once before. Forgive me the deception; I wanted to introduce myself to you and Lord Adamo. But I couldn't betray my identity then, for it would have raised far too many questions."

"You're an outlander, and you're working for a Lethean leader?"

"Working *with*," she corrected me. "Aye, Xia is a friend of the outlanders, though she hides her allegiances well, along with the hint of outlander blood that runs in her veins. Even Lord Adamo, perhaps her closest friend, is unaware of her connection to us."

I suppressed a flinch at the reminder of Xia's long-lived friendship with Dorian. "I didn't think I meant so much to her."

"Xia has been searching for you for months. You've proved difficult to find."

"I don't understand. Why didn't Xia send *you* to assassinate Lord Draven? Why bother searching for me?"

"She doesn't know I'm a *mem*." Aleria's eyes twinkled. "Some secrets, I still keep to myself. Besides, I don't believe that murdering Draven is the answer to our problems. If we kill him, his son will only rise up in his place." She glanced at the door. "I wish there was more time, so I could explain everything."

"But you can escape. You can leave right now."

Aleria pursed her lips. "Listen, you have to trust me. If I stay here, they'll drug me, and I won't be able to transform. I may not be able to leave for a long while. In my eagle form, with eagle eyesight, I can cover more ground and track people more easily. I'll get a message to Xia, and to Lord Adamo. Then I'll return for you."

"Nay." I shook my head violently. "If you come back, he might capture you again, and this time, you may not be able to escape."

She reached through the bars and clasped my gloved hand. "I'm not afraid of him, Sephone. I'll find your Dorian and Cass—"

"They aren't *mine*—"

"And then we'll come find you. I won't be dissuaded."

I blinked away tears. "Xia must consider me a valuable piece for you to go to such trouble."

"You are a valuable piece. But you're also a friend, Sephone Winter. I won't forget you, and neither will Xia and Lord Adamo. We promise."

A tear slipped down my cheek, and she smiled sadly. "Remember the white bird," she said, squeezing my hand. "There is always hope." And then she was transforming into her golden eagle form. I watched as she flew to the window and alighted on the ledge. Though I hadn't seen eagles except in memories, I thought she might be smaller than those birds usually were.

Still, it was quite a feat to force her body through the bars, and my stomach tightened as she released the aquiline equivalent of a muted cry. Then she suddenly shot through to the other side. I hoped she wouldn't be injured when she returned to her human form.

She flew to my window and remained there for several seconds, shuffling her wings.

"Go," I said. "I'll be all right."

Yellow eyes blinked once, as if to acknowledge my answer, and then Aleria Vega was gone.

6

DORIAN

"This change in the weather can't be coincidence," Dorian ventured as they walked hesitantly through the gloom, their hands on their weapons. "Surely we're getting close now."

The gray had descended soon after Cass had found the lock of hair and the footprints, veiling the gorge with an unnaturally heavy mist. For two days, they had followed the meandering path, finding more footprints and signs of life, including a campfire that morning with the ashes still warm.

Asa's men were not far ahead of them.

Of course, following their trail meant missing the planned rendezvous with Bear, Bas, and Jewel, but they had agreed that in the event of finding Sephone or a significant clue to her whereabouts, they would continue on. The others would stay where they were, at the agreed meeting place, and Dorian, Cass, and Spartan would return to them once they had found Sephone.

Cass paused, eyebrow raised. "How do you figure that, Thane?"

"Remember that Asa Karthick had a man who could create thick, black smoke?"

"Ah, yes. I remember. Smoke shaped like your worst nightmares. Cheery fellow."

"Well," Dorian replied, "maybe Asa has another *alter* who can manipulate the gray."

Cass scowled. "Stop calling him Asa. He's an *ignis*, remember? An *ignis* who might just kill us all before the day is done."

Dorian glanced at Spartan, who hadn't spoken. He rarely intervened in Dorian and Cass's arguments, and this one was proving to be no exception, even though it concerned his own brother.

"I don't like it," Cass grumbled, pulling his cloak more tightly around his shoulders and adjusting his hold on his blades. "If they're manipulating the gray, they must know we're coming. And there are only three of us against the gods know how many of them."

"What happened to 'it depends on the men'?"

Cass glowered at Dorian. "And what if Ignis is with them? It was Sephone who overpowered him last time, as you recall."

Dorian sobered at his words. Asa would have no trouble lighting a fire, even with this oppressive mist. "He's the leader of his father's army. Right now, his priority is defeating Lethe. I doubt he would have come after Sephone himself."

That left the woman who could blind her assailants, the one who could turn into a ferocious wolf-lion—Zaire—and the man who could toss people into the air like stringless puppets. And whoever else they'd brought with them. Unless Lethe's new weapons had finished them off, which Dorian doubted. More likely, they had undertaken a temporary retreat.

"Need I remind you," Cass went on, "that while we have weapons, our gifts are not offensive in nature." He eyed Dorian's quarterstaff dubiously. "We don't have that impressive wolf of yours this time, and even the monk can only do shields."

Was Cass remembering the Nightmares that Zaire had controlled? The ones that might have killed him the night they fled Calliope, if not for Sephone's intervention?

"Don't call him a monk," Dorian said stiffly.

"That's what he is, isn't he?" Cass retorted. "We don't have Sephone *or* Jewel. Maybe we shouldn't be sneaking up on an enemy who could annihilate us with a single fireball."

"We'll be careful. And we're not after Asa; we're after the hooded man. I have no intention of fighting Asa's *alters* if I can help it. Now, keep your voice down, or they will hear us coming."

That night, they lay wrapped in their cloaks, unwilling to make a proper camp lest they be caught off guard. It was Spartan's turn for the watch—the acolyte stood not far away, searching the gloom for movement—but both Dorian and Cass remained wide awake, neither of them able to sleep. For the hundredth time, Dorian wished for Jewel's presence, for she would be able to sense if someone was coming.

Or perhaps not. The gray had only grown denser as they travelled, and the warm days had become oppressively cold. Cass was even moodier than usual, snapping at Spartan when he'd suggested they stop for the night and at Dorian when he'd said it was too dangerous to start a fire. Dorian tried to remind himself that Cass was Marianthean, and used to long days in the sun, but his temper shortened at each waspish quip and heated scowl.

Spartan returned and sat cross-legged beside Dorian. "Naught is out there. At least, not yet. But this gray is indeed unnatural. I sense trouble afoot." He darted a look at Dorian and lowered his voice. "Are you all right? You've been downcast all day."

He was right: not even Spartan's gift had managed to shift the shadow on Dorian's soul. And for good reason.

Dorian glanced sideways at Cass, who was now watching the river drift silently along the floor of the gorge, carrying all manner of helpless debris with it. "The company isn't exactly cheerful."

"Yet I sense it is more than that."

The youth was uncanny. He was also right. Dorian took a deep breath. "I lost my wife and daughter two years ago today."

Spartan bowed his head. "I am sorry to hear it."

"Don't be. They say the burden becomes lighter with every passing year."

"Nay," replied the acolyte. "You just become stronger at carrying it, and therefore feel the heaviness less."

He spoke as if his experience of grief were personal . . . and then

Dorian abruptly remembered that it was. "I never asked what happened to your mother. How did she die?"

"My father didn't kill her," Spartan said quickly. "She died in her sleep. I think her heart had broken years before, when she realized that my father would never marry her and that I would always be illegitimate. She was never the same after that. I do wonder if . . . well, if she had actually fallen in love with him."

Compassion overtook Dorian for the slave woman—always loving, but without any hope that her feelings would ever be returned. Loving a monster past all reason, even to her death.

"I am sorry," he said, somewhat woodenly. Draven had taken everything from both of them, which made them brothers of sorts.

Dorian glanced at Cass and found the *lumen* watching them, his features impassive. His gloved fingers twitched in his lap, and Dorian remembered that Cass had once offered to share Dorian's sorrow. Dorian doubted Cass would renew the offer, even if he'd overheard what Dorian had said to Spartan. But for once, Cass's customary scowl was gone, and he hadn't mocked Dorian for his loss.

"None of us are sleeping," Cass said eventually. "Why don't we press on?"

He was right: there was no point trying to rest. They had maintained a brisk pace all day; each of them now sensed how close they were to Asa—and to Sephone. Her features flashed into Dorian's mind, along with the distinct recollection of how it had felt to hold her. Then the memory was replaced by a vision of the blood draining away from her face, only to be replaced with poison . . .

"Aye," Dorian said, running a trembling hand through his hair. "Let's go on."

"Thane. Stop."

Dorian halted at Cass's whispered command, knowing the *lumen's* ears were more finely attuned than his own. Carefully, Dorian put down his pack, wincing at the faint *clink* of the copper arm cuffs within. The other men followed suit.

Dorian gripped his staff tightly. It was sometime in the early morning, though the gray remained as thick as ever. They had been traveling all night, following the trail left by Asa's *alters*.

"I hear voices ahead," said Cass in an undertone. "I think we've found them."

The briefest of suspicions flashed across Dorian's mind. He could hear naught. What if Cass was leading them into a trap?

Dorian glanced at Spartan, and he nodded. "I hear them, too."

Cass lifted an eyebrow, and green ribbons drifted between him and Spartan, tangling with the unearthly fog. The sudden reappearance of Cass's gift always took getting used to; now, Dorian hoped it wouldn't give away their position.

Holding his staff, Dorian crept forward. Past a veil of rock, which was draped sideways across the path, there looked to be a clearing ahead, and the walls of the gorge were not as high. Perhaps they had finally come to the end of it.

Dorian squinted. Several dark figures lay strewn around the clearing—no more than four, he thought.

"I count five," Cass whispered, startling Dorian.

Surely the *lumen*'s eyesight wasn't better than Dorian's, too.

"We're outnumbered," Dorian replied. "So, we keep our distance for the time being, and follow them. They may lead us directly to Sephone."

"Maybe they'll take on the hooded man for us." Cass's teeth gleamed. "Better they risk their necks than we risk ours."

"That's not very kind," remarked a voice from behind them, and they whirled. A middle-aged man in dusty traveling clothes stood there, his arms sheathed in black leather gloves to his elbows. Dorian stepped to the fore and raised his staff defensively, though the newcomer carried no weapons.

From what Dorian had seen of this man's gift in Nyx, he didn't need them.

"For your information, there are six of us. And I would caution you against following us. We're not to be trifled with." The *alter* blinked as green light materialized in the space between them, causing the fog to glow eerily.

"Listen," Dorian said quickly, before Cass could offer some taunting reply or the *alter* decided they presented a significant threat. "We're both after the same thing, are we not?"

The man raised an eyebrow. "And what is that?"

"Sephone Winter and the Reliquary." Dorian wouldn't reveal their names—not yet. Best the man not realize that Asa was hunting them, too.

The *alter* crossed his arms. "You seek the Reliquary and the girl?"

"Aye." Dorian indicated the green ribbons drifting from Cass toward him on an invisible current. "The *lumen*'s gift declares I am speaking the truth. Is your master, Asa, here?"

He studied Dorian carefully, and Dorian knew he had guessed correctly. Asa wasn't present, but this man wasn't going to reveal that easily, especially now he knew Cass was a *lumen*. "Why do you ask?"

"Because the man you seek—the hooded man—is no more our friend than he is yours. He has taken one of our number against her will. Why not attack him together?" Dorian poured both his gifts into his words, mimicking the man's accent as best he could in the hope that he might consider Dorian an ally.

The *alter* laughed thinly. "Why should we have need of *you*?"

"There are only six of you," Dorian pointed out. "The prey you seek was strong enough to take a powerful *mem* against her will." The *alter* didn't need to know that Brinsley had drugged her in order to do it. "Are you so confident in your abilities that you would refuse our help?"

He appeared to be considering the offer. Then he looked beyond Dorian to Spartan, and his eyes suddenly narrowed. "I know this boy."

Without warning, the *alter* raised his hands and flicked his wrists. A gust of wind slammed into Dorian, knocking him backward. Grasping his staff, he staggered to his feet, looking around for the others. Cass had been thrown as he had, but Spartan was still standing, a shimmering crystalline shield attached to his right arm.

"Peace, Tobin," he was saying. "We are not the enemy."

"You became the enemy the day you left," Tobin spat through gritted teeth. He raised his hands and sent another blast at Spartan, who blocked it easily with the shield that was now as tall and wide as he was. The *alter* continued to advance, but his back was turned to Dorian, who crept toward him just as a large shape streaked through the gap in the rock.

Spartan shifted and flung out his hand; an iridescent wall of crystal appeared behind the creature. It took Dorian a long moment to realize why the acolyte had erected the shield *behind* the creature instead of between them: the other *alters* had noticed the commotion and were advancing, too. They stabbed and shoved at the barrier, but it remained firm, preventing them from joining the fight.

How long could Spartan sustain the shield? The moment it failed, they would all die.

Dorian spun to face the creature. It was a smaller version of the animal which had terrorized Nyx—it had to be to fit through the gap in the rock—but no less vicious looking. Its jaws still dripped poison, and it had the lithe body of a wolf with the powerful shoulders and head of a lion, though both were grossly disfigured. It tossed its head as it advanced, iridescent black mane rippling. Yellow breath puffed from between rows of bared teeth.

So, Asa had sent his lover to track down Sephone. It was hard to believe that in her human form, Zaire was a stunningly beautiful woman.

Dorian glanced at Spartan. His back was against the wall as Tobin pummeled him with blasts, but both his shields were holding steady. Still, Cass and Dorian were now at the mercy of the beast, and until he dealt with Tobin, Spartan could do naught to help them.

Judging by the way Cass held his head, he had hit the ground much harder than Dorian had. He was still sitting where he'd fallen, looking slightly dazed. Dorian moved between Cass and Zaire, brandishing his staff.

The creature's black lips curved in a garish smile. *That flimsy piece of wood will do naught to stop me, Dorian Ashwood.*

He flinched as her menacing words seared his brain. Was she telepathic, too? "Get out of my head," Dorian growled, quickly erecting his mental wall. But she made no advance against his mind, and he concluded she could merely project her thoughts in monster form.

No matter—even if she couldn't take control of his mind, she would soon destroy his body. As she stalked toward him, the gray cleared, knifing the gloomy gorge with sharp, golden daggers. Cass had gotten his wish: the space around them would soon be flooded with sunlight. Was Spartan's shield keeping out the *alter* who manipulated the gray?

Zaire lunged at Dorian, and he twisted sharply to the side, narrowly avoiding a swipe of her deadly claws. Once again, she pounced, and again he jerked away. Again and again. His breath came short as the cold air punctured his lungs; sweat beaded on his hairline. He could only play this game of cat and mouse for so long. His limbs screamed weariness, and he was swiftly regretting the many sleepless nights.

Too late, he realized that Zaire had successfully maneuvered him away from Cass. When Dorian dodged her, she lunged for the *lumen* instead. Thankfully, Cass was on his feet, but he only narrowly missed the swipe of her jaws. Dorian heard the tearing of his sleeve and his yelp of surprise. Cass stumbled backward and once again hit the ground on his backside.

His sleeve was red—had he been injured after all?

With her attention diverted, Dorian threw himself at Zaire. The iron tip of his staff caught her beneath her ribs, and she growled, twisting midstrike at Cass to come for Dorian instead. She caught his staff in her jaws and bit down, but it didn't break. With a violent jerk of her head, she wrenched it from his hands and flung it away.

Snarling, she leaped at Dorian. He fell flat on his back, the breath smacked from his lungs by the rocky ground. He attempted to regain his feet, but she pinned him with her heavy paws, crushing him with her weight. Her claws raked his chest. Blood welled, quickly soaking his ribboned shirt. He closed his eyes, not wanting to see the moment she ripped out his throat.

Against the haze of red, Sephone's face materialized. He wished he could have told her the truth about how he felt this side of the grave, but it was not to be. Cass would have to find her and rescue her in Dorian's place. He could tell her—if he condescended to—what Dorian had never admitted, though Dorian doubted he would. Even if Dorian were dead, Cass would still consider him competition.

I'm sorry you won't get to save the girl, Zaire said in his mind. *Your heroism is admirable, Ashwood, and I will admit I'm a bit of a romantic, myself. But Asa's father was clear: we are not the future; they are.*

Dorian opened his eyes. He was a *calor*; he would be brave even if she tore his heart to shreds. Zaire's poison dripped onto his face, splashing his neck. The liquid was nearly hot enough to singe his skin. "I wonder that you would give up on Asa so easily."

I am not *giving up on him,* she snarled in reply. *The girl changes naught. Asa will always be mine.*

With his weak third gift, Dorian could feel her fury . . . and her passion. She loved Asa. Somehow, Draven had convinced her that she could still have him, even if he belonged to another woman.

Now, Dorian Ashwood, I am going to kill you. She lowered her jaws, and Dorian braced himself for the killing strike. But at the very moment she bent her head, golden-brown flashed above her. The shape spiraled down with the current, its enormous wings partially retracting as it entered a shallow dive.

The eagle shrieked—a cry loud enough to raise the dead—and its talons extended, swiping at one of Zaire's eyes. She howled with pain and recoiled, her weight lifting from Dorian's chest just as lightning flashed overhead. He sat up and saw Spartan whirling above him, brandishing what looked like a bolt of crystal. Tobin lay on the ground nearby, either dead or unconscious, and Cass sat in the dirt, blinking and clutching his bloodied arm.

Together, Spartan and the eagle drove Zaire back; Spartan with his sword of light, and the eagle with its sharp beak and claws. The wounded Zaire whimpered, blood gushing from one eye and her glossy flank. Only when she was nearly to the gap in the rock did Spartan release his shield, quickly re-erecting another barrier between him and Zaire. The other *alters* clustered around her as she regained her human form and collapsed.

The sword of light vanished, and Spartan rushed back to Dorian's side. "We don't have much time," he said urgently, kneeling. "That barrier will only hold them for so long."

"The s-sword," Dorian stammered. "How did you—"

"There'll be time for questions later, Dorian. Now, we must flee."

Cass joined them, holding his arm awkwardly. "We're trapped. There's no way out of this gorge."

"Not to the naked eye," came a voice behind them, and they turned.

A young woman stood there, her clothes grimy and a little shabby, but the woman herself was strong and sure. She was holding Dorian's staff; as Cass continued to gape at her, she inspected it closely.

"Ash wood," she said, amused. "How very appropriate." She bent and handed it back to Dorian with the smallest dip of her head.

"Thank you," he replied, quickly gaining his feet. "For the staff and for saving my life."

It was easy to see that *she* was the eagle; her mane of golden-brown hair was almost feathery, and her eyes were a striking topaz yellow. Her chin jutted forward proudly, and Dorian could see how the animal whose shape she readily assumed had imprinted itself on her nature. Or perhaps it was the other way around.

Cass reached instinctively for one of his blades, and Dorian put out a hand to stop him. "Nay, she's a friend."

She nodded briskly. "I'm Aleria Vega, and we've met before." Her head tilted, and Dorian recalled Siaki Xia's messenger eagle. "I will explain everything as soon as I can, Lord Adamo, but right now, we have to escape. Sephone's life may well depend on it."

He straightened. "Do you know where she is?"

"I last saw her two days ago. I've been trying to track you, but your movements have been masked by the gray."

She peered up at the side of the gorge. Was her human vision as sharp as her eagle form's? Sunlight streamed down on them, and after so long in the near dark, it blinded.

"Do you see that path there?" She pointed, apparently oblivious to the yells and threats coming from behind Spartan's shield-wall. Dorian squinted and made out the faintest of trails, no more than a goat track. Steep, but it would bring them to the top of the gorge.

"Can you manage it?" Dorian asked Cass, seeing how he cradled his arm.

"Of course," he said smoothly. "Can *you*?" He glanced pointedly at Dorian's bloodied shirtfront.

"Of course," Dorian responded. He couldn't pause to examine the wounds now; they were smarting badly, but that would have to wait until they were well clear of Zaire and her fellow *alters*. There didn't seem to be a great deal of blood, but poison covered his face and throat, which could seep into the open wounds. And of all the things he couldn't afford right now, a delusional fever was near the top of the list.

"Come," said Aleria Vega, and they retrieved their packs and followed her to the base of the goat path. She took the lead, remaining in her human form. Spartan's crystal shield expanded and turned opaque as they began to climb, effectively concealing their escape.

"The barrier will weaken the further I go from it," Spartan explained. "We should move as fast as we can."

The gray thickened once again as they climbed upward. Miss Vega's upper arms were bare, and Dorian glimpsed large, coal-black bruises on the outsides of both. In which form had she been injured? Still, she moved more quickly than any of them, reaching the top well ahead of Cass, who came next. Dorian heaved himself over the edge, Spartan close behind him.

"You said you saw Sephone," Cass was saying to Miss Vega. "Where?"

"We were imprisoned together in a concealed stronghold not far from here. I would take you there, but there's no use. Sephone was moved two days ago." Green vines wove themselves into the breeze between her and Cass. If they surprised her, she didn't show it.

"Moved?" Dorian repeated.

"Aye. The hooded man—our captor—knew Asa's *alters* were close. He decided to move us before they arrived."

Cass eyed her as he hugged his arm to his chest. "And how come you escaped and she didn't?"

"There will be time for this later," she said impatiently. "For now, you just have to trust me."

"I think you'll find we're less trusting than we used to be."

"Cass," Dorian intervened, "you can see she's telling the truth."

Her eyes flashed, and Dorian caught a glimpse of the aquiline fierceness. "I can do one better than that." Peeling off her gloves, she reached out to both of them. "I can show you."

Cass hesitated, then nodded. Dorian extended his ungloved hand as well. With a sigh, she briefly gripped their hands. A rapid sequence of images flashed across Dorian's mind.

A meeting with Siaki Xia, and the mention of Sephone's name. Soaring on the updrafts, heading for the mountains. An unexpected—or perhaps not so unexpected—abduction. Aleria Vega, fighting the guards with everything she had. And then Sephone . . . hurt. Aleria splinting her wrist as she grimaced in pain. Sharing tales of the outlands—becoming friends. Then a face . . . a man whose eyes were the only thing visible in a swath of white.

The hooded man.

Her fingers tightening on Dorian's wrist, she showed him a final frame: Squeezing through the bars of her cell window as an eagle. Then, hovering on the ledge of another window, looking down at a young woman with pale hair grown to her shoulders. A woman they'd both promised to return for, who carried a world of grief in her desolate eyes.

After a few seconds, Aleria drew back. "There," she announced, seeming more fatigued than before. "Are you satisfied?"

Dorian turned to hide his expression. Sephone might look whole physically, but sharp-eyed Aleria had gazed into her soul and seen what few could.

When we find her, Sephone may not be the same woman who left us . . .

"All right," said Cass, who seemed just as shaken. "Lead the way."

"I'll need to return to my eagle form." She glanced at Dorian, and he knew what she'd seen in him.

"Aye. We'll follow you."

Her figure dissolved and assumed an eagle's shape. Extending her enormous wings, she dived off the cliff they'd just ascended and appeared seconds later, soaring on an updraft. Dorian tracked her spiraling form, only then realizing what she'd shown them, and what it meant.

Aleria Vega was a *mem*.

7

DORIAN

By the time Aleria called a halt for the night, they had put a significant amount of distance between themselves and Asa's *alters*. Even so, they had just retraced many of the steps they'd taken over the past few days . . . had it all been for naught?

But they had found Aleria—or rather, she'd found them—and she seemed to know where she was going. She covered five times the distance they did on foot, staying as high as she could without vanishing completely, searching the patches of gray that still concealed much of the mountains. Only at the end of the day did she descend for more than a brief rest.

"Did you see her?" Dorian asked as soon as she was her human self again.

She shook her head. "Only signs of their trail. We are two days behind them at least. And they're not easy to track. The hooded man knows what he's doing."

"At least Asa's *alters* don't yet know Sephone has been moved."

"Aye, but they'll discover that soon enough, and then they'll be on our tail again. We may find ourselves sandwiched between enemies before the week is out."

They made camp in another mountain cave, this one little more than a rocky overhang which kept out the damp, but not the wind. At least this time they could risk a fire—with the gray so thick, the smoke wouldn't be noticeable. Dorian thought of the Mardell brothers and Jewel as they collected all the wood they could find. Were they still at the meeting place, as agreed? Was Jewel keeping them well-fed with game while they waited?

Dorian's stomach grumbled at the thought—the evening's pickings would not be nearly so glamorous. But Cass, fortunately, had put aside his sour mood for once, and even rations seemed like a feast when accompanied by long-awaited news of Sephone.

Aleria, though weary, seemed to feel their need for answers. As soon as the fire was blazing, she tilted her head at Dorian and Cass. "Those wounds look serious. Before I tell you everything, you should probably tend to them."

She was right. Dorian directed Spartan to help bind the gash on Cass's arm while Dorian removed what remained of his own tattered shirt. The gashes beneath were superficial and didn't require bandaging, but on seeing the poison once again, Dorian washed his face, neck, and chest carefully until no trace of the inky black remained. If he had been poisoned, he would know in the coming hours. He gingerly lifted his arms and shrugged on another shirt.

When he rejoined the others, Cass was speaking with Spartan. "I thought you could only do shields."

"Whatever the situation requires," came the acolyte's vague reply.

Maybe after all of this, Cass would no longer call him *monk*.

Aleria settled herself on the ground, leaning back against the cave wall. Dorian, Cass, and Spartan seated themselves around her like children about to hear a tale of grand adventure.

"The first thing you probably want to know," she began, "is that Sephone is well."

"Why did you splint her wrist, then?" Cass asked, beating Dorian to the question.

"Because one of the guards broke it," she replied. "Well, her brother broke it first, and then, after it had healed, the guard—"

"Her *brother*?" Cass exclaimed. "The foul scu—"

"Aye, the same day she was captured. Brinsley Winter is with them now."

Rage swept through Dorian, eradicating any lingering awareness of pain. To treat one's own sister so contemptibly . . . then again, Brinsley had never cared for his sister, nor her return from the dead. He only cared for the profit she could bring him.

Dorian should have seen that sooner. "Where has she been kept all this time?" he asked. "We've been searching these mountains for months."

"I'm sorry to say that you probably would never have found them on your own. Asa's *alters* only came close because they had Brinsley's trail to follow. And it is a stroke of good fortune that they even found Brinsley in the first place."

Dorian briefly met Cass's gaze. Had it been Brinsley's hair they'd found, then, not Sephone's?

"The hideout was mainly underground," Aleria went on, "and only a few cells were exposed to the elements . . . mine and Sephone's included. Of course, the hooded man didn't know I could change into an eagle, or he would not have made such a mistake."

In a low tone, she related the details: How she was an outlander, sent by her people to bring down Draven at any cost. How she had joined forces with Siaki Xia, who—to Dorian's astonishment—carried outlander blood in her veins. How she had allowed herself to be captured in order to get close to the hooded man and Sephone, but then her plan had backfired, and Sephone had given in to their captor to save Aleria from the Reliquary's poison.

"I don't know who this man is," Aleria admitted, "and try as I might, I never saw his face. But he's powerful—very powerful. He has extensive resources. He's using Sephone and the Reliquary to interrogate his enemies, then to erase their recent memories so they have no idea they've betrayed their master." She paused, then took a breath. "Once, he had her wipe the mind of one of Draven's advisors. She didn't know it would happen so, but the woman . . ."

She trailed off, but Dorian understood. The woman had died. He closed his eyes briefly. How had Sephone, a woman with a heart so tender she felt the smallest of sorrows, endured such a procedure? How could she go on with such a weight on her conscience? Now he knew the reason for the desolation he'd seen in her eyes through Aleria.

"We know about the missing people," said Cass uncomfortably. "And we know what the Reliquary demands in exchange for its power."

"Aye." Aleria seemed reluctant to say anything more. "She tried to protect me from it, and though I didn't understand at the time, now I know why."

She met Dorian's eyes, and he realized she knew about the poisonous marks on Sephone's chest, the curse which was slowly draining her life. But she must have also sensed the rising tension between him and Cass, because she swiftly changed the subject.

"I learned very little about the hooded man during my captivity. But enough to know that soon he will strike at Draven himself. We have to rescue Sephone and the Reliquary before he does."

"Is he an *alter*?" Spartan asked. "The hooded man?"

"I don't know. Sephone wasn't sure, either."

"You're working for Siaki Xia," Dorian said. "Does she know that you're a *mem*?"

Aleria shook her head. "Sephone asked the same question, but nay, Xia is unaware of my secondary gift. The thaness and I are like-minded on many subjects, but I believe it will take more than an assassin to defeat Draven. The hooded man evidently knows it, too, else he would have sent Sephone after Draven himself."

"Have you any news from Xia?" Dorian tried not to dwell on the fact that his supposed ally had kept Aleria's existence a secret. But Xia had sent her to look for Sephone, and in the past, he had kept secrets from Xia, too.

"Some," Aleria replied, "though it's probably outdated now. Lethe's army has clashed with Memosine's again, but presently, they're at a stalemate. With the outlanders pushing back in the north, Memosine is fighting a war on two fronts, and Draven's army is stretched thin. If ever there were a time for someone to make his move against the new king, it would be now. Draven's hold on Caldera is tenuous at best, and the unrest he's created by using *alters* to do his bidding has generated fires that are not easily put out. Asa Karthick is not exactly a popular leader."

Her gaze strayed to Spartan's, and by the way her eyes sharpened, Dorian could see she knew who the acolyte was. But, unlike Tobin, no anger simmered in her expression. "You're a member of the Order now?" she asked him.

Had they met before?

Spartan nodded, and her eyes lit up. "I would speak with you of the Three."

Another group of potentially powerful people Dorian had unintentionally alienated—if they existed. He moved away, leaving Spartan and Aleria to converse privately. They could make more plans in the morning, once each of them had rested and recovered their strength.

"I'll take the first watch," Dorian said and wrapped himself in his cloak a short distance from the others.

As Cass lay down on his bedroll, Spartan and Aleria kept talking, apparently not as weary as Dorian had first believed. After a while, Spartan wished her goodnight. Dorian stood and stretched, trying to regain the feeling in his legs, then walked silently toward Aleria. She glanced up as he approached, but didn't look surprised.

"If you're not too spent," he said softly, "I would speak with you alone."

She nodded and followed him to a spot further away from the others, where they could talk without being overheard. When Dorian didn't speak immediately, she turned to look out at the mountains. They were high up—no doubt as Aleria preferred—but the gray still veiled much of the landscape, even at night. Only a handful of stars was visible.

Dorian wet his lips. "Was it Xia or Sephone who told you about me?"

"Both." She brought her sharpened gaze downward—she seemed to understand why he had asked to speak privately. "Though they differ greatly in their accounts of you, Lord Adamo."

"Dorian," he insisted, even as his stomach clenched. "And how so?"

She studied him carefully. "When she looks at you, Siaki Xia sees a man of power, persuasion, and ambition . . . practically a war hero. But Sephone—"

"I know I failed her. I *betrayed* her."

"Let me finish my sentence before you spend the rest of our conversation wallowing in self-pity, Dorian. When Sephone looks at you, she sees the boy who saved her as a child. A boy who risked everything to save a girl he didn't even know."

"Then she told you what happened. How we met."

"Aye. Like I said, I'm her friend—no less a friend for such a short acquaintance." She eyed him. "Isn't that what you wanted to ask me? What she thinks of you now?"

"I'm not sure you answered that question, even if it was the one I asked."

"She spoke well of Cassius Vera and of you. If I read her correctly, she cares for you both. But if you want to know more than that, you should speak to her yourself."

"It's not that simple," he objected. "But then, you already know she is dying."

"Aye." Her lips turned down. "But why should it not be simple, Dorian, to declare what Sephone still doubts but I see clear as day?"

"And that is—"

"That you love her. That you love her so much, you're planning to die for her."

He jerked back, stiffening. "I shouldn't have let you in my mind."

Her face softened in shades. "I'm sorry. I didn't mean to see it. But such life-altering plans have a way of leaping out at you. That is, at *mems*. If you want to conceal your intentions from her, you're going to have to do better than that, or else stay away from her altogether."

Reluctantly, he acknowledged that she was right. He would have to practice keeping any thoughts of the future well behind his walls.

She came closer and grasped his wrist—fortunately, both their hands were gloved. "What you plan to do is impossible without the Reliquary. And even if you get that back, she will never agree to it."

"She doesn't have to."

"Her heart is already fractured. What you propose would break it entirely."

"Only if she loves me back," he said, remembering the letter she'd written. "And she doesn't anymore." He retreated again, shaking off Aleria's firm grip. "There is only enough life between us for one of us to live. Even if I cared naught for her, the decision would still be easy. She is light; I am shadow." He had told her that the day he had rejected her, beside the stream, and it was as true now as it had been then.

"If you think she could ever thank you for such an exchange, you don't know her at all."

"Fortunately, I will have no need of her gratitude where I am going."

The *mem*'s *altered* eyes searched Dorian's with startling acuity. He tried not to flinch or shy away, but the way she studied him felt almost painful. Even Cass's gift did not probe so deeply.

"You are an admirable man, Dorian Ashwood," she said at last. "I should not have seen what I did, so I will keep this confidence. But before you do anything, you should speak to her. There is much between you that needs to be resolved."

He nodded, and at last, her eyes released his.

"There is one more thing I can give you." She removed her glove before extending her hand to him.

He pulled back, wary of her after the last time.

"There's no need to shy away like a spooked horse. Trust me. I won't go near your memories again."

Hesitantly, he peeled off his glove and lightly grasped her fingers. Warmth stirred in her palm, bleeding into his cold fingers. It was exceedingly strange, seeing Sephone's gift bestowed on an entirely different woman.

"Close your eyes," she ordered, and he obeyed.

She offered him a memory, something she had not shared earlier in the day, shaped like a child's snow globe. He took it in both his hands. It was a simple scene, brief in its duration. Sephone lay asleep on her bed, her hair streaked with silver moonlight. In his dreams, she had been sickly and skeletal when they found her, but the woman on the bed was neither. She lay half on her side, half on her back; the slender, splinted forearm slung across her chest rising and falling with each gentle breath; her head turned toward the window where a white raven perched on the other side of the bars, looking down at her.

Aleria Vega let go of his hand.

"You see?" she said softly when his eyes opened. "There is still hope, Dorian Ashwood."

"Hope?"

"Aye. There is always hope." She squared her shoulders and replaced her glove. "Now get some sleep," she commanded, though looking thoroughly exhausted herself. "And please, for the sake of those circles beneath your eyes, limit the wallowing in self-pity . . . just for tonight, at least."

"'Wallowing in self-pity'?" he repeated, with one of Cass's sudden grins. "It's like you don't know me at all, Miss Vega."

"Aleria."

Even once his watch was over and he lay on his bedroll, Aleria Vega's words continued to echo in his head. *There is always hope,* she had said, with enviable conviction. She had seen Sephone's suffering, and she hadn't given up. The women were more alike than either of them knew.

Even before his eyes closed, he was bolstered by a renewed sense of optimism. If she could continue to hope, then so could he.

But in the early hours of the morning, he awoke—something was wrong. Heat licked through his body, and he wondered how he had inadvertently swallowed one of Asa Karthick's fireballs. It burned through his chest, searing everything it touched. His mouth was painfully dry, yet his shirt was soaked with sweat.

Aleria, who was on watch, glanced at him and paled.

"Fever," she whispered.

8

SEPHONE

I was dreaming, once again, of the white stallion.

We stood in the Garden at night, and though no moon shone, there was more than enough light to see. He was bigger than he had been when I'd seen him last, and somehow more real. His mane and tail shimmered like white silk; his iridescent coat rippled like the sun shining on gentle waves. When he came to me, he snorted softly, and I felt the puff of hot breath against my palm, even through my gloves. Distant echoes of high, almost ethereal notes reverberated in my ears.

I quickly discarded my gloves, wanting to feel his coat with my bare fingers, the tickle of his long whiskers. The fear I usually felt at touching another human being was absent with him, for he was just a horse, wasn't he? And, by the depth in his liquid black eyes, he understood me completely. He saw me—all of me, and still he came, as he had done every night since Aleria had left. Around him, I felt as warm as I had the first time I met Dorian. Warmer, even. I could do anything, so long as this new friend was beside me.

He was now far too tall to ride, but the moment I thought so, he lowered his body to the ground so I could climb on his back. When I settled myself, he regained his feet, tossing his glossy head, as if he wanted to run.

Go, I thought. *I want to run, too.*

In response, he broke into a graceful canter. I should have been afraid, since the saddle, reins, and stirrups were missing, but I merely gripped his mane and flattened myself against his back. The longer we rode, the more I surrendered myself to the rocking movement, becoming one with his even stride.

Ivy and Marmalade had nothing on this horse.

Once more, the stallion brought me to the vines, the only tamed part of the wild Garden. By the look of the plants, it had not rained here for some time. But the man still walked among them, studying them closely, occasionally pausing to snip a withered leaf or prune back a branch too heavy for the trellis to bear. Such care, such devotion, and yet I could see how the shoots were suffering.

I slipped from the stallion's back. The man must have seen us—the horse would be hard to miss—but it was some time before he came to greet us. I tried to conceal my anxiety, but my hands shook, and a lump filled my throat. I wished I hadn't lost my gloves.

Why had he delayed? Was he was wondering how best to punish the accomplice of a thief?

Dorian was wrong. The Mountain wasn't empty. The Three weren't a figment of my imagination.

The man—the son of the powerful *alter* I'd heard so much about—stopped in front of me and extended both his hands. He wasn't exactly smiling, but warmth emanated from him, just like I'd felt from the horse. It sank deep into my bones like liquid over parched ground, soaking all the way to my soul. I thought I heard a few warbling notes.

I stepped back. "I want to apologize." Wetting my lips, I fixed my gaze on my muddy boots. "Dorian stole from you . . . *I* stole from you. I didn't know what he was going to do, but I let him do it, and therefore, I'm just as deserving of the blame as he is."

He hadn't summoned a lightning bolt to annihilate me—yet—so I hastily went on. "We thought Spartan was mistaken. That the Mountain was unguarded, unoccupied. I see now that I was wrong. We stole something that belonged to you."

Still, he reached out to me. The regard in his eyes was steady, unchanging. But he said naught. Perhaps he didn't believe I was truly sorry.

"There's more," I confessed, this time hardly above a whisper. "Someone died because of what we stole. Someone died because of me." Tears slipped down my cheeks, and the white horse nuzzled my shoulder. "If I had known what the Reliquary could do, I would never have used it."

"Not even to save yourself?" the man asked, gently.

A second question was embedded within the first. This man might be the son of an *alter,* but I suspected he was one himself. At the very least, he seemed to possess a gift of foreknowledge. Maybe telepathy or dream-walking, too, given how he'd twice appeared to me while I slept. He must know that I was dying, that the Reliquary was the only thing capable of saving me. He must understand the temptation.

"Not now that I know what it will cost," I replied at last.

But that wasn't the whole truth. From the beginning, I had known about the curse, even if I'd refused to heed it. He'd told me the truth before, the night we fled the Mysterium's sanctuary.

What is required, Sephone, Dorian cannot give. For one to live, another must die . . .

He had told me what price the Reliquary demanded, and I hadn't listened.

Despite what I'd confessed, he hadn't withdrawn his hands. I glanced at them. They were large, coarse, and bare. He was probably more powerful than any *alter* I had ever met, and yet he exuded a quiet, reserved strength. I didn't think he wanted to harm me, but he wasn't exactly safe. Even if one of his hobbies apparently included gardening.

"You have questions, Sephone. Why not ask them?"

Aye, I had questions. About the Mysterium, about the Mountain, about *him.* But at that moment, my courage deserted me.

"I am sorry," I said breathlessly. "I have to go." I ran from the vineyard into the wild of the Garden, branches slapping at my face, brambles clawing at my clothes. Neither the *alter* nor the horse followed, and the Garden grew steadily darker until shapes were keeping pace with me through the trees. I shivered as I realized what they were.

Wolves.

I ran until my legs gave out, sinking to the ground in a small clearing as I gasped for breath. The wolves were circling now, close enough for me to see the hard glint of their eyes. As the wolves came closer, I realized they had human faces. Cutter, Lord Guerin, Silas Silvertongue, Rufus and Asa Karthick. And now the eyes of the hooded man.

I screamed as the foremost of them lunged for my throat.

I jerked upright, still feeling the jaws that had clamped around my neck, the teeth that had so easily crunched bone and severed sinew. But I was alive, and apparently intact, and for the first time in days, I felt the presence of my gift flickering in the back of my mind.

It was of little use to me, for I was imprisoned within a circle of sleeping men, including my brother and the hooded man. My wrists and ankles were tightly bound with thick rope. Behind me, a pair of guards sat together on watch, speaking in low voices. If I made even the smallest noise, they would turn and see me.

The hooded man had been furious after Aleria's escape. When I claimed not to know how she'd done it, he'd struck me in the face, knocking me to the floor. But we did not have much time, according to Brinsley, and the hooded man could not spare men to search for her. He'd promised to deal with me later.

We'd made haste through the mountains, moving as quickly as daylight—and sometimes night—allowed. I soon wished for my drafty cell, for I had the shortest legs of all of them, and my hands were bound constantly. Every muscle ached, but nothing hurt more than my throbbing wrist. The hooded man had removed Aleria's splint out of spite, and for most of the day, I had no feeling in my fingers. His men had only to seize my right forearm and I would double over in agony. Sleep was the only relief from the torment, and it was always in short supply.

I blinked, suddenly remembering the white horse . . . the Garden . . . the *alter*.

It had to be the drug they had given me—helmswort—to suppress my gift. Maybe it brought on vivid dreams. Even hallucinations. But that didn't seem right. The first time I'd dreamed about them, I had been at the Mysterium, not under the influence of helmswort. And the world of the dream felt far more real than the world I woke to each day. The white stallion—I had touched him, felt his hot breath. Looked into his liquid eyes. And the wolves—

I shook my head. It wasn't real. At least, it was no more real than memories.

But memories are *real, Sephone,* a voice insisted.

A fluttering near my right shoulder interrupted my thoughts. The shape alighted gracefully on my thigh . . . the white raven. I'd not seen him in days, and now he had arrived in the middle of a circle of enemies? Though the sight of him ordinarily filled me with joy, now my chest tightened.

"Go," I whispered urgently. Thankfully, the guards hadn't seen him yet. "They'll kill you for sport if they see you."

The raven remained where he was, intelligent eyes flickering as he balanced easily on my leg. When I tried to shake him off, he merely hopped to my ankles.

I turned to look at the guards—they were still looking the other way. Feeling a loosening of the ropes around my feet, I looked down.

My mouth dropped open. Something had sawed through the thick ropes, freeing my legs. The raven's sharp beak?

"Nay," I murmured. "Even if I'm free, there's no chance I could run." In response, the raven moved soundlessly to my lap, where he began working at the ropes around my wrists. Seconds later, they, too, fell away. Perhaps the bird had his own kind of magic.

My brother snorted in his sleep, and I jolted, but the raven wasn't startled. I stiffened in the darkness, hoping that the guards wouldn't look our way, wouldn't notice the large white bird perched on my lap. But when no shouts sounded, I relaxed. Yet only by a degree.

I could escape tonight. Could I?

The raven met my gaze, inclining his head in a way that reminded me of Aleria. When I didn't move, he hopped off my lap and away a few paces, as if beckoning me to follow. I bit my lip. He might be able to fly, but I would need to step over a sleeping body to escape this circle. And then there were the guards. But they were seated side by side, and my gift had re-emerged. Would it be powerful and stable enough to render them unconscious? I had no Reliquary this time to direct my gift nor to keep it under control and support me when my own energy reserves failed.

The image of the dead woman was enough to propel me to my feet. I wouldn't kill again for the hooded man, not if I could help it. The raven was in the air now, circling above as he waited for my escape.

Pulling my cloak tightly around myself, I quietly removed my gloves, stuffing them inside my shirt. There was no time to retrieve the Reliquary. The artifact was somewhere in this circle, in one of the packs, and it would be far too risky to search them. Keeping an eye on the guards, who were still deep in discussion, I stepped over the sleeping form of my brother. My heart rose to my throat as I imagined him waking, grabbing my ankle, and wrenching it as he had my wrist. But he remained asleep, snoring softly.

Farewell, brother.

I crept up behind the two guards, mimicking Jewel's stealth. The men sitting on the log had removed their face coverings, and their necks were exposed.

Foolish.

Summoning my gift, I extended both hands. The moment I touched their skin, the men stiffened, their lips frozen in a silent cry, every limb paralyzed. I had never used my power on two people at once—not without the Reliquary's help—and I was overwhelmed by the feel of two minds simultaneously. Two minds which were ugly, cold, and savage.

Still, my gift rose to the task. A little too enthusiastically, for suddenly my own memories were rising to the surface . . . years of nightmares from all the minds I'd ever visited. It would be so easy to push them through the mental link.

I leaned forward, black threads advancing ominously across my palms. It would be no less than these men deserved. No one else knew what they'd done, but I saw . . .

Nay, I couldn't torture these men with my memories. At the last moment, I tried to pull back, but my gift didn't respond. Power surged through my fingers, the black marks thickening and expanding. A fist squeezed my heart and I gasped.

Stop . . . please.

I struggled against the pull of my gift, even as it tugged me onward. *This isn't what I wanted.* But I was completely helpless.

Just as I began nudging the first of the horrors—one of Lord Guerin's most sordid memories—into their minds, a wave of heat swept through my body, and my power was suddenly snuffed out, like an extinguished candle. A vision of the white horse danced across my mind.

Sephone, he seemed to say, with a toss of his majestic head. *This is not the way.*

I drew back, and the two guards slumped soundlessly to the ground. My hands shook uncontrollably. What had I just tried to do? What had I done? This wasn't who I was. This wasn't me at all.

Or maybe it is, a voice said. *Maybe this is who you really are, deep down.*

But I wanted to stop. I tried to stop.

The first voice grew louder. *Maybe you really are what Cutter and Asa believed you to be.*

Shivering, I pulled my gloves back on and looked at the circle of men, still sleeping soundly. Then I turned and fled into the mountains.

The next night, my heart gave out before my body, though my body was not far behind. Several times, I had felt the urge to stop, but I'd forced myself onward, knowing that the hooded man would hunt me down ruthlessly as soon as he noticed I was missing.

I tripped and stumbled over the rocky terrain; my heels were soon rubbed raw, and my wrist hurt like it had broken all over again. I tried to splint it with a couple of sticks and a few torn strips from the hem of my cloak, but it was difficult to accomplish this task one-handed, and the end result was nowhere near as sturdy as Aleria's handiwork.

I had no idea where I was. The white raven still flew above me, and he seemed to know where we were going, though I had no other plan than to get as far away from the hooded man as possible. Admittedly, the bird might be leading me into another trap, but he was my only ally, and it was far better to follow him than to go in circles. Occasionally, he led me to fresh water or through a green patch where I found nuts and berries. The raven ate them, so I ate them, too. He seemed to know when I needed to rest.

When night fell, he found me a shallow cave, high on the mountainside. I lay down and fell asleep nearly instantly, waking some hours later to the raven tapping on my shoulder. I blinked away the last vestiges of sleep and emerged from the cave into a weak sunrise.

I had nothing on my person, not even a waterskin.

But I was alive. I was free.

Why, then, did I feel so empty? Why did I feel as if I had left a part of myself behind, somewhere in these wretched mountains? And the exchange was for naught. I didn't even have the barest scrap of information to give to Xia or Dorian when I finally found them. If I found them. I hadn't discovered the identity of the hooded man, for even his guards had never seen his face.

Nearly four months had passed, and I was lost. Hopelessly lost, in more ways than one.

For two days, the raven led me through the mountains. I was hungry and thirsty, but not enough to collapse; lonely, but not exactly alone. At night, the raven remained beside me, as if standing guard. I was too tired to do anything but fall asleep right away.

"I wish you could speak," I told him when I woke the next morning. All I had to look forward to were sharp taps on my shoulder and a slightly angled, beady set of eyes. I had quickly learned that the raven's presence was not always comforting; sometimes, the tap of his beak was hard enough to bruise.

On the third day, we came to the end of the mountains. If my internal map was accurate, we were a little north of Nyx. Nyx, which had been destroyed by Asa Karthick's army. I stood on the edge of the heather-covered moorland, the white raven perched on my shoulder. The vast expanse still bloomed a vivid purple, though I had been gone a long time, and in my absence, spring had given way to summer.

I had no idea where Dorian and Cass were, no idea if Aleria had found them, as she'd promised. I had no way of finding them myself. They might not even be in the mountains anymore. Thebe was far away, and I wasn't sure I remembered the way. I couldn't return to Nulla with the bounty on my head, and besides, no one waited for me there. I only knew of one place, one man I could still perhaps call a friend, if I were of a mind to do so.

Regis Symon.

Orphne was only days away. I could make it, I knew I could. Would Regis and his wife welcome me, even now?

Excitement rose. Regis was part of the lowborn resistance against Lord Draven. The Sons of Truth, they called themselves. He would know how to contact Dorian and Cass . . . or Aleria.

I straightened my shoulders, and the raven flew off.

"Sorry," I said at once, thinking I'd jolted him. But when I looked around, the raven had disappeared.

My heart skipped a beat. Where had he gone? He'd not left me once since I'd escaped the hooded man. Even while I slept, I could feel his comforting presence nearby. And now I was truly alone. I resisted the familiar urge to fall to my knees and weep. Instead, I turned my face northward. Orphne lay in that direction, past the River Lethe. I just had to cross the edge of the moorland, and I would be under the cover of the woods.

A series of foreign sounds alerted me to the intrusion of company. I hastily retreated behind a scraggly clump of trees, my heart rate hammering as a troop of men on horseback came into view. I had not realized I was so close to the road.

Friends? Or foes?

At the front of the procession rode an old man dressed in finery—the dress of the Memosinians, if I was not mistaken. Or perhaps he wasn't so old; his hair was silvery-white, but then again, so was mine. Nevertheless, something about him gave the impression of a great many years, and I shuddered as I realized who he was.

Silas Silvertongue. The same merchant who'd lured me away from my friends, first in Idaea, then in Thebe. An *alter* with the gift of persuasion, rumored to be working with Rufus Karthick, Lord Draven, now the king of Memosine.

That realization dawned a second, and my eyes went to the man riding next to him. He was young, with familiar red-blond hair and hard blue eyes. My legs weakened, sending me to my knees.

Asa Karthick.

I waited until the company had passed and then some. Such good fortune, for if I'd crossed merely a few minutes earlier, Asa's soldiers would have intercepted me directly. The hooded man might be heartless and cruel, but to fall back into the hands of the sadistic new king of Memosine . . .

Where had they been headed? Had Nephele fallen to Lord Draven's army already? I hadn't heard any news in over a fortnight. Perhaps Regis would know more.

After tending to my blistered heels, I started in the direction of Orphne. The long days of travel had worn on me, and I was hot and filthy, but I was also strong. I had survived far worse than this in the minds of Nulla's ruling elite. There was plenty of water, and Bear had taught me which plants were safe to eat. They wouldn't fill my stomach completely, but they would do until I reached Orphne.

The nights were the hardest. I was fortunate that it was summer, for the temperature, though cool, was not unbearable. But at night, my thoughts were full of Dorian and Cass and Jewel, my parents, Spartan, the Mardell brothers, and Lady Xia. Between nightmares of what I'd tried to do to the guards, I was plagued with visions of the white stallion, and the *alter* patiently tending to his vines.

The Mysterium was not much farther than Orphne. Several times, I considered adjusting my heading, reasoning that they would offer no less a welcome than Regis and his wife, Magritte. Perhaps even more so.

You're a fool, Sephone, a voice would remind me. *You would seek refuge from the same people who know you as a thief? Think what they would do if they knew you were a murderer, too.*

So I set my shoulders and continued on, trying to forget what the *alter* had once offered me—an unexpected gift I could never accept.

When the time comes, you have only to call for me, and I will come to you . . .

Dorian would have been proud of my navigational skills. Without a map, I managed to find the River Lethe and cross it at a shallow point, pausing only to soak my aching ankle—the same ankle which had once been broken in my altercation with the wolves. Then I plunged once again into forest, retracing our steps from months ago.

Though the gray still lingered, the forests of Lethe had come alive since I'd seen them last. Water chattered nearby as songbirds dipped in and out of the babbling current; beavers swam in the deeper pools, patrolling carefully constructed dams; even herds of roe deer were visible through the trees. The lush green was almost shocking after so many months among a palette of iron-gray, umber-brown, yellow, and red. Twice, I saw a golden eagle and thought of Aleria, but even after it glimpsed me, it came no closer.

Fearful of wolves and Memosinian soldiers, I spent the nights in the most hospitable trees I could find, but I encountered nothing more dangerous than a cluster of honeybees guarding a patch of wildflowers. The landscape would have been exquisitely beautiful if I had not desperately wanted to be somewhere else. It was hard to believe that Memosine and Lethe were now at war, that it might not be long until these woods were overrun with soldiers, the ancient trees cut down and hacked apart for fortifications and firewood.

The forest thickened and darkened by shades, and finally I came across one of the spiral entrances to the underground city of Orphne. Regis had given directions to the settlement where he lived in case we ever returned, and I was glad that despite my anger at him, I'd seen the wisdom of listening. Few people were about, and none of them spared a glance for a bedraggled stranger. Still, I kept my hair tucked inside my hood.

Orphne seemed much the same despite the more guarded glances of its inhabitants, and most of the buildings that had burned the last time I'd visited had been repaired. I'd forgotten how eerie the city felt, situated in its enormous dark cavern, with only the oil lamps to give the illusion of day. How did its citizens live in this perpetual state of intrigue, this constant shadow and mystery? I was already hungering for the sunrise.

Passing through the city, I found the underground river which connected the caverns. It should have been impossible to barter passage to the settlement where Regis and Magritte lived without money, but the boatman on duty agreed the moment he heard Regis's resistance name of Symon. With me lost in a haze of fatigue, the boat ride lasted what felt like mere minutes before we were gliding from the smooth tunnel into another cavern, this one smaller than the one that housed Orphne. I stammered my thanks to the boatman and stepped gingerly onto the rickety jetty.

Three days after leaving the mountains, I found myself standing on Regis's doorstep. To my great relief, the settlement where he lived had been largely untouched by the war. His three-story house was almost identical to the others in its row, except for the dark greenery someone—Magritte, presumably—had planted outside the front window in a long, rectangular box. The oil lamps cast pools of light at regular intervals down the narrow road.

I knocked softly on Regis's door, steeling my trembling knees. I was exhausted, thirsty, and famished. My ankle throbbed. My hair was covered in a thick layer of grime from days of traveling, and my clothes . . . I wouldn't even consider the state of my clothes. Would Regis recognize me?

Regis hadn't hesitated to leave me behind in Nulla the day he left with Magritte. And now I was wanted by Xia, the Karthicks, and the hooded man. What if he didn't help me? Or worse, gave me back to my captors?

The door opened before I could worry that possibility further, and a tall man stood there with short, roughly cropped hair and eyes that burrowed into me. My knees gave way a little, and he shot out a hand to steady me. His dark gaze swept me from head to toe.

"Miss, you don't look very—*Seph*? Seph, is that you?" He dived forward and caught me beneath my elbows.

"Aye," I said, trying to focus on his face, which kept duplicating unhelpfully. "It's me." I pushed back my dusty hood.

"I, uh . . . I didn't recognize you with longer hair."

I smiled weakly at him. "Aye, that's it. It's the hair."

"What happened to you?" He frowned. "Where's Lord Adamo?"

"Actually," I said, my vision starting to blur. "I was hoping you could tell *me.*"

Magritte appeared beside her husband, her fair eyebrows knotted, her dimples less pronounced than usual. "What are you doing keeping her out here, Reg? Bring her inside. Can't you see she's about to pass out?"

"Nay," I replied, shaking my head—which only made the dizziness worse. "I'm perfectly well."

Seconds later, I felt the ground rush to make my acquaintance. Regis arrested my fall, catching me up in his arms.

"Poor dear," Magritte clucked sympathetically, stroking the hair back from my face. "Never fear, Sephone. You're among friends now. We'll take care of you."

Friends, I thought dimly. They were my friends. I could stop running. I could stop walking. For the first time in days, I took a slow, deep breath. Surely, neither Asa nor the hooded man could find me here, deep underground.

"Won't you . . . tell Dorian . . . I'm here . . . with you?"

Regis nodded. "Aye, I will. Magritte's right, Seph. Rest now. You'll be safe with us. We'll take care of everything."

There was more to say—so much more. But at that moment, the details vacated my head like a flock of startled birds. I was suddenly acutely aware of my blistered heels, my leaden legs—and my aching soul.

Safe, I repeated, and once again, I thought of the *alter.*

Call to me . . .

My head slumped sideways against Regis's chest as I went limp in his arms.

"You must understand, Seph," said Regis, leaning forward in his chair, "everything is different since you were here last."

An entire day had passed since I'd collapsed on their doorstep, and I was still in bed. They'd showed me uncommon care, feeding me and drawing a bath so I could wash my filthy body and matted hair. When I had dried off and changed into clean clothes, Magritte had propped up my sore ankle on pillows and gently reworked the splint on my wrist. I'd done little else but sleep and dream until I'd woken the next morning.

Magritte had been still sitting in the chair beside my bed, her head tilted back, a now-dry cloth held limply in her lap as her free hand rested on her stomach. She had looked exhausted herself, and I hadn't wanted to wake her, but she'd jerked upright at the quiet knock on the door.

"Oh! I must have dozed off," she had exclaimed as Regis entered, his face a careful mask. He'd treated me like porcelain ever since I'd arrived, as if fearful that if he looked at me too long or asked too many questions, I would shatter into pieces. And maybe I would.

While Magritte slipped past her husband and hurried below to prepare breakfast—likely keeping busy in an attempt to evade any more awkward conversations—Regis sat in Magritte's chair.

I met his gaze, surprised to find it deeply troubled. But at least it seemed he would finally talk to me.

"Our *healer*, Jillane—who healed your burned arm last time—was one of the first *alters* to disappear."

"Disappear?"

"Aye. It's why Magritte tended to you herself—she knows that the bones in your wrist require resetting, but we have no one left who could do it."

"Was it Lord Draven?" I asked shakily. "Who took them?"

"Aye, some of them, certainly. But the others . . . " Regis fidgeted with his hands, then shifted in the chair. "There're no heroes in this war, Seph. We've heard rumors that Lethe has been experimenting on their own *alters*. You see, people have been going missing for some time."

I remembered the *altered* girl who'd been executed outside of Iona, the same day I met Cass. "What do you mean, *experimenting*?"

"They had to test their weapons on something," he replied.

"Do you mean to say that Lethe's weapons target *alters*?" I had heard a whisper of that particular rumor in the mind of the advisor whose memories I'd erased. But until this moment, I hadn't thought it possible. Lethe didn't value its *alters* as highly as Memosine valued theirs, but surely they wouldn't—

"There are some in Nephele who believe our race has been corrupted by the gifts. That the future is only for those who most resemble our ancestors. And besides," he emphasized when he saw my incredulous expression, "with their numbers divided between a northern and southern war, Memosine is attacking Lethe mainly with *alters*. Lethe's only way to fight back is to level the playing field by attacking the *alters* themselves."

"Without you? What does your resistance think about all of this?"

Did he remember that he had once hoped to use my gift to eliminate Lord Draven? He shook his head. "It is difficult to take sides when both Calliope and Nephele have shown they're capable of ruthlessness and terror. We are divided on so many fronts: Lethean or Memosinian, *altered* or normal, Calderan or outlander. It is becoming impossible to be both Lethean and *altered*, except if one joins the Karthicks."

"I am Lethean and *altered*, and I will never join the Karthicks." I struggled upright, trying not to put pressure on my broken wrist. "You haven't really answered me, Reg. Where do *you* stand?"

His brows lifted, then he looked at me intently. "I could never serve a Lethe that would selectively destroy its people. But neither can I sit by and do naught while Memosine takes Caldera for its own."

"What of Lady Xia and the League? What of Dorian and his friends?"

"Your Lord Adamo has not been seen in weeks, Seph. As for Lady Xia, it is no longer clear where her loyalties lie. In the beginning, I would have said she supported the Sons as an extension of her League, but now there are rumors she's allied herself with the outlanders."

I thought of Aleria. "The outlanders are enemies of the Karthicks. Perhaps we can count them as our friends."

His eyes flashed suspiciously. "Forgive me for saying so, Seph, but you're still far too naïve. If the outlanders defeat the Karthicks, they'll want whatever they can get of Caldera. They aren't our friends."

"Then what have you decided?"

He shifted his body in the chair again. "The Sons are lying low until more pieces are in motion. When the time is right, we will make our move, depending on how those pieces fall."

Meaning, they wanted to see who won the next battle before they decided their loyalties. "So, you no longer want to assassinate the new king."

"This has become so much bigger than Lord Draven, Seph." He studied me closely. "You said you were kidnapped by a man who wanted to know everything about the king. Did you—"

"I don't know his name or anything about him. He never showed his face. And I didn't recognize any of his guards."

Reg laughed. "There you go again, trying to read my mind so you can finish my sentences. I wanted to ask if you caught any glimpse of his plans."

I shook my head. "All I know is that he wanted to capture Lord Draven. I couldn't . . ." I stilled, remembering how I'd grabbed his hand, how I'd tried to use my gift on him, but felt naught. Naught but cold, empty space.

Did you think I would make it so easy for you to overpower me?

A long pause stretched between us.

"He knows about me," I said at last. "About the ice. Maybe even about Dorian." I wrapped an arm around myself, cradling my wrist. "He may come for me here. I don't want to put you and Magritte in any danger, so I'll leave tomorrow."

"*Leave?*" For the first time, he sounded like the old Regis. "I won't hear of it. You're completely spent, and you're injured, too. And besides, I've already sent for Lord Adamo. If you leave, he won't know where to find you."

I straightened, ignoring the answering stab of pain from my propped-up foot. "What do you mean? Do you know where Dorian is?"

"Not exactly." He leaned forward again. "Did you know that the gifts can sometimes appear later in life? When they do, they're not quite as strong as if they arrived during childhood, but still, they are there. No matter how much it scares the living daylights out of the person when they first notice it."

I stared at him.

He nodded. "Magritte's nails. You would never see it, of course, because she's always frenetically busy in company. They're slightly iridescent."

"Are you saying your wife is an *alter*?"

"Aye. We discovered it a couple of months ago. The poor thing fainted dead away when she discovered it." He glanced at me. "And so you see, Seph, there's another reason why I cannot fight only for Lethe. I cannot believe in a future where both my wife and my friend are feared and even despised."

"Your friend," I repeated, testing the word for sureness.

"Aye," he said, more firmly this time. "My friend. Magritte's gift is unusual, but it just so happens to be a perfect gift for the wife of a resistance leader. You see, she can communicate with people at extended distances. Though she works daily to hone her abilities, they're fairly weak, and her range is still somewhat limited. But if she's met someone before, she can touch their mind across a distance of many miles and communicate a short message—no more than a few words. The better she knows the person, the more she can communicate."

"Then Magritte has contacted Dorian?"

"Yesterday morning. Just after you arrived. She doesn't know if he heard her. Of course, it is impossible for people to answer back, but if he got the message, then he knows to find you here."

Hope blossomed in my chest. This very moment, Dorian and Cass could be on their way to find me. Aleria, too.

"You're right," I agreed. "It's a perfect gift for the Sons."

Another lengthy silence. I found myself wishing for more light. The lamps outside had been turned up, indicating morning, but it was nothing like the real thing. I pulled my gaze from the window to find Regis watching me.

"I'm glad you sought us out in your hour of need, Seph."

"I didn't have much of a choice," I replied honestly.

He flushed. "I've been so foolish. I see that now. If I could do everything over, I would do things so differently. And I . . . well, we want to be your friends again, if you are willing."

Magritte chose that moment to enter the room. I wondered if she'd been listening outside or if Regis had somehow signaled that she was needed. I noted how her hand rested, once again, on her abdomen. A burst of understanding swept through me. Magritte smiled faintly.

I see that very little escapes you, said a woman's voice directly into my mind. *Aye, the baby is due come winter.*

I started visibly, and Regis laughed. Magritte's real voice was high-pitched and bubbly; her mind's voice was far more serious, but with a distinct streak of mischief. The sudden intrusion into my thoughts should have been unpleasant—unwelcome, even—but I recognized Magritte's intentions. She was offering me her friendship. For real, this time. Just as Regis was.

Asking for another chance.

"My congratulations," I said, a little breathlessly. "I know you will be wonderful parents."

They smiled and nodded but continued to look at me expectantly, waiting for me to answer Regis. They didn't know about the Reliquary and the Three. They had no idea about the poison marking my chest. It was impossible to explain what the hooded man had forced me to do, and how, when I looked in the mirror, a very different woman gazed back at me. They saw the same Sephone they'd left behind in Nulla and found again on their doorstep, but I was completely, utterly changed.

The Sephone they knew had died in the mountains, the very moment she'd stolen another person's soul. Lifetaker. *Soul-letter.* An *alter* who was losing control of her gift. But they couldn't know that. And perhaps they didn't need to. The fewer people who knew what I was capable of, the better.

"I am willing," I said, letting my gaze encompass them both, radiating warm acceptance and unconditional forgiveness, or so I hoped. "Let us leave the past where it belongs. In the past."

10

DORIAN

The nightmares followed him into a brightening dawn. His skin still burned hot, and shadows jostled for precedence at the edges of his vision, but he gritted his teeth and pushed on, driven by the words which had woken him from a feverish sleep two mornings before.

We have Sephone in Orphne, Lord Adamo. Come to us when you can.

At first, he thought it was Zaire inside his head. How had she found Sephone? How had she gotten inside his mind again?

But then he realized that the voice belonged to Magritte—the wife of Sephone's friend, Regis. How Sephone had come to be in Orphne, so far from the mountains, Magritte didn't say. But she was there. She was safe. She was alive. He'd told the others, who thought him delusional from the lingering fever. But when the message came again, an hour later—there was no mistaking it this time—they finally decided to believe him and agreed to set a course for Orphne. After all, they had no other options.

Before Magritte's contact, they had been all but wandering in the mountains. Aleria Vega had done her best, but the hooded man and his party had vanished into the gray, and it was impossible for even an eagle to track them. Something Aleria had eventually admitted, with no small amount of despair. They'd retraced their steps to the meeting place where the Mardell twins and Jewel should have been, only to find it abandoned. Bas had left a note pinned under a rock.

*We waited for you as long as we could, but we fear
something terrible has happened. If you get this,
follow us to Thebe. — B*

Dorian hid his disappointment. They had agreed, of course, that if the other party didn't show for some time, those waiting would retreat to Lady Xia's forces in Thebe. That would be safer than lingering in the mountains. And Dorian's group *had* been delayed in returning due to finding Aleria and attempting to track the hooded man.

But Dorian had hoped that they would be reunited with Bas, Bear, and Jewel, and that they might have lingered past the agreed time. He missed the easy company of the Mardell twins; most of all, he missed Jewel. It had been Jewel who'd gotten him through the terrible months after his family's deaths.

Nevertheless, they would be safe in Thebe until Dorian could get a message to them. Jewel would alert them to any dangers as they crossed the moorland, enabling them to steer clear of Asa Karthick. And once Dorian, Cass, Spartan, and Aleria had rescued Sephone from Orphne, they could go to Thebe directly.

They had managed to acquire horses at a small town on the edge of the mountains, albeit for an exorbitant price. There, they also heard the latest news: Lethe's army, led by the vice-regent, Algar Spath, had retreated to defend the capital and the thousands of refugees who'd sought its protection, including the former citizens of Nyx. Asa Karthick's army was encamped outside Nephele, but so far, he had made no move to attack the city.

What was he waiting for? Did he only hesitate because he feared their weapons?

Once they'd left the mountains, Dorian had glimpsed the extent of the devastation the Memosinians had wrought. Asa Karthick had burned nearly every town and outpost in his path to the capital, perhaps as retribution for Lethe's new weapons repelling his *alters*. The damage was unmistakably fresh: Fires were still burning in places; the crops were smoldering in the fields; the bodies of the dead had not yet been burned. Charred corpses of both humans and animals filled the air with a nearly unbearable stench.

"How could Nephele not come to their defense?" Cass had wondered as they lingered amongst the ruins of a small settlement. It looked as if every inhabitant had been murdered where they stood. Even children hadn't been spared. Dorian closed his eyes, trying not to think about Emmy.

"Perhaps they thought this place not worth the trouble to save," Aleria ventured. "It is far from the capital, after all."

Opening his eyes, Dorian swayed slightly, quickly reaching for his horse's bridle to steady himself. He could barely stomach the horror of the sight, but more than that threatened to undo him.

"Are you all right, Dorian?" Spartan grasped his arm. "Perhaps you should rest."

"Nay," Dorian replied with an emphatic shake of his head. "Every minute counts."

"Forgive me for saying so, but you look as if you're about to collapse."

"Then I'll collapse in the saddle," Dorian muttered. His neck felt hot, and he was sure his face was flushed. Every limb burned. Despite his best efforts, Zaire's poison had wormed its way into his wounds. But a few more days and he would be well. Besides, they couldn't afford to waste a single moment. Dorian didn't trust Regis Symon not to use Sephone to his advantage.

The further they went from the moorlands, the more the landscape regained its untouched, pristine state. Asa's army hadn't come this way . . . at least, not yet. His soldiers had probably crossed the border south of Idaea before attacking Nyx. Then, Dorian guessed, his route had skirted the mountains before heading directly for Nephele. Dorian had often wondered why it had taken so long for Asa to attack Nephele after taking Nyx so easily. It had been months now since the city had fallen.

But then, perhaps Lethe's army had kept his forces at bay. Or Asa had been waiting for reinforcements, especially with Lethe's new weapons in play. There had been numerous reports of skirmishes in the mountain towns they'd passed through, though many seemed more fiction than truth.

In the meantime, hopefully they had done enough to outrun Zaire and her *alters*. Where the hooded man was, however, was anyone's guess. Even Aleria had no idea where he could have gone. For now, though, their next step was clear. The rest could be decided on after finding Sephone.

A few hours from Orphne, Aleria called a halt.

"It's only twilight. Why are we stopping?" Dorian lifted his head from his horse's mane to find Aleria dismounting. The gelding he rode was no Marmalade, but the horse had done well to follow the others with so little direction from Dorian.

"Because if we don't, you're going to pass out."

Dorian slid from the horse's back, gripping the saddlebow to disguise the wobble of his legs. But Aleria's eyes narrowed. Apparently, she'd noticed.

"Just a few hours, Dorian. Then we'll continue on."

"Every moment—"

"We know," Aleria interrupted, "every moment counts. But a few hours will make no difference to Sephone; whereas to your fever, they will do a world of good."

Spartan glanced at Dorian wryly. "She's right, you know."

"I know," Dorian said, then mumbled, "but I don't have to like it."

Spartan helped him to the base of a tree. Dorian leaned on him heavily; without the acolyte's assistance, he would have slithered to the ground. He sat there weakly as the others tended to the horses, unpacked supplies, and started a fire. He had never felt so useless in all his life. Cass shot Dorian mocking glances across the small clearing, wordlessly reminding him of the fact.

"Have pity on yourself, Dorian," said Aleria, sitting beside him. "You've been poisoned."

"The poison should have left my body by now."

"That woman, Zaire, isn't a Nightmare. Perhaps her poison has greater potency."

Perhaps. Dorian plucked a tuft of grass. So close to Orphne, and yet so far—

"May I see your quarterstaff?"

Nodding, Dorian passed the compacted staff at his belt to Aleria, who stood, studying it carefully.

"You have to—" he began.

With a jerk of her wrist, she snapped it to its full length. Her eyebrows shot up. "Impressive." She grasped one of the iron tips and twisted sharply. A blade appeared at the end, approximately the length of a hand and shaped like a jagged diamond. With a twist of the other end, a second blade appeared. Both looked wickedly sharp.

Dorian's mouth fell open. "How did you—"

"This staff is of outlander design." She handed it back to him. "Who gave it to you?"

"My father," he said, still looking wonderingly at the quarterstaff. How many more secrets did it conceal? "His father gave it to him as a coming-of-age present. And so my father gave it to me."

"It was made by my people." Aleria's voice betrayed a hint of pride. "Their craftsmanship was once beyond compare, even in the days of the world-that-was."

Cass stopped in front of them and whistled, studying the staff admiringly. "*Nice,* Thane. And here I thought you were little more than a glorified shepherd." He smirked. "Bet you wish you knew about this when Zaire attacked."

"I had no idea," Dorian said to Aleria, ignoring the *lumen*, "about the blades."

"It is no less a weapon as it was," was her surprising reply. Dorian twisted the iron tips and both blades disappeared, retracting into the wood. Remembering how it hadn't broken in Zaire's jaws, he wondered if the shaft within was made of metal, not wood. The staff's exterior was not even scratched. Superior craftsmanship, indeed.

"It won't be a match for Lethe's weapons," Dorian said.

"I don't know," she replied, with a small shrug. "So far it seems full of surprises."

They rested for several hours—longer than Dorian wished to, though he later had to admit that the forced break had done him good. Despite

Aleria's reassurances, his unease was growing steadily. Perhaps it was because his dreams were so full of Sephone, but he also increasingly felt like he was connected to her in a tangible way.

Some kind of trouble was afoot, and she was in danger. He was sure of it.

"Come on," he said when he couldn't stand it anymore. "We must be going." His legs were no longer shaking, and his hands were steady. Most of the heat had left his body. Even his vision had cleared.

He was halfway to his horse when he heard the voice in his mind, confirming his worst suspicions. *Come quickly, Lord Adamo. Orphne's settlements are under attack by* alters.

"Asa," he muttered. He had thought the *alter*'s forces behind them, not in front. But then, they may have left the countryside intact. How had Asa found Sephone so quickly? Or had he attacked the underground city and its satellites without knowing that she was in one of them?

Dorian glanced up to find the others staring at him. He swiftly relayed the message, and they reacted at once. In moments, they were all mounted and riding through the trees as quickly as the forest would allow. The pendant resting against Dorian's chest—partially entangled with the heavy chain bearing the gold rings—was warm, as if it knew how close its mistress was.

I'm coming, he declared, though it was unlikely Magritte would hear his reply. He didn't have her gift.

Dorian only hoped that their delay hadn't cost them dearly.

"We'll need to move fast," Magritte said as she hastily wrapped a firm bandage around my ankle, then moved to my wrist to do the same. "They will be here within the half hour, if not before. It's fortunate we were even forewarned." For a brief moment, her eyes glowed with wifely pride. "Regis didn't believe it would be long before Memosine came for us. He has had the scouts and sentries in place for some time now."

After she'd woken me, I had dressed quickly in the traveling clothes she'd brought: a white, front-lacing shirt; tight black leggings; a black tunic that reached halfway down my thighs; a fur-lined cloak; and sturdy black boots. Since Magritte and I were roughly the same size, they were a perfect fit. She had even replaced my gloves with new ones that fit me like a second skin. I had instantly admired the black leather, even though I'd briefly bemoaned the putting aside of the old ones. They were scuffed and worn, but they had served me for a long time.

After I'd slipped the glove over my bruised right arm, Magritte had refastened the splint over the top of the leather, a tight bandage fixing both pieces of wood in place and immobilizing my wrist. She hadn't wanted me to continue wearing the right glove, but I'd insisted. I didn't want to risk coming into contact with another person's skin, particularly with my gift so chaotic of late. Unless they were an enemy. In which case, I could easily use my left hand.

"What direction have the *alters* come from?" I asked as Magritte leaned back. Awkwardly, she tried to stand, and I moved to help her.

"Thank you," she said, pressing my gloved left arm before letting me go. I bent to pull on my boots, aware that little time remained. "It seems they have come through one of the tunnels. These caverns hardly make for a defensible position, especially since there are limited passages to the surface. As best we can tell, some of the outer settlements are already under attack. They will come at Orphne last."

"But surely," I said, my brain working furiously, "there are enough tunnels down here to hide us."

"Perhaps," Magritte replied, "but we cannot *all* hide, especially not if the Memosinians try to burn us out. Besides, Regis must pass some important things to his contacts in Orphne. Once we've done that, we will flee with the rest." She indicated my hood. "Hopefully we will blend in among the other refugees."

We, she said. But she meant *you*. Me.

I realized, then, the nature of the dilemma they faced. If it were just the two of them—soon to be the three of them—they could perhaps flee with the rest of the resistance. But if Asa or his *alters* knew I was here, my presence would only endanger them. I would lead the enemy straight to Regis and Magritte's friends.

I pulled my hood over my hair. It had grown past my shoulders now, and it would be more than obvious what I was, even in the dark.

"Leave me," I urged. "You'll stand out even less that way."

Magritte began to shake her head just as Regis's voice sounded from behind her. "Of course we're not leaving you, Seph. Now, are you ready to go?"

I nodded, and he passed me a small sheathed knife attached to a short belt. Despite the circumstances, a smile danced on my lips as I realized what he'd given me. I strapped it around my upper thigh, the sheath on the outside of my leg. It was very much like the blade he'd bought me in Nulla when I was a young girl, so I didn't have to rely on my gift to defend myself.

"Thank you," I said, and he grinned in return.

"Not that you really need it, or me, to protect you. At least, the way I used to."

"You're right." I stood erect. "I can protect myself. You'll be far safer without me, and as you say, there are more important things you must do. For the Sons and for your men. And for your wife and child."

"Magritte has already sent messages to the remaining members. We will regroup outside of Thebe. How each of us get there—and who we travel with—is not important."

"Messages?" I repeated, and glanced at Magritte. "Have you sent word to Dorian?"

She nodded. "If you stay with us, I can keep him informed of our whereabouts."

I hesitated. If Asa's *alters* attacked us, Regis and Magritte would be dragged into another war not their own. But if I left their company, I would have no way of finding Dorian and Cass and the others.

"Stay, Seph," said Regis, his eyes almost pleading. "At least for now."

Finally, I relented. "Lead the way, then."

I expected Regis to escape via the underground river, but instead, he returned us to Orphne by way of another passage. This one, I guessed, was known only to a few, since it was practically abandoned.

"These tunnels are dug from softer dirt," Regis explained when he saw the question in my eyes. "They're prone to cave-ins. It's best not to use them unless absolutely necessary."

I shuddered. I didn't mind heights, but the thought of being crushed beneath several tons of dirt and rock, slowly suffocating . . . I thought, almost longingly, of the underground river. Thankfully, the tunnels came to an end soon enough.

In Orphne, the streets were clogged with people, and as we moved toward the town square where I'd once battled Asa's *alters,* we quickly blended into the crowd. Sensing the undercurrent of panic, and knowing how quickly a mass exodus could become a stampede, I held tight to Magritte's arm as Regis forged a path for us both.

On the edge of the town square, several men waited under a shadowed eave. Regis veered in their direction, then passed a number of items, including what looked like a sheaf of papers, from his pack to theirs. Distributing secrets, in case one of them was caught or killed?

I suppressed a smile. I'd always thought Regis would become a politician someday, but he made a good resistance leader. Like Dorian, he was driven and deeply passionate, though I'd once feared that Regis cared more about his cause than the people who fought beside him.

But perhaps not anymore. Despite the danger, Regis and Magritte had taken me in, clothed me, fed me, and protected me. Even when they could have run, they'd chosen to stay with me. They might have let fear lead them before, when they'd fled Nulla, but no longer.

Regis murmured a few words to his men, and then they scattered. Returning to Magritte and me, he shouldered his pack and took his wife's arm. "It is done. Now, we find the surface."

"Can we not fight?" I asked. "Could not the Sons—"

"There aren't enough of us to make a stand," Regis replied. "And besides, Seph, what could we do against *alters*? Nay, it's far better that we flee and live to fight another day. That is exactly why I put the early warning measures in place."

I accepted his logic. Regis wasn't a coward, even if his loyalties weren't completely decided. But eventually the resistance would encounter a battle from which they could not run.

The inhabitants of Orphne and those who'd escaped the surrounding settlements moved as a single mass toward the surface. Some were carrying packs, sacks, or even boxes, while others had naught but the clothes they were wearing. Many wore nightclothes, as if they'd been roused directly from their beds. Only a few carried lanterns, which considering the crush of people, was probably wise. As we climbed the spiral staircase leading out of Orphne, a hushed silence fell over the group, which up to this point, had remained oddly calm. Somewhere below us, a child wailed and was quickly quieted.

The three of us had nearly reached the surface when yells sounded from below.

"They are coming!" a woman screamed.

"Move!" another voice shouted from somewhere near the bottom of the ancient well. "They're nearly here!"

A tangible wave of fear rippled through the crowd, and it was as if a dam wall had broken. The mass of people surged forward and upward as one. Screams and cries of pain shattered the night all around us. Regis's hand shot out and grabbed my upper arm; with his other, he pulled Magritte close. We formed one rigid, immovable unit as we were swept along by the panicked crowd, stumbling up the slippery stone steps. I clung as tightly as I could to Regis. If not for him, I almost certainly would have fallen.

The crush of people finally spewed us into the clearing surrounding the old well. Regis quickly guided us to the side, where we took shelter beneath an old oak. Lanternlight illuminated a scene of absolute chaos. The inhabitants of Orphne continued to well up from underground like an unstaunched flow, hardly aware of who or what they trampled in their bid to escape. Those who reached the surface were rapidly dissipating into the surrounding forest, while others stood like rocks in the stream, calling the names of their loved ones.

A lump formed in my throat.

"Come on," said Regis breathlessly, still holding onto us both. "We have to get out of here."

I barely heard him. Mere yards from our position, a tiny boy was lodged in the middle of the river of people, bawling for his mother. The crowd continued to flow around him as if they were immune to his cries. Any moment, he could fall and be trampled.

Not far away, a lantern crashed to the ground, and fire raced along the forest floor, further scattering the fleeing people. The *whoosh* of flame galvanized me into action, and I pulled myself from Regis's hold.

"Go!" I cried and raced toward the child.

"Seph!" Regis yelled, his call quickly drowned out by the screams of the crowd.

Come back! Magritte shouted in my mind, her voice splintered with fear.

It was nearly impossible to move against the current, and arms and shoulders clipped me on all sides as I struggled forward. I made myself as small as possible, but twice, I was nearly thrown to the ground. If I survived this, bruises would mark every limb.

Finally reaching the boy, I quickly circled him and put my arms around his tiny body, lifting him against my chest and presenting my back to the current. The constant wave of people continued to buffet us, but something was happening—something was different. The onslaught from below had thinned. Now, as I huddled around the boy, I turned to find that it had slowed to a mere trickle. The clearing was still thick with bodies, but only a few people now issued from the top of the spiral staircase.

I clutched the boy tighter. Had Orphne's inhabitants all escaped? Or was this—

Five figures appeared on the uppermost stair, three bulky and two with narrow builds. All of them wore black, with gloves sheathing their hands and heavy hoods pushed back. The growing fire behind me threw their faces into sharp relief. Smug, confident expressions surveyed the panicked people of Orphne. But none of the *alters* appeared to have red hair. I released the breath I'd been holding.

At a tap on my shoulder, I turned to see a young man, barely a few years older than myself.

"He's my son," he said urgently, pointing at the child. Blood streamed from a slash at his temple, but he extended his arms.

Seeing the close resemblance, I passed the child to his father.

"Thank you," he breathed before he caught sight of the hair beneath my hood. His slender throat cording, he shrank away and quickly melted into the crowd.

Did he think me one of *them*?

Slowly, I turned to face the advancing *alters*. The inhabitants of Orphne fled before them like woodland animals before a storm. The *alters* made no attempt to give chase as they stalked through the crowd, giants among ants. None of them looked familiar—perhaps Asa wasn't here after all. Which was fortunate, considering that—

An agonized scream tore me from my train of thought.

One of the foremost *alters*—a woman with iridescent yellow hair—had halted a few yards from the staircase. A man lay crumpled at her feet, clutching his lower leg. As I watched, she raised her gloved hand

and snapped her fingers. The man screamed a second time, this time holding his arm. The limb was now distinctly misshapen, the elbow at an unnatural angle. The woman smiled and raised her hand again, her cold gaze zeroed on his face.

"Mercy," he spluttered. "*Mercy, my lady.*"

The blood surging through my veins chilled. Once again, I moved without thinking, barely aware I'd slid the glove from my left hand and stuffed it into the pocket of my coat. The darkness allowed me to come at the *alter* from the side, and the man's whimpers kept her distracted until I was almost upon her.

I slammed into the *alter*, knocking us both to the ground. Her body broke my fall, but she recovered quickly, shoving at my midsection before I could get a grip on her exposed neck. She was heavier than I was, and she swiftly rolled me onto my back, pinning my injured wrist while she raised her other hand.

This time, I was the quicker one. My left hand grabbed her around the neck, and my gift responded at once. Cold poured through my hand into her skin, and in her mind, it turned to ice, hardening everything in sight. I caught a glimpse of a dark-haired woman and a pair of freshly dug graves before my gift coated her memories with bluish white. Her head lolled, and she slumped, sliding away from me. The man I'd saved had gone still, staring at me with a shocked expression—my hood had fallen away.

Panting, I regained my feet. The other *alters* had seen us. Four of them now advanced on my position, hatred and fury in their eyes. I was dimly aware of the fire at my back; the clearing was filling with smoke, making the *alters* look like wraiths approaching from the underworld. Where were Regis and Magritte? Had they escaped into the surrounding forest?

I should be thinking of myself. Power still thrummed through my bare fingertips, and a strange energy built in my chest. But I couldn't take on four *alters*—not by myself, and certainly not at this distance.

"You'll pay for that," said a man with glossy brown hair and a thick build, the jerk of his chin indicating the woman I'd felled.

"She isn't dead." I stepped back. "She'll only sleep for a while."

"Look at her," urged another voice. "It's the *alter* King Draven is searching for. Sephone Winter."

"I don't care who she is," snarled the first man. "She killed Zephya." Reaching beneath his cloak, he pulled out a knife.

I dove to the side, narrowly avoiding the blade as it whistled past my shoulder. Whatever the man's gift was, it wasn't precision with weaponry. The *alter*'s face contorted, and he produced another knife, even as his fellows called out for him to stop.

This time, he aimed for my heart. I twisted away again, but my foot tangled with something—a tree root?—and I wasn't fast enough. The knife nicked my right side, slicing through my tunic and the shirt underneath. Sucking in a breath, I fell to my knees. Maybe if I stayed where I was, the *alter* would get close enough for me to bring him down. His upper arms were exposed, along with his face and neck. He had only to let down his guard.

"How does it feel to be helpless?" the brown-haired man hissed, stopping before me and drawing a third knife.

Worse than you know, I mentally replied, then pushed onto my tiptoes. But before I could reach his skin, his gloved hand closed around my throat. He held me away from him, grinning as his fingers almost completely encircled my neck. My hands thrashed in the air.

"Oh, we know all about you, Miss Winter," he said as my eyes began to bulge and black spots appeared in my vision. "And I'm afraid your tricks won't work with us."

"They worked . . . on your master," I choked out.

He squeezed harder. I felt my feet leave the ground. Was he going to kill me? Why would he, if Asa and his father were still looking for me? Didn't they want me alive?

"That's enough," insisted one of the *alters* behind him, but the man only gritted his teeth. The white horse danced across my vision, and I suddenly knew.

This was the end.

Golden-brown appeared above my head, and I thought, dimly, that perhaps the fire had overcome us at last. But then I felt the beat of wings, the rush of air against my flushed face. The *alter* throttling me screamed and dropped me, batting at something above him.

I staggered back, somehow managing not to fall. One of the other *alters* aimed a crossbow in my direction. I saw the weapon too late, and my arms flew up to protect my face. The bolt loosed, and I braced myself.

A brilliant wall of shimmering crystal suddenly appeared in front of me, and this time, I did fall onto my backside. The bolt glanced harmlessly off the surface of the shield, and just as quickly, the light evaporated.

I struggled to my feet as a horse and rider came into view. No, three riders and four horses. Most of the crowd had dissipated, leaving behind only stragglers and the fire that threatened to engulf the clearing. Thick smoke spiraled upward into a darkened sky.

Ice and fire. Were they always to be my greatest strength and my greatest weakness combined?

The foremost of the newcomers rode directly up to me, wedging his horse between me and the *alters* who were still being harried by their winged assailant. Leaning down, the man stretched out a gloved hand.

"Get on," he commanded, and my gaze collided with his.

"Dorian!" At once the warmth of his presence surrounded me, as if I had rapidly downed a succession of spirits on a cold afternoon. I grabbed his hand with my uninjured one, expecting him to haul me up behind him, but instead he pulled me up in front, curiously mindful of my splinted wrist as I settled myself in the saddle. He briefly hugged me from behind, and I tried not to melt against him. All these months, and he was *here*. My chest expanded, threatening to burst.

"Did you do that?" I asked.

"Do what?"

"The crystal shield."

I felt him shake his head. "Nay, that was Spartan."

"*Spartan?*"

"There's a lot to catch you up on. Can you take the reins?" His warm breath puffed against my ear. "We're about to have company."

"Of course."

He placed the reins in my hands and fumbled at his belt.

His staff—of course. Two of the *alters* approached, and my heart seized as I realized they'd been joined by five more. Five more *alters* of unknown strength and giftings. And Dorian and I were practically defenseless.

As I wheeled the horse around, Dorian turned in the saddle. He lashed out with his staff, and blood spurted in a wide arc. Cries of pain punctured the night. I caught a flash of silver and realized that the quarterstaff now had blades on each end. Serrated blades, shaped like diamonds.

Apparently, there was a lot to catch up on.

"Spartan!" Dorian yelled. "We could use another shield right about now!"

Seconds later, a blinding wall of crystal appeared between us and the *alter* who'd been mere inches from stabbing Dorian's thigh. The man lost his balance and fell back. Expecting the horse beneath us to revolt from the nearness of the barrier, I braced myself, but the animal merely tossed his glossy head. Maybe it didn't work on animals the way it did on humans. This time, the crystal shield remained in place, effectively separating us from the other *alters*. There was no sign of the man I'd saved from the yellow-haired *alter*. Hopefully he'd gotten away.

Dorian wrapped his arm around my waist, and I winced, feeling blood beginning to trickle down my side toward my leg.

"Let's go," he directed, "before they follow."

As we turned, I saw Spartan on horseback, his hands devoid of any weapon. He was focused on the forest fire at our back, sweat sheeting down his face as he manipulated his hands. Another crystal barrier appeared between us and the advancing blaze.

"It will not contain the fire forever," Spartan told us, dropping his hands. "Nor the smoke." His gaze turned distant. "The shields will trap them here. By the time they fail, the smoke may have overwhelmed the *alters*."

I stilled, understanding what he was saying. To leave them behind was a death sentence. There was grim irony in the fact, since their own leader was a master of fire, and yet it was fire, or smoke at least, which would consume them.

"There's no other way," Dorian replied. "We cannot allow them to pursue us, especially now they know we have Sephone. Besides, we must think of Orphne's people and the time we buy them to escape."

"I know," Spartan replied, but an air of misery shadowed his admission as he took up his reins again.

I pulled Dorian's horse up short. "Regis and Magritte. They're somewhere nearby. We can't leave them."

"It's all right," Dorian assured me. "Cass and Aleria have them. They're going to ride Aleria's horse. They're over there."

I blinked. Aleria? So that was the golden blur who'd saved me from being strangled. I turned and saw Cass helping Magritte into the saddle in front of her husband, who was already seated on a jet-black horse. When she was secure, Cass mounted his own horse, a dappled gray. His eyes connected with mine and flared; I tried to resurrect a smile for him, but my face suddenly felt like it was made of wax. None of my muscles would move.

Dorian leaned forward and took the reins from my still fingers, kicking the horse into motion again. His staff was once more fastened to his belt. When we joined the others, Aleria flying above in her eagle form, Regis shot me a look equal parts stern and relieved.

You shouldn't have done that, Magritte chided me on her husband's behalf. *You are too brave for your own good, Sephone.* But a hint of pride lurked in her voice.

She didn't know, of course, that there was a reason why I couldn't let the boy die. Once, I had been that child. And nobody had come to my aid except Dorian.

You have no idea, I wanted to tell her, *how afraid I am. How cowardly I can be, if the right things are threatened by the wrong people.*

Even now, as Dorian's arms surrounded me, I felt the familiar fear rising in my chest, mingled with joy. Joy that I was not alone anymore, but fear—terrible fear—that a single moment could steal every one of them away. I was beginning to understand why Dorian held everyone at a distance, because once you'd known what it was like to be completely alone, sometimes it was easier to remain that way forever.

A loss suffered twice was far worse than one endured only once.

But I could say naught of this to Magritte, even if she could hear me. I merely leaned back against Dorian's chest as his horse took us far from Orphne and the fire that raged at the underground city's front door.

And the anguished bellows of Asa's thwarted *alters* followed us into the night.

After nearly four months of thinking she was lost to him forever, it was pure bliss to have Sephone back in his arms. Pure bliss and sheer torture.

Dorian had seen the heated look Cass had given her across the forest clearing. Dorian might have been the first to reach her, but she didn't belong to him.

You're her friend now, remember? But the awareness coursing through every cell of his body was far beyond what he would ever feel toward a friend.

Thankfully, the speed of their flight prevented them from talking much—or at all. As soon as they could, they slowed the horses to prevent them from tiring too quickly, since two of them were now carrying a double burden. In case some of the *alters* lived to follow them, Dorian directed them through rivers where possible, hoping that the prints made by the fleeing populace of Orphne, as well as their abandoned belongings, would disguise their other tracks. Still, naught could mask the horses' hooves.

Dawn broke as they rode through one particularly deep stream, which reached just past Dorian's horse's stirrups. He could feel the weariness in Sephone. Despite his attempts to impose a distance between them, she'd all but slumped against him an hour earlier, her head falling back onto his shoulder. She started awake as the water lapped against the heels of her boots.

"Where are we?"

He avoided a low-hanging tree branch. "Somewhere in the wild. Not far from the no-man's-land, I would think."

"Are the *alters* . . ."

"Nay, they're not behind us. At least, not yet."

She let out a breath. "You arrived just in time. Another second more, and I would have—" She shuddered and broke off the sentence.

"It was Aleria and Spartan who saved you, not me. And it was Magritte who kept us appraised of your whereabouts." When she didn't reply, Dorian brushed her arm with his. "You can take the reins, if you like."

"Nay, I'll only fall asleep again."

An odd note filled her voice, as if she wanted to stay where she was. As if she enjoyed being held by him as much as he enjoyed holding her. It almost made him forget the dark looks that Cass, who rode in front of them, kept shooting in their direction. Dorian reminded himself why he had to be indifferent to her.

As dawn lightened the surrounding landscape, tiny shafts of sunlight piercing the gray canopy, the water turned to dappled gold. The river had deepened, and though it wasn't cold, it would be hard work for the horses. They would need to rest them soon. Exhausted as well, Dorian let his right arm encircle Sephone's waist while his left held the reins.

She gave a soft gasp and arched away from him.

"I'm sorry," he began, just as he noticed spots of blood swirling in the water. Had they stumbled upon another massacre? But a dark, wet stain covered Sephone's side.

"You're bleeding," he exclaimed, dropping the reins.

"It's nothing," she insisted. Ignoring her, Dorian turned her body toward him, pushing back her cloak. His hands were gloved, but she still flinched as he probed the wound, gently moving the torn layers of shirt and tunic to expose a horizontal slash just above her hip. Not long, but it was deep enough to require stitches.

"Were you injured by my staff?" His voice was taut.

"Nay, a blade thrown by one of the *alters*."

He relaxed, then remembered one of Asa's men who had the power to create wounds which would never close. She must have remembered, too, for she took his hand and squeezed it. "It's all right, Dorian. I would be dead by now if it were that kind of weapon."

"I think it's time to call a halt."

"Nay, I'm fine—"

"We've pushed as hard as we can today, Sephone. Even if you insist you're all right, we risk laming the horses if we go on."

Cass chose that exact moment to glance behind his shoulder. He scowled. "Comfortable, Thane?"

Dorian quickly let her go. "Pass the message to Spartan, Cass. We need to rest."

Despite his ire, he did as Dorian asked, and minutes later, they emerged from the river into a small clearing framed on every side by willow trees. Aleria flew down from a branch and began the process of transforming into her human form. Spartan, Regis, and Magritte were already dismounted; Spartan was introducing himself to the others. Dorian realized that Spartan had never met the resistance leader and his wife. He had joined their company after they left Orphne.

Cass strolled over as Dorian guided the horse into the clearing. Dorian held Sephone's good arm to help her down, pursing his lips as her long hair shifted to expose bruises wreathing her neck. Before she could dismount, Cass reached up for her waist, and she slid from the horse into his waiting arms. Failing to notice her ensuing wince, he bent and kissed her forehead.

Dorian looked away, only to find that both Aleria and Regis were staring at him; the former with an almost somber expression, the latter surprised.

But at Sephone's gasp of pain, Dorian turned his head in time to see her pushing Cass away. "Careful," Dorian intervened. "She's injured."

"You're injured?" Cass echoed, now all smooth solicitousness. He kept an arm around her waist as Dorian dismounted wearily. "Where?"

"My side," she began, then sighted Aleria standing next to Magritte. The tawny-haired woman came forward with a smile and clasped Sephone's good hand. Abandoning her usual formality, Sephone flung her arms around Aleria.

"I told you we'd come for you." Aleria smiled. Her sharp gaze found the bloodstain. "Let's get that seen to."

"The Mysterium are not far," Spartan offered. "We could take her there."

At that, Sephone turned to Dorian, a stricken look on her pale features. "I'm sorry, Dorian. I couldn't retrieve the Reliquary."

"It doesn't matter—" he started, but Cass cut him off.

"We can't return to the Mysterium. They want us for thievery, remember?"

"Thievery?" Regis raised a brow. "What did you steal?"

Aye, there was *much* to discuss.

Spartan crossed his arms, a flicker of uncharacteristic defiance in his blue eyes. "Sephone's lost a good deal of blood. And you yourself are still feverish, Dorian. It would be wise to seek help."

Sephone looked at Dorian. "What does he mean, 'feverish'?"

"From Zaire's poison," Cass added unhelpfully.

"Poison?" she repeated, her voice rising. "What poison? And who's Zaire?"

"It's a long story," Dorian said.

"Where's Bas and Bear?" She looked around, as if she'd suddenly noticed them missing. "And Jewel?"

"Also a long story," said Cass.

Her shoulders stiffened. "You could have told me on the way, Dorian."

"You didn't ask," he returned, beginning to lose his temper as a familiar heat once again swirled in his chest.

"I didn't think—" she began, then swayed, clutching her side.

Dorian started forward, but Cass, who was closer, scooped her into his arms.

"You can fight it out later," Aleria declared, scowling at them both, "when none of our lives are in mortal danger." She looked at Dorian. "I, for one, am in favor of visiting the Mysterium. We need to recoup our strength and tend to our injuries. It would be better if we could do so without having to constantly watch our backs."

Dorian shook his head. "For reasons I can't presently explain, we will not be welcome there."

"Of course, you would be welcome—" Spartan started.

"Why not?" Aleria demanded of Dorian.

When he hesitated, Cass quipped, "There really aren't many *short* stories we can tell."

"I hate to point it out," commented Regis, "but Lady Xia and Thebe lie in the opposite direction to the Mysterium."

Dorian silently thanked the man for his input. Neither Aleria nor Spartan would understand why they couldn't return to the monkish order, not since Dorian had stolen and lost their most precious artifact. If Sephone or any of the others were at death's door, Dorian wouldn't hesitate. But they could manage these injuries on their own.

"You will both need a *healer*," said Aleria, looking between Sephone and Dorian. Could she see the sweat beading on Dorian's forehead? The shivering that was beginning to overtake his legs? "If there are any to be found, that is."

Dorian started to shake his head, to say that he would be fine, then saw that Sephone was nearly unconscious in Cass's arms. She had a deep cut, a bruised neck, and a badly broken wrist. What was he thinking? Of course, she needed a *healer* before they pushed on to Thebe. And Dorian couldn't deny that he was once more feeling the effects of the poison.

"We shouldn't move her," said Cass. "The bleeding seems to have stopped for the moment, but walking or riding may cause it to start again."

"I saw some shelter nearby," offered Regis. "If one of you will stay with Magritte, I will go in search of an *alter*. There is a village not far from here. They may know of someone willing to come."

"Nay," said Aleria, taking charge. "You stay with your wife, Master Regis, and protect Sephone and Dorian. The three of us"—she looked at Cass and Spartan—"can go. If we spread out in different directions, we have a better chance of finding a *healer*."

Spartan inclined his head, and Cass nodded begrudgingly. Both of them could see what Aleria had: Regis's wife was expecting. She would want her husband close. Looking faintly mutinous, Regis led the way to a small shack not far from the grove of willows. It looked as if it had been abandoned weeks ago; the crude furniture within was tossed about, suggesting someone had left in a hurry. An *alter* fleeing Memosine's armies—or Lethe's?

Inside the shack, two tiny bedrooms abutted a small living room. Cass carried Sephone into one of the bedrooms. Dorian followed them, watching Cass lay her on the thin straw pallet that served as a bed. While Magritte slipped past Dorian and began tending to Sephone, Cass came to where Dorian stood in the doorway.

"I'll look after her," Dorian said.

"I know you will." For once, Cass's expression was serious. "She will need your courage, Thane. Just for tonight, she will need it more than the truth."

He was gone before Dorian could puzzle out his meaning.

As Dorian knelt beside Sephone, her eyes fluttered open, and she struggled into a sitting position. When he reached out to help her, she lifted her hand to his forehead. He stilled, but her hand was gloved. She couldn't feel his mind.

"You're burning up." She frowned. Her voice was slightly hoarse from the attempted strangling.

"You can't possibly feel that through your gloves."

"They're new gloves. Better than the ones I had. And besides, you're sweating."

"Maybe I'm just thinking about my answers to all the questions you asked me before."

Her hand slid to his cheek. He wondered if she had any idea what she was doing, but her eyes were sharp, not glazed over. Still, perhaps the blood loss had lowered her inhibitions.

Dorian found himself thankful that Regis and Magritte were in the other room. After the others had left, Magritte had bandaged Sephone's side and checked the splint on her wrist, but then she'd left them alone.

"You were attacked by a woman named Zaire?"

"You were right," Dorian told her. "Asa Karthick is in love with a woman. She's a rather beastly sort, if you ask me." At her bewilderment, he explained their two encounters with the *altered* woman, finishing with how she'd swiped him with her vicious claws and doused him with her insidious poison.

Her eyes held dismay. "I'm so sorry," she said when he finished. "I wish I could have been there to stop her. Is the poison . . ."

Her gloved fingers trailed down his neck and snagged on the collar of his shirt, setting his skin on fire. She was young—perhaps she didn't know what she was doing. Or she still thought he was indifferent to her.

He caught her fingers up in his hand, tugging them away and squeezing gently. "They're not mortal wounds." *Not like yours.* He looked at her. "May I see?"

Understanding him, she eased apart the laces of her shirt—not low enough to be indecent, but far enough that he could see the webbing over her sternum. He hissed and drew back. The marks had advanced and thickened since he'd seen them last. It was now impossible to deny the intent of the poison. The curse of the *mems* sought to consume her.

She was dying a little more each day.

Dorian lifted a hand to comb a lock of long, pale hair back from her ear. His mind warned him that he was in dangerous territory, but he told himself that he was inspecting the five or six thin streaks of black that had appeared when he shifted her hair. Never mind the fact that they'd appeared after he'd decided to move it.

She swallowed visibly. Was he making her uncomfortable? He hastily withdrew his hand and focused his attention on the bandages around her middle. They were suitably tight, and so far, there didn't seem to be any seepage.

"What are you looking at?" she asked.

"Checking Magritte's handiwork."

"You needn't worry. She's become quite skillful in Jillane's absence."

"Jillane?"

"The *altered healer* who repaired my burned arm." She gave a wan smile. "I seem to make a habit of requiring *healers*."

He leaned back and set his jaw. "I haven't forgotten my promise, you know. I *will* find a way to save you." She didn't need to know that he already had.

"You're forgetting two things," she replied. "We don't have the

Reliquary, for starters, and even if we did . . ." She faltered. "You don't know what it does."

"I know. At least, I do now." He took her hand. "I swear to you that I didn't know before."

She raised deep brown eyes to his, and even though both their hands were gloved, it felt like she looked directly into his soul. "I believe you, Dorian. I wish it had turned out differently, if only for your sake. Your family . . ."

Her voice was filled with infinite depths of pain and regret. Not for herself—for him. "It's no matter, Sephone. Even if the Reliquary worked the way we hoped it would, I wouldn't ask you to erase my past. Not anymore. I release you from any obligation in that regard."

Her eyes widened. "You've changed your mind?"

"It was your parents who changed it. When I saw how lost they were without their memories, without you . . ." Her eyes fell away from his, and he was sorry that he'd reminded her.

He was lost without her, too, but he could never say so. She didn't owe him anything. It was he who owed her everything.

"Are they well?" she asked quietly. "My parents?"

"They're safe in Thebe, with Lady Xia. I made sure of it before I came looking for you."

"Thank you."

How much he had to tell her—and how much he needed to know. What had happened to her during her nearly four months of captivity, what the hooded man had done to cause the deep hollow in her eyes, why guilt radiated from her like a fever.

"I should never have asked you to take those memories." Dorian stared at the floor. "And I should not have been so angry when you refused. I've been selfish, Sephone. Selfish, arrogant, and thickheaded." He glanced up at her. "Might you forgive me?"

She smiled. "Of course I forgive you."

"You were right, you know. About the Reliquary and about me. But I can't bear to think of what would have happened if you had agreed to what I asked and—" His voice choked to a halt.

"But I didn't." This time, he saw it in her expression: the terrible, crushing guilt . . . the shame. What had happened to her? "So there's naught to apologize for, Dorian. We both know better now."

Tears filled her eyes. Without hesitation, he took her in his arms. She slid her arms around his waist and buried her face in his shirt. He barely felt the pressure of her head against his wounds as muffled sobs issued from the vicinity of his chest.

"It's all right, Persephone," he murmured. "It's all right."

He stroked her hair, marveling at its color and length . . . the gentle wave of it, more obvious now it was longer. She no longer looked like a slave. She was a free woman—or she would be, if it was the last thing he did.

All going well, it *would* be the last thing he did.

Eventually, Sephone raised her head and gave a tremulous smile. "You regrew your beard."

Their faces were only inches apart, and it took every ounce of self-restraint he possessed not to lean in closer. Instead, he fingered the growth on his chin. Belatedly, he recalled that she'd seemed to prefer his face without a beard.

You idiot, said a voice in his head that sounded remarkably like Cass. *She doesn't prefer your face at all.*

Sephone's cheeks were slightly flushed. "I'm sorry. I couldn't help noticing."

"I guess it was just easier," he said, wondering if she thought he looked overly wild. "Good haircuts are hard to come by in the mountains."

"As I found out," she replied, tugging on a strand of her own hair.

They laughed together, and he tried not to notice how her eyes danced . . . how they made his heart dance, too. Much too late, he recalled Spartan's advice. *If you don't intend to claim her, you should tell her.*

But even if, against all reason, she still cared for him, it was impossible.

He had already made his choice. Once they found the Reliquary, once Sephone and Caldera were taken care of, he would use it one final time. Spartan would help him arrange everything; he was sure of it.

"Dorian? What's wrong?"

He looked at her and found her looking at him anxiously. In the face of certain death, the temptation to steal a kiss was difficult for any man to withstand. "I'm fine," he said quickly, just as Magritte called from the next room.

I'm coming to check on Sephone's wound.

Sephone pulled away as he did, as if she'd heard the same message, and he found himself grateful for both the warning and the interruption. The woman bustling into the room smiled as if naught had happened and knelt beside Sephone. The questioning, nearly suspicious light had left Sephone's eyes. Dorian was safe.

But words from long ago—from Cass, of all people—churned in his head. *Sephone Winter isn't the kind of lass you can easily lie to, even without a truth-revealing gift present in the room.*

Dorian headed for the pallet in the adjacent bedroom. Sephone was right: his skin was hot enough to brand cattle. He would rest for a short time while Magritte and Regis watched over Sephone. It wasn't difficult to see that something had eased the tension between them of late. She was in far better hands than his.

By the time night fell, bringing with it a summer storm that shook the shack walls and rattled the windows, the others still weren't back. Dorian hoped one of them had found an *altered healer.* Perhaps they had been forced to seek shelter on the return journey.

As he stretched out on the pallet, shivering beneath his cloak and an extra blanket, he felt Sephone's fear through the wall between them. She might have been afraid of the storm, the hooded man, or any number of nameless evils. If he were here, Cass could have shared her sorrow, but Dorian had only one way to comfort her. And so, as he slipped into the dreamworld, he reached out with his gift, surrounding her with the only thing he could give.

The gift of a *calor.*

13

SEPHONE

Dorian's fever was getting worse. When I woke around midnight, I heard him thrashing through the wall, occasionally uttering a low, guttural moan. Gingerly, I stood, pulling a cloak over my clothes. As I tiptoed to his room, the whole building quaked in the wind. Only an ordinary storm, but I was still glad we weren't outside in the elements.

Regis knelt beside Dorian, pressing a damp cloth to his forehead. Magritte crouched beside him. Both of them looked up as I entered. They appeared utterly exhausted.

"How is he?" I whispered.

"Not good," said Regis. "He shivers and sweats in turn."

I looked down at Dorian as he writhed on the floor. By the light of Regis's lantern, his face was sheened with moisture, and his shirt was soaked. The buttons at his neck were partially undone, and my throat tightened as I caught a glimpse of my pendant, tangled with the chain that looped through his wedding ring—his and Lida's. How long had he been wearing my necklace? And why?

I dropped to my knees. "What can I do?"

"You can go back to bed," said Magritte sternly.

"I'm feeling better, I promise." I reached out and took the cloth from Regis. "I can sit with him awhile. I'll wake you when I'm tired."

Regis eyed me doubtfully, but Magritte sighed. "As soon as you feel tired, Seph. Even if it's five minutes from now."

"Aye, I will."

Magritte climbed to her feet with her husband's help. Regis looked over his shoulder as he guided her from the room. "Magritte's right. Call us if his condition worsens."

I spied Dorian's pack beside his bed. "Oh wait. Can you help me get him into a fresh shirt? It might make him more comfortable."

Regis nodded and remained behind as I quickly grabbed Dorian's pack and rummaged through it, pulling a clean shirt from within. At the sight of something gleaming near the bottom, curiosity got the better of me, and I reached for it, holding it, or rather, them, up to the lanternlight.

I dropped the coiled bracelets like hot coals, and Regis exclaimed softly. We had both worn the serpentine copper cuffs as one of the marks of a slave, but these were mine.

"Why does he have those?" Regis asked, frowning.

"Because he was the one who bought me from Cutter." Seeing his shocked expression, I hastily continued, "He would have freed me if he could have returned to Calliope. But the Memosinians have branded him a traitor."

"I didn't think Dorian Ashwood was the type to own slaves."

"He doesn't. At least, none besides me. He only bought me because Cutter refused to free me." I stuffed the hated cuffs back into Dorian's pack and held up the shirt. "Shall we?"

Dorian was out of his mind with fever, and it proved a difficult task to partially undress him. He was broad shouldered and strong, and his body convulsed when Regis peeled away his shirt. As my eyes found the bandages around his chest, Regis's strayed to my pendant at Dorian's throat.

"Another thing of yours," he noted, his expression deeply veiled.

"I gave it to him for safekeeping. When I was going to surrender myself to Asa Karthick."

Regis nodded—I'd shared the barest details of my abduction and captivity with him before—but something stained his gaze. Suspicion? Or disapproval? He didn't know, of course, that I'd also once offered Dorian my heart. But Regis was a man of the resistance, a man with eyes in his head. Maybe he did know how I felt about the former thane of Maera.

"What did you do with your wrist cuffs?" I asked to distract myself from the sight of Dorian's mostly bare chest. I'd never seen him shirtless before. I hoped Regis couldn't see the high color in my cheeks. Only when he was fully dressed again did I let out the breath I kept captive.

"I buried them outside of Nulla. No use holding on to the past."

"You're right." Cutter was dead, which meant Regis was free. As I would have been, if Cutter hadn't sold me to Dorian.

Regis stood and reached out to pat my shoulder, then stopped halfway. "I'm sorry. I'm always going to forget."

"It's fine," I said with a weak smile. "I'll always be here to remind you."

He smiled back and left me alone. Dorian was no longer thrashing, and when I wrung out the cloth and placed it on his forehead, I saw the sweat had dried. Now, he lay on his back, shivering uncontrollably. I hurriedly covered him with his cloak and the blanket that had been tangled up in his legs. When he continued to shake, I retrieved the blanket from my room and laid it over him. "Sleep, Dorian. You must sleep to heal." After a while, he calmed, and I laid my hand on his forehead, keeping it there for a long time.

I looked around the meadow, realizing I'd been here before. It wasn't the same meadow where I'd first met the white horse, but the one where I'd faced Dorian across a moving sea of emerald green, just before he'd rejected me. This time, it was night, and moonlight silvered the grass. I was looking on as an observer, watching the dream version of Dorian approach the dream version of Sephone. He wore the same clothes he had at the winter festival in Nyx, as did I—or rather, my dream self did.

"I've been waiting to ask you to dance," he said, stopping in front of me and looking down.

"I thought you didn't want to," Dream Sephone replied.

"Wanting to and not being able to are two very different things." He bowed at the waist, then extended his hands. "May I?"

Dream Sephone nodded and was ushered into his arms. The scene shimmered and changed, and suddenly they were dancing beneath the snow-blossom trees near Nyx, under branches strung with rows of lanterns. It was the height of summer, but the warm breeze still carried the scent of the blossoms, which reached me where I stood. It was the scent of dreams, of impossible expectations, of unrequited love.

Sorrow pierced me, for the blossom trees must have been destroyed along with the city. Asa Karthick would not let anything so beautiful remain standing. And this dream . . . this dream was only a figment of my imagination, the playing out of a long-buried fantasy. Even the silvery-gold light limning my now-long hair as Dream Dorian bent to kiss Dream Sephone was just a silly fancy on the part of my subconscious. There had only been one woman in Dorian's mind who deserved that glow.

Enough.

I forced the dream to end. In the real world, I came awake to find I had fallen asleep by Dorian's pallet. His eyes were open . . . wide and panicked.

"Dorian," I said quickly, "I'm only here because you were cold. I accidentally fell—"

"How much did you see?" he blurted.

I blinked at him, not understanding. "Did I see?"

"The meadow." He raked a hand through his hair. I comprehended the significance of his question. The realization made my heart pound.

It was not my dream, but his. An arm must have flung out while he'd slept and brushed against my face. My gift must have worked on him, even in the dreamworld, giving me a window into his private world. Which meant that—

"How much did you see?" He was rigid, his back against the wall. I had never seen him so vulnerable, not even in his worst nightmares.

"Enough."

It was different than what I'd seen in Cass's mind—far more honorable—though the shape of Dorian's thoughts was the same. It was what I'd hoped for the day I practically declared myself beside the stream.

He loved me.

I felt dizzy, as if an avalanche had caught me up and swept me down the side of a mountain.

"Why, Dorian? Why now?" I asked when he said naught, and I could see he grasped the unspoken question. Why now, when it was unlikely that I would live for much longer?

"Because I'm a fool." He shifted uncomfortably. "I never intended to tell you."

"Why? Because you were ashamed of your regard?"

His eyes flared. "Of course not." He crossed his arms, then scrunched his brow at his sleeves. "I wasn't wearing this shirt when I went to bed."

"Don't change the subject," I snapped. Red crept up my neck, and I was glad the lantern was burning low. "Why wouldn't you tell me? Why wouldn't you . . ."

"You wrote me a letter," he said. "A letter that made me realize how blind I'd been . . . and for how long."

How long had he hidden his feelings—from me and from himself? Nevertheless, I sagged at the reminder of my letter. "Dorian, I was angry. And hopelessly lost. I had to write what I did, or I would never have been able to leave you behind."

"You were right to say it. All of it."

"Was I?" I touched his hand. "What was between us isn't finished."

He got to his feet, a little shakily. I stood as well, wishing I hadn't spoken. I likely had his *calor* gift to thank for my bold statement. I retreated to the other side of the room to give him space. For good measure, I closed the door, though sound might yet travel through the thin walls to where Regis and Magritte had bedded down.

Dorian was still for so long I thought he would reject my statement, but then his eyes flickered. Uncertainty was suddenly replaced by firm resolve.

"You're right. It isn't finished." In three strides, he crossed the room and gathered me in his arms. It was nothing like the possessive, almost bruising embrace Cass had enfolded me in earlier. And when Dorian took my face between his hands, I knew he was seeking my permission. In response, I slipped my arms around his waist and lifted my head.

"Persephone," he whispered, and nothing was more intoxicating than hearing my full name from Dorian's lips . . . those same lips gently pressed themselves against mine.

All at once, I felt him in my mind, and myself in his, the silvery-gold light from before wending between our bodies like Cass's truth gift. I could feel his memories, see his mental image of me glowing even more vividly than before, but he must be able to feel all of my emotions . . . to feel the warmth that swept through me at his touch, crimping my fingers and curling my toes. His love for me ran deep, to the very bottom of his soul. Even my gift remained in check as I stood on the threshold of his mind and poured myself into him.

Until he abruptly pulled away, breathless, his brown eyes shadowed once more. "That was wrong of me. I'm sorry, Sephone."

"What are you talking about?"

"I should not have done that."

"Why not?"

He looked at me directly, exposing the raw anguish tormenting his soul. "Because you are young and lovely, and I do not wish to take advantage of you . . . especially not when you are still affected by my gift. And I will not destroy you with my darkness."

"*Darkness*? What darkness?"

"You forgave Regis."

"Aye, but I fail to see the relevance—"

"But you will not be able to forgive me."

"Forgive you? What are you saying, Dorian?"

"I was the one who betrayed you to Brinsley." His voice was pained. "You were abducted because of *me*."

Invisible daggers sliced into my heart, far more deadly than the one which had cut my side. "What do you mean?"

"At the winter festival in Nyx. Perhaps you didn't realize it, but I was drunk that night. Very drunk. I told Brinsley about helmswort. How in Nulla, someone had used it to suppress your powers. Brinsley used it to capture you."

Is that all? "I don't see how you can blame yourself for my kidnapping, just because my brother got you drunk—"

"Nay, I got myself drunk."

"—and you shared something by accident. You had no idea what Brinsley would do with that information. You're not responsible."

"You don't understand." Dorian shook his head. "But you will, later, when you have time to process what I've told you."

I released an exasperated sigh. "Why did you get drunk?" I knew from his mind that he'd never indulged in anything to excess. He had always been a man of moderation and restraint . . . barring the passionate kiss he'd just given me.

"Because I was jealous," Dorian admitted. "After that, I promised myself I'd give you the space to decide what you truly wanted."

"To decide if I preferred Cass, you mean."

He nodded.

"And if I told you that I cared only for you?" I was hedging my bets, I knew, by not confessing how I felt. But surely, I didn't need to. He was an empath; he must know.

"There are other reasons, of course."

"Other reasons?"

"Why nothing can ever come of this." He gestured to the space between us, as if the reasons he spoke of had assumed physical form and now crouched there in the semidarkness, waiting to spring if either of us moved. At least the wind had now risen like a siren, masking our conversation from the occupants of the next room.

I crossed my arms. "Like what?"

"I'm an empath. You're an uncommonly powerful *mem*. Love is an intimate affair, even when the parties are not *alters*. If you become my wife, we will both be at a disadvantage, albeit in different ways. I have nightmares, Sephone, just as you do. If we marry, you'll be tortured by my past, just as I would be affected by yours."

My heart skittered at his mention of marriage. "Then you would reject me simply because I'm a *mem*?"

"Can you deny that it is difficult for you to be in my mind?"

"It's not as difficult as you might think." I thought of Lord Guerin. Some minds were infinitely worse, and this was Dorian. I'd known him since I was four years old.

"You said yourself that your gift is becoming more unpredictable. What if the difficult soon becomes impossible?"

I gulped, because he was right. I *was* losing control. "This is not just about me. You have better mental control than anyone I've ever met. Many times, you've kept things from me without me realizing. I could teach you how to keep me out of your mind altogether."

Sorrow lined his brow. "You are already in my mind, Sephone, whether you're touching me or not. My every waking thought, and most of my dreams, are full of you. If you were mine—and you should know that I want nothing more—you would see all of me . . . *all*. And it would destroy us both."

My chest simultaneously expanded and deflated at Dorian's bold declaration of his feelings. He wanted me, more than anything else, but not enough to risk the inevitable pain our union would bring.

"Is it so terrible to have me in your mind?"

"If you had any other gift, it might have been possible, but I . . . *we* are not meant to be. You must forget me."

"Dorian, I—"

"Think about what I'm saying, Sephone. It is impossible in every respect. Telepathic ability runs in my veins already. My daughter was a *mem*, the same as you. If you and I . . . if there was a . . . any children we had—"

I blushed, but he pressed on doggedly.

"—could you imagine their gifts, Sephone? Could you imagine how powerful a child we created would be? Remember, after all, that it was that which led Asa to come to you—"

"Against his wishes."

"Perhaps. But he was still willing to do as his father wanted. I know this sounds callous, but think on it. *Alters* are only ever considered valuable or dangerous. Our son or daughter would be hunted wherever we went."

"Then we would protect them. Together."

He made an exasperated sound in his throat. "If you had lived in the world as long as I have, you would understand."

I stiffened. "You see me as a child."

He shook his head emphatically. "Nay. It is a long time since I thought of you as a child . . . if I ever did, beyond our first meeting. But I am as old as the hills, Sephone."

"And just as disinclined to budge, I'd wager," I countered. "You aren't old."

"Age is not a number but the state of a soul."

"Then we are both alike in that respect. I feel a hundred years old and twice as weary."

He smiled faintly, as if remembering the time he'd told me that himself. Then his lips pursed in a grimace. "You forget that I've already lived an entire life, whereas you have yet to live yours."

"I'm a *mem*, Dorian. I've witnessed much in twenty-one years. More than most, perhaps. The births of children, the embrace of lovers . . ." I trailed off, then went on, "You're forgetting," I was still smarting from his reminder of my youth, "that *I'm* the one who's dying."

His head went up sharply. "Not if I have any say in the matter."

"And what say do you intend to have in the matter, Dorian? I thought you didn't want any part of me."

Hearing the anger and hurt in my voice, his own voice became softer. "If you think I can make this decision without feeling the pieces of my heart shatter inside me, you're mistaken. If I cared for you less, I would have accepted the heart you offered me that day at the stream."

"If I cared for you less, I would not have offered it." I closed my eyes. Rejection, like abandonment, hurt so much more the second time around.

When I opened my eyes again, Dorian's hand was extended, my pendant on his bare palm.

I shook my head. "I don't want it."

"It belongs to you."

When he insisted, I took it, absently fastening it around my neck. The weight and shape of it, which had once felt so familiar, was now strangely foreign. A red substance had worked into the deepest recesses of the pendant . . . a substance I suspected was blood.

It wasn't mine.

"The man who died to save me," I murmured. "I didn't even know his name."

"But he knew yours," Dorian replied, somewhat cryptically. "And that was enough for him to sacrifice everything to save you, even if he never knew you."

I glanced at him. "You make it sound like he cared about my life."

"I know he did." Dorian presented his back to me again. When he spoke again, his voice was uncharacteristically cold. "You should go, Sephone."

I slowly came back to myself. The wind whistled through the loose boards and sheeted under the door, reminding me of Nulla. Once again, Dorian Ashwood was shutting me out of his life. Denying me his love . . . even his friendship. Whether it was for the reasons he'd given earlier or because of something else, I knew I couldn't convince him otherwise. Nevertheless, perhaps because his courage still ran in my veins, I had to try one final time.

Hesitantly, I reached out and touched his shoulder. He stiffened, but shivers were once again wracking his body.

"There may be only a few months left. Months I would gladly share with you, if you were willing. Would you deny yourself that?" I swallowed my pride. "Would you deny *us* that?"

A long silence stretched between us, punctuated only by the sound of his shivering and my own serrated breathing. Then he drew himself up.

"It is impossible," he said, and even though I'd prepared myself for his reply, tears still fell at the certainty of the declaration.

He would not be moved. He would never be moved. He couldn't allow me into the space Lida and Emmy had vacated so abruptly.

"Then perhaps it's for the best," I replied, unable to keep the bitterness out of my voice. "Perhaps it's best that I know, right up front, that I am not worth the sacrifice."

He opened his mouth to answer, but before he could do so, I was gone.

14

DORIAN

Though the fever left his body for good in the early hours of the morning, he didn't sleep again that night. He was still awake when the storm died down just before dawn, the others finally returning soon afterward. He replayed it all in his mind: the dream he'd unwittingly shared with Sephone; the perfect, inevitably doomed kiss.

The expression on her face when he had rejected her so completely.

Sacrifice, she'd said, as if he were at liberty to claim her heart and simply forget about the threat to her life. As if he had not already decided to pay the ultimate price to free her. But he had led her to believe that he didn't care to risk his heart for the sake of a few months of happiness. That he could not do so because of her gift, because of who she was.

And if he were to proceed with his plan, she could never know the real truth of the matter: that he loved her more than ever.

As if he somehow guessed what had transpired between Dorian and Sephone, Cass was even more unbearable than usual. The three of them had brought back a middle-aged man, shabbily dressed and of decidedly uncertain levels of sobriety. Aleria had found him on the outskirts of a small village, living in a hut much like the one where they'd sheltered for the night.

"I don't know," Magritte whispered to Regis as the man squatted beside Sephone. "He seems a little . . ."

"Unsteady," Regis agreed.

"You have payment?" the man barked at Aleria.

She nodded, and he shifted uneasily, setting a silver flask on the ground before leaning over Sephone. When he saw the gash in her side, he shook his head, unsettling greasy strands of hair Dorian guessed were usually iridescent black.

"Not much good with flesh wounds. You'll need to stitch that one up yourself. I'm much better with bones."

"Marianthean," Dorian murmured to himself, hearing the strong accent and noting his deeply tanned skin.

"He wasn't my first choice," Cass retorted.

Aleria sent Dorian and Cass a look that said, *He was the only choice.*

"How are you with poison?" Cass asked the man.

The *alter* shrugged. "Hopeless."

At least he was honest. Nevertheless, Dorian glared at Cass. It wouldn't do to alienate the only man who could help ease Sephone's discomfort.

"We are grateful for whatever you can do for her," Dorian said, avoiding Sephone's gaze.

Magritte had unwrapped the splint on Sephone's arm and eased off her glove. Seeing the deeply bruised, swollen limb for the first time, Dorian stifled an utterance. The *alter* merely laid his ungloved fingers over her wrist; Sephone closed her eyes, as if she were concentrating, though she showed no signs of being in pain. Perhaps she was trying to stay out of his mind.

The *bonesetter* huffed. "Lots of bones in a wrist. Some of them are in the wrong place. They'll need to be rebroken and set properly."

Magritte's eyes widened. "Are you sure?"

"Nay, mistress, I just said so for the fun of it," said the man gruffly. He nudged the flask toward Sephone's knee. "Have at it, girl."

Expecting her to refuse the offer, Dorian was surprised when she reached forward to claim the grubby offering. Thankfully, Cass intercepted her, bending down and passing her his own flask.

"Have as much as you like," he said in a low voice. "I restocked with the help of a passing stranger near the village. Trust me, between this fellow and the stitching later, you're going to need it."

She smiled at him, and Dorian's gut wrenched.

She drank a good amount of the liquor, appearing a little glazed and unsteady by the time she returned the flask to Cass. Dorian forced himself to watch as the *bonesetter* leaned over her wrist again. Holding it more firmly this time, he closed his eyes.

Dorian reached out with his *calor* gift at the same time as Spartan drew on his *pax* gift. Together, they filled the room with a strange mixture of peace and courage. Sephone raised her head and smiled at the acolyte appreciatively. Dorian had heard them speaking together early that morning, a conversation that had begun with *So, you do shields now?*

She didn't look at Dorian.

There were several small cracks in quick succession, and Sephone uttered a sharp gasp, her left hand clutching her right elbow. Cass gripped her shoulder, though his sorrow gift could do little to relieve her agony. Still, Dorian sensed that every person present shared her pain. A wave of nausea surged up his throat.

"Now for the big one," said the man, and there was a loud *crack*. Sephone screamed and collapsed against Cass in a faint.

Holding her firmly, the *lumen* glared at the *bonesetter*. "Are you done yet, man?"

"Almost."

By the time he was finished, Dorian's stomach roiled like a restless sea. Cass had eased Sephone onto the floor, and Magritte was preparing to stitch up her wound while she was unconscious. Sephone's white-blond hair pooled around her ashen face in a silken approximation of blood. With a hurried whisper to Regis, Dorian left the room.

Lord Adamo? Magritte called after Dorian, her voice filled with concern. But he didn't turn back. He'd barely made it twenty paces when the nausea made good on its earlier threat. Spasm after spasm left him doubled over and trembling. When there wasn't anything left to throw up, he wiped his mouth and staggered to his feet.

Cass stood watching Dorian, an odd expression on his face. "You know, Thane, you surprise me. I didn't realize she meant so much to you."

A faint air of mockery edged his statement. Dorian wiped his mouth again. "Say what you came to, Cass."

His eyebrows lifted. "I came to say naught."

"No sly jabs? No contemptuous comments?"

"You have me pegged all wrong." Something appeared in his gaze that made him look almost sincere. "Were you reminded of your family?"

"Sephone *is* my family," Dorian snapped, disliking the sincere Cassius Vera even more than the mocking version.

"Ah, yes, the old 'sister' ruse." He smirked, but his eyes flashed. "I know something happened between you and her. The way she refuses to look at you now, as if she cannot bear to see your face. You broke her heart when you rejected her the first time. Will you break her spirit, too?"

Though indignation flared, Dorian said nothing.

"Perhaps it's time we go our separate ways, Thane. You are surely bound for Thebe with the resistance leader and his wife, and I . . ." His meaningful look, followed by the patting of his coat pocket where he kept Sephone's letter, left no doubt as to his intentions.

"She's still dying, Cass," Dorian said heavily.

"Meaning what?" he retorted. "You won't abandon the chase until she's dead?"

"You know that isn't what I meant." Dorian came closer, not wanting the others to overhear. "We both want the same thing. For Sephone to live."

"So?"

"So, let's divide our forces. One of us will search out an *alter* strong enough to endure the Reliquary. The other will hunt down the hooded man and retrieve the artifact."

"A truce," Cass said, apparently contemplating it seriously. "To save Sephone?"

"Aye."

"I will find the *healer*," he said, nodding decisively. "You can find the hooded man, since the lady of Thebe desires an alliance with him anyway."

Dorian nodded. "I'll find him." Feeling more bile rise, he began to leave.

"There's one great flaw in your plan, Thane," Cass said, and Dorian turned to find the *lumen* looking at him more thoughtfully. "If both of us succeed and we finally have the Reliquary and the *healer* at our disposal, what next? You must recall what the Reliquary demands in return for its power."

Dorian hesitated. Cass was the last person in whom he wanted to confide his real plan. But Cass remembered what Brinsley had told them about the Reliquary. He knew that to save a life, someone had to die.

And, by the look in his eyes, he knew it would have to be one of the two of them.

"I made my decision months ago," Dorian said quietly. "Sephone will be yours forever, if you only do as I ask."

Cass's eyes widened as Dorian briefly outlined his plan. How he would need Cass's help to arrange the procedure, possibly even to restrain or sedate Sephone. Shock paled Cass's tanned features as Dorian spoke.

"She must never know what we're planning," Dorian insisted. "You must promise me that."

Cass regarded him. "She will never forgive you if you die in her place. She will never forgive *me*."

"All going well, she won't even know you were there."

"But she'll know I helped you."

"I doubt it. You are going after the *healer*, are you not? It's me who's going after the Reliquary. Do whatever you think is necessary to discredit me after I am gone."

Cass continued to look at Dorian closely. "You haven't said why."

"Why what?"

"Why you're doing this."

Dorian stilled. There were a thousand reasons why, the foremost of them being that he loved Sephone with every fiber of his soul. But there was only one reason Cass would accept. "I have naught left to lose."

A long silence. Dorian could see that he understood, in his own way. Cass was younger than he was, less troubled by the world. He hadn't lost his wife and daughter; he hadn't lost years of his life to a cause he was no longer sure he believed in.

He hadn't purposefully destroyed Sephone's love for him.

"Then you did reject her. That's why she refuses to look at you."

"I told her anything between us was impossible. Does that satisfy you?"

Cass's eyes sparked. "It does."

Dorian already knew what Cass would say next, but his acceptance was still a long time coming.

"All right. When were you thinking we would do this?"

"She doesn't have much time left. It won't be years now, possibly only months. But I will not abandon her while Draven is still alive. As soon as he's dead, I'll . . ." Dorian trailed off. No need to explain further.

Cass swallowed. He seemed to be about to say something, but then he shook his head and returned to the shack. After a few minutes, Dorian followed.

Aleria had arranged payment for the *alter,* who had swiftly departed. Meanwhile, Magritte had finished stitching Sephone's wound, and as the others prepared the horses, Regis lifted his childhood friend into Cass's saddle, where the *lumen* wrapped his arms around her semiconscious form. Dorian ignored the gazes of both men and went to Magritte.

"Could you send a message?" he asked the woman, ignoring her sympathetic look.

"Of course, Lord Adamo. Who to?"

"Do you remember my bodyguards, Bas and Bear?"

She nodded.

"Please tell them that we will shortly join them in Thebe. And then, if you might also notify Lady Xia that we are coming, and that we have Sephone."

"I will, my lord."

"Just Dorian," he said, feeling how easily the words came now. The months of stumbling over formalities were long past.

As Dorian went to mount his horse, he found Spartan at his elbow. "If you are about to argue that we should return to the Mysterium, save your breath."

"Nay, Dorian," he replied, handing him his pack. "I was merely going to give you this." He hushed his voice. "And to ask how you fare."

"Thank you for your concern, but I'm fine."

"Are you sure?"

Dorian placed his boot in the stirrup and hauled himself up, feeling every one of his thirty-one years, and more besides. "Never better."

"My head hurts," I said as soon as I opened my eyes, surprised to find the world lurching to-and-fro. We were on horseback again, passing through another grove of nondescript green. Where had they said we were headed? Thebe?

"That would be the liquor," Cass replied from behind me. "You get used to it."

"I don't want to get used to it." I shifted in the saddle, but Cass held me closer than Dorian had, his arms snug around my waist as he held the reins in my lap. My mouth was dry, my body ached, but my wrist . . . my wrist was distinctly better. I forgot the pounding in my head as I flexed my gloved limb.

"Careful," said Cass in my ear, a smile in his voice. "Last I saw, it was still nicely bruised. You don't want to do any new damage."

Would it become like my injured ankle or my burned arm? Mostly healed, but always a memory of the original accident? A shadow of the old pain?

"Did I drink your whole flask?" It certainly felt like it.

"It's all right. We passed through another town, and I restocked."

"How many towns have we passed through?"

"Only three."

"*Three*?"

"You've been in and out most of the day." He lowered his voice. "You didn't miss much, Seph. The thane is as grouchy as ever, the monk as quiet as ever, and your childhood friend and his wife keep to themselves." He squinted through the gray. "I can't see the eagle-woman at present, but she insists she's scouting ahead."

Hearing the wary note in his voice, I stiffened. "Aleria is our friend."

"She's also an outlander," he replied, somewhat offhandedly.

"She saved my life."

"So did the monk."

"Spartan isn't a monk." I thought of the *alter* that Spartan hoped would be king. If anything, Spartan was more of a soldier, fighting for an impossible cause. If Spartan wanted his captain to be king of Caldera, he would have to go through his own father. And his brother. Neither of whom would give up the throne.

"Be careful, Seph," Cass warned me softly. "There's not a soul in Caldera without an agenda."

"Even you?"

"Aye, even me. Though I should think my purposes are more obvious than most." If it were possible, he tugged me closer. Color poured into my cheeks—what would Dorian think of me if he saw?

Pain wrung my heart. Dorian didn't care. He had told me as much last night.

"The thane and his friends go to Thebe," Cass was saying. "To Lady Xia. You know she will consider us mere foot soldiers in her war with Memosine."

"I won't run, Cass." I knew what he was going to suggest. That I should flee with him to Marianthe, to find refuge on the sea. "Not while Lord Draven and Asa and the hooded man live to terrorize Lethe."

"Rest assured Lethe is doing its own spot of terrorizing. You've heard about their new weapons?"

"Aye."

"And you know how they tested them?"

"Regis told me about the experiments."

"Ah. Then you know our great friend Siaki Xia is not as noble or as innocent as she seems. And, by extension, neither is the thane, nor Xia's new outlander ally."

I resented his implication. "You have no proof any of them were involved in the *alters'* disappearances."

"I know that Xia is pursuing an alliance with the same man who held you captive for nearly four months, Seph."

I twisted in the saddle. Cass was too close; his stubbled jaw brushed against my cheek. "What do you mean?"

"It was one of our objectives in finding you. The enemy of our enemy is our friend, aye? At least, Xia supports the logic."

"That can't be true." How could Xia do such a thing? The hooded man was a sadist and a murderer. He might despise Lord Draven, but that didn't make him our friend.

Then again, the same argument applied to the outlanders. As much as I wanted to believe that Aleria Vega was an ally, we had no guarantee that she would stand with us if it meant going against her people. Especially when Lord Draven's rule now encroached on their lands.

The world may not be so kind in reality as it appears in your imagination . . . Regis's warning, given so long ago, flashed into my mind once more.

Forgive me for saying so, Seph, but you're still far too naïve . . .

"Aleria said Dorian wasn't aware of Xia's connection with the outlanders," I told Cass. "You cannot doubt *his* loyalties, even if you doubt hers."

"He's still a politician, Seph. And that comment was made months ago, right?"

I reluctantly nodded.

"They seem to have had much to speak about since then."

"What are you saying, Cass?"

"Only that I have observed long conversations between them, sometimes late at night. Perhaps it is because Aleria is a *mem*, or because she is an ally of Xia. I don't know. But you must be careful. Things change quickly in a time of war, and oftentimes people who thought themselves to be on the same side suddenly find themselves facing each other across the field of battle."

My heart was now pounding instead of my head. Whether Cass was implying a secret alliance between Dorian and Aleria or a romantic attraction—or simply sowing seeds of doubt—I didn't know. But he was right to put me on my guard. My naïveté had allowed Brinsley and the hooded man to capture me. Was it possible that my love for Dorian had blinded me to his other purposes? Was that why he had rejected me, even if he'd confessed that he returned my feelings?

"It matters not," I said at last. "Whatever happens, I may not be around to see it."

Cass's arms around me tightened, his chest pressing firmly against my back. "Nay, Seph. The thane and I have made a pact. Once you are safe—I would prefer it not be in Thebe, but if that is your choice, I will honor it—we will renew our search for an *altered healer*. We'll find someone who can extract the poison."

Cass and Dorian had made an agreement without my knowledge? Irritation mingled with gratitude, but the quest was futile. "There are few *alters* left in Lethe, Cass. And those in Memosine are either dead or working for Lord Draven. Besides, even if you're successful, there's no remedy."

"The thane said there was a *healer* who could mend the impossible."

I thought of the Mysterium and the Three. I had never asked Spartan if his captain had a healing gift, though it was likely he had been the one to whom the *alter* in Idaea referred. But then I remembered the Garden, fading into deadly shadows . . . the wolves . . . the woman I'd killed.

Why would that man save a murderess?

"It is hopeless." Feeling Cass deflate, I added, "But thank you for entertaining hope nonetheless."

"You can't dissuade me, Seph. Though you should have told me the truth about the curse . . . from the very beginning."

I felt rather than heard the hurt in his voice—that I hadn't confided in him that I was dying. That I had confided in Dorian. My own omission had sown the tension and discord between them, and my reluctance to be honest with either of them had only exacerbated the situation. I should have known better, for it was not the first time Cass had loved a woman who'd belonged to another man.

"Did you think I would not care?" he murmured in my ear.

"Nay. I feared you would care too much."

Ahead of us, Aleria swept across the path, alighting on a branch just above Dorian's horse. At once, Dorian called a halt, and the others guided their mounts from the road. Dozens of tracks imprinted the trampled forest. Many of the inhabitants of Orphne would have fled this way. I was dimly aware that we'd encountered some of them on the road, bound for Thebe like we were.

Aleria began morphing back into her human form. When she was finished, she spoke quietly to Dorian. My stomach tightened as I remembered Cass's warnings.

Cass slid from the saddle and reached up for me, holding me beneath my armpits to avoid brushing against my wounded side. I stumbled a little as my boots hit the ground—I'd never had enough liquor to feel its aftereffects. In response, Cass stepped even closer, his hands now spanning my back.

"One can never care too much," he whispered and then released me. I looked up and found Dorian glaring at Cass. Despite Cass's suggestion of an alliance between them, a mutual quest to save my life, the tension in the air was palpable.

Dorian had no right to feel anything, not after what he'd done. I'd been starkly honest with him: I loved him. And I had offered him the remaining months of my life. I had chosen him over Cass, and he'd spurned me outright. He could not judge me—or despise Cass—for the company I kept from this moment forward. Though the way Cass was returning Dorian's glare would hardly help the situation.

Neither man wore jealousy well. I watched Aleria beside Dorian, her mane of golden-brown hair and tanned skin so like his.

Aye, and neither did I.

The next day, I rode double with Spartan. Cass had objected to the arrangement, but even he could see that riding double with him again would tire his horse. Dorian had swapped mounts with Regis and Magritte to give Aleria's horse a rest. I had wondered if Aleria ever tired of flying so far in her eagle form, but she never seemed overly exhausted, and I guessed she stopped for rests while waiting for us to catch up.

Of course, none of that mattered anymore. Aleria had decided that she would return to the outlands, for she had not seen her family in months.

"They will be wondering what has become of me," she had explained the night before as we sat around the fire. "Now that I know you are all safe"—she glanced at me—"I must return to the north."

"What about Lady Xia?" Cass had asked, his arm brushing against mine, as if to rouse my suspicions. "Doesn't she need you in Thebe?"

"I've already spoken to Dorian at length," she replied. "He will share with her everything I have gleaned."

Once more, jealousy pinched my gut.

"And besides," Aleria continued, "eagles fly faster than horses can travel. I will return soon, when Xia sends for me again." This time, her look included Magritte.

Reg's wife had a valuable gift, indeed.

Our parting, just after dawn the next day, had given rise to mixed feelings. During our weeks of shared captivity, I had come to see Aleria Vega as a friend. But then I'd learned that she had never been a prisoner at all. I had sacrificed myself for someone who'd been free to come and go as she pleased.

I tried to remind myself that she had done so for my sake. But Cass's insinuation that Xia wanted an alliance with the hooded man, his remarks about Dorian and Aleria's private meetings, together with Aleria's own admission that she had been gathering intelligence in the mountains, all combined to birth a pervasive sense of new mistrust. Despising myself for it, I did my best to conceal my suspicions as I bid Aleria farewell, instead thanking her for saving my life outside of Orphne, and for finding Dorian and Cass, as she'd promised she would.

"I will see you again soon, Sephone," she said, her features already melting away, replaced with glossy feathers. "Take care, my friend."

Then she was gone, into the gray. She had said naught of the Mysterium, though I'd seen her talking to Spartan on several occasions. Had she truly desired to visit the Three? Or was the visit only a smokescreen for other agendas?

Fortunately, Spartan was a quiet companion. I'd insisted on riding behind him, and he said very little, though I knew that he saw much. The countryside was littered with signs that a great many people had passed this way recently, including the occasional discarded item of ragged clothing or abandoned belonging, and even the corpse of a horse.

"What will you do when we reach Thebe?" I asked, after an entire hour of silence had passed. Dorian, Regis, and Magritte rode ahead of us, while Cass brought up the rear. "Will you fight for Memosine or for Lethe?"

"It is not so simple, Sephone," Spartan replied. "First and foremost, I heed orders from another captain."

"The *alter* from the Garden."

He straightened. "You have met him?"

"Twice now . . . but it was only a dream." I expected him to contradict me, but he said nothing. I hoped I hadn't insulted him. "And will your captain ride to war against Lord Draven? Or even the hooded man?"

"The battle he fights is not one of this age, but *every* age. And the throne he seeks is not the one now occupied by my father."

My brow creased. "You're saying he is for Lethe, then, not Memosine?"

"For neither."

"I don't understand."

"A man is only ever marginally better than the badness of what he's rebelling against, Sephone. It is the pattern of this world that every revolutionary eventually becomes precisely the thing he hates. For that reason, this war will come to naught, as the last came to naught, and the one before that. It has been that way since the beginning, even in the days where the Three were widely accepted. No country has ever served the Three for long, no matter how much of their presence was revealed."

It was a curiously long speech for the acolyte. Not for the first time, I wished Spartan was not so enigmatic. Aleria had known about the Three, and I guessed that they were longer-lived than ordinary men . . . maybe even old enough to have seen the world-that-was. "If your allegiances lie with them, then why are you riding with us?"

"I promised that I would not leave Lord Adamo until the end."

"But why? He's already forgiven you for your father's crimes."

"Aye, he has. But I gave my word to the Three that I would not abandon him."

I wondered if Cass, who rode closely behind, was listening. "Why didn't you stop him from taking the Reliquary? For surely the Mysterium was aware it had been stolen, given they sent you after us."

"Aye, they were." He drew in a long, deep breath. "Everyone born into this world partakes of its curse, Sephone. We are all born into slavery; we are all cursed men and women. And we are all given a choice in how we seek our freedom."

It was eerily similar to what Aleria had said to me, just after I'd given in to the hooded man for her sake.

We are cursed, as cursed as we are gifted . . .

"Then the Reliquary is evil," I declared. "A cruel trick played on us by the Mysterium and the Three. It does not give without taking something precious in return."

"Nay." Spartan shook his head vigorously. "It is not evil. Not in itself. It was not designed for humans, but for animals, so that people would not pay the price for their wickedness. So that they would realize that their choices carried a cost. But it was twisted and corrupted, like everything else in this world. It was distorted by evil-natured men, just like the memories you carry."

Once again, he reminded me of Aleria. What had she told me about the war between Caldera and the outlanders? *You may not have known what you saw. And you were not there. But you have felt the guilt, have you not?*

"Nevertheless," continued Spartan, "the Reliquary's purpose is complete. For the lesson of the artifact is that only one can endure it. Only one can pay the terrible price it exacts."

"Only one?" I repeated. "You mean the *alter* from the Mountain?"

He nodded.

Impossible. No one would choose to willingly shackle themselves to the Reliquary, to bear its poison. Not even Spartan's noble-hearted captain.

And even if he chose that path, no *alter* could endure it without dying himself.

The guilt Aleria had seen so easily threatened to overwhelm me. "I can never return to the Mountain, Spartan. I have done the hooded man's work, his wrong. I will never be free."

"So I once believed myself."

I recalled in that moment that he was not just Spartan of the Mysterium, but Jerome Karthick—Rufus Karthick's son and Asa Karthick's brother. A child born of violation and heartbreak. Raised to serve a man he despised, a man he'd fled to join the Order.

"I once shared your shame, Sephone. I will freely admit that I never felt worthy of the Order, or of the Three, who claimed me as their own. I have struggled, many times, to convince myself that I belong to them. I have tried, so often, not to become the man my father shaped me to be."

I wished I could see his face. "You are nothing like him."

"Oh, but I am, Sephone. I am every bit like him. In every way but one. I have turned from the path he wanted me to walk down, and not for anything will I turn back again."

Another long silence stretched between us. I wanted to ask him more—to ask him about the *alter*, and what would happen if I reached out and took his hands—but that would mean returning to the Garden on the Mountain. The same Garden from which I fled every night in my dreams, only to be devoured by the wolves.

Instead, I watched the changing landscape around us. Summer was at its height, and signs of life emerged everywhere: a cluster of snowdrops, oddly late to bloom; a woodpecker chattering high in a tree; a glint of silver revealing a distant stream caught in a rare sunbeam.

It was the strangest thing. The world was so beautiful—so magical and perfect—it was hard to believe that it was cursed. But then something would shift, like a mirage in the desert—the sun slipping behind the gray, plunging the world into darkness; a baby rabbit captured in the jaws of a weasel—and I would see the truth. I would see what most people had forgotten.

It wasn't perfect. It was deeply, terribly wrong.

An ache built in my chest. The ache of seeing the world as it truly was, and people as they truly were, and wanting the illusion back again. Wanting everything to be the way it was before, even knowing that *before* was a lie.

In that moment, I understood why the Memosinians bought memories and the Letheans selectively erased their past. Memosine, unsure of its future and ill at ease with its present, was quick to reach back into the past for a surer foundation. They were obsessed with ancient stories, legends, and tales that praised their ancestors' valor, courage, and fortitude, relying on them to supply all the things they now lacked. Meanwhile, Lethe, my own people, saw only the future—its bright potential and endless possibilities. But to move forward, they had lost something of themselves. They had forsaken their souls.

I attempted to share these reflections with Spartan, who nodded as if he understood. "Past and future are echoes of each other," he said. "Memosine has forgotten what they are and Lethe has forgotten who they were. After all, half of the truth is the same as a lie. Together, they might remember, but they have long been divided."

"Then this war," I was beginning to comprehend him, "this war we fight now will not be the last."

Spartan gazed around at the quickly fading day. "Nay. It isn't the first, and it won't be the last. The land groans for peace and for redemption, but it will be so until the end of time."

We were both silent for the remainder of the ride. When I dismounted, Spartan handed me a small vial. "You left this behind in Nyx."

I studied it—the plain exterior, the tiny cork, the fading label. The iridescent liquid within. *Taste and see.*

"So I did." I hesitated. "Is it true, Spartan? Or are they only dreams?" The vial was the smallest memory potion I'd ever seen. How could it be enough? How was it big enough to hold the truth about everything?

"I can only tell you what I told you before." He reached out and closed my fingers around the vial. "You must see it for yourself."

"Get up, Sephone," said a voice in my ear, and I jerked awake.

I had fallen asleep by Magritte, but when I sat up, I was completely alone. The clearing was identical, down to the patch of iridescent-capped mushrooms three feet from where I'd laid my head. But there was no fire, no packs, no horses.

No friends.

A shiver needled my spine. "Hello?" I called, getting to my feet and realizing I wasn't wearing my boots . . . or my gloves.

The tiniest of warbles sounded above me, and I looked up. The white raven balanced on a low branch, his sleek head inclined in my direction. Even his beak and feet were white.

"You," I whispered. It was the same bird who had led me through the mountains. Why had he come back now?

Seeing me, he flew off. When I didn't follow, he circled around and came back, beating his wings to stay aloft. *Come on*, he seemed to beckon me. *Come and see.*

I hesitated. I didn't want to leave the others—but there were no others. The clearing was empty. Was it possible that the bird was leading me to them? He had, after all, guided me to safety once before.

"All right," I relented. "But I don't like it."

Following the raven, I walked through the forest on bare feet, the damp grass as cool as freshly fallen snow. Winged shadows soared above, blocking out large sections of the canopy of stars. *Bats,* I thought. But the raven didn't appear to mind them. It never flew beyond my line of sight, sometimes alighting on a branch or bush while it waited for me to step over a tree root or cross a stretch of spiky pine needles.

We headed, bit by bit, uphill. The raven led me up a steep rise, fluttering close by as I climbed on hands and feet, mourning the lack of both gloves and boots. Finally, the hill leveled out, and I saw that we had ascended well beyond the forest canopy. A sea of endless green stretched in every direction, rippling in the warm breeze.

A lone man stood at the edge of the cliff, gazing out, and at first, I thought it was Dorian, for he was tall with broad shoulders, and in his presence, my unease fled. The white raven alighted on his shoulder, and he turned slowly.

It wasn't Dorian, but the *alter*. "It was you," I said wonderingly. "You sent the raven."

"Aye," he replied in a deep voice that reminded me, inexplicably, of the Mountain cavern.

"You freed me from the hooded man."

He didn't answer this time, but I knew the truth. The white raven was also the white horse? An animal shapeshifter?

A flicker of resentment stirred to life in my chest. "I thank you, my lord"—how did one address a candidate for a kingship?—"but I will admit, I could have used the horse better than the raven. I was so weak, I barely made it to Orphne." It would have been nice to be carried there instead.

"What was needed most was given," he replied, and I felt the gentle rebuke, layered with infinite compassion. "You needed to walk the path, as it was."

"But the raven left me."

"Nay, Sephone. You were never alone."

My disgruntlement faded, and guilt constricted my throat. If he had sent the raven, and the raven could see me even when I couldn't see *him*, he would know—

"The hooded man's guards. Did you see what I tried to do to them?"

"I did."

"I saw the white horse. You stopped me, didn't you? You stopped me from destroying their minds."

"It was not your place to judge them."

How powerful was this *alter*? He apparently had gifts of foreknowledge, mind-reading, dream-walking, and matter-manipulation. Already more than the maximum of three Cass had once mentioned. I knew, somehow, that he was exceedingly old, though he appeared little more than Dorian's age. Spartan said he had walked the earth in the days of the world-that-was and that our ancestors had known the Three, even though they were strangers to Caldera.

The *alter* beckoned me to join him at the cliff top, the raven still on his shoulder. Unlike the members of the Order of the Mysterium, he wore rough, ordinary clothes. He could not look any less like a king, and I had seen kings before, in memories from minds who'd lived long ago. They wore crowns and long robes and possessed jewels of every color. Despite his powers, the *alter* didn't even have any signs of the gifts: no iridescent hair, eyes, skin, or teeth.

When I reached his side, the *alter* waved his hand, and night turned to day. Immediately, sun drenched us from above, bathing us in golden warmth. My toes curled into the grass, encountering the soft, loamy earth beneath, and I breathed in air so sweet it even tasted like sunshine. I bent and picked a small yellow flower, but as I twirled the stem between thumb and forefinger, the flower quickly bruised, the petals wilting. Butter-yellow faded to gray and then black, and then the entire flower disintegrated in my palm.

"I thought it was real," I whispered, staring at the place where the flower had been.

The *alter*'s voice was almost tender. "Can you not see, my daughter? When you get a little closer to the copy masquerading as the original, when you truly look at it and hold it in your hands, can't you see that there is something terribly wrong with this world? That it is not as it was meant to be? You drink of it, but it does not satisfy; you hold it tightly in your hand, and it slips away; you clutch at it, and it only fades all the faster."

I had observed as much to Spartan earlier in the day. Caldera, like iridescence itself, was a handsome magician who never revealed his true form, though he appeared in many guises.

"Then it's all a lie." I looked into his deeply lined face. "An illusion, a trick."

"Nay. This world is only a copy of what was—and what will be. But it remains to show you what you lack. For the real truth is forever stamped on your soul. Your kind was born in a perfect world, and you will always be hungering to return to it."

Humankind was born in a Garden, Spartan had told us once. *Their souls will always thirst to return to it thereafter.*

"Then this feeling," I said slowly. "This feeling, that I don't belong anywhere in Caldera . . ."

He smiled. "Aye, you do not belong to this world. This world, and the one before it, and the one before that, were all built by human hands. You belong to a different world. A better one."

I suddenly remembered the vial Spartan had given me. Had I drunk of it before I fell asleep? Aye, I had. "But this is a dream, too. You are a dream. You're only telling me what I want to hear."

"Is this what you truly want to hear?"

A shiver stole through my body. "Nay. It isn't."

"I am here, Sephone. For real."

It certainly felt real. More real than any of the memories I'd extracted or consumed. "But how can I tell? What if you're just a figment of my imagination telling me that?"

"It is difficult to tell the difference between the original and the copy, especially when both appear so convincing." He waved his hand again, and night fell once more. "But one good test is that the real thing, unlike the copy, never leaves you wanting. No matter how bitter the draught, it satisfies to the very depths of your soul."

I frowned, not understanding him.

"A memory," he said, as the raven shuffled its wings on his shoulder, "shows you only part of the whole, does it not? It has the shape of the truth, an approximation of its form, but it does not fulfill. It does not satisfy." He gestured to the print my bare foot had made in the dirt. "It is an indication of what once was, an outline of what used to be, but it is only a shadow."

Even this, the crippled veteran in Nulla had told me as he prepared to show me what real strawberries tasted like, *is only a shadow of the real thing.*

"Then what *is* the truth?" I asked.

"Do you want to see it?"

"I do."

He extended his hands to me. "Then come with me, and I will show you."

I hesitated. I already knew he was an *alter,* a very powerful *alter.* If I went with him, what could he do to me? Would he be like Lord Draven and Asa Karthick? Or the hooded man?

"Can you not simply tell me?"

"You will not see unless you are shown."

I stared at his outstretched hands. He was asking me to trust him. To follow where he and the white raven led. Could I do it? Not for the first time, I wished I could feel Dorian's gift.

"This choice requires a different kind of bravery," said the *alter,* as if he'd read my mind. "One that must be discovered, not given." As he spoke, the white raven hopped onto my shoulder, and I felt it: the warm reassurance, the gentle sense of peace. Similar to what I felt in Dorian and Spartan's company, but different, somehow. More potent.

Surely I will be safe with him.

I reached out and took his hands.

Light flashed overhead, and then darkness descended. The darkness was so complete it felt nearly palpable, an oppressive force weighting my chest. I heard myself cry out, and I would have been lost but for the *alter*'s hands in mine, tethering me to himself.

I couldn't feel his mind, or his memories, or anything but the warmth of his roughened skin. Were his mental defenses so impregnable? Thinking of Dorian and Cass, I envied him that. A *mem*'s mind was never truly their own.

One by one, lights winked into being. It took me a long moment to realize that we were in a cavern, and that the lights were actually bioluminescent glowworms.

"The Sacred Grove," I murmured. The *alter* and I stood on the rim of the enormous subterranean lake Spartan had called *Memoria*. Gnarled, twisted trees surrounded us on every side, the bluish-green light flinging garish, misshapen specters against the cavern walls. The water itself was undisturbed and perfectly clear, though I remembered how it had turned to viscous black when stirred. Once again, my attention was drawn to the lone tree which sank its roots into the poisonous pool. The tree which, against all odds, was still alive.

When there was light enough to see, the *alter* let me go. The white raven flew from my shoulder to perch on a branch which extended over the water. The *alter* knelt beside the pool, and—though I exclaimed loudly—swirled his brown fingers in the water. Filth and muck stirred in their wake, reminding me, once again, of Nulla's canals. I could have sworn that a shape glided beneath the surface, a shape with ragged wings.

As the *alter* withdrew his hand, the water seemed to suck at his fingers, tugging them back down. He flicked his wrist, and he was suddenly freed. As he shook his hand, splotches appeared on the grass, black as pitch, oily and oozing. A foul smell issued from them.

"What is it?" I asked, hoping he would not be affected by the poison.

"It is the meeting of the Rivers Lethe and Memosine."

"It looks . . . alive."

"It *is* alive. In fact, you might think of it as living memory. A record of all the pain and evil that has existed in the world since it first began."

"Pain and evil?"

"Pain is but one kind of evil, aye."

I closed my eyes, and for a few seconds, I could almost hear it: A woman's haunting scream. A bloodcurdling war cry, followed by a child's sobbing. The clash of weapons, a sinister cackle, the deep, guttural moan of someone in agony. A series of *cracks*, like the splintering of bone.

When I opened my eyes again, the *alter* was gazing at the pool, his expression somber.

"How long has it been like this?" I ventured.

"Since the beginning. It was beautiful once." He looked around the cavern, his gaze turning wistful. "There was no darkness then, no cavern, and this whole place was covered with lush forest. On a sunny day—and never a day dawned that was not—you could see clear to the bottom of the lake."

I glanced at the crooked specimens behind us. "I don't understand. How could you possibly know that?"

"Because my father and I planted the forest, an age ago now."

My jaw temporarily unhinged. "But you're only a young man. I mean . . ." I trailed off as I met his eyes—his deeply creased, ancient eyes. Surely he wasn't one of the gods the first Calderans had left behind to perish with the world-that-was. But that would make him hundreds—*thousands*—of years old.

"We planted the Garden for the first of your race," the *alter* continued. "It was intended to be a sanctuary for them. A place of completion, of utter perfection. But it was poisoned."

"Poisoned?" I thought of the webbing.

"Aye, poison infiltrated it, corrupting the soul of the world-that-was. Memoria is all that is left now of what once was. The rivers join together here, and from this place, the infection spread. What was intended as a gift has become a stain on the soul of Caldera."

"What about upstream? Surely there the water is clean."

"The Rivers Lethe and Memosine are not ordinary rivers, Sephone. They do not flow just one way. Memoria may be the place of their meeting, but it is also their source. Their lifeblood. The poison comes from the heart. And it is there that the cleansing must take place."

"Are you saying that the rivers themselves are poisoned?" I remembered the potions I had once made with Cutter. The water came from the River Memosine, just as the water for Lethe's potions came from their namesake river. Potions which caused forgetfulness.

"Aye."

"Who would do such a thing?"

And then the *alter* looked at me. Looked at me as no one had ever looked at me before. I felt his gaze peeling back the layers of my soul, exposing my shattered, bleeding, poisoned heart.

I closed my eyes, attempting to keep him out. Hadn't I done good with my gift? Hadn't I tried to save the world? But the *alter*'s gaze probed me even through my eyelids, and I remembered. The men and women who'd endured the mind-bleeding, who'd become mere husks of themselves as their souls faded away, piece by piece. I'd thought I was doing them good, removing the pain of their difficult lives, helping them to survive each waking moment.

Lord Guerin. I'd chipped away at his horrific past, numbing his conscience, helping him to forget. Only when I met Dorian did I realize how much the mind-bleeding cost a soul. How pain could not be created or destroyed, only transferred.

And the young woman, the woman who had died to erase a past. I hadn't known of the Reliquary's price, but I had allowed myself to become the hooded man's tool, the instrument of his vengeance.

The guards. I'd been so angry at the hooded man, so embittered. I had wanted them to feel my pain as deeply as I felt it. To suffer as I had suffered. But in the process, I had become the monster Asa insisted I was.

Who would do such a thing? I had asked so disbelievingly.

But *I* had.

I fell to my knees. "We poisoned this world. As we poisoned the last, and we will poison the next. It was us."

"Aye."

I opened my eyes and found the *alter*'s full of compassion. The compassion made me remember other things: my childhood as Cutter's slave; Regis and Magritte's betrayal; the loss of my parents. It was as if he reminded me simultaneously of the wrong that I had done and the wrong that had been done to me.

I had tried so hard to save the world that, in the process, I had lost myself.

"Are you familiar with Silas Silvertongue?" the *alter* asked.

I nodded.

"Then you know he has the gift of persuasion. That he seduces people to do his will by telling lies that seem like truths."

I remembered how he'd nearly captured me in Idaea and again in Thebe. "He is no ordinary merchant, is he?"

The *alter* shook his head. "He was once in my father's service. But now he is our enemy, seeking revenge on both us and the world he helped to poison."

"*He* was there?"

"Aye, long ago. He led your ancestors astray, and he continues that mission to this day. He bestows his own gifts, but they are twisted versions of the original ones."

"Is he . . . is he human, then?"

"Nay, he is not. But though he is immortal, his days are limited."

"What do you mean, *limited*?"

"His influence on this world, in time, will come to an end."

I retrieved the glass vial Spartan had given to me, which, oddly enough, was still in my cloak pocket and still full—and showed it to the *alter*. "Is this poisoned, too?"

"Nay, not in the way you mean, though it contains some things that are hard to stomach. It will show you the truth, Sephone, no matter how difficult it is to see."

I thought of the Reliquary. "The poison in the artifact that Dorian stole." I swallowed. "That *we* stole. Is it the same as the water of Memoria?"

He nodded. "You must not use the Reliquary again. It carries a burden another must bear—a poison more potent than any other poison. If you try to wield it, it will only bring you death."

"But . . ." I was suddenly acutely aware of the marks on my chest. "I am already dying." I met the *alter*'s tender gaze, only to find it grave.

"I know," he said gently. "My father has a plan to restore Memoria, Sephone, but you must trust us. You must trust me." The white raven flew back to his shoulder, and I felt it: a strange mix of peace, courage, and truth, as if Dorian, Cass, and Spartan's powers had all been rolled into one. If only I could spend my entire life basking in that warmth, letting it soak into my soul.

The real thing, unlike the copy, never leaves you wanting . . .

The *alter* stepped closer, and at the same time, the Sacred Grove began to fade. His voice now carried the faintest of echoes.

"It will not be easy," he said, and once more, I felt his hand on mine. "Before the end, everything you love will be threatened. But when that time has come, and you are in your hour of greatest need, you will call on me, and I will answer you. Everything I am and everything I have will be at your disposal. At the very moment death claims you, you will begin to live."

His voice rang with the sureness of prophecy. Bold and unafraid, as if he had not just predicted that my friends would abandon me and I would die.

"Impossible," I whispered.

"The impossible," he replied with a smile, "is my specialty."

"I don't understand." My voice was beginning to quake. "I am already fading, a little more each day. It will not be long before I lose control of my gift completely. How am I to go on alone?"

He clasped both my hands in his, and I was glad I was not wearing gloves. His strength flowed into mine, warming my soul.

"Because you are not alone, Persephone Winter. No matter what your heart tells you, you are not alone. And because"—his eyes once again bored into my soul—"my father has yet to bestow his greatest gift."

He was nearly gone when I remembered the question I should have asked from the very beginning. "Please, would you tell me, who are you?"

"I am he who was and who is and who always will be."

It's your fault for asking such an obscure question. "I still don't understand."

"I am an *Infinitum*—one of Three. My father, the raven, myself. We have neither beginning nor end."

I blinked. If what he said were true, no wonder Spartan and the Mysterium revered him. "And what is your name?"

A deep voice lingered. "I am Aedon."

And in that moment, I understood. Aedon, a word from the world-that-was, had only one meaning. I recalled a song—a rich, beautiful song of simple melody and exquisite pitch. A song that, until recently, I believed would never be heard in Caldera again.

Aedon.

He was the nightingale.

"Dorian?"

As Sephone came awake, he leaned back. "Aye, it's me."

Her eyes widened, adjusting to the light of the lantern beside him, which illuminated her tiny room and narrow bedroll. He hadn't wanted to wake her, but it was time for him to make good on his promise to Cass.

They had arrived in Thebe the night before. The tree-bound city was in chaos, the outskirts crowded with hundreds of people, many of them refugees from Orphne. Xia's soldiers were attempting to keep the order, but a general atmosphere of barely restrained panic saturated the place, and food and other resources were beginning to run short. It would not be long before hunger made enemies of friendly neighbors.

Dorian had gone immediately to Xia, hoping to find the Mardell brothers and Jewel, but to his dismay, there was no word of them. A multitude of scenarios had swept through his head, each one more dreadful than the last.

While the rest of their small group snatched a few hours' rest in one of the tree houses reserved for visiting dignitaries, Dorian and Regis had debriefed Xia. Aleria had told Dorian everything she believed would be of value, which turned out to be very little that Xia didn't already know. Asa Karthick's army was still encamped outside Nephele, apparently finding satisfaction in starving out the Letheans. Xia planned to ride to their aid, but it would be some time before she could recoup her forces, which had taken a severe blow with the fall of Nyx. The League was nervy and divided. Many Letheans were moving past Thebe, seeking refuge in the northern mountains.

"What are you doing here, Dorian?" Sephone rubbed her eyes and struggled to a sitting position.

"I came to tell you I'm leaving."

"So soon?" She came fully awake. "But we've only just arrived."

"And you will stay."

She stiffened. "Cass told me about your pact to find a *healer*. It isn't necessary."

He tried to mask his surprise. Cass had told her about their plan? "It's not only that. We must also retrieve the Reliquary."

If it had been possible, she would have recoiled from him. But the room Xia had assigned her was not much bigger than a closet, and she was forced to remain in his proximity for the time being. "Why would you want to do that?"

"So long as the hooded man has it, he is a danger to us. When we find it, we will make sure it is destroyed." *Forgive me the lie.*

"Cass also told me about your other mission." When he eyed her, she elaborated. "Xia wants an alliance with the hooded man. When were you going to tell me that?"

Dorian gritted his teeth. Clearly, Cass had been a little too loose-tongued since they'd left Orphne. What else had he said to her? "That was Xia's mission, not mine."

"You expect me to believe you want nothing more than to remove the Reliquary from the hooded man's reach?"

"It's more complicated than that." Haltingly, Dorian told her about Bas, Bear, and Jewel. Her features softened in sympathy.

"I am sorry, Dorian." She shifted, pushing the blanket away. "I can help you look for them—"

"Nay!" Hurt spilled across her pale face, and he tried to make her understand. "You're safe here. Well, as safe as you can possibly be at present. I won't risk that for anything."

"Safe with the woman who wants to join forces with the man who abducted me?"

"I've already thought of that." Xia wouldn't be happy with Dorian, but it had to be done. "I've spoken with Regis. There's an underground resistance safe house not far from here. A place where you will be safe. And Magritte, too. Spartan has agreed to stay with you, since he won't receive the warmest of welcomes from Xia, either. She won't know where you are, which is for your own good. And hers."

"So you're not just leaving," she observed coldly. "You're sending me away."

"I'll come back. Cass will return, too."

"What about Lady Xia? Doesn't she need you here? Doesn't the League need you?"

"I'm Memosinian. I'm the last person Xia wants near the League right now."

"But you were an ambassador."

"This has gone far beyond ambassadors, Sephone. We are at war. They will only need me if there's a peace treaty to sign." *And even then, they will be fine without me.*

"I was a captive of the hooded man. Maybe I can help you find him."

"Nay. I won't give him a reason to recapture you. You must stay here, or nearby, where no one but us knows where you are."

"You would make me a prisoner again."

"Not a prisoner. *Alive,* Sephone. Spartan's gifts are far more useful than mine. You will be safe with him."

"I don't care about safe," she all but snapped. "Don't you know that by now?"

A silence stretched between them, deeper than any sunless gorge. Every time he tried to protect her, he deepened it further.

"So," she finally said, "this is goodbye."

"It is." He turned to leave.

"Dorian?"

"Aye?"

She stood directly behind him, the blanket around her shoulders. She toyed with the pendant at her throat. It would be so easy to erase the distance between them, to reunite everything he'd torn apart.

Except that he couldn't. And it wouldn't be.

"Stay safe," she whispered.

Dorian smiled wryly. "Maybe I don't care about safe, either."

Regis and Spartan were waiting for him outside, at the base of the tree house. Cass, Dorian surmised, would make his own farewells to Sephone when he woke. Dorian tried not to dwell on the how or what of that particular scenario. It was barely an hour before dawn, but the people of Thebe were already stirring. Many of them had set up tents around Thebe's tree houses or simply bedded down in the grass. It was summer now, and warm enough to sleep in the open, but what would happen when winter came? Was it too much to hope that the war would be over by then?

"Your horse is saddled," Regis said when Dorian approached. "But I still think you should take a couple of men with you."

"I could go," said Spartan at once.

"Nay," Dorian replied. Xia had already offered to go, as had Spartan previously, several times. "I will travel faster on my own. An extra set of weapons will make no difference against the hooded man. And besides, once I find the twins and Jewel, I won't be alone."

Regis glanced up at the tree house, the top of the dwelling veiled by mist. "I'm surprised she let you go."

"She very nearly didn't. I had to persuade her to stay." Dorian narrowed his gaze at Regis. "Keep her safe, Symon."

"I will," he vowed.

"Consider this your second chance. To do what you should have done before."

"My second chance or yours, Dorian?"

Dorian met his knowing gaze, uncomfortable with his perceptiveness. "Both, perhaps."

"We have a history of disappointing Sephone in common."

"Aye, and we both lost the regard of a woman before we were aware it existed."

Regis's eyes widened, and Dorian realized that this was news to him. Maybe Regis wasn't so perceptive as he'd first thought.

"If you care for her," Regis ventured, "why would you leave?"

No easy answer to that question existed. "Because I cannot stay." Dorian pivoted and strode away, only to feel a hand grasp his arm. "Symon—"

But it was Spartan. "Dorian—"

Knowing what he was going to say, Dorian interrupted him. "When I return with the Reliquary, after everything is done, I want you to take it to the Mysterium, and tell them to destroy it."

His blue eyes sparked in uncharacteristic anger. "Why must you be so stubborn? There is another way—"

"I will not go anywhere near the Three. And there is naught you can do to persuade me otherwise."

The acolyte shook his head. "I know what you're planning, and it won't work."

"Thank you for your counsel." Dorian bowed and tried to move, but Spartan continued to grip his sleeve.

"You're only one man, Dorian. One man against enemies whose powers you cannot possibly match or even understand."

"Thanks for the vote of confidence." Riled, Dorian considered adding the word *monk*, as Cass would have, but thought better of it. Spartan didn't deserve his anger.

"At least let me come with you."

Dorian pulled on his arm, and this time, Spartan released him. "The best thing you can do for me is look after Sephone."

"To keep her safe until you're ready to die for her, you mean."

Dorian looked at him sharply. "Did Aleria tell you that?"

"She didn't need to. You have the look of a man walking to his execution." Spartan skimmed a hand over his stubbled head. To the best of Dorian's knowledge, he had never once worn gloves. "You cannot save her, Dorian. Not like this. Forsake your pride, and call on the only one who can."

Pride? Dorian glared at him. *Stubborn*, Spartan had called him. And he knew nothing about women.

Well, Dorian knew one thing at least. He had no need of an arrogant, self-righteous monk. He spun away and strode into the mist.

"Dorian! Come back!"

He kept walking.

18

SEPHONE

Every night I spent in the Garden on the Mountain, it became a little more real. Sometimes I stood with the raven at the cliff top, or rode the white horse through the sunlit forest, or simply sat and watched Aedon tend his vines. The Garden was far bigger than the one Spartan had first showed me. Big enough, even, to contain several Calderas. How could I have ever thought the Mountain was empty? Or that the world had ended?

Day would have been a pale contrast to my nighttime dreaming if not for the glass bottle Spartan had given me. Just like the Garden, a world of memories was contained within that tiny reservoir, and unlike normal memories, they were never completely consumed. No matter how deeply I drank of the iridescent liquid, the bottle was always full when I reached for it next.

And the memories themselves were impossible to describe. I had been used to dealing in mere fragments: the first taste of strawberries, a kiss in the rain between lovers, watching sand dunes shift and re-form in the desert. No memory ever lasted longer than half an hour, and when they were consumed, they were completely spent. The memory could be extracted again, albeit with diminishing returns.

But here, at last, was the *whole*. At first, the stories contained in the bottle were strange to my mind, which had grown up in a world covered in gray mist, a world whose most basic instinct was to covet moments. There were songs. Songs of grief, of poignant lament, echoing across thousands of years of pain. Stories of strange people doing strange things I didn't truly understand. The beautiful, ethereal city I'd glimpsed the night I'd been bitten by the Nightmare. And Aedon, his father, and the white horse, throughout the long ages. Always there, always watching over us.

The more I drank of the memories, the more I began to see patterns: a common thread of gold running through each of them like the one I'd first seen in Dorian's mind. But this current was richer and more vibrant. It called to me across the thousands of years which had been captured in the glass bottle, linking me to the millions of souls whose stories had been preserved, as if just for me. Sometimes they were so vivid it almost felt like they were still alive—living, breathing people who might leap out of the vial and assume warm, quivering flesh.

Though each person was unique, I began to see the same faces. Since the world began, there had been thousands of Brinsley Winters and Lord Guerins, hundreds of Cutters and Lord Dravens, maybe even dozens of Dorian Ashwoods and Aleria Vegas and Cassius Veras. There were only ever a few Spartans. And there was only one Three.

But what was most surprising of all were the effects of drinking from the vial. Those who imbibed memories usually found that the more they consumed, the more the world around them seemed to fade until the present had lost much of its zest and color. The more time they spent in the minds of others, absorbing their most precious moments, the more small pieces of themselves were lost. As I drank of Spartan's tiny bottle, the real world didn't seem as impressive or big as it once had, but I never lost myself. If it were possible, I felt more myself than ever. I had begun to return to certain stories, but with every viewing, they became more, also. It was starting to dawn on me that no matter how deeply I drank, I would never reach the bottom of Spartan's vial.

"I don't understand," I said to Spartan when we were alone. I held up the bottle. Even now, in the lanternlight, it hinted of more colors than was possible to name. "What kind of *mem* could perform such a series of extractions? These are no ordinary memories."

"Aye, they aren't. And therein lies the miracle." Spartan sat beside me on one of the low couches. The underground safe house where Regis had brought us had a room which was intended to approximate the outdoors, with dark-leafed plants and a glass porthole that let in the barest of light. It reminded me of the atriums in Idaea. I had thought, wistfully, that the sound of water would not go amiss. To be so long underground took its toll, even if Regis's resistance contacts meant that we received constant updates about the war.

"Where did you get it?" I asked him.

"It was given to me by the Mysterium, who received it from the Three."

"And you have drunk of it for yourself?"

Spartan nodded.

"Then you've seen the stories. Seen the people from the world-that-was."

So much of it, I didn't yet understand. The Three were in everything, enough for me to realize that what I'd believed about them was barely a fraction of the whole. In every stage of history, the world-that-was had come to know of them—or as much of them as they chose to reveal. When the world ended, our ancestors had journeyed to Caldera, forsaking gods and kings, vowing that they would never repeat the same mistakes which had led to their downfall, little realizing that they brought the ingredients of another catastrophe with them. As war tore the fledgling world of Caldera apart, the ancestors had descended into violence and bloodshed.

Aleria had been right. We were just like them.

For a brief time, the Three had been forgotten. But the efforts of a small, devout Order known as the Mysterium had preserved their memory, and a year ago, Aedon had appeared, inviting the Order's members to visit the Garden on the Mountain for the first time in history. More and more Calderans had rallied to them, drawn by the kindness and renowned gifts of its members. The more I discovered about the Three, the more I understood why the Mysterium had built a home around them—why Spartan now called Aedon his captain and his king. The powerful *alter* was known as an *Infinitum,* but in Spartan's vial, I came to know him as an uncommonly good man.

"Aye," said Spartan in answer to my question. "I have seen them." Bright blue eyes searched mine. "Have you seen it yet? The truth about Memoria?"

I sank back against the cushions. "Aedon showed me." I stroked my pendant; the habit increasingly brought me no comfort. The webbing on my chest grew larger every day, while the black streaks in my hair were thickening.

"Then you know that a great battle is coming."

"We're already at war."

He shook his head. "I'm not referring to the one my father now wages."

"Is that why you follow him? Aedon, I mean."

"Because war is coming?"

"Because he wants to be king."

Something in Spartan's gaze flickered. He might be three or four years younger than I was, but in that moment, he seemed far older. "He didn't come here to be king," he said. "Though he would make a better king than anyone."

"He's not a warrior. What does he hope to do against your father?"

"My father is not the enemy, Sephone. Neither is my brother. As I said, Aedon has not come to be king. He has no interest in Caldera's throne. Nay, he has come for us."

"For us?"

"To free us."

I remembered, then, that Spartan had been born a slave, just as I was. "For him to achieve that, we would have to belong to him."

"Aye," he replied, with the slightest of smiles. "We would."

I thought of everything I'd seen in Lord Draven's mind. In Asa's. Neither of them would rest until every threat to the kingship had been eliminated. Did that mean that, eventually, they would wage war on Aedon and the Mysterium?

"For you to be free," I pondered, "your father and brother would have to be defeated."

His shoulders stiffened.

"They will not let either of us go without a fight, Spartan."

"I know."

I reached out and brushed his arm, surprising myself with my willingness to touch him. "At least you have Aedon on your side. He is a powerful *alter*."

He gave a reluctant smile. "Surely you see by now that Aedon is much more than just an *alter.*"

I fingered the bottle in my hand, unsure of what to say. "And what is he to you? What are *they* to you?"

"He is my true father," he replied, more at ease now. "My brother. My general in a time of war, my king in a time of peace. But more than that, he has become my friend."

I voiced the question that had been on my mind for many weeks now. "You believe the old gods have come back, don't you?"

Spartan's smile became broader. "There is only one God, Sephone. And he never left."

"You're worried about Dorian."

I looked up as Spartan lowered himself to the ground beside me. Magritte was somewhere, and Regis was not at home. I hadn't seen either of them in days. Asa was yet to attack Nephele, but it was only a matter of time. The city could not withstand a siege forever.

"He's been gone for a fortnight now," I said. "And we've had no word. Of any of them." Anxiety about Dorian and Cass's whereabouts had temporarily driven thoughts of Aedon and the Mysterium from my mind.

"They will return," Spartan reassured me. "Aedon has told me as much."

"Can he see the future, then?"

Spartan didn't need to answer. I already knew that he could. Did Aedon come to him in his dreams, too?

"I wish I had gone with him," I said miserably.

"With Dorian? Or Cass?"

"Either. Both." Except that Dorian hadn't wanted me with him, and even Cass was reluctant to risk my safety. I glanced sideways at Spartan. "You must think me a fool."

"Not a fool. Just a little crossed in love."

"What does an acolyte know about love?" I bit my lip at my harsh tone. I was doing to Spartan exactly what Dorian had done to me. "Forgive me. My temper's a little frayed at present."

His blue eyes only twinkled. "You're hardly the first to remind me of my age." He leaned back against the wall, and I felt the brush of his *pax* gift. If Dorian's gift felt like a sip of liquor and Cass's gift resembled temporary weightlessness, Spartan's was like a cool drink of water in the middle of a hot day, slaking a heavy thirst. To be in his presence was to be at ease, and the more time I spent with him, the more my anxiety faded.

"Your gift," I observed. "It's different. It's not so temporary as some." And though Dorian and Cass had never once felt the effects of their own gifts, it often seemed as if Spartan was as much at peace as his hearers.

"It wasn't always so. It used to draw on my energy, draining me, and I could never sustain it for long. But when I came to the Mysterium, it changed, sharpened. The longer I lived with them, and with the Three, the stronger it became."

"And your shields?"

"That was a gift I only discovered after I escaped my father." He shook his head ruefully. "He would have used it to his benefit, if he had known." His eyes on me were uncomfortably direct. "I cannot advise you on your heart, Sephone. But I think I can advise you on Dorian's. He does love you"—he seemed to look past me—"more than his own life."

"I cannot believe that," I protested. "He only ever pushes me away."

"It's not that simple." His face shuttered a moment, and then he said, "Trust Aedon, Sephone. He has a plan."

That night, the white stallion came to me in my dreams. Aedon stood beside him looking oddly haggard, his fingers entwined in the horse's mane. The Garden behind him was dark and still.

"Aedon," I said, concern brimming in my voice. "Are you all right?" He looked so different—so human—that I forgot, for a moment, that he was an *alter*. An *Infinitum*.

"A great battle is about to begin, Sephone. You must be ready."

"I am ready."

He extended his hand. "Come walk with me."

We had been walking for some time when I realized that despite everything that had kept me away from him in the beginning, the ancient *Infinitum* had become a friend.

"Sephone, wake up," said a voice in my ear, and I sat up to find Spartan hovering over me with a lantern, fully dressed. Had he even gone to bed? I knew he sometimes went for late night walks in the forest; if Regis had known about them, he would have forbidden it, but since Spartan was more powerful than the rest of us put together, I hadn't betrayed the confidence. He could look after himself.

"What is it?" I asked, alarmed.

"I was coming back from my walk when I found a guard outside. He'd been knocked unconscious. Someone knows we're here. We have to leave."

Adrenaline surged through my body, eradicating the last traces of sleep as I reached for the gloves I had removed when I went to bed. I usually slept with them on, but since I never had them in my dreams, I had taken them off.

"There's no time," Spartan urged. "We must go *now*."

"The boy's right, you know," said a deep voice. A gloved fist streaked through the air, and at its impact, Spartan's eyes rolled back in his head. As his body went limp, I stumbled forward to catch him, easing him to the ground before turning to face his attacker. My gift was already licking through my veins, hungry for release.

"Touch me and you'll regret it," I warned, surreptitiously easing my knife from the sheath I'd left strapped over my leggings.

He lunged for me. Why had Spartan not tried to get away? I moved and felt my knife encounter flesh, and the man grunted in pain and grabbed my upper arm. Seeing that his hands were ungloved, I dropped the bloodied knife and seized his wrist. I reached for my gift and attacked his mind.

Nothing. I blinked and tried again, but it was as if I'd never even summoned my power. Did he have some kind of mental wall? Some barrier to protect himself? I grasped his wrist with both hands. But it was for naught. I could discern no sign of my gift, no telling power in my fingertips.

A low, chilling laugh. "Foolish girl," said the man. "Did you think I would knowingly make myself defenseless against you?"

"What have you done to me?"

"You might think of my gift as *your* lack, Miss Winter. In my presence, you are nothing more than an ordinary woman." His cold fingers closed around my wrist.

I jerked back, trying to pull him into the lanternlight, and I saw the white hood and mask . . . a sight I would never forget if I lived to be a hundred.

"*You.*" I tried to wrench myself from his grip, but it was my right wrist he was holding, and if I wasn't careful, he would break it again.

"Cease your struggling," he demanded, twisting sharply until I obeyed. He dragged me from the room into the main living area, where a circle of similarly anonymous men awaited him. One of his guards had bound Spartan's hands and feet and slung the acolyte's limp body over his shoulder.

"Bring Mistress Magritte," the hooded man ordered. Two guards left the room and returned a minute later, dragging Magritte between them. Her eyes filled with panic when she saw me, and she tried to struggle, to no avail. Where was Regis? I tried to ask the question with my eyes.

He's away from here, she said into my mind. *I don't understand. How did they find us?*

Facing Magritte, the hooded man withdrew a knife and angled it against my throat. "I want you to send a message to Lord Adamo."

"Nay, Magritte, don't—"

The blade pressed more firmly. "Silence. Now, mistress, if you will oblige me. Tell Lord Adamo to return to the safe house as a matter of the utmost urgency. Nothing more, nothing less. If you tell him anything else, or put him on his guard in any way, I will kill Sephone Winter and your husband. Who, you might be interested to know, is also in our possession elsewhere."

Magritte's eyes widened further, and I guessed she had already contacted Regis. Ignoring the slight shake of my head, she scrunched her eyes closed. After a few seconds, she opened them again. "It is done." She swallowed. "I don't exactly know, but I think . . . I think Lord Adamo is close."

"Very good." The blade left my throat. "Now, my friends, there is naught to fear. All we have to do now"—it seemed he smiled—"is wait."

19

DORIAN

One thing was becoming obvious: he was dangerously close to failing to fulfill his half of the bargain he'd made with Cass. In a fortnight of searching, he had not even come close to finding the hooded man. As always, whispers abounded: a report of a party of masked men who'd come through a village near Orphne asking questions about Asa Karthick's *alters*; another missing girl, stolen from her bed in the middle of the night.

But no clear trail remained, no indication of where they had gone. Dorian didn't even know if they were still in Lethe. And since he was accused of high treason, he couldn't cross the border as easily as he had once done.

Nor had he seen Bear, Bas, or Jewel. They must have met with trouble after leaving the mountains, perhaps even been captured by Asa Karthick. But if that were true, wouldn't Asa have sent a ransom by now? Or sought to use them against Dorian in some way? If there were few traces of the hooded man, there were even fewer of Dorian's friends. The only thing he had learned was that a giant had been sighted northeast of Nyx. But the Lethean man who'd seen him had only done so at a distance and had understandably not ventured any closer.

The pointless pursuit of another clue had led Dorian close to Thebe again, but he was reluctant to return with nothing. Even now, Cass might have found a *healer* who could save Sephone.

He just had to push on, to keep looking. His perseverance would eventually be rewarded.

It was now around midnight, though, and he needed to sleep. Beneath a large oak tree, he dismounted from his exhausted horse, allowing it to graze while he retrieved a few strips of dried meat from his pack and leaned back against the tree trunk to eat them. His fingers felt like blocks of ice in his gloves. It might be summer, but a chill wind had arisen, too much like the restless sprites that tormented the canal-bound city of Nulla.

He closed his eyes and allowed himself, foolishly, to think of the fateful night he had entered that city. He hadn't noticed Sephone as anything more than a servant who could introduce him to Cutter's famous *mem*. It was only after he'd detained her in her master's shop that he'd realized she was the one he sought. She had surprised him with the depth of her feeling—the sense he had, after only a few minutes in her company, that she understood his troubles. That she shared in them, somehow, even though he was a stranger.

That sense had only grown as they travelled to Iona, and then Calliope. Against Dorian's wishes, she had become a friend to him. Apart from his wife and daughter, the only other soul he had been as close with was his younger sister, Kaesi. But the bond he shared with Sephone was anything but sisterly, though it had taken him months to see it.

If it had been possible, he would have taken her to Maera, where the rest of his family could keep her safe. His parents would adore her; his younger brothers would be in awe of her. Even Kaesi would like her.

But Maera, too, was now at war. His family still believed he was the traitor to Memosine that Draven had painted him to be. And the current thane of Maera, Dorian's replacement, would now be preparing the city to defend itself against the outlanders.

If Draven had released Dorian's family from house arrest, Dorian's father might be helping to protect Maera, never knowing that his eldest son had allied himself with one of the feared invaders. What would he think of Dorian now, stripped of his title, wealth, reputation . . . everything that had once made him a respected man and a formidable opponent? He was no longer Lord Adamo, thane of Maera. Most days, he didn't even feel like Dorian Ashwood.

"You need to sleep, Ashwood," he told himself. He had recovered from the fever, but he was still exhausted. He could do naught until daylight, anyway. So why did he feel so on edge?

He had barely closed his eyes when he heard a voice inside his head. *Return with all haste, Lord Adamo. You are needed here.*

Dorian jolted upright. Magritte. He could feel her concern, her urgency . . . her fear. Had something happened to them? Was Sephone all right?

As if she'd heard his question, she spoke again. *Sephone is well. But you must come.*

He jumped up, galvanized into action. Perhaps Siaki Xia wanted to see him. She would be almost ready to march on Asa Karthick's forces by now. In seconds, he was mounting his horse . . . his poor, exhausted horse, who felt the miles far more keenly than him.

"Sorry, my friend," he murmured. "But we must go."

He was less than a day's hard traveling from the resistance house where Regis and Magritte had taken Sephone. If he rode through the night, he could be there by midday.

Please be all right, he repeated over and over. He had left her thinking she would be safe. But if anything happened to her or Spartan or even to Regis and Magritte, he would never forgive himself.

Dismounting, Dorian immediately reached for his quarterstaff, snapping it to full length. After a moment's consideration, he exposed the twin blades as well. It would be wise to be prepared. Especially if his friends had been compromised and this was a trap.

The forest surrounding the small mound of earth was unnaturally quiet. Beneath the mound was buried the house which had been taken over by Regis Symon's resistance—a perfect place, he'd assured Dorian, to hide Sephone and Spartan from Lady Xia while remaining close to Thebe.

There would be guards, but they would be carefully hidden. They had probably seen him by now. He moved on silent feet to the hatch set into the side of the miniature hill. It was covered with undergrowth, but once he found the latch, it opened easily on well-oiled hinges, exactly as Regis had described.

The urge to call out as he entered the earthen house was strong, but he remained quiet. Not for the first time, he wished he had his faithful bodyguards and Jewel at his side.

The mound housed a tiny space with a large hole cut in the center of the floor. A sturdy ladder led to the rooms below, which were completely underground. To go down the ladder meant temporarily letting down one's guard, but there was nothing for it. Clutching his staff, he quickly descended the rungs.

He turned around in almost complete darkness, his throat constricting. Something had happened . . . somebody was there. He found the wall and hugged it, easing along the shadowed corridor. If only Magritte would speak again, but she had said naught since last night.

A door was open, and he followed the corridor until he reached it. The faintest trickle of light from a porthole far above illuminated a woman sitting in the middle of the floor, her ankles roped together and her wrists bound behind her. A gag covered her mouth.

She was alone.

"Sephone!" he exclaimed and rushed to her, dropping his staff as he knelt beside her. Her eyes went wide as she saw him, and she began shaking her head vigorously. He focused on removing her gag.

"Nay, Dorian!" she said as soon as she could speak. "Get out of here! This is a trap!"

The blow to the back of his head sent him toppling forward, plowing into Sephone. His vision winked out, and he rolled, encountering cold stone instead of soft flesh.

He groaned and tried to reach, blindly, for his staff. He had been on his guard, but when he'd seen Sephone, all thought of caution had fled. He was a fool.

A booted foot settled on his chest. "Don't worry, Lord Adamo. I have your staff here in my hand." A soft murmur of approval. "My, my, these blades are wickedly sharp."

"If you hurt her, I will—"

"Oh, I don't think you're in a position to deliver threats, my lord." The deep voice ricocheted painfully in Dorian's skull. "Besides, I'm not here for Sephone, Dorian Ashwood."

Someone bent and pressed two fingers against his exposed neck. At once, he felt his awareness fading. He lost consciousness to a grating, sinister chuckle.

"I'm here for *you*."

When Dorian woke again, he feared that the world was shaking violently. An earthquake? Nay. He was lying on his back in a dark box. A carriage, by the looks of it, shuddering and jerking as it bounced along a rutted road.

His head lay in . . . a woman's lap? He caught a glimpse of white locks, the only source of light in this gloomy place. Gloved fingers were in his hair, stroking it back from his forehead. *Sephone.* She was leaning against the corner of the carriage, crammed on the very edge of the seat. And no wonder, for the length of his body occupied the majority of it. Her eyes remained closed, as if she slept, but her hands still moved.

He lay there, savoring her touch, then the carriage went over a particularly large bump, and he couldn't help but groan as it resurrected the throbbing ache at the back of his head.

The fingers in his hair stilled.

"You're awake."

Dorian sat up and nearly tumbled onto the floor. His hands were bound in front of him. Sephone steadied him the best she could, her own hands tied together at the wrists. On the other seat lay another woman—Magritte. She was sleeping, or maybe unconscious.

Sephone followed his gaze. "The hooded man has an *alter* who can put people to sleep or wake them up again."

"The hooded man?"

"Our captor."

All this time searching for him, and he had found Dorian first. "Are you hurt?"

"I'm fine."

He exhaled. "How long have I been out?"

"Only a few hours." She turned to look out the window, but dark fabric covered it. A few cracks here and there let in light, but barely enough to see by. "I think it's near twilight."

"Do you have any idea where they're taking us?"

"Nay, but I think I may have injured him."

"The hooded man?"

"Aye. I'm not sure where. I cut him with my knife."

Conflicting emotions churned in Dorian. Pride at her bravery, fear for the potential consequences of it. "Where's Spartan? And Regis?"

"The hooded man said he had captured Regis elsewhere. I don't know where they took Spartan. I woke up here ten or fifteen minutes ago, and it was just you and me and Magritte."

Who had betrayed them? It could have been Cass or Regis or even Aleria. Not likely to be Regis, given Magritte was also a prisoner. Because of Regis's secrecy, Lady Xia didn't know about the underground safe house. But what if one of the guards, loyal to Lethe and the thaness of Thebe, had revealed its location?

But that would imply that Siaki Xia was working with the hooded man. Even if Dorian believed her capable of this kind of treachery, she couldn't have found the man so quickly.

Dorian should know. He had been looking for him for a fortnight.

He turned in time to see Sephone shiver. She wasn't wearing a cloak, and it was freezing. He scooted closer to her on the seat. "Don't be afraid," he said, summoning his gift. "I won't let him hurt you."

She paid no heed. "Didn't you hear what he said? He didn't come for me. He came for you."

None of it made any sense. Sephone was the *mem*—the one the hooded man had captured in Nyx and forced to do his bidding. From what Aleria, and later Sephone, had told him about her captivity, her kidnapper's main object had been intelligence-gathering, and Sephone's gift allowed him to do so undetected.

What could he want with Dorian?

"Did you find any trace of the twins and Jewel?" Sephone asked.

"*Only* traces. It's as if they've vanished from Caldera. But we'll find them."

She didn't say anything to that—maybe she doubted they could. As the carriage rumbled on and darkness fell completely, they both relaxed by degrees.

"I wonder if this is the same carriage as before," Sephone remarked sleepily.

A bump jolted him awake.

Sephone stirred, and across the carriage, Magritte groaned, rubbing her head.

"Are you well, Magritte?" Dorian asked.

"Aye." She moaned again. "Or I will be, soon."

"Your gift—"

"I think they already thought of that, my lord. They gave me something back at the safe house to suppress it. I'm yet to feel its return."

The carriage had stopped. He spoke hurriedly. "The moment you do, would you send a message to Cass?"

"To tell him to stay away?"

"Nay, tell him to come. As soon as we know where we are. And tell him to bring help."

The message was long enough already. The *lumen* could figure out the rest on his own.

The door was flung open; outside, it was almost completely dark. A black-clothed man reached in and grabbed Magritte, who yelped as she was dragged from the carriage. Another figure seized Sephone.

Dorian was pulled from the carriage after her. He thought about fighting back, but the tiny courtyard was swarming with dark figures, and his eyes hadn't fully recovered from the blow to his head. What had they done with his staff? Somebody held a lantern. Dorian caught the briefest glimpse of a closely shorn head—Spartan.

The youth looked dazed, supported by the men on either side of him. Had he been struck on the head, or had they suppressed his powers as well? Dorian turned to look for Sephone again. A foul gust slammed into him, and his blood turned to ice. There was only one place where the breezes smelt so foul and froze a body almost to its very soul.

Nulla.

A blindfold was secured over my eyes, and someone gripped me tightly by the shoulders, fingers biting into them like steel.

"Bring them," barked a deep voice.

I was shoved forward, nearly stumbling over rough cobbles. The wind picked up, carrying the stench of mold and refuse. My mind froze.

I knew this breeze. Surely not . . .

We walked for only a few minutes before a door creaked open and I was pushed over a threshold. My captor steered me several directions before forcing me down into a chair. My bonds were cut. I felt a moment of exhilaration before my arms were wrenched behind my back and tied together again.

"Take the other woman upstairs," the same voice commanded. "But leave the boy." Boots filed obediently across the floor and pounded up a creaking staircase.

Spartan? Magritte? I strained against my bonds as the blindfold was snatched away, revealing a shadowy room I would remember to my dying days.

Nay . . .

"Cutter's tavern," murmured Dorian beside me. I turned my head to find him similarly restrained, as was Spartan on his other side. The acolyte's head tilted forward, blood trickling from a gash near his temple. His eyes were closed.

My stomach twisted. I looked around. Thebe was not far from Nulla—and given its reputation for villainy, it came as no surprise that we would be brought here. But Cutter's tavern? Why this place? Why now?

It had seen better days. It looked to be abandoned, with boards over the windows and ash spilling out of the fireplace. Most of the furniture, save the few chairs that restrained us in the middle of the room, had been piled in untidy heaps near the walls. A rat scampered across the bar where I had first exchanged banter with Cass; the sole lantern in the corner of the room illuminated a trail of droppings. The door to the shop—which had once boasted shelves bearing hundreds of multicolored memories—was closed, but the wood was deeply scored, as if someone had laid siege to Cutter's supply room.

Had no heir claimed Cutter's property? How he would twitch if he could see his beloved establishment now. A tidal wave of memories spilled over me . . . Regis, standing hesitantly beside the fireplace, waiting for instructions from Cutter. Me, flinging open the door on a gust of wind and slamming it closed, then leaning heavily against the wood. Rattled by an unassuming old man who claimed to know the real taste of strawberries. Cutter, sweeping across the room to interrupt my conversation with a truth-revealing *lumen* . . .

"Do you remember this place, Miss Winter? Lord Adamo?" A man strode into the pool of light, his boots crunching over broken glass, and stood there before us. It was the hooded man, clothed in the black I remembered from Nyx. If he'd been injured by my knife, he didn't give any indication of it. Slowly, he divested himself of his garments . . . the fabric covering the lower half of his face, the hood concealing his hair, the heavy cloak. He handed them to the two guards who stood at attention next to the door, the only ones still remaining in the room.

Finally, he pivoted. I studied the long face, the dark-blond hair and slightly lighter eyebrows. The penetrating gaze that had bored into me for so many months, forcing me to erase pasts. Forcing me to kill.

I hadn't thought this vile man from the mountains would be so young. I didn't recognize him, but Dorian must have, for he swore under his breath.

"Remon," he muttered to me.

"Who?"

"I know him. Remon from Maera." His voice tightened. "Once upon a time, he admired my sister, Kaesi."

"I am not Remon, Lord Adamo," said the man, who could obviously hear us. "But you're right on one count, at least. You do know me."

I bit back a gasp as all at once, the figure before us began to change and re-form into another shape, just as Aleria's had. It shrank in stature, then became narrower and leaner. Gentle curves appeared, and I realized I was looking at a woman.

A woman?

The woman standing in the hooded man's place was tall and willowy, with long blond hair curling to her waist and dark-brown eyes. She was as beautiful as Lida Ashwood had been—maybe even more so.

Her mouth curved wryly as she looked at Dorian. "I'm sorry about your head, brother."

Brother?

"Kaesi," he said, his eyes going wide. Kaesi, his favorite sister, his *talented* sister, who had been locked away in the dungeons of Maera for her attempt to overthrow Dorian's father and the other thanes.

The hooded man was not a man, but a woman. And that woman was Dorian's own sister. I could hardly breathe.

"How did you escape?" Dorian asked in disbelief.

Kaesi smiled thinly. "Is that it, brother? No expressions of regret? No sorry for all these years of distancing yourself from me? Not a single visit in eight years, as I recall."

"I had my family to think of."

"Your family or your career?" Her eyes flashed.

"You threw away everything we believed in, Kaesi."

"Nay, I threw away everything you believed in, Dorian. You and Father. And in return, you cut me off completely. You cut me out of your lives like a cancer and tossed me away as if I'd never even existed."

Dorian took a breath—I knew how deeply he regretted his actions where Kaesi was concerned. "You cut us out of your world first."

"Did I? My ideas would never have harmed you, brother."

His face was stony. "How did you escape?" he asked again.

"I didn't. At least, my decoy hasn't." She beamed.

"Your decoy?"

"Aye." Kaesi's head lifted proudly. "Our mother continues to visit her most diligently. Brings her food, cares for her occasional illnesses,

clothes her nearly unrecognizable body. Meanwhile, I've been free
for years."

Years?

Dorian's voice held a sharp edge. "You would leave an innocent to
suffer your sentence in your place?"

"Didn't you?" Kaesi retorted, and he stiffened. "I seem to recall
a certain bodyguard who suffered your sentence for quite some time
before you rescued him."

"That's irrelevant. But you didn't answer my question. How did
you escape?"

Kaesi smiled haughtily. "For that, you can thank our mother. The
supplies she smuggled me—unwittingly; you needn't look so horrified,
brother—were more than enough to facilitate my freedom. After that,
with my newly discovered gift of shapeshifting, it was impossibly easy to
make the switch. If you'd visited, you would have known straightaway
that my replacement wasn't me. But you didn't. So, I suppose I should
thank you for your negligence. It is, after all, what has allowed me to
roam free all these years."

Dorian was silent. Had he known of Kaesi's gift? Or had it, like
Magritte's gift, appeared only in her adulthood?

"Nevertheless," she continued, "I am not one to hold grudges, at
least not against my most favorite brother. I didn't bring you here so I
could exact my vengeance."

"Then why did you bring me here?" His mouth firmed. "If you hurt
Sephone—"

She gave an airy laugh. "I won't hurt her, brother. At least, you
needn't fear that I will hurry things along. She is already dying,
is she not?"

Dorian's face blanched, and I went still.

"How do you know that?" Dorian asked softly. Dangerously.

"She was my prisoner for nearly four months, remember? It's rather
hard to miss those marks on her chest." She paused to glance at me.
"You see, I came up with the plan after learning of her powers. You
recall how isolated Maera can be, Dorian . . . how detached from the
grand workings of the world. Well, I knew I needed information, and
at the time, my followers were few. When I heard of a *mem* who could

read minds and manipulate memories and an artifact that could make those changes permanent, I knew exactly what I needed to achieve my ends. I just had to follow you until the time was ripe to steal her away."

"Information?" Dorian repeated. "To what end?"

"Our plans. The ones we made as children—don't you remember them?" She gazed off in the distance. "We were so young, so bold. We had questions, challenges, ideas. We thought we could rule the world one day. I promised myself, even back then, that I would bring such a grand thing about for *you.*"

Dorian frowned. "What are you talking about, Kaesi?"

She looked at him, her eyes filled with a strange, feverish energy too much like madness. "Father was right, you know. You were born to rule. With your gifts, you could have been anything you wanted. Even the arch-lord."

"That future is past now."

"Aye, it is past. Because you won't be the arch-lord, Dorian, nay. You will be king."

"*King?*"

"Aye, king." The bold façade shifted, revealing a hint of vulnerability. She spread out her arms. "You see . . . I did it all for you, brother."

Dorian regarded his sister uncertainly. "What did you do?"

She looked at him pointedly. "You have acquired many enemies over the years. Various lords and thanes, Cutter, Silvertongue, Lord Draven and his son."

"How do you know about Silvertongue?" I blurted, but she ignored me.

"I knew that you couldn't do it all on your own. You needed help. And so, when my gifts first appeared—a lone light in a very dark dungeon—I realized that what you needed was me."

Gifts? Kaesi had more than one?

"So, as soon as I escaped, I set about forming my plans. When you were nearly killed by Draven, I knew he was more dangerous to you than the rest of them put together. So, I put in motion the pieces to bring about his downfall."

"Kaesi—" he began.

"It was difficult, aye, but as it turned out, Draven had many enemies.

Many who were willing to serve someone else simply because they despised their present master." Her gaze ran critically over me. "Miss Winter's help was instrumental for the rest. One by one, I have been removing your enemies, Dorian. Members of the Council of Eight—Lord Enver, Lady Alba. Former and current allies of Draven. Every person who has ever opposed you, or ever will oppose you. I did it all for you."

Dorian sucked in a breath. "I never asked—"

She released a high, almost girlish laugh. "Of course you didn't *ask* me to, Dorian. No doubt you wouldn't have approved of my methods anyway. But I did it because it needed to be done. Because you would never become king without my help."

As I listened, I fiddled with the ropes binding my wrists behind the chair. Were they a little loose this time? The guard who'd tied me must have been in a hurry. He hadn't even bound my ankles, and I wasn't secured to my chair as Dorian and Spartan were. While Kaesi focused almost exclusively on Dorian, I worked on loosening the ropes further.

"I did it all in your name," she was stating. "When you are king of Caldera, you will thank me for it."

"I thought you hated governments. Kings, worst of all."

"Aye—other kings. But this isn't just any king. This is you. This is *us*."

Dorian shook his head. "This is madness, Kaesi. Madness." His eyes were grave; his forehead was deeply lined. "If you think this is what I want, you do not know me at all."

"Oh, I know you, brother. I know you better than anyone."

Kaesi sent me a patronizing look, and I froze.

She quickly turned back to Dorian. "All our lives, you have spoken of our greater purpose. *Your* greater purpose. I know what you want most, and it's right in front of you, ripe for the taking."

"There is only one thing I want," Dorian said, and he looked directly at me. My heart stuttered, and my breath caught.

"I wasn't speaking of romance," Kaesi scoffed and turned to her guards. "Bring him to us." Both men nodded and left the room.

Pulse racing, I focused on the ropes again, working furiously despite the ache in my previously broken wrist. This was my chance. Unlike

Magritte, I hadn't been drugged. My gift was still awake. I simply had to get to Kaesi before she noticed me.

Dorian had evidently registered my efforts, for as Kaesi's back turned, he gave a sharp incline of his head, then nodded at his sister.

I understood his meaning: *I'll distract her.*

"I don't understand," he addressed Kaesi. "You say you've been free for years. Where have you been all this time?"

There was a hint of a smile. "Oh, here and there."

"With your revolutionary friends? The ones whose company put you into prison in the first place?"

"Ha!" She scoffed. "Nay. I did cross paths with some of them again, only to find that I'd rather outgrown their antics. Once I discovered my gifts, it took time to refine them. I desperately needed practice. Fortunately, I found others who were similarly gifted and like-minded and had likewise been misunderstood by the world. Through them, I found ways to use my gift that some might consider, let's just say a deviation from the norm."

"Dark magic," ground out Dorian. "Like Asa Karthick's *alters.*"

I kept working, trying not to think about the *alter* who'd burned my arm in Orphne, or the lion-wolf, Zaire, who'd nearly killed Dorian in the Grennor Mountains.

"Once we were numerous enough, we found an instructor to teach us the deeper wisdom. But though he was wise in the Dark ways, he was a cruel master."

"Silvertongue," intoned Dorian, and I bit down on an exclamation. *Of course.*

Kaesi grinned. "Aye, Silvertongue. You know him already. He tried to steal Sephone away from you in Idaea and again in Thebe."

Dorian scowled at his sister. "Silvertongue is working for Lord Draven. If you are Silvertongue's friend, then you cannot be the king's enemy."

A shadow passed over Kaesi's face. "And this brings us to the conclusion of the matter." She looked around, as if wondering where her guards had gotten to.

I tugged hard on my ropes, and one of my hands slid free, then the other. Carefully, I eased the glove from my good arm.

Kaesi focused back on Dorian. "I have missed eight of your birthdays, brother. Did you know that? Well, here at last I will make it up to you. Consider this a belated birthday gift—two long-awaited dreams rolled into one."

In one swift movement, I rose to my feet and lunged at her. Fortunately, her back was turned, and I had the element of surprise. As I knocked her to the ground, I was surprised by how sluggishly she reacted. She didn't turn midair, instead hitting the floor on her stomach. Straddling her back, I reached out for her exposed neck and . . .

Naught.

My gift? But nay, it was there, potent and powerful in my fingertips, sparking to life. Black tendrils wreathed my hand like the last threads of shadow before dawn. But they refused to sink beneath her skin.

I don't understand. You should be unconscious by now.

Beneath me, Kaesi began to laugh. A low, chilling laugh that sounded like Cutter's.

"Foolish girl," she said. "Is that the best you can do?"

21

DORIAN

Tied firmly to a chair, Dorian could do naught to help Sephone as she crouched over Kaesi's crumpled form and summoned her gift. But something was wrong. His sister was still fully conscious—cackling, even. Suddenly, she twisted beneath Sephone. Her hand darted upward, striking Sephone in the face, knocking her backward. Kaesi leapt to her feet and stood over her.

"Stupid girl. I thought you learned your lesson the last time. You cannot touch me."

Gift or no gift, Sephone threw herself at Kaesi, but Kaesi stepped neatly to the side, grabbed Sephone's healing arm, and twisted sharply. Sephone gasped and fell to her knees. Kaesi plucked a dagger from a small sheath at her belt and angled it against Sephone's throat, simultaneously wrenching her head back by her hair.

"Nay!"

Kaesi shook her head at his exclamation. "Oh, brother, you certainly have a penchant for weak women. Don't you see she is unworthy of you?"

"Hurt her, and I will never speak to you again."

"Is that a threat?"

"You know it is." He held her gaze until Kaesi finally retracted the knife and shoved Sephone away. Sephone crouched on the floor, clutching her arm.

"If you hurt my friends, you are no sister of mine," he spat.

"I have no intention of hurting her," Kaesi retorted. "It was she who lunged at me. And besides, only one person is going to die today."

At those words, she turned toward the door of Cutter's shop—the same one Dorian had once hidden behind in an attempt to question Sephone—where four black-clothed guards were emerging, dragging a man between them. His head was covered with a black hood, but he was fighting wildly, muffled cries emanating from beneath the fabric. The guards brought him to Kaesi, who murmured something, and he stilled.

The man was forced to his knees before her.

"Your birthday present, brother." She snatched the hood from his head.

The old fear rose in Dorian's throat like a ghost, up from the grave. Behind his back, his hands curled into fists. It was as if every vein in his body was suddenly filled with shards of dagger-sharp ice, aiming directly for his heart. He forced himself to look into the gagged face only ten or fifteen years his senior: the pleasant features; the tousled, reddish hair; the brilliant blue eyes that, to the unassuming eye, would seem synonymous with everything kind and good.

The face of a devil.

"Draven."

Across the room, Sephone uttered a cry and shrank into a ball. Beside Dorian, Spartan stirred with a low moan, though he did not seem fully conscious yet. Kaesi was the only one who remained nonplussed.

"Aren't you pleased with me, Dorian?" Kaesi was looking at him like a cat who had brought a rabbit to the feet of its master. "Your archenemy, the would-be *king* of Caldera, on his knees."

"What have you done, Kaesi?" Dorian managed.

"Why, I have brought him to you." Grabbing the man's hair, she pulled back his head, exposing his blistered, bruised neck. The gag muffled the elder Karthick's words—presumably a threat or muttered oath—but did naught to mask their venom.

Kaesi paced behind Draven, twisting his head from side to side like a ridiculous puppet, the point of the dagger in her free hand tracing invisible circles in the air, the occasional jab and thrust of it punctuating her words.

"He was *very* hard to find, you know. But Miss Winter's intelligence once again proved invaluable. My men finally tracked him down in Ceto about a week ago now. He didn't come willingly, but then again, freshly minted kings can be rather stubborn at times."

Was that why the hooded man's minions had been sighted near Orphne?

"Kaesi . . ."

Above the gag, Draven's eyes bored into Dorian's, sparking with familiar hatred. His features were even more like Asa's than Dorian remembered. With discomfort, Dorian could even see the resemblance to Spartan. Judging by the way the elder Karthick's eyes had darted to the slumped figure beside Dorian, he had realized his youngest son was present. And the hatred there as he gazed upon Spartan did not diminish in the slightest.

"You know," Dorian's sister continued, as if this were merely a play and she would not pause until they had all played their parts, "Rufus Karthick and I met long before you did, Dorian."

Wrenching his head so that she and Draven appeared to nod in unison, her lips quirked. "I can see you're surprised by that. Aye, back in the day, we were friends, even. You will be even more surprised to learn that he is an *alter*—not a very good one, mind you, just some minor gift in rearranging the content of dreams. Silvertongue was never easy on him—always pushing him, forcing him to refine his abilities. But despite his dark aspirations, our dear, sweet Rufus was not touched by the gifts in the same way the others like myself were. He hated that he could not manage even the slightest expenditure of his gift without suffering greatly afterward. He hated that he was essentially ordinary, when he wanted to be extraordinary."

Dorian exchanged a glance with Sephone. Was that why she had concluded Draven was ungifted? Because his power was too weak for even her to discern?

"Of course, that was the reason why we became friends, at first. He liked that I rendered other *alters* ordinary. Well, with the exception of one. And in me, he began to see his way forward, his future. Only, I didn't see it like that. I was far stronger than he would ever be."

Dorian recalled how Draven had abducted a woman—Spartan's mother—to produce a gifted child. Had he made similar advances toward Kaesi?

"Did you never wonder why he hated you so much?" she asked Dorian directly.

"It was a political negotiation." Dorian glanced at the man. "Things soured, and Draven swore his vengeance on me and my family."

"Oh, he swore it long before that. I was honest with him about my feelings, as I always am. I told him I wanted no part in his future because I had already planned mine." She smiled condescendingly down at the man, but deep sorrow lingered in her eyes. "He didn't take the rejection well."

Dorian's heart thudded painfully. He knew what was coming next.

"It was because of me that he went after you," she said more earnestly, searching Dorian's face as if she wanted to know what he thought of her admission. "That's why I had to be the one to save you. It was because of what I did that he struck out at you. When I learned about it, I swore that I would have my vengeance. That *you* would have your vengeance."

With a rising dread, Dorian watched as she laid the knife against Draven's throat. "Nay, Kaesi, this is not what I—"

"Not what you want? Shall I remind you how he murdered your family? What he did to them, because of me?" She choked. "This is our right, Dorian. No one has suffered more at Rufus Karthick's hands than you have. And because of that, no one will suffer more than he at yours."

Dorian stared at her, remembering her wild nature as a child, often explained away as mere high spirits. The way she would fixate on things—odd things. Her endless, zealous determination to succeed, no matter the cost.

A paralysis stole over him. Of course he had wanted Draven to die. But in his most private imaginings, it had been in a public place, after an extensive reading of Draven's crimes and a unanimous conviction by the Council of Eight. He wouldn't be treated kindly, but he would be executed humanely. Wretch as he was, he was a thane, after all. Dorian wouldn't become the very tyrant he was trying to depose.

"You will not want him to die slowly, of course," Kaesi said, her eyes glinting. "He has been my captive for a week now, and rest assured we have not treated him as an honored guest. But I have saved him now, for you. You will finish what I have only started." She nodded to the corner of the room, and two more guards appeared. They sliced through Dorian's bonds and brought him to his feet. He approached his sister hesitantly, flexing his wrists and trying to get the circulation going again.

"Are you ready?" Kaesi murmured softly, passing him the dagger.

"Ready for what?"

"The death of a king."

A low cry came from the corner. Spartan had awoken. His eyes were wide with dismay. "Nay, Dorian. You mustn't."

I won't, Dorian almost reassured him, but as he stood over Draven, who glared defiantly up at him, the words fled Dorian's lips. Here, at last, was his living nightmare. Was it time for absolution? For closure?

"Every night," Dorian told him, "every night, in my dreams, you kill them. Lida, Emmy . . . Sephone. I have to watch them die, over and over again. And every night, you stick this knife between my ribs, and you laugh while I bleed out on the ground. You stole my future. You corrupted my past. You are a destroyer of worlds, of lives, of innocence. There is naught you deserve more than death."

He tightened his grip on the hilt, and Kaesi leaned forward expectantly. The guards flanking them remained unmoving. Draven wouldn't be the first man Dorian had killed, but he would be the first Dorian had killed in cold blood.

Still, it would be so easy—

"Dorian." Sephone's voice. He looked at her, and she shook her head. "He does deserve to die. But not like this."

"Don't listen to the weak woman." Kaesi snorted. "She is spineless."

Dorian kept his focus on Sephone. "If I do this, it will all be over."

"Will it?" she asked. "Or will it just be the beginning of something far worse?"

"What would you have me do? If I let him go—"

"I never said you should let him go." Sephone glanced at Spartan, who remained mute. "But it's as you told me from the very beginning. Justice must be satisfied. If it is circumvented, you will never be at peace."

Peace. Dorian glanced at Spartan, remembering the boy's gift. No trace of it remained now.

"Quiet," barked Kaesi. "You'll muddy his head with your foolish talk."

But Sephone's words had done exactly the opposite. His head was clear. Dorian looked into his enemy's eyes, felt the full force of his loathing, recalled every way he had hurt Dorian. Then Dorian turned away.

He returned the dagger to Kaesi. "Thank you for your efforts in finding him. But I will not kill him . . . not today. He must be brought to trial, and then he will be punished as the Council sees fit." He went back to Spartan and Sephone.

"The Council? Half of them are in Draven's pocket, and the other half are dead"—she pointed at Draven—"murdered by him. Don't be a fool, brother. This is your right. Don't you want to avenge your wife and daughter?"

"I do. And they will be avenged. But not by me."

"Very well." Before Dorian could react, Kaesi grabbed Draven by the hair again. Grinning widely, she drew the dagger in a half circle beneath his throat.

"Nay!" Spartan shouted. Her guards released Draven, and he slumped forward, blood pooling beneath his motionless body. Face down in the dirt, the way Dorian's family had died in his dreams.

Dorian instinctively reached for Sephone and pulled her to him to keep her from seeing. She was shaking.

Spartan wept aloud, the brokenness of his cries piercing the depths of Dorian's soul. Had he loved his father that much? Or did he weep because of the father Draven might have been?

"I thought you had more courage than this, brother." Kaesi idly wiped the bloodied blade on the edge of her tunic.

"I'll admit to not comprehending what constitutes bravery at times," Dorian said as Sephone straightened and stood at his side, "but surely killing a gagged and bound man in cold blood is not courage."

"You cannot be sorry for the loss of such a beast," Kaesi replied disbelievingly. "He was a viper, a spider." Her eyes narrowed on Spartan. "A spider who left behind a rather large web."

Raising the dagger, she advanced on him.

Dorian started forward, but Sephone was faster, darting in front of Spartan. "If you touch him—"

"You'll what?" Kaesi demanded. "We have already established, Miss Winter, that you cannot hurt me."

Dorian stepped next to Sephone, blocking Spartan from his sister's view. "Leave the boy be, Kaesi. He is nothing like his father."

"He is devil spawn. He must die."

"Nay." On a whim, Dorian added, "If we are to work together, you must trust me on things. Trust me on this."

"Work together?" she repeated, going still. "You mean to say you will join me?" Her eyes lit. "Oh, Dorian, say you mean it. We will rule together. Side by side. Brother and sister." She spoke in a rush. "A void exists now Draven is dead, and we will step into it before others seize their chance. We will save Memosine—we will save Caldera. Miss Winter will be our tool of salvation."

He refused to look at Sephone. "You must let me think about it."

"Dorian, you can't seriously be considering—"

He shot Sephone a look, and she had the sense not to question him further. If they were to escape and save Spartan's life, they needed whatever time Dorian could buy them.

Kaesi's excitement morphed into solicitude. "Of course, brother. It is nearly midnight; you must be tired. My guards will take you to your room."

"Nay, put us together," Dorian said. "I must discuss this with them. I know they will support my decision."

Kaesi studied Sephone. "Ah, yes. They will follow you to the end, correct? Just like those revolutionary brothers you once freed to serve your cause?"

Dorian hoped Sephone understood. "They will."

By the time Kaesi's guards left them, Dorian was ready to collapse from weariness. He heard the distinct sound of a bolt sliding home—Kaesi evidently didn't trust him completely—and leaned back against the door. Despite his request, Magritte hadn't been included in their small group. Kaesi must be afraid of the woman's gift resurfacing.

Spartan sat on the bed, his head in his hands. Hesitantly, Sephone lowered herself to the mattress beside him. She had reclaimed her gloves, but Dorian could see she was reluctant to touch him.

Dorian looked around at the tiny room that had taken two long flights of stairs to reach. Dank and moldy, he suspected there would be little change to the amount of light come morning. Kaesi's guards had left a couple of lanterns, illuminating dusty window panes, a single, sagging bed, a wooden crate covered with a scrap of cloth, and a tiny side table bearing a pitcher and basin. The room had no fireplace, and even now, in the height of summer, it was cool.

He met Sephone's gaze and saw recognition there. "This was your bedroom?"

"Aye, for seventeen years."

He was unable to help comparing it to the luxury he had grown up in. Her entire bedroom could have fit into his childhood wardrobe. Spartan lifted his head to numbly look around.

Dorian shook his head. "How did you bear it?"

"One day at a time, I guess. Until I met you, I didn't know people lived any differently."

"The first time we met? Or the second?"

"The first. In your mind, I saw your home . . . Maera . . . I saw the sun." Her eyes were faintly luminous, but she didn't elaborate further. Instead she winced, gingerly adjusting her arm.

"You're still injured." Dorian knelt before her and peeled off his gloves.

She flinched and pulled away. "Nay, Dorian, you can't. My gift will . . ."

He reached for the corner of the threadbare sheet. When she saw what he intended, she relented, allowing him to ease off her glove. Carefully, he slid the sheet over her arm, keeping it between his skin and hers as he felt the limb from elbow to fingertips. It was red and slightly swollen. Months of captivity had rubbed the skin of her wrists raw in places.

"I don't think it's broken again," he remarked at last, leaning back on his haunches. "I'm no *bonesetter*, but the bones seem to be in their proper place. All the same, you should rest it as much as you can."

She nodded and picked up her glove, relaxing only when it was safely covering her arm once more.

Spartan spoke up. "You did an honorable thing, Dorian, sparing my father."

Looking at the boy's hollow eyes, his mouth went dry. "He still died."

"Aye, he did. But his blood is not on your head. And for that, I am thankful."

Dorian met Spartan's eyes. "The fact remains that Memosine now has no king. My sister is right in part; we must act quickly if we are to secure the throne."

Sephone didn't appear to be listening. "It was her," she said suddenly. "Kaesi saved your life in Idaea."

A memory came to Dorian's mind. A night as black as this one, but illuminated by dozens of blazing fireballs. A rearing, shrieking horse. A crossbow bolt aimed at Dorian's heart, until a man from the shadows intervened.

Had that been Kaesi preventing Draven from killing Dorian that night? Her blade had struck Draven's forearm—and Kaesi was more than proficient with weaponry, especially knives. If she was aiming to kill, she wouldn't have missed.

Even then, she had been preserving Draven's life until the day she could capture him in person, alive. She'd been saving up all her revenge for Dorian.

In that moment, he felt every hour of his thirty-one years. He sank to the floor.

Rufus Karthick, Lord Draven, was dead. Dorian's greatest enemy in the world was gone. Why didn't it feel the way he thought it would?

Why didn't he feel free? Instead, his chest felt hollow, the echo of his heart decaying into inevitable nothingness.

"Dorian," said Sephone quietly. "Do you mean to claim the throne?"

He sprang to his feet and crossed to the window. As expected, the night outside was as black as Nulla's main canal. There were no stars, no moon. Nothing to grab hold of. No hope.

"Dorian?" At Sephone's hand on his arm, he turned.

"Do you think I would make a good king?" he said abruptly.

She withdrew her hand. "Aye, I think you would."

If Cass were here, Dorian imagined his green ribbons would have a tiny thread of black at their center. She was holding something back. "But it troubles you to realize how tempted I am by the idea, just as I was tempted to kill Draven before."

"I would be surprised if you weren't." She shifted uneasily. "Your sister does not intend for you to rule alone."

"You're right. She doesn't."

Kaesi had made that very clear. Whatever she said about securing the throne for Dorian's sake, Kaesi's self-interest was obvious: she intended to be co-regent. If Dorian claimed the kingship, he would be sharing the throne with a madwoman.

"She's changed, you know. She was never like this as a child, not even as a young woman." The Kaesi he'd known would never have murdered a man in cold blood.

But he had to admit that the ingredients of her destructive choices had been there from the very beginning. Her love for dissembling and disassembling. Her forceful, yet always-endearing personality. It had yielded to a callous disregard for life, a belief that any and all means were in ultimate service to a glorious end. That same mind had plotted the downfall of Dorian's father and the other lords without a second thought for their family's welfare.

Wisely, Sephone said naught in reply.

"No matter how tempted I am by the chance to save Caldera," he said, "I cannot join forces with a woman who treats innocents as Kaesi has treated you. She would have let you die alone in the mountains."

Seeing a red mark on her temple where Kaesi had struck her, Dorian covered it with his hand. "I am sorry for everything she did to you in my name." He couldn't bear the thought that it was his own sister who had hurt and threatened her. His sister who had stolen the light from Sephone's eyes.

"You didn't know."

He changed the subject. "Before I left Thebe, I sent word to your parents. They were relieved to know you were safe."

Sephone's eyes lit. "They wrote back to you?"

He nodded. "They have not forgotten you, Sephone. No matter how hard they tried." Would she catch the hidden meaning in those words?

Tears pooled in her eyes. He looked around. "We have to escape this place. Tonight, if possible. Is there another way out of here?" Dorian glanced at the bed. "Perhaps the sheets—"

"We're on the third floor. It's a long way down. I don't think we can do it without help."

He turned to Spartan. "Has your gift returned?"

The youth shook his head.

Now would be a good time for shields and swords of light. But Kaesi must know of Spartan's gifts.

Dorian turned to the window, but it had been bolted shut from the outside. Cutter's doing? Or Kaesi's? He tried not to think of how many years Sephone had been a prisoner in this place. "Right. Then we need another plan."

Just as he said it, a tiny *crack* sounded at the window. Another came barely five seconds later, followed by a third. Someone was throwing stones.

Spartan leaped to his feet. "What was that?" he asked, coming over to the window.

Dorian grinned. "I think help just arrived."

Just a couple of minutes after the last stone, a face appeared in the darkness outside the window. A series of low *thwacks* ensued as a succession of bolts were drawn back, then the face disappeared. Dorian and Spartan pushed at the tiny window, and it eventually gave way, creaking outward on tired hinges. A foul-smelling breeze immediately rushed into the room, and I was grateful I'd never managed to get the window open before.

Dorian leaned out the window and said something I didn't catch. Seconds passed, and then a man was easing over the sill, sans rope. Boots thudded onto the floor, and Cass leaned down to brush the dust from his clothes.

"You received Magritte's message?" Dorian asked when Cass looked up.

"Aye," Cass replied. "The very moment she was captured, I think. And then another message was sent, only a few hours ago. Fortunately, when she sent the first one, I was close by, and by the time I got to the safe house, Symon was already there. We must have missed your departure by a matter of hours."

"Then Kaesi was lying about Sy—"

"Who?"

"I'll explain later. Regis is with you?"

"Aye, waiting below, with some of his resistance folk. We saw the light and guessed this room was where they were keeping you." He reached behind his back and withdrew Dorian's staff. "You left this behind at the safe house."

Dorian took it from him, visibly relieved. "I never thought I'd say this," he said with a half smile, "but I am glad to see you."

Cass grinned. "I'll take that as a *thank you*, Thane." Looking past Dorian and Spartan, he winked at me. "Ready for more climbing, Seph? You can come with me again, if you like. I think you enjoyed it better that way, last time."

Dorian frowned at Cass's comment. "Did you bring rope?"

In response, the *lumen* hefted a coil from his shoulder.

I stared. Cass had free-climbed up the side of the building?

"Sailor, remember?" he said, noticing my incredulous look. "Besides, this building is so badly decayed that there are plenty of holds. You just have to watch where you put your hands."

Together, Dorian and Spartan dragged the bed to the window, where they set about securing the end of the rope. Cass seized the opportunity to sidle closer to me.

"Did you miss me, Sephy?"

I opened my mouth to rebuke him for the overly familiar address, only to realize the truth: I *had* missed him. That realization awakened an uncomfortable sensation in the pit of my stomach.

Fortunately, he saved me from answering. "Nice place," he said, looking around the room. "Your room or Symon's?"

I frowned. *How does he—*

"I recognized the building," he said in a softer voice. "Just as Mistress Magritte did when she was brought here. I know this is where you grew up."

"The room is mine." I caught sight of the mirror shard on the bedside table, the same one I'd once used to check the length of my hair. "There are good memories, too, along with the bad ones."

"Such as the day we met?" he offered, with another wink.

"We're ready," said Dorian from the window, and I inwardly thanked him for the interruption.

"What about Magritte?" I asked.

"It's all right," Cass replied. "She's on a lower level. Symon is probably getting her as we speak." He indicated the window. "Monks first, then thanes. I'll come last."

"Sephone's arm is injured," Dorian informed him as Spartan swung his legs over the sill and began climbing down. The bed held steady, counterbalancing his weight surprisingly well.

"I'll help her down," Cass replied easily. "After all, it won't be our first climb together."

The two men exchanged a look of silent challenge until Dorian finally nodded—though something smoldered in his eyes.

The door suddenly swung open. Three men entered the room, only one of them unmasked.

"Dear sister," Brinsley said when he saw me. "I came to enquire as to—"

But whatever he'd come to enquire about would remain a mystery, for when Dorian saw my brother, he dove at him.

Just then, Brinsley saw the open window and the bed beside it. His eyes went wide before Dorian tackled him, knocking one of the guards back into the hallway. Brinsley and Dorian rolled, while the second guard came at Cass.

None of the four were armed with anything more than daggers—not that they paused to draw them. There wasn't even room for Dorian to extend his staff, even if he had wanted to do so. As Cass engaged the second guard and Dorian pinned Brinsley to the floor, I wove between them to the door, where the stunned first guard might re-emerge any moment. I slammed it shut and reached up to the bolt Regis had secretly installed when I turned fifteen, so I could lock my door from the inside. I had barely shot it home when a weight fell against the door. The wood shuddered but held firm.

We had minutes—maybe seconds—before the guard alerted Kaesi and the rest of her men. How many were there? There had been at least a dozen in the courtyard.

My ears registered the sound of breaking pottery, and I turned to find that the pitcher and basin had smashed on the floor. The door shuddered again as something heavy hurled itself against the wood. My heart thudding, I grabbed the small table that had borne the pitcher and shoved it up against the door, followed by the crate with the mirror shard still sitting on top.

"Open up!" a voice bellowed. "Open this door *now*!"

He wasn't half as scary as Cutter. I swiveled to see Cass and his assailant grappling together, a succession of dents in the plaster suggesting that the fight was nearing its zenith. But it was Dorian's low grunt of pain that brought my attention to the floor. I cried out. My brother had drawn a knife, and as I watched, he slashed at Dorian's chest. Dorian recoiled instinctively, and Brinsley seized his opportunity, knocking Dorian onto his back.

I grabbed the mirror shard and moved without thinking. Brinsley turned at my approach, and I stabbed blindly. My brother shrieked and fell to the floor, dropping his knife in the process; I stepped back, blinking at the mirror shard embedded in my brother's left shoulder.

I had stabbed my own brother—

Dorian didn't waste a moment, grabbing Brinsley's knife and bringing it down in a silver arc, aiming for Brinsley.

"Nay," I whimpered.

Cass caught Dorian's arm midstrike, panting. "Perhaps you should let Sephone decide her brother's fate." He planted his boot in Brinsley's chest, pinning the struggling man to the ground.

Dorian's arm dropped.

Another *thud* came at the door, followed by metallic scraping sounds.

"They're taking the door off its hinges," Cass said. "Make your decision, Seph."

"Nay," I said reflexively. "I don't want him dead."

"The lady has spoken," Cass announced. Leaning down, he grabbed Brinsley's shirtfront before punching him in the face. Brinsley slumped to the ground. "He'll live," he said, seeing my wide-eyed stare. "Now come on. We have to move."

Blindly, I made my way to the window, dimly aware of the body of Cass's assailant lying propped against the wall, blood trickling from his mouth. Would he live?

"Go, Thane," Cass was saying.

"Nay," Dorian insisted. "Take Sephone first."

I gazed at the room that had been mine for seventeen years, now a mess of broken pottery shards, upturned furniture, and bleeding bodies. Was this the last time I would see it? Memories rushed in like the icy winds of Nulla.

Cass took my arm. "We have to go."

Numbly, I let him guide me to the window, where he climbed over the sill and grabbed hold of the rope.

"Now you," he instructed, talking me through every movement. Dorian must have been using his own weight to counterbalance mine and Cass's. My arm screamed with pain, but it held as well.

"That's it," Cass encouraged. I clung half to the rope and half to him as we shimmied down the thick rope, finding the occasional extra holds on ledges or outcroppings of bricks. Never in a million years had I thought I would one day abseil down the side of Cutter's house.

How long had we been descending? Any moment, the door could burst open and Kaesi's men would surge into the room. Would she hurt her own brother?

My boots encountered stone—the narrow street behind Cutter's house—and Cass pried me from the rope. "Well done, Seph. We made it."

But everything else pushed to the periphery as I watched the dimly lit window: the small cluster of cowled men, the lingering stink of the canal that ran alongside the street, the long boat tethered to a wooden post.

There, at last—Dorian climbed over the sill and began to shimmy down the rope. He moved quickly, hand over hand. But voices emanated from above, growing in intensity.

"Where are they?"

"They've gone out the window!"

Dorian reached a quarter of the way down—then halfway. I held my breath.

The rope went slack, the end of it snaking over the sill and tumbling past Dorian. He tried to grip the side of the building, but there were no handholds in immediate proximity. A cry tore from me as he fell.

But hands rose beside me. There was a blinding light, and I blinked, dazzled.

A shimmering crystalline shield hovered midair, barely three feet above us. On it, Dorian lay, arms and legs flung out like a starfish. Spartan stood beneath, his arms lifted above his head, sweat beading on his temples with the effort of sustaining the barrier.

"You idiot!" a voice screeched from above. "How dare you cut the rope! What if my brother was on the end of it?"

He was. Spartan's shield shrank and began to descend, lowering Dorian safely to the ground before it snuffed out. Dorian clambered to his feet and grasped Spartan's shoulder.

"Thank you," Dorian said fervently. "I thought I was a goner."

"Seph!" Regis appeared, Magritte behind him. "You're safe."

"Not yet," Cass warned, indicating the room far above, where a face framed by long blond hair watched us with mounting fury. "We should get out of here."

"Aye," said Dorian, with one last look at the window. "Let's go."

Lanternless, our boat glided almost silently through the filthy canals of Nulla. Peering over the side at the opaque water, which sucked at the craft like clinging mud, I thought of the pool under the Mountain, Memoria.

They weren't so dissimilar.

This late at night—or so early in the morning—the canals were practically abandoned, and I saw only moored, covered boats as we traversed one of the lonelier tributaries. It would lead us to the south side of the city, where we could regain land.

"So," Cass said conversationally to Dorian, who was sitting across from us. "Who was that woman back there?"

Dorian slowly raised his head. I understood his discomfort. Ten of us were present. Myself, Dorian, Cass, Regis, Magritte, Spartan, and four of the Sons. Whatever he said, it would be heard by all.

"My sister."

"Your *sister*?"

In a flat voice, Dorian explained how Kaesi had turned out to be the hooded man, who had captured me in order to learn Draven's whereabouts. Then, how she'd used me via Magritte's gift as bait to lure Dorian. And, finally, how she'd murdered the king of Caldera in front of us. In front of his youngest son.

A hush had stolen over the boat by the time he finished. Cass broke the silence. "So"—he looked at me—"your brother and his sister."

I didn't answer, and he threw out his hands.

"Well, why all the glum faces? Shouldn't we be rejoicing that Draven is dead?"

Spartan's shoulders jerked, and I sent Cass a reproachful look.

"It's not that simple," gritted Dorian. "Draven might have been evil, but he was a known evil. Kaesi, unpredictable and powerful as she is, may end up being far worse."

"Powerful?" Cass echoed.

"My sister's gift, besides shapeshifting, is to rob others of their powers. In her presence, an *alter* is no better than an ordinary human."

Another long silence ensued. An enemy against which no gift could function, not even Asa Karthick's. How large was Kaesi's range? Spartan had been able to conjure a shield, so it couldn't be longer than the height of Cutter's house.

"She mentioned one who was immune," I remembered.

"Aye, so she did." Dorian considered this thoughtfully.

"Wait a moment," interrupted Cass. "You're saying she offered you the chance to rule, Thane. Why didn't you take it?"

Dorian's expression was unreadable. "I'm not the right man to rule Caldera. But even if I were, I could not claim a throne with so many strings attached."

"Never thought I'd hear you say so."

But Dorian's eyes were on Spartan. I wondered if he was thinking about Aedon.

"So," Cass repeated, "the pretender king is dead, but now we potentially have a queen on our hands. A powerful, shapeshifting *alter* who just so happens to render every single one of our gifts useless, including the monk's."

"That's about it," said Regis.

"And in addition to the thane's crazy sister"—Cass ignored my eyes this time—"we may just have alienated Lady Xia by keeping Seph and

Spartan away from her. All possibly in vain, since we're no closer to retrieving the Reliquary or finding an *altered healer* who can help Seph."

Dorian sat upright. "You weren't successful?"

Cass shook his head. "Nay, thanks to Draven's recruitment and Lethe's purges. The only surviving *alters*—including that scruffy-looking *bonesetter* who healed Seph's wrist—have all been taken to Calliope."

My stomach turned. If only Cass's gift were present. There was something they weren't telling me. Some aspect of their plan that was still in shadow.

"So what now?" Magritte asked, interrupting my train of thought. "What do we do?"

"For now?" Dorian said as all eyes swept to him. "There is only one option, really. We are exhausted, wounded, and running low on supplies . . . and allies. We must return to Thebe."

23
KAESI

"So," I concluded, watching the young man kneeling at my feet, "I have your fealty, then?"

Asa Karthick raised his head, his face an inscrutable mask. No sorrow had appeared in his eyes when I told him of his father's fate. Would he express his grief later? Or had he hated his father as much as I had?

"In theory," he said carefully. "Though we would need to discuss terms." He glanced to my right, where Brinsley Winter stood beside the arch-lord's chair, which I now occupied, snug and comfortable in his new general's uniform.

I forcefully quenched my rising temper. *The nerve of the boy.* But at least Asa had a backbone, unlike his pathetic father.

I stood, to gain the height advantage, arraying the short train of my dress with regal flair. Fortunately, I had no more use for masculine disguises. Feminine forms afforded greater opportunities now. It had been easy—laughably easy—to enter Memosine's capital and take control of the arch-lord's castle in the Karthicks' absence. Foolishly, they had surrounded their inner sanctum with *alters*, and the Karthicks' brand of *alters* were so confident in their gifts that they rarely bothered training with weapons.

Unlike my own men, who had been training for this day for years.

By the time my loyal followers had secured the castle, there was no longer any Council of Eight. Now, there would only be a Council of One.

I shook myself and focused on Asa. "What terms?"

"Permission to stand, my lady?"

I nodded curtly. I was still on the dais, and he was no danger to me.

He gained his feet slowly. "You recalled me from the siege of Nephele, Lady Adamo. And since you're asking me to pledge you my loyalty rather than ordering my execution, I think I can safely conclude that there's a reason why you want my fealty. Perhaps even why you need it."

Folding my arms, I tapped my gloveless fingers against my upper sleeve. "I might have killed you, aye. But, unlike your father, I'm not wasteful." I studied the grimy, dusty, travel-weary face of the boy Draven had spawned, and inwardly despised him. "Arrogant upstart that you are, you're right. You are something of a symbol among the Memosinians, Asa."

"I prefer to be called Ignis."

"I care little what you prefer, boy. Now, the throne your father established is tenuous at best. Memosine is surrounded by enemies: the outlanders to the north, the Letheans to the southeast. The Mariantheans will join the fray, should we prove ourselves to be weak. And you have failed to subdue even one of those enemies thus far."

"The siege of Nephele is progressing as expected," came the reply.

"As expected, meaning that you are failing dismally. You have thousands of men at your disposal, including several dozen *alters*, and the city yet stands."

The *ignis* darted a look at Brinsley. "If I am such a failure, why not have me replaced with another?" He met my gaze boldly. "Ah, of course. Because as the king's son, the Memosinians will expect me to be named the next ruler."

"Perhaps," I mused, making a show of studying my fingernails instead of the man who believed himself my superior. "These are young traditions, you must see. And you are an *alter.* Nevertheless, with your open support of my claim, any potential critics will be silenced forever."

"And if I refuse to support it?"

I smiled. "I control Calliope, young Asa. Which means I also control its dungeons. And that includes every single one of its prisoners." I paused to allow the realization to take hold.

And it did. Asa sucked in a breath. "Zaire."

"Aye, Zaire. That was what your father used against you, wasn't it?

The life of your lady love? He would give you time with her, so long as you obeyed him."

Asa looked ashen now. He scraped a nervous hand back through longish red-blond hair. "Have you hurt her?"

In response, I reached for my gift, watching as the shape I assumed widened his eyes and shadowed his expression. When the transformation was complete, I fingered a long, glossy black curl, stretching it out to its full length before letting it spring back.

"Exquisite beauty," I mused. "A pity her only other form is so beastly."

Asa straightened and clapped his hands together. When naught happened, he frowned and tried again.

I laughed at his lost expression. "Foolish boy. Your gift will not work in my presence. If it's any consolation, she cannot change in front of me, either."

Twice more, he attempted to summon the blazing fireballs that constituted his gift. Giving up, he tilted his chin defiantly. "I control Memosine's forces. In the north *and* the southeast."

"There's no need to boast, young man." I let Zaire's shape dissolve, assuming my natural form again. "I drive the same bargain as your father, Asa. If you will pledge me your loyalty, and be my faithful general all the days of your life"—if the prophecy proved authentic, that might not be long—"I will allow Zaire to live. Depending on your actions, she may even enjoy relative freedom and comfort. Even luxury."

How had Draven done it? How had he blackmailed them? He was no *alter*, not really. His eldest son was far more powerful. Zaire was more powerful. Either of them could have killed Rufus Karthick in a heartbeat, no matter what he threatened. Had patricide felt unthinkable to Asa? Or was there another reason why he had refused to challenge his father?

No matter, my own power came from another source. So long as Asa and Zaire were in my presence, they would pose no more threat to me than any other pair of star-crossed lovers.

"Well?" I said when he remained silent. "You cannot doubt my generosity. I am even willing to overlook the fact that you would have killed me just now."

"I accept, Lady Adamo." His throat bulged. "And I thank you for your generosity."

I smiled my satisfaction. Brinsley, because of his Lethean heritage, would always be distrusted by the Memosinians. And he was no soldier. But Asa, with his formidable gift and his position as the former king's son, would give me the victory I sought. And not just against Lethe, but the whole of Caldera.

"Shall I return to my—to your army, my lady?"

I shook my head. "Nay, Lord Draven."

"Lord Draven?" he repeated, looking discomfited.

"It was your father's title. As his eldest son and heir, it belongs to you now. Do you not want it?"

He hesitated, his jaw working, then bowed. "Aye, thank you."

"Well, then, I have other plans for our forces in Lethe. A change of leadership might do us good. Or a change of strategy. Meanwhile, I will need you here." Close by, where he couldn't scheme and plot against me. Until I was sure of his allegiances, or he understood what would happen if he shifted them elsewhere, he would stay in Calliope.

Perhaps, when the time was ripe, I would send him north. By all reports, Draven had dropped an angry beehive on his northern subjects by engaging and antagonizing the outlanders. If Lethe joined forces with them against us . . .

"You are dismissed," I told Asa, who bowed again and departed the great hall.

A tiny cough came from the man behind me.

"Spit it out, Brinsley."

The former merchant stepped forward, eyes narrowed. "He's plotting something. I just know it."

"Then earn your keep and ensure we're abreast of whatever he's planning."

Brinsley nodded. "My lady, will you go after your brother? And my sister?"

"Ah, you seek to make amends for your earlier failure." I sniffed. "All in good time, Brinsley. All going well, they will come to *us*."

"The Reliquary?" He looked around, as if I were foolish enough to hide it in plain sight.

"It is safe."

Brinsley bowed and melted into the shadows.

I paused, thinking. Dorian had been searching for the relic for months. But he had continued to search, even after he knew what it could do and what it would cost. What was he planning?

It came to me in a flash. *He wants to save the girl.*

Only a blind man could have failed to see the affection between them. Apparently, my brother had finally found a woman to replace the irreplaceable Lida Ashwood. And now that woman was dying. The only thing that remained was to see how far he would go to save her. Who he might join.

I sank into the arch-lord's uncomfortable chair and suppressed a sigh. Over all this, my brother could have been king. *Ungrateful, idiotic . . .*

Perhaps Dorian had done me a favor. This way, I didn't have to answer to anyone. I had killed Draven and the remainder of the Council of Eight, so why should I not reap the rewards for myself? Why should I not rule?

Lady Adamo, they called me. It had been my title before I was thrown in prison. The eldest daughter of the former thane of Maera, and younger sister to yet another thane. A mere woman, while the men wielded the real power.

But I was more than Lord Adamo's sister now. More than Silvertongue's protégé. I was a powerful *alter* who none could rival, not a *mem* nor an *ignis*. I was seated in the arch-lord's chair, the chair that Draven had not yet replaced with a true throne, like the ancestors might once have sat in. I had the famous Reliquary in my possession. Why should I wait for my brother to claim what I wanted?

This castle, this country, this world—all were mine.

And, as soon as the ceremony could be arranged, I would be queen.

I sat up and looked around the darkened room—not unlike the one I had occupied before Dorian requested Regis take me to the safe house.

I blinked the sleep from my eyes as the present came flooding back. We were in Thebe again. Lady Xia, despite her anger at Dorian and Regis's underhandedness, had accepted us back, granting us refuge in a tree house recently vacated after its occupants moved northeast. When I emerged from my room a few minutes later, appropriately attired, Cass tilted his head, studying me. "You're not one to sleep in."

"I had bad dreams."

His eyes softened. "Would you like to walk a bit?"

I nodded, and soon we were out of the tree house and walking through the trees. The forests of Thebe had an ethereal beauty to them; even at midday they were shrouded in mournful shadows. A few birds called to each other through the gray, but other than that, the wood was almost completely still.

"Eerie place," remarked Cass.

I wondered if he was cold without the sun. "But better than Orphne?"

He grinned. "Infinitely." He reached inside his cloak and extracted a small silver flask. He raised it in my direction like a toast before taking a deep swig.

"What?" he said when he caught me frowning. "It's midday." He smiled wickedly. "Somewhere."

"Cass! A *lumen* should know better—"

"Aye, but that's exactly what this is for. So I'm not a *lumen* at all."

"It's your gift. How can you deny it like you do?"

His eyes flicked toward my gloves. "You're one to talk."

I crossed my arms. "These gloves help me to preserve a person's privacy."

"Aye, and this little flask helps me to preserve a person's integrity." At my scoff, he tucked it away.

"That little flask is getting bigger."

"It takes more and more of it to hold the world at bay."

My anger evaporated. "Is the truth really so unbearable, Cass?"

He studied me. "It can be, wouldn't you say?" Memories flickered in his eyes. His mother, who he'd been unable to save? His younger brother, who'd stolen the title and inheritance Cass was owed, and the woman he loved?

"I'm still your friend," I said. "Whatever sorrow troubles you, I can help—" I broke off, realizing I couldn't fulfill that promise. I couldn't share his sorrow, not when my gift was increasingly unreliable. I thought of Kaesi's guards and shuddered. What would I do to Cass if I entered his mind?

Cass nodded soberly, as if he understood. "Don't you ever wish for an ordinary life, Seph?" He took my hand in both of his, studying the leather glove. "A life free from all of this?"

"A life without the gifts?"

"Aye."

"Sometimes," I admitted. "But I didn't think you wanted to be ordinary."

"Maybe it's the type of gift that counts. Maybe I want to be like Asa Karthick, capable of summoning fireballs with a clap of my hands."

At the thought of Asa, my stomach tensed. Two weeks had passed as the Letheans calculated their next move. According to Dorian, who had heard it from Lady Xia, Asa had joined forces with Kaesi. The two together would make a formidable opponent. And Nephele had only just held Memosine's army at bay . . .

"Or maybe I just want to be a simple man, strolling through the woods with a simple woman at my side."

I covered my nervousness with a laugh. "You're calling me simple?"

He smiled, but his heart wasn't in it. "If I were, would you still push me away?"

I extracted my hand from his, uncomfortable. It was altogether too easy to imagine a simple life with him. He was a devastatingly attractive man who had put aside womanizing ways to pursue me. He was a faithful companion with a wicked sense of humor. Unlike Dorian, he'd never once hesitated to call me his friend. He'd declared his feelings rather than attempting to conceal them, and he'd even prevented Dorian from killing Brinsley, for my sake. The mocking veneer concealed a man of deep feeling and even principle.

"There is another road, you know," Cass continued when I didn't respond. "Kaesi Ashwood's powers are unequaled. And she has the Reliquary in her possession. If she can temporarily render an *alter* ordinary, she may be able to do it permanently."

I stared at him. "What are you suggesting, Cass? For starters, Kaesi will kill us before she helps us."

"Don't say you haven't thought about it."

"Actually, I hadn't." But I had to admit the offer was tempting. To leave behind my gift forever . . . Would the nightmares diminish? Would my memories of other minds eventually fade into nothingness, like long-forgotten dreams?

Surely even Aedon did not have such power. Only a god could bestow gifts and take them away. But the gods had given us the Reliquary. It might be possible . . .

And then I remembered the price.

"You're forgetting," I said, "that the use of the Reliquary would cost a life."

By the look in Cass's eyes, he hadn't forgotten. "What if it's just any old life that will do? A person on their death bed, perhaps, willing to give their life for a good cause? Or a plentiful sum of money for their surviving family?"

I recalled Aedon's warning. *You must not use the Reliquary again. It carries a burden another must bear—a poison more potent than any other poison. If you try to wield it, it will only bring you death . . .*

"Aren't you sick of being used, Seph? Sick of being chased, hunted down across half of Caldera, without home or hearth to return to? Don't you want to be free?"

My father has a plan to restore Memoria, Sephone, but you must trust us. You must trust me . . .

I looked into Cass's face, seeing his anguish. "Aye, I do want to be free. But you can't take this away from us without stealing from others."

It was the same choice Dorian had faced, back in Nulla. He had craved freedom from Lord Draven, but not Kaesi's way. Never Kaesi's way.

"Our methods define us as much as our choices," I told Cass. "If we chose that path, there would be no turning back."

Cass laid his hands on my shoulders. At such proximity, the iridescent color in his eyes was startling. "Deny it," he murmured. "Insist you're unmoved by my presence."

Had he forgotten about the Reliquary, or was he still trying to convince me to choose him? "Is this a test?"

He tapped the interior pocket containing his flask. "No gift, remember?"

I met his gaze. "I—"

"Sephone, Cass!"

We turned to see Magritte hurrying our way. How had she found us here in the forest? We had long since left the trail. And why had she come after us personally, rather than simply sending a message? Nonetheless, I was grateful for the interruption.

"What is it, Magritte?" I said, moving away from Cass.

She reached us, breathing hard and clutching her swollen abdomen. "You must come to Lady Xia. She has convened a Council of War."

"And we're invited?" Cass raised an eyebrow. "Both of us?"

She nodded breathlessly. "You must come."

"Well," muttered Cass when we finally stood in Lady Xia's war room, crushed together at the back against a wall that was more tree than anything else, "this is a happy gathering."

As bodies shifted, I searched the room for familiar faces. Siaki Xia stood at the center in front of her war table, dressed in a simply cut gray gown with a scalloped hem. White-blond hair fell to her waist in lengths of perfect symmetry. Dorian stood beside her, his hands clasped behind his back, his hair and beard recently trimmed to a uniform length. He was dressed in Lethean gray, his broad shoulders filling out a snugly fitting tunic, and his brown leather boots had been exchanged for polished black ones. He looked powerful and commanding, with no trace of uncertainty or desperation.

Arrayed around the table was a smattering of intimidating-looking people, including some members of the League as well as Regis and a few of his Sons of Truth. Some thirty or so people had been crammed into the treetop war council.

"Why do you think they invited us?" Cass mused in my ear. "It would seem they have this whole thing well in hand."

"Shush," I told him. "I think they're about to start."

Just as I said it, a bare head, glinting with auburn stubble, moved into my periphery. I smiled at Spartan, who returned the smile with a faintly troubled expression.

Since returning from Nulla, I hadn't drunk from Spartan's vial again, nor had I seen Aedon in my dreams. A shadow had returned to disquiet my sleep, and nightmares crowded in where there had only been light before. The days blurred together, just as they had during my captivity. It was becoming increasingly difficult to distinguish between real and unreal. To ascertain if Aedon was anything more than a figment of my imagination, a product of my own wishful thinking—or if the visions I'd seen of the world-that-was were real.

Magritte appeared on the other side of Spartan just as Lady Xia began to speak.

"Thank you all for coming," she said in a strong, clear voice. "Each of you is here because you stand against the darkness that comes at us from the northwest."

"Ah," Cass said beneath his breath. "So that's why."

"Now," Xia continued, fortunately not having heard him, "we have news from Calliope. Kaesi Ashwood of Maera has recently assumed the late Lord Draven's newly established throne, with the support of his eldest son, Asa Karthick. She crowns herself Queen Adamo."

There were low murmurings, and some dagger-sharp glances at Dorian, whose face was stoic. "Fortunately for us, the death of Lord Draven left a temporary power vacuum that worked to our advantage. Asa Karthick has been recalled to Calliope, and in his absence, Nephele has been able to consolidate its defenses."

"Put out all the fireballs, you mean," muttered Cass.

"However," Xia said, "word has just reached us of another development, a far more troubling one. It seems that Lady Kaesi—I refuse to call her Queen—has withdrawn Memosine's army altogether. They are marching back toward Calliope as we speak. They will be home within the week."

Kaesi was withdrawing from Lethe? Might she want peace? Somehow, I couldn't reconcile that idea with the woman I'd met in Nulla. That woman had been hungry for Memosine's throne. And she'd wanted Dorian to be king of Caldera. Surely, she wouldn't be content to stay within her borders now.

Evidently, the others thought the same.

"This is an opportunity," said a flush-faced man I recognized as Lord Viorel. "If we move quickly, we can cut them off before they reach Calliope. Ambush them on every side."

"We don't have that kind of strength," said a tall, dark-haired woman with iridescent fingernails. "If we had marched to Nephele's aid, we might have been able to overcome them together, with Nephele's weapons and our reinforcements. But remember that Asa Karthick's *alters* are still with them. They will be watching for an ambush. They may even be hoping for one."

"Lady Samaire is right," Xia stated. "But the question remains, why is she withdrawing in the first place?"

"Perhaps she realizes that taking Nephele is impossible," offered Regis. "It has been weeks since the siege first began."

"Nay," contradicted Lord Viorel. "We have had word from the capital. They were nearly at the end of their supplies. Vice-Regent Spath would have surrendered if we had not promised to come."

"There is another possibility."

All eyes swiveled to Dorian.

"I have had word from Aleria Vega of the outlanders," he announced. "They are moving against Memosine, against the northern cities and towns."

I wondered if he was thinking about Maera. Would his home city be at risk?

Aleria. I remembered Cass's insinuation about the time they'd spent together. I pushed it away.

"The outlanders," said a man I didn't recognize, shaking his head in disgust. "We can trust them even less."

"Nevertheless, they have as much to lose at Memosine's hands as we do. They have expressed interest in an alliance." Dorian looked around the room. "It may be the only way to remove my sister from power. And neutralize the forces responsible for putting her there."

Was he speaking about the merchant, Silvertongue? The *alter* who had turned out to be a master of the Dark gifts?

"You so readily enter into agreements and alliances, Lord Adamo," sneered the same man. "A shame you are not capable of keeping them."

Dorian's eyes sparked, but he kept his temper. "This is not about me, or even you, Andrius. This is about Caldera's future."

"And yet Xia expects us to participate in a council attended by the very brother of our enemy! Who's to say you wouldn't sooner join your sister than remove her from power? Or assume the throne after she is gone?"

"That's enough, Lord Chaske," Lady Xia snapped. "Lord Adamo has proven himself to this League a dozen times over. If he wanted to join Kaesi, he would have done so in Maera, eight years ago.

"Now that we've cleared that up nicely," Xia continued, "we can decide our course of action. I, for one, am in favor of an alliance with the outlanders. If they were to approach Calliope from the north and us from the south . . ."

I leaned against the wall, feeling the ropy outline of tree branches at my back. Shapes danced and spun in my vision. They spoke of a war like it was a simple matter of strategy: matching Memosine's greater numbers with Lethe's new weapons. But waiting for us in Calliope was a man who threw fireballs that could incinerate people, a half-human beast with teeth and claws sharp enough to tear a person to shreds, a merchant who could persuade someone to do anything he wanted, and a woman whose gift not only allowed her to assume any form she chose but made it impossible for any gifted person to approach her.

Even if the outlanders joined us, or we joined them, we had no chance. I doubted even Lethe's weapons would work on Kaesi. Only one, she had said, was immune. Cass? He had proved to be immune from Silvertongue's gift . . .

"Seph?" A gloved hand touched my arm. Seeing Cass's concern, I straightened and tried to collect myself.

"Then it is settled," Xia was saying. "We march on Calliope within the week, with whatever forces and weapons Nephele can spare."

What? How long had I been lost in my thoughts?

"We will not reach their capital in time," Lady Samaire warned. "Not before their army returns. We will have to fight Memosine at their full strength."

"That is where the outlanders will come in," Xia replied. "Providing they attack from the north, via the river, there will be sufficient cover for a smaller force to penetrate the city." She looked at Dorian. "Your mission will be to take the castle, and everything inside. The rest of us will provide the distraction."

Did Lady Xia realize that she could be sending him to his death?

"I volunteer for this mission."

The crowd broke into a low hum. I watched in shock as Spartan stepped through the tightly packed bodies to stand beside the war table.

"You?" Lady Xia said. For once, the façade of her iron composure had slipped. "Jerome Karthick?"

"Aye," replied the acolyte, matching her level gaze as the whispers grew.

Jerome Karthick. The younger son of the dead king . . .

Dorian inclined his head. "I accept your offer, Spartan, with my gratitude. After all, if you wanted to join your father and brother, you would have done so in Argus, eight years ago."

The surrounding lords and ladies looked discomfited at the clever reversal of Lady Xia's logic.

"Dorian, you must reconsider," she began.

"You've appointed me leader of this mission," Dorian reminded her. "At least allow me to choose my own men."

"Will Spartan be able to kill his own brother when it comes down to it? To resist the temptation of the throne left behind by his father? He is only a boy, you know."

"Nay," countered Dorian. "He is a man. And he possesses more courage than anyone in this room."

They exchanged a look: the former thane and ambassador, and the young acolyte whose father was responsible for the destruction of Dorian's entire world. Spartan seemed to grow taller, as if fortified by Dorian's acceptance.

I forgive him, though in my eyes, he does not bear his father's guilt . . .

Dorian looked past the acolyte to Cass. "I could use a *lumen*'s help, particularly if Silvertongue is present."

Cass cocked his head. "Aye, Thane, I'll consider it."

"Count me in," said Regis, several bodies away, and Dorian nodded his thanks.

I spoke up. "You can count me in, too."

Dorian's dark brown eyes were inscrutable. "Nay, Sephone. You must stay here. In Thebe, where it's safe."

"I'm a *mem*. I can help." Even if I couldn't exactly control my gift right now.

"For reasons I do not quite understand, you are the key to my sister's plans. I won't take you into the heart of the dragon's lair once more."

"It's not your decision," I said defiantly. "It's *my* life."

"Nay, it's all our lives, Sephone. Or have you forgotten how Kaesi used you? How you became her weapon, her tool of destruction? I won't let that happen again."

My cheeks flamed, and tears sprang to my eyes. I was dimly aware that Cass was glaring at Dorian. But all I could think about was the chamber under the mountain, the Reliquary, the advisor whose mind I'd erased. The woman who'd died.

I spun and fled the room. Somehow, I found the stairwell and blindly felt my way down it, ignoring the surprised looks of Xia's guards at the bottom. Leaving the tree house, I headed for the forest, stumbling once as my weakened ankle caught in a thick tuft of grass. I ran until I was out of breath, sinking to the ground in a small thicket.

I closed my eyes and gave into my grief.

Guilt and self-recrimination followed him through the trees as he tracked Sephone. Rain had fallen the night before, and it was easy to see her footprints in the soft earth. After he'd excused himself from the Council, which had been near to concluding anyway, Xia's guards had pointed him in the direction she had gone.

She had to understand why she needed to remain behind. Allowing Cass to come was one thing—not only was he a *lumen*, but he was their sole defense against Silvertongue. Sephone was another matter entirely. If she came, she would be as much a danger to them as to herself.

The sound of quiet weeping reached his ears long before he saw her. Not wanting to startle her, he reached out with his gift. She turned at once, swiping the tears from her face and getting to her feet.

"I don't want it," she said, her eyes alight. "It isn't what I thought it was."

"My gift? Or me?"

"Both of you."

He obeyed half of her request, retracting the invisible tendrils of his gift. Seeing a rough scrape on her cheek, he came closer, extending his gloved hand. "You're bleeding."

She swatted it away. "Is that what it takes for you to stop avoiding me? An injury?"

"I haven't been—" Honesty compelled him to break off the statement, and she thrust out her chin, reasserting her point. "I've been busy."

"Aye, busy making plans to save Caldera that don't require my presence. Busy building alliances and resistances and leagues. Busy receiving secret messages from outlanders."

Dorian frowned. Was that jealousy in her voice?

"Why did you come, Dorian?"

He met her gaze squarely. "To apologize."

"For showing Xia's Council how despicable I am?"

"That's not what I said or implied," he said. "I'm only trying to protect you, Sephone."

"From your sister? Or from myself?"

He sighed. "If Kaesi captures you again, one more session connected to the Reliquary could kill you. And even if it doesn't, I'm afraid of . . ." He took a breath. "I'm afraid of what she will force you to do."

His voice cracked, and Sephone thawed, if only slightly. "Your concern is admirable, Dorian, but I'm one of the few *alters* on Lethe's side. If we are to win this, you will need every *alter* and every *mem* you can get."

"I'm not sending a dying woman into war."

"You're not sending me. I'm coming of my own volition. As will Aleria." Her expression turned determined. "Please. You can't leave me out of this. What the Karthicks and Kaesi started, we have to finish. Together."

He hesitated. "You can't ask me to risk your life."

"It's not yours to risk, Dorian. And just as you would never abandon your friends, you cannot ask me to abandon mine."

He closed his eyes. To let her accompany them was unwise, especially if Kaesi found a way to use her against them. Against Sephone herself. But Kaesi also had the Reliquary. If everything went to plan, and they were able to recapture the Reliquary, it would be helpful if Sephone was close by. Then, once Kaesi was defeated . . .

Dorian's eyes opened. "If I allow this, you must remain with the army. It's too dangerous to let you infiltrate the castle with us. That will only play into Kaesi's hands."

She paused, then nodded. "I'll do as you say."

He frowned at her ready acquiescence—was she preparing to disobey him later? He gentled his voice. "You've been avoiding me, too."

Her head dipped, and he knew he was right. Not just him, either, but her parents, Regis and Magritte, and any discussion of what had happened in Nulla. "Is it because of Brinsley?"

"Nay, Dorian. I know you weren't thinking."

There was a long pause.

She swallowed. "Do you dream of Aedon?"

Dorian started at the name. He knew who she was referring to—the *alter* from the Sacred Grove beneath the Mountain.

"I see you know what I'm talking about. I dream of him, too, Dorian. Spartan gave me a vial of old memories, and I see it all. It feels more than just a dream. It feels real."

He shook his head. "So do memories, Sephone. You should know that better than anyone."

"This is different. You must see that."

He listened as she spoke to him of forgotten pools, cryptic prophecies, white ravens, and immortal gardeners who could change day to night. He could see the shadows haunting her as she spoke, the same shadows that stalked him, flitting like wolves beyond the tree line.

"It's naught but fantasy," he said when she finished. "If this *alter* were real, you would have asked him to heal that webbing on your chest."

She hesitated. "We did great wrong, Dorian. We stole what wasn't ours to possess. How could I ask him to heal me?" Her face fell. "But you don't believe me."

"I believe you," he said. "I believe that you are telling the truth. But remember Nulla. Remember Silvertongue. It is easy to be persuaded by something you desperately want to be true."

"Then that's it? You think I've just deluded myself?"

"What else could I think? You've never been to any of these places and have never seen this man in the flesh. All you have is a vial of old memories, given to you by a fatherless acolyte longing for a family. If Spartan knew for sure that the Mountain wasn't empty, he could have produced this Aedon or another of this mysterious Three."

She glanced at him curiously. "And if he had, would you have believed him?"

"I would have considered it." He put out a hand. "The whole world is full of magic, is it not? Remember the Mysterium and their tricks.

This man, if he truly exists, is only a gardener at worst, and an *alter* at best. This is naught but a fantasy to make sense of your reality."

"Maybe." She chewed her lip. "But what is the alternative? Despair? There's nothing down that road I haven't already seen."

"You don't have to despair," he said, taking her hand. "I will find a cure."

She sobered. "Between saving the world and defeating your sister, I don't believe you have the time."

"I'll make time."

"Oh, Dorian. Only you could arm wrestle with Fate himself and still believe it possible to win."

"Don't you?" He intended the question to be playful, but she frowned and changed the subject.

"Thank you for letting me come with you. But there's one thing I still don't understand. Why would you bring Cass along? You still distrust him. Is it the idea of keeping your friends close and your enemies closer?"

"Someone betrayed your whereabouts to Kaesi, Sephone. The list of potential candidates is very short. And Cass has been with us since the beginning."

"I've been inside his mind. I would know if he was a traitor."

Yet she hadn't seen that Draven was an *alter*, albeit a weak one. He chose not to remind her of that. "Didn't you once tell me that your gift is biased where you are concerned?"

Her eyes narrowed. "What are you suggesting, Dorian?"

"Maybe your feelings cloud your judgment on the matter."

Regret blossomed in him, along with an internal groan. He was being unfair. She glared at him and stalked away.

He caught up to her just as the forest path came into view, revealing a small crowd of people who had gathered around a tall man.

Sephone stopped and gasped as Dorian exclaimed.

"Bear!"

He saw them a moment after they glimpsed him, his features filling with tangible relief. A loud bark, and the crowd parted to reveal Jewel beside Bear. The faithful wolf's coat was matted and dirty, and gone was the queenly air that had given her the title of Lady.

But she was alive.

Rushing forward, Dorian fell to his knees and opened his arms as she came to meet him. He was dimly aware that Bear had caught up Sephone in a similar embrace. After he had hugged Jewel, he released the wolf to greet Sephone, while he grasped Bear's hand. Breaking the rules of accepted decorum, he hugged the bodyguard as well. Sephone's arms were still around the wolf.

"I feared the worst," Dorian told him breathlessly. "I've looked for you throughout Lethe, but all I heard of you were whispers."

Bear's clothes, like Jewel's coat, were mussed and crusted with filth, and a long scratch down one cheek extended past his jaw to the edge of his collarbone. He looked absolutely exhausted. "We were attacked. Ambushed by Memosinian soldiers," the large man told him.

Dorian's stomach knotted. Sephone scratched the wolf's ears and straightened. Jewel's eyes were their usual iridescent blue, but they held a familiar warning.

"Bear." Dorian looked around. "Where—"

To his great surprise, the giant's shoulders quivered, and a great tear rolled down his face.

Dorian froze. "Bear, where is Bas?"

If anyone ever doubted that giants could feel the same range of emotions as ordinary men, they had only to look upon Bear as he sat in an armchair in the main room of the large tree house Xia had assigned to our party. Dorian had wrapped him in blankets, and Magritte had placed a mug of hot tea in his hands, but he merely gazed into the liquid as if he wished he could plummet into the steaming depths and never surface again.

I took the seat beside Dorian and Jewel, while Spartan, Regis, and Magritte occupied the other sofa, and Cass remained standing on the opposite side of the room. Bear's crossbow had been placed on the small table near the window, along with the remainder of his gear.

"Take your time," Dorian said, one hand on the man's shoulder and the other arm draped around Jewel, who sat between us. "Only speak when you are ready."

"That's just it, my lord. I don't know if I'll ever be ready." Tears ran down the man's face, striping his dirty cheeks and collecting in his thick beard. He set down the mug. "There's no easy way to say this."

He looked miserably at Dorian. "Bas was the traitor."

Bas?

Magritte gasped; Cass straightened and uttered an exclamation as Dorian caved inwards, as if he were collapsing from within. He covered his face with the hand that had been on Jewel.

Finally, he looked up. "What happened, Bear?"

Bear accepted a handkerchief from Regis and blew his nose noisily.

"In the mountains—the Grennor Mountains—I wanted to wait for you. I could tell that Lady Jewel did, too. I felt in my bones that you had found Sephone, or at least were close. I told Bas that we should delay heading back to Thebe. But he was adamant that we were vulnerable so long as we stayed there. He was persuasive, so I eventually gave in. We wrote you a note and left. Jewel dragged her feet all the way across the moors."

I hugged the wolf and held onto her. Her loyalty was unparalleled.

"But by the time we reached the river, I knew something was up. Bas was different. He barely spoke to me or Jewel. It was as if he'd been replaced by a stranger. One night, he insisted on taking the watch out of turn. I let him, but I kept one eye open, just in case. For Bas's sake, if naught else. It was fortunate that I did."

Bear's eyes went to Jewel. "The lady wolf came awake as she heard them. Eight or nine men appeared from all sides like wolves in the night. They were ordinary men, but heavily armed. Jewel and I fought them, only to realize that Bas wasn't doing any fighting. It was almost like . . . like he knew they would come. And that was when I realized . . ." His voice faltered, and pain filled his eyes. "He was with them."

He gave a shuddering breath as Dorian squeezed his shoulder. "Lady Jewel was magnificent. I've never seen her take on so many enemies at once. Between us, we managed to take them all down. Bas was surprised. He underestimated us." Bear bowed his head, and tears dripped off his face. "He attacked me, and I was furious." He choked on a sob. "I didn't mean to fight back, but he would have killed me."

"So you had to kill him," Dorian said quietly.

I held back a gasp. The room was deathly still.

"I had no choice, my lord."

"I know you didn't." Dorian's hand stayed on Bear's shoulder.

Bear's gaze on Dorian was intent and pleading. "Bas wasn't the traitorous sort. You know him. We dabbled in revolutionary ideas when we were younger, but he would have given his life for both of us a dozen times over. It must have been Silvertongue. He got in his head somehow and convinced Bas to turn."

"Except that Silvertongue's gift doesn't work at such a distance," commented Cass. "How could he keep your brother persuaded in his absence? As soon as he was gone that time in Thebe, the effects of his gift faded."

"Not to mention," Regis added gently, "that you had a *lumen* with you almost the whole time you were traveling across Caldera. If Silvertongue were nearby, Cass's presence would have negated his gift."

Bear slumped and buried his face in his hands.

"Draven would have been persuasive," ventured Dorian. "We don't know what he promised Bas in order to get him to betray us. He may even have threatened him."

"It wasn't just Draven." Bear's head rose. "Maybe in the beginning. But later, it was someone else. Bas once mentioned a hooded man."

Dorian froze. "Kaesi."

Bear looked at him, puzzled. "Nay, he spoke of a man—"

"They are the same. My sister is a shapeshifter."

As Dorian explained, I looked into Jewel's eyes and saw sorrow reflected there.

"We've spoken enough," Dorian said at last, giving Bear a pat on the back. "Eat some food, have a bath, and take your rest. You, too, Jewel. We will revisit things in the morning."

Bear stood slowly. "My lord, I already buried Bas, back at the place where we were ambushed. But I thought . . . that is, if you were willing—"

"Aye." Dorian nodded, understanding him. "We will have a service to remember him, as he was. Tonight, if you're feeling up to it, and if Siaki approves."

"I would appreciate that, my lord." Bear's gaze grew distant. "Aye, as he was."

Cass's eyes were on Bear. "I have one more question. It is weeks since you left the Grennor Mountains. Why is it that you are only arriving here now?"

We all looked askance at him. Was he really questioning Bear's story?

"He was injured," Dorian answered for his bodyguard, lifting sorrowful eyes to Cass's. "He wasn't well enough to travel until recently. Does that satisfy you?"

Cass had the grace to look ashamed. Regis and Magritte escorted Bear to his bedroom, for a nice warm meal and a steaming hot bath.

Jewel nuzzled at Dorian. I realized Spartan hadn't said a word throughout the entire conversation.

Dorian sighed. "At least we know now why Asa Karthick's men kept finding us, town after town." He glanced at Cass. "Forgive me for doubting you."

Cass inclined his head a fraction. "You are forgiven."

"It would also explain," Dorian added, "how Asa Karthick found Sephone in Nyx. Bas was his informant."

"But he must have betrayed the *ignis*," said Cass, taking the vacated seat next to Spartan. "It was your sister who captured Sephone in the end, not Asa."

"Bas might have had a change of heart, toward the end," I suggested. "After all, Kaesi didn't want you dead, Dorian. Exactly the opposite. Maybe that's why he went over to her side."

"You're forgetting he tried to murder his own brother to cover his tracks." Dorian buried his hands in the lady wolf's fur. "And Jewel, too."

"But why?" Cass mused. "He didn't know what you would do. He didn't care to test his brother's loyalties, either."

"It does no good to speculate," said Dorian. He patted Jewel and stood stiffly. "Excuse me. I must speak with Siaki." Jewel followed him out of the room, her tail between her legs. After a minute, Cass left as well.

I sat beside Spartan. "Are you all right?" I studied his pale, drawn features. His blue eyes were dull and lifeless.

"Aye. I will be."

"Are you grieving your father?" I winced. That was a little blunt.

"Of sorts." He shifted uneasily.

"Your brother, Asa," I said, suddenly understanding. "You fear that before the end, you'll have to kill him, too."

"Nay, Sephone." He shook his head. "I will not kill him."

"If you don't, he may kill you."

"Then so be it. My life is in Aedon's hands."

"After everything your brother's done, Aedon wouldn't ask you to spare him."

"Wouldn't he?" He searched my face with unnerving acuity. "I didn't give Asa his life, Sephone. Nor his title. I won't be the one to take it."

"Then you will die."

"Then I will die," he agreed, this time with more color in his face.

"Aren't you afraid?"

"Of the Aeternum? Nay. This is the shadow; that is the true reality. I am not afraid to go home at last. In fact, sometimes I yearn for it."

"The Aeternum?" I had heard this word before from Spartan's lips. It was the world beyond this one—the life beyond the veil. Letheans never spoke of it since their only future was the present, and Memosinians rarely thought of it. "Then you really believe what Aedon says?"

"Aye," he said, looking more like his usual self. A familiar peace radiated from him. "Though I admit that I can be as forgetful as the next person."

"But you never doubt."

"There is sometimes doubt, Sephone," he said. "But the path of doubt, if walked honestly, leads only to greater faith."

I recalled Dorian's words. *This is naught but a fantasy to make sense of your reality . . .*

"You speak of faith. But it's so . . . hard."

His gaze flickered with compassion. "It may be hard to walk the path, to believe. But it is harder to go our own way, as you have discovered. We choose our hardship, do we not?"

But what is the alternative? Despair? There's nothing down that road I haven't already seen . . .

"Aye," I consented reluctantly, for my own attempts to make sense of everything thus far had come to naught. "We do."

"What is required will be provided, Sephone. I promise you that."

Xia's people were busy preparing for war, but she gave her permission for Dorian to host a modest service deep in the woods, away from the rest of the Thebans, who might not take well to the idea of mourning a traitor. As night fell, we trekked there, a small procession of a dozen funeral-goers carrying lanterns. The whole thing reminded me of

Nyx and the snow-blossom festival. But that memory was best left undisturbed.

Dorian and Spartan walked up front with Bear, and together they constituted the only ones who appeared to be truly mourning Bas's passing. Regis and Magritte had not known him well, and Cass had disliked him almost as much as he disliked Dorian. As for me, I remembered my suspicions of the bodyguard and how he had distrusted and feared me from the first. Because I could see into his mind? Or was he afraid that I would guess his true motivations? Had I only imagined that I'd finally earned his respect in the end?

We reached a clearing where dozens of candles had been lit, the amber glow pushing back against the haze of the gray. We had no body to bury, but waxy stubs formed the approximate outline of a coffin in the center of the clearing. Near the head of the glowing coffin, Bas's throwing knives had been thrust into the earth to their hilts; when he saw them, Bear began to weep. Tears streaked Dorian's face, and even Jewel appeared moved. Had the wolf been forced to assist in overcoming the murderously inclined Bas?

My heart bled for Dorian. This, after all, was the slave he had freed. The servant who had once pretended to be Dorian to save his family from harm. Dorian had trusted him with his life, with all our lives. He had not questioned him once. This betrayal would be a hundred times worse than anything Lord Draven had done. For all that Jewel could sense danger, she had never sensed the treachery that rode with us. Perhaps that was the natural limitation of her gift.

A short eulogy was given, the first half by a choked Bear and the second half by Dorian, short but eloquent and heartfelt. This was followed by a prayer to the old gods that Bas's soul would be safe in the hereafter. The Aeternum. Somebody sang a song—a woman I didn't recognize, with dark brown hair. It must have been in Lethean, for the words were unfamiliar.

Finally, the gathering disbanded until only Dorian, Bear, Jewel, Cass, and I were left. Bear was squatting on the ground, his eyes shuttered with pain. Dorian flanked him, Jewel on his other side.

Cass came up beside me. "Come on, Seph. Let's go."

"Just a moment." I stepped forward and placed a tentative hand on Bear's shoulder. "I'm so sorry, Bear. I'll be here for you, as long as you need me."

Still looking at the ground, he mumbled something in reply, and Dorian glanced at me gratefully. "Thank you, Sephone."

I nodded and walked back with Cass to the base of the tree house. He looked at me. "Thinking about the servant or the master?"

I raised my head and glowered at him.

"I'm sorry," he said, and I knew he meant it. "My tongue gets carried away sometimes."

"Why do you always try to provoke me?"

"I only prod at embers that are already alight." He sighed. "I really am sorry, Seph."

"I know." I mirrored his sigh. "And you're right. I am thinking about him. About Dorian. I'm sorry, Cass."

The skin around his mouth tightened, but he nodded. "At least you're honest."

"How can you tell?"

"After all these years, I think my gift has trained me to just know." He shrugged and bid me goodnight.

Bas's betrayal and death were still raw, and Dorian thought too often of Sephone. But fortunately, there were plenty of available distractions. Lethe was marching to war, and soldiers didn't care for such petty matters as love. Dorian spent most of the day in Xia's war councils, planning and strategizing from just before dawn until well after midnight, when he would finally collapse on his bed, snatching a few restless hours of sleep before the whole cycle began again.

Bear had thrown himself into the preparations with zeal. He was to be involved with managing the weaponry. Specifically, the new technology that had arrived from Nephele under heavy guard, closely watched by Lethe's best scientists. Nephele had sent whatever men they could spare, but the city had been heavily damaged before Asa Karthick's retreat. If the outlanders didn't agree to the alliance, the Letheans would be greatly outnumbered when they reached Calliope.

Three days after Xia's first war council, Aleria Vega arrived, summoned by Magritte's gift of long-distance telepathy. The outlanders had agreed to join them, on the condition that their existing lands and borders would be protected and that they would be recompensed from Memosine's treasury for everything they'd lost during Draven's raids.

Xia, with a few terms of her own, happily agreed to the arrangement. Aleria Vega joined their meetings, while Magritte, whose powers had grown, communicated the results of their strategizing to the outlanders' equivalent *alter* across hundreds of miles. Regis was busy mobilizing the Sons of Truth, who had agreed to march with the Letheans—at least for now.

"Are you still coming with us?" Dorian asked Spartan when he glimpsed the boy between meetings, striding down the path that connected Xia's tree house to the one where they were staying.

"Aye, Dorian. I gave my word."

Dorian fell into step beside him. "And if we meet Asa during the fray?"

"I still believe that Asa can be swayed. He will be uneasy after—" Spartan broke off suddenly, flushing.

"After my sister Kaesi killed his father." A growl emanated from Dorian's stomach. He hadn't eaten all day, and it was midafternoon.

Hearing it, Spartan smiled, and the tension dissipated. "Shall we get some lunch?"

"That's a good idea."

They passed a pleasant half hour until Xia summoned Dorian again. Aleria was in attendance this time, as were Regis, Magritte, Bear, and a few others. Dorian wondered if Sephone and Cass had been invited, though he knew the presence of a *lumen* made Xia uneasy.

"The outlanders are ready," Xia told Dorian in her usual brisk tone. "We must march on the morrow. Are you ready, Lord Adamo?"

Dorian paused, considering her question. He was Memosine-born and the former thane of Maera. His father had trained him for ambassadorial duties, wisely concluding that his gifts would make him the perfect candidate to bind the three countries of Caldera together in peace and prosperity. He had advised Dorian to learn how to defend himself and kill, if necessary. But the staff at his belt was no longer a tool of peacetime. It was a weapon of war. Instead of iron tips, it had wicked edges, designed to draw blood.

The attempt to infiltrate Calliope could only go ahead if the new alliance provided a diversion, which meant engaging the forces of Memosine and Asa Karthick's small army of *alters*. Even if they succeeded, many lives would be lost. And what if Siaki Xia fell? Dorian barely knew Algar Spath, the vice-regent of Lethe, or any of the other currently elected thanes and thanesses. It was terrifying to consider what would happen if they lost.

But it was even more frightening to imagine the future if they won.

"Dorian?" Xia looked concerned.

In his mind, he posed the question Xia was really asking. Was he ready to betray his own country? Was he ready to be the traitor his people had painted him to be? Whatever he did now would reflect on his family, on Maera.

There would be no going back.

Unbidden, he thought of Sephone, and his resolve hardened. Kaesi had the Reliquary. And the Reliquary was the only way to save Sephone.

"Aye," he said evenly to Xia. "I am ready."

He tried to memorize the landscape as they travelled, since it was probably the last time he would see this part of the world. After leaving Thebe, they crossed the seam south of Nulla—the soldiers on Memosine's side were easily overwhelmed—and then the river that flowed out of the same city. It was thick with sludge and refuse. Surely, he didn't imagine it, but the water seemed tinged with red. Blood?

The border towns were of no consequence to Lethe—Calliope was their target. But later, after they'd achieved a victory, Xia planned to secure the Memosinian towns, mainly Argus, Iona, and Ceto. Dorian tried not to think about the day they would march on his home city of Maera.

It was now late summer, and autumnal gold was beginning to gild the leaves on the deciduous trees. Though the days were still warm, the nights were crisp, and he was reminded of that first journey to Calliope, which now felt like a lifetime ago. After a short trek through pine forest, they reached the moors. They were beautiful in summer, covered with purple, white, pink, and even red heather. Bracken, moss, crowberry, and cotton grass grew as far as the eye could see. Wildflowers ran rampant over small, gently undulating hills.

Without the thick forest to hinder them, Xia's army picked up speed. All going well, they would attack Calliope within the week, laying siege to Memosine's capital just as the Memosinians had laid siege to Lethe's. The outlanders would come from upstream on a horde of boats, attacking the city from the northeast. Meanwhile, a small force, led by Dorian, would infiltrate the arch-lord's castle and attempt to secure it from within. It was Xia's hope that they could turn many of the *alters* to their side before it was too late. A *lumen*'s gift might break whatever hold Draven and now Kaesi had over them.

Again and again, Dorian pondered Kaesi's reasons for withdrawing her forces. Calliope was situated on an island, with limited supplies and resources. Memosine's larger army would do them no good cooped up within the ancient walls. With more soldiers to feed, the people would starve even more quickly than the citizens of Nephele had. And though Kaesi did not know it yet, the outlanders would come by river, roused by the raids on their lands.

If Kaesi was hoping to draw them out and thus weaken their defenses, she would be sorely disappointed. Many of Lethe's cities were well protected in their remoteness. And while the outlanders rallying against Memosine had not been of her doing since Draven was responsible for that mess, she had inherited the legacy of his choices. Superior numbers or not, she would have to find a way to keep the people of Calliope alive and the outlanders at bay.

You're assuming she even cares for those people, a reasonable voice reminded him.

But Kaesi had been as well schooled in the art of governance as Dorian had. She understood the value of a farmer or butcher or baker—not just the value of a soldier. If she wanted to make Memosine formidable, she would need the Memosinians on her side. Draven had been popular in his time, since his son had carried out the most brutal and unforgiving tasks. But would Kaesi command the same loyalty? Would the woman who'd once spoken so eloquently about uprooting governments be able to establish hers?

Not far from Calliope, they set up their nightly camp for the last time. Lethe's army consisted of a motley assortment of fighters: survivors from the siege of Nephele; men from the border towns who were fearful of Calliope's reach and influence; several hundred lowborn folk who comprised the Sons; even refugees from Orphne and other places who had decided to fight for the chance to return to their lands or to avenge lost loved ones. Few had come from the towns in the no-man's-land. Most of them would remain neutral, as they had for over sixty years.

Nephele's weapons would arm barely a fifth of their assembled forces. And they were mainly useful as protection against *alters,* of which Lethe now had no more than two dozen. The rest carried weapons that might have belonged to the Old Times: crossbows, pikes, staffs, spears, axes, daggers, crude swords, and even farming tools. Many of them carried secrets, like Dorian's staff. But they were still ordinary weapons.

Against Asa Karthick and his colorful fireballs, they would amount to naught.

As the army erected tents, tended horses, and started fires, Siaki Xia led Dorian a short distance away from the others, Jewel trailing them by several paces. The gray pressed closely all around them, fading Lethe's army into near anonymity as night fell, and rendering the last warmth of the day nearly stifling. A hot breeze picked up, more oppressive than refreshing.

Siaki extracted something from beneath her cloak. Two things, rather. She held them up for his inspection. The first was shaped like a bow, minus the string and two-thirds of the usual size; it was made of some curved, sleek wood and had a grip at the halfway point. The second could be likened to the hilt of a sword, though the actual blade was missing.

"I suspect you may not like this, Dorian," Siaki remarked, "but these will keep you alive when you enter the city tomorrow."

Was this . . . a weapons demonstration? Wisely, Jewel remained at a cautious distance.

"Allow me." Sweeping her long hair onto one slender shoulder, Siaki raised the bow-shaped object first, extending it out from her body and shaking it twice as she squeezed the grip. An amber-tinted, crystalline shield—not unlike Spartan's—appeared, perfectly matching Siaki's height and width. The shield was curved like the surface of the bow, which formed the horizontal plane, so that it fit naturally around a body.

Jewel yelped and bounded further away. Apparently even *altered* wolves had their limits when it came to magic.

"It will automatically adjust to your dimensions," Siaki explained, eyeing Dorian's greater height. "That is, it will adjust to the dimensions of any wearer."

He was staring. "Siaki, this technology . . ."

She smiled at his astonishment. "Wait until you see the sword." Gripping the hilt, she swished it back and forth in a figure eight, and an amber-colored blade appeared to match the shield. Even in the gray, with night falling, it shimmered and sparkled.

"Both the blade and the shield were constructed by harnessing *altered* lightning, with some help from the technology of the world-that-was. Our scientists have been working on them for decades, ever since the first *altered* storms appeared." She looked uncomfortable. "This is the part you won't like. They are designed to work on *alters*, though they can function as ordinary weapons if need be."

Dorian took in a breath. He'd had this conversation with Siaki a dozen times over. Nephele had sacrificed Lethe's own *alters* to test these weapons. Siaki didn't like Nephele's methods any more than he did, but she maintained that it was too late to be choosy. If they were to stand a chance against Kaesi and Asa, they would need whatever advantage Nephele could give them.

Though, ironically, if Lethe hadn't sacrificed so many *alters*, Asa's small army of them would not pose as much of a threat now.

"Impressive, aye?" Siaki watched Dorian closely.

He nodded, though he couldn't help but compare the weapons to Spartan's extraordinary gift of summoning light from nothing. Remarkable as they were, they almost seemed like a childish imitation of an adult weapon.

"These are just a sample of the weapons we've brought with us," Siaki informed him. "There are *altered* spears, bows, axes. Your men will have whatever they need. The shields are designed to protect the wearer from the powers of any *alter* who attacks you."

"Will they work in Kaesi's presence?" A shadow crossed Siaki's face, and Dorian understood. "You don't know."

"I am sorry, Dorian. I have armed you as best as I can. But when you enter that castle, providing your sister is within, I have no idea what you will face. My only consolation is that Kaesi is more interested in recruiting you than killing you."

"And you're not afraid that I will join her?"

She gave him a rare smile. "I've never once doubted you."

That night, the men were restless, as were the few women who'd accompanied them. Rumors swept like wildfire through the camp of the outlanders and their savage methods of warfare, of the dreadful things the Memosinians had done on their way to Nephele, and of Nephele's deadly weapons that would help Lethe exact revenge. Even so, victory was far from assured. More than once, Dorian had heard Kaesi described as the demon shapeshifter queen. Grief and regret churned in him for his lost sister.

The little sister whose bloody machinations could well bring their world to its knees.

He hadn't seen Sephone for two days. He had been riding near the front with Xia, Regis, Aleria, Bear, and the other leaders, but that hadn't included Sephone, Cass, or Spartan. Siaki was still hesitant to trust the younger son of the former king, not the least because his gift easily rivaled Lethe's new weapons. Dorian had finally convinced Siaki that Sephone's presence on their secret mission would be more of a liability than an asset, since Kaesi wanted her so badly. Siaki had promised to assign Sephone bodyguards when the battle began in earnest, and after her failure in Nyx, Dorian knew she would hold to her word this time.

Even so, he had instructed Jewel and Bear to remain with Sephone, knowing they would give their very lives for her. It pained him to lose Jewel's presence on what felt like the loneliest night of his life thus far, but Sephone would need her more than he did.

A few hours after Siaki's demonstration, Dorian returned to his tent, stashing her weapons beneath his bedroll. He had removed his mantle and was bending to take off his boots when someone cleared their throat outside.

"My lord, I come from Lady Xia." It was one of Siaki's guards.

He straightened. "What is the message?" he called through the canvas.

"She requests your presence in her tent."

"I'll be there shortly."

Leaving behind his mantle, since it was too warm for it anyway, he made his way through the camp to Siaki's tent. It wasn't far, situated on a small outcrop that looked out over the entire army. Eyes watched him as he passed, and he registered the whispers.

Lady Xia's closest advisor, the kindest ones said. *The former thane of Maera.*

Others were not so generous.

The shapeshifter's older brother.

The Memosinian traitor.

He stiffened his spine, not looking to the left or the right. He had been called far worse during his ambassadorial days.

Two guards stood to attention outside Siaki's tent, but inside, the lady of Thebe was alone. She looked as queenly as Kaesi, though her hair had been bound into a tight bun with only a silver circlet to adorn her head, and she was wearing men's clothes instead of her usual modest dresses.

"Ah, Dorian," she said, looking up at him from where she leaned over a table scattered with parchment, weapons, and several lanterns. "Good, you're here."

"You wanted to see me?"

"Aye." She came around the table, her gaze briefly flicking to the chain around his throat with its two rings, then to the doorway where the canvas flaps had been folded back. "I'm sorry to rouse you; I know it's late. But this is a private matter. I don't wish the Council to know what we're about to discuss."

He waited, knowing she would get straight to the point.

"I meant what I said earlier today. The truth is that there are few people in this world that I can really trust, and you are one of them, Dorian."

He inclined his head. "I take that as a great compliment."

"But," Siaki went on, "I cannot say the same for the rest of the Council. We may all march on Calliope tomorrow together as Letheans, outlanders, and resistance fighters, but I am not so naïve as to believe that we all desire the same outcomes. Should we win this fight, Calliope and, soon after, Memosine will be ours. But everyone will want their piece, their cut, and maybe even their own king to lead it."

She sighed. "We have inherited many of the problems of the world-that-was, my old friend. And many of the flaws of our ancestors. We are restless, hot-headed, and arrogant, though we imagine ourselves to be precisely the opposite." She shook her head. "Aleria tells me that thousands of her people will come. And though this bodes well for our victory tomorrow, I fear what will happen in the aftermath. Lethe will need to be strong, Dorian. And so will Memosine."

She straightened and looked at him squarely. "We have been friends for over a decade. I would not change that for the world, so know that what I suggest now is only in consideration of the interests we both serve."

It wasn't like Siaki to ramble. "What exactly are you suggesting?"

"An alliance"—she watched him carefully—"not based on love, but mutual admiration. If we were to wed, my old friend, it would strengthen our position as leaders of this new era and strengthen the bonds between Memosine and Lethe. The Letheans would trust you more than they do at present, and the Memosinians would respect you and any claim you asserted to their throne."

Dorian stared. Siaki was proposing marriage? "You're forgetting that Memosine has branded me a traitor."

"Draven branded you a traitor, along with the Eight," she corrected. "And they are no more. Their members are either missing or dead. When your sister is removed from power, there will be another opportunity to step into that void and restore peace and order to Memosine. And with it, peace to the rest of Caldera."

He retreated a step, trying to comprehend everything she was saying, what she was offering. He watched the light of the lanterns flicker eerily on the walls of the tent, banishing the night outside while simultaneously conjuring shadows of their own. "I told you once before, Siaki. I have no interest in Memosine's throne. The kingship ought to be dissolved, not re-established."

Was Siaki being completely truthful? Or was she tempted by the opportunity to be queen, rather than a mere thaness?

She took a step toward him. "You were once the most respected man in Caldera, Dorian. With my help and my support, you will be so again. With your character, your fortitude, and your gifts, you would make the very best of kings. You would lead us into a better age."

He couldn't tell her that he was sorely tempted by the thought, just as he had been back in Nulla. *Anyone can be tempted,* a small voice told him. *It's how you respond to it that counts.*

He eyed Siaki. "Then this isn't just about defending Lethe. You want Memosine, too."

"So black-and-white, Dorian," she chided. "The situation is more complicated than that. If we do not claim Memosine, the outlanders will."

"Aleria gave her word that they wouldn't."

"And you believe her?"

Dorian recalled the sharp, topaz eyes belonging to both the eagle and the *altered* woman. "I trust her."

She snorted disbelievingly.

A gust shook the tent, which trembled on its moorings but held firm. The parchments stirred in the breeze, while the lanterns flickered.

It would be easy, so easy, to claim the throne. To attempt to unify their world. But for one thing. "I'm sorry," he said after a lengthy pause. "We cannot be wed, Siaki. Not even for Caldera's sake."

"And why not?" She studied him critically. "It's the girl, isn't it? She's the one you wish to marry."

"Aye . . . and nay."

Her eyes widened. "You can't be planning what I think you're planning." She came closer until she was peering up into his face. "You would sacrifice yourself for her?"

Siaki was his oldest friend—his closest ally. It was time to be honest with her. "Even if there was no poison and no Persephone Winter, I couldn't take the throne. It would only corrupt me, as it has corrupted my sister and a thousand kings and queens before her. But since you ask, aye, I have plans for the Reliquary. Since I cannot find a *healer* for Sephone, there is only one other way. The moment we have the Reliquary and Kaesi is defeated, I will transfer my remaining years to her."

"And she knows about this?"

Dorian shook his head. "She knows naught."

"She will never agree to it."

"She doesn't have to." Cass would uphold his end of the deal. Dorian's sacrifice, after all, would give him what he wanted most.

Siaki shook her head. "I would forbid it, except that I know your stubbornness, my old friend. You would only find a way to disobey me again."

Dorian cringed inside, remembering how he'd deceived her regarding Sephone's whereabouts, though Xia had forgiven him for his actions. "I am sorry." He tried to smile. "You would have made a fine queen. And a very fine wife."

He meant every word—Siaki Xia was an admirable woman. Clever, quick-witted, and brave. Any man would be fortunate to marry her.

She tilted her face and sniffed. "There's no need to pander to my feelings, Dorian. I don't love you, and you don't love me." Her eyes met his. "But I will not promise not to try and persuade you otherwise on the matter of Sephone Winter. We will need you in the days ahead. Caldera will need you."

Siaki's manner was almost warm, and his smile became more genuine. "I have already made up my mind."

"Has that ever stopped me before?" She waved her hand in dismissal. "Get some sleep. You will need it."

He bowed to her and was almost to the door when she spoke again. "Dorian?"

"Aye, my lady?"

Her lips curved. "I always believed you would never find a woman to equal Lida Ashwood. But I am happy, just this once, to have been proved wrong. If there is a future where you both live, and you are able to marry the girl, I will do everything in my power to bring it about."

"Thank you," he said as sincerely as he could, and left.

On the moorlands of Memosine, smoke rose from campfires in lazy spirals, with the mingled scents of horses, sweat, and aging stews. Though it was far from pleasant, he inhaled lungful after lungful, hoping his nightmares would dissipate more quickly.

He thought he had slept for hours, but not everyone had bedded down yet, and a few shadowy figures were moving about the camp. It must still be before midnight.

Catching the scent of smoke, he looked up to see the gray horizon glowing orange. He knew how the moorlands could burn—there had been plenty of fires to observe over the previous few days as they travelled. But hopefully this summer blaze wouldn't come much closer. Rain fell periodically, extinguishing the fires as quickly as they began.

Coming to the edge of camp, he was surprised to see a slight figure standing there, watching the glowing sky.

Jewel sensed his presence first, and Sephone turned, her hand reaching instinctively for the knife at her thigh.

"Dorian." His name was flat on her lips.

Jewel bounded happily to his side, making up for Sephone's reticence. He scratched the wolf's ears and chest, avoiding the long scar, then glanced at Sephone. "Can't sleep?"

She shook her head. "I see you can't, either."

Dorian shrugged. "Bad dreams."

At his quiet command, Jewel returned to Sephone's side. The smoke thickened, trapped beneath the gray. He thought of the night at the bridge, the night he'd first seen the iridescence in her hair beneath a sky of stars. It wasn't iridescent anymore—it was more black than white—but she was still beautiful to him. He struggled with himself, desperately wanting to be as honest with her as he had been with Siaki, to explain why he had pushed her away.

"Sephone," he began. He had to say something—this might be the last conversation they ever had, alone or otherwise.

She gazed steadily out onto the moors as if she hadn't heard. "The men say that you will join with Lady Xia."

His carefully constructed explanation crumbled to ash.

The moment I said it, I regretted it. Better to continue believing a lie than to uncover the truth.

By the stricken look on Dorian's face, the rumor circulating among the men—that Lord Adamo had met alone with Lady Xia earlier in the evening, and that there would be an alliance between them—was indeed true.

"What did you hear?" he asked after a moment.

"That you and the lady of Thebe are to be married, forging a permanent bond between your countries."

"It is false," he said firmly. "There is no alliance. At least, not of that nature."

I didn't need Cass's gift to know that he was lying. If they weren't yet engaged, they very soon would be. Dorian had admitted to being tempted by the prospect of the throne. And Siaki Xia was ruthless and clever. Together, they would make a formidable combination.

The mere thought of it tore shreds from my heart.

I could no longer see the boy from the ice when I looked at him. That boy had grown into a man who valued political ambition and power above all else. His future lay with the influential and beautiful Xia, not with a dying slave from Lethe.

The smoke had found its way into my lungs. I coughed violently, trying to expel it, but my lungs squeezed tighter, pain shooting through my chest. Jewel whined, pawing the ground.

"Persephone?" Dorian turned me to face him. "I'll get water." He sprinted away and returned seconds later with a flask.

Still coughing, I sank to the ground, dimly aware of the musky scent of heather and the loamy earth beneath. Dorian knelt beside me. With one ungloved hand, he supported the base of my head, while with the other, he held the flask to my lips. The water was lukewarm, and somewhat marshy to taste, but it eased the strangling feeling in my lungs. Wrapping my arms around my ribs, I leaned forward, the pendant around my neck nearly touching the ground.

"When did the cough return?" Dorian asked, a deep line between his brows.

"A few days ago."

"Why didn't you tell me?"

I met his gaze reproachfully. "You weren't easily found."

His lips compressed. "I had my reasons." His face shuttered. Whatever he had been going to say earlier, he wouldn't say it now.

I coughed again, and my heart beat erratically at the hollow rattle—like I'd heard from Cutter's chest toward the end. I tried to stand, but my knees gave way, and I almost fell.

Dorian kept me upright. "Where's your tent?"

I tried to push him away. "I don't need your help."

"I think you do." Bending, he slipped one arm beneath my knees and another under my back and lifted me easily. "You'll have to give directions."

"Dorian—"

"Don't tell me to put you down. If I do, you'll only collapse. Now start directing, or I'll stop and ask someone."

If it had been anyone else, I would have laughed at the ludicrousness of the situation. If one of the men saw us now, serious doubts would be raised about the authenticity of Lord Adamo's engagement to Lady Xia. Or maybe they'd just think I'd become his mistress. After all, in the eyes of Caldera, I still belonged to him. It wouldn't be the first time a master had taken advantage of his slave.

Dorian set off in the direction I now indicated, Jewel following behind. Fortunately my tent wasn't far, and in no time, he was setting me on my feet again. He whistled softly to Jewel, and the wolf went obediently to my side. I knew I wasn't imagining the forlorn expression in her sapphire eyes.

She would rather be with him.

"Thank you," I said as my palms grew clammy. "For carrying me, and for Jewel."

"She belongs with you."

I frowned. What was he talking about? The loan was only for a few nights or weeks, surely. Until I—

Dorian lifted a hand toward my cheek. At the last moment, he pulled back.

"Soon," he said, "soon you will be free."

I frowned. Perhaps death was a kind of freedom to him—I had certainly seen his hunger for it at times. But why would he remind me? The poison was advancing more each day. My hair was streaked with black. In a few months, maybe less, I would be dead.

He bent his head. "Sephone—"

"Goodnight, Dorian."

He stepped back, and I told myself I didn't miss his warmth—the courage his presence always brought me.

"Goodnight, then."

And then he was gone, leaving me standing with Jewel in the smoky dark.

The next morning, I rose early, only to discover from Bear that Dorian and his party had departed well before dawn. Lady Xia's forces were mobilizing, the first waves now marching the remaining distance to Calliope, where they would cut off the city and mount an assault on the main entryway, if Kaesi hadn't blocked it off already. The attack, combined with the outlanders' arrival from the river, would keep the city distracted while Dorian's band did everything in their power to end the battle before it began. Magritte would remain with Lady Xia, funneling intelligence to the outlanders' *alter*.

Though I had bid farewell to Aleria, Regis, and Spartan the night before, as well as Cass and Dorian, those goodbyes had been unfinished.

Until now, I hadn't allowed myself to consider that I might never see them again. The Lethean weapons might not work against Kaesi or Asa or Zaire. Kaesi may have different plans for her brother.

Even now, they might be riding to their doom.

Though I'd argued against it, a small contingent of men remained behind to guard me, on Lady Xia's—and, I suspected, Dorian's—orders. I didn't know their names, but one was an *altered* Lethean woman with silvered hair, like Cutter would have had if he hadn't shaved his head; another was a member of the Sons, wearing a long beard and a determined expression; and two more were from Xia's personal staff, both armed with Lethean weapons. Together with Bear and Jewel, that made six guards to watch a woman who was already dying.

Six warriors who could hardly be spared.

Xia had ordered us to remain at the rear of the army, where it was safest. I could tell that Bear resented the command, though it wasn't aimed at me.

"You're an *alter*," he had rumbled yesterday when the order had come. "More powerful than a dozen of the others put together. She shouldn't coddle you so. Nor should Lord Adamo. He, at least, knows better."

His confidence in me had bolstered my spirits . . . and set me to wondering. I had promised Dorian to remain behind, but what if I could still assist? There would be hundreds or even thousands of injured once the battle began in earnest, men and women in need of pain relief and oblivion. Could my gift help them, as I'd once helped Bear?

A minute later, my enthusiasm faded. My gift was unpredictable and unreliable. What if I tried to help, only to accidentally mind-wipe or even kill someone instead? Without the Reliquary, I doubted I could focus my powers enough to maintain control. Even *with* the Reliquary, it would be difficult. The poison working through my body made it nearly impossible to access my gift as I once had.

Discouraged, I focused on helping the others pack up camp. Jewel appeared as lost as I was, pivoting on the spot in a small circle, her sapphire gaze constantly probing the soupy gray.

The tents around us were dissembled in no time at all. Supplies were loaded onto pack horses, while horses for riding were saddled, their girths tightened and stirrups adjusted. The last of Xia's army had mounted up and were receding into the gray. Even now, Dorian and his band might be scaling the walls of Calliope—

"Lady Nightingale," said Bear with a courteous bow. "We are ready to leave. Lady Xia outlined a path we might follow through the forest, to watch the battle from a safe distance." The twist of his lips as he spoke the word *safe* revealed exactly what he thought of that plan.

"Aye, let's go."

Bear helped me into my saddle, and I flicked my braid over my shoulder and reached for the reins. At least the mare was placid and wouldn't be easily spooked. Jewel appeared beside us, still looking morose. I hoped she wasn't ill, as she had been in Idaea. I'd been careful not to overfeed the wolf, but she was prone to sneaking second helpings when I wasn't looking.

My guards fanned out, the silver-haired *alter*—who I'd learned could manipulate moisture—in front, together with one of the Lethean men with his amber-tinted shield and long spear. Bear and Jewel took up positions either side of me, with Regis's man and the other Lethean guard behind. Five horses snorted and stomped the ground restlessly.

We moved out. At this sedate pace, Calliope was only a few hours' ride away. Leaving behind the moorland, we plunged directly into forest, taking the route Bear had mentioned, which would follow the army until the last part, when we would detour slightly south, away from the fray.

It was midmorning when we reached the chosen place, a peaceful little cove where the waters of the River Memosine lapped gently against a narrow stretch of sand. The gray, along with a densely forested rocky outcrop, blocked any chance of seeing what was happening further north. The air was thick with smoke. From the moorland fires? Or from the battle for Calliope? I wished I'd asked Magritte to send me updates as well. Not that she would have the time.

I dismounted and looked around. The ground was already trampled with hoofprints, indicating that Lady Xia's men had scoured the area before we arrived. She had been impressively thorough. Other than Thebe, there could not be a safer place for me to wait.

I pointed at the rocky outcrop. "We might see better from there what's going on."

"Doubtful with this gray," said Bear, "but it's worth a look." He indicated for the others to secure the horses and follow.

Jewel edged closer to me as we walked. The temperature had plummeted, and the breeze that wended through the trees felt almost wintry. No birds sang, and though the current was swift, even the surface of the river seemed as smooth as glass. It was almost as if I was back in Aedon's garden, waiting for something to happen.

Waiting for the world to wake up.

I reached the top of the little cliff, slightly winded. Jewel's ears were flat against her head as she surveyed the area, but she didn't growl. Bear appeared uneasy, his fingers ready on his crossbow. The silver-haired *alter* muffled a cough.

I told myself to relax. Whatever danger was about, Jewel would sense it long before it arrived. And whatever danger we faced, it would be nothing compared to what awaited the others in Calliope.

Peering through the gloom, I could see naught of the city or anything beyond a dozen or so yards ahead. There was an almost sulfurous tinge to the density, giving the vague impression of a rotting marshland.

"I can't see a thing," I concluded, reluctantly turning to face the others.

"Are you sure?" came a voice from further down the rise, and a figure emerged from the gray. "Look again."

Asa Karthick strode out of the forest, a beautiful, raven-haired woman at his side. It was the same woman who had once tried to seduce Cass—Zaire. Asa wasn't wearing gloves, but he hadn't yet summoned one of his fireballs.

Where had he come from?

The hackles on Jewel's spine rose, and she growled, planting herself in front of me. Bear did the same, raising his crossbow. The other members of my guard closed ranks between us and the approaching *alters,* the silver-haired woman removing the glove from her right hand.

"Nay," I told them, "let me face them."

They all ignored me.

Asa and Zaire halted, barely a few paces away.

"They don't answer to you, Miss Winter," remarked Asa. "Or haven't you worked that out already?"

He clapped his hands together, and a violet-colored sphere appeared. Almost casually, he tossed it over his shoulder. The trees behind him burst into flame. Zaire's lovely form dissolved, and an enormous beast mushroomed in its place, black poison dripping from her fangs onto the grass. I shuddered, remembering the slashes on Dorian's chest and the feverish heat of his skin. A twinge of pain in my ankle reminded me of another night, months ago now, that I had faced such deadly weaponry.

I dragged off my gloves just as Zaire pounced at the first man, the one with the beard. He yelled and stabbed out with his blade, but Zaire was preternaturally fast, knocking him onto his back and slashing once with her deadly claws. The man went still. The Lethean guards moved into position, locking their shields together and grabbing their spears, while the silver-haired *alter* reached behind her to the river. A current of water rose upward in a spiral and barreled toward Asa, who had summoned a sphere the color of hot coals.

Bear and Jewel lunged forward just as a cloud of steam obscured the fighters. Blinded, I stepped back, trying to swat away the smoke with my hands. I could do naught unless I got close to Asa. But where was he? I searched the cloud, desperately looking . . .

Suddenly, it cleared. The silver-haired *alter* lay on her back, a crossbow bolt in her chest. One of the Lethean guards was crumpled on the ground, his face a mess of blood and ragged flesh, while the other was pinned beneath Zaire's claws. The Lethean weapons lay nearby, abandoned and useless.

With rising dread, I stared at the *alter.* A crossbow bolt? But that would mean—

I reared back. Bear had dropped the crossbow and was advancing toward me, holding up his gloved hands in a placating gesture.

"Steady now, my lady," he soothed. "We mean you no harm."

We? Bear was with Asa and Zaire?

"*You* were the traitor," I spluttered, suddenly understanding. "You were the one who betrayed Bas."

His face was impassive, with none of the easy smiles and camaraderie I'd come to expect from him. No clever verses or kind words.

"I didn't have a choice. If Bas had kept his nose out of my business, he would still be alive."

"You killed your own brother. Your *twin*."

Hollow eyes met mine. "I did what I had to."

I was nearing the edge of the cliff, and still he approached, Asa behind with Zaire. In a few seconds, I would run out of land.

A white shape streaked past Bear. I let out a breath. Jewel. The wolf spun and faced Bear, her hackles raised. How had she not sensed Asa and Zaire's approach—and Bear's treachery?

But then Jewel turned, her sapphire eyes brightening as they focused on me. I watched with horror as her body dissolved, shortening and then lengthening, growing upward. Fur became creamy white skin; the glossy mane grew longer until it was spilling over slender shoulders; the teeth became smaller and less sharp, although two canines either side of the front incisors retained a sharp point.

Jewel was human.

The glittering sapphire eyes remained as they were, while a dress of the same color cascaded down around elegantly booted ankles. Low-necked and one-shouldered, the dress exposed the rise of a thickly knotted scar which slanted diagonally across her chest, paralleling the single strap and eventually stopping near her right collarbone. It was far more prominent against her skin than it had been against white fur.

I stared into the foreign face, which was strangely familiar. The only difference was the eyes, which had been deep brown before, like Dorian's. Now, they were shimmering, iridescent blue.

Blue like Jewel's.

Kaesi smiled. "Are you not pleased to see me again, Miss Winter?"

"What have you done with Lady Jewel?" This couldn't be Jewel. This was just Kaesi borrowing the wolf's form.

"Lady Jewel?" Kaesi uttered an abrupt laugh. "I assure you, that isn't the name I would have chosen for myself. My brother chose it for me the day I appeared to him in this form."

Then it was true? There was never any lady wolf?

How else did she know where you were going, that morning in Nyx?

My heart beat an impossibly fast rhythm against my ribs. I was trapped. Kaesi was Jewel. Or rather, Jewel was Kaesi.

"Impossible," I breathed, still refusing to believe what my eyes were telling me.

She chuckled deeply. Behind her, Bear and Asa waited side by side; Zaire had returned to her human form. This close, I could see the ragged slash across Zaire's eye—Aleria's earlier handiwork. Had it cost the *alter* her sight? It certainly hadn't cost Zaire her beauty.

My guards were all dead. Beyond their prone bodies, the forest burned with purple vengeance, blocking off an escape that way, even if I could get past them.

"Did no one teach you the nature of the gifts, Miss Winter?"

Aye, they had. I knew that gifts almost always came in pairs. Sometimes, even in threes. Except for mine, of course.

I already knew Kaesi was a shapeshifter. But *this* shape . . . I had never once considered . . .

The edge of the cliff crumbled a little beneath my heels. A hasty glance over my shoulder revealed a drop far deeper than I had imagined, and a cluster of wickedly sharp rocks below. If I jumped, there was a good chance I might not survive.

Three *alters* and a giant stood between me and a rapidly spreading forest fire. The only thing I could think of was to try and buy more time.

I looked past Kaesi to Bear. "Why did you do it?"

He glanced briefly at Kaesi. "I owed a debt," he said, but didn't elaborate any further.

"You knew all along who she was."

He was silent.

"And you killed Bas because he discovered your treachery."

A shadow passed across Bear's face. "He saw her change from wolf to human. I couldn't let him live with that knowledge."

"Then you made it up. The ambush, your injuries, all of it." My eyes went back to Kaesi. "This whole time, you've been not just following us, but actually *with* us."

The corners of her lips winged upward. "I would explain everything, of course, but we're rather time poor at present." She glanced pointedly at the blazing trees.

I edged as far back as I could without plummeting over the cliff.

Kaesi's smile faded. "I don't wish to kill you, Miss Winter. At least, not yet."

"I will never join you."

"Oh, I don't require a pledge of fealty from you. Not from a slave." She regarded me as if I were no more significant than a smear on the bottom of her boot. "But before you jump, you might think of your friends. My brother and the rest."

My throat tightened. She was Jewel. She had been at Dorian's side for dozens of war councils. She would know everything, including the Letheans' alliance with the outlanders. The operation of the Lethean weapons. Their every weakness.

The intimate details of Dorian's plan to infiltrate the arch-lord's castle.

She extended a pale, ringless hand in my direction. "Come, Miss Winter, and I will take you to your friends. I wouldn't try your luck with the rocks. It's a grisly way to die."

When I didn't move, she *tut-tutted* under her breath and called out to Bear. "Bring her." To me, she added, "Don't bother trying your gift on him. With a mere thought, I can suppress it."

She drew back. Bear approached, cornering me at the cliff edge.

"Don't do this, Bear," I begged him. "This isn't the man I know you to be."

Once again, he said naught.

Kaesi was right. Even though my hands were bare, I couldn't feel my power. I fumbled for my knife in the sheath strapped to my thigh. I had stabbed Brinsley. Could I stab Bear, a man I had considered to be a friend?

A man who killed his own twin.

I drew the knife, brandishing it. "Stay away. I don't want to use this."

Bear shook his head at me. "That blade will do naught against me, Lady Nightingale."

But I couldn't jump.

Bear seemed to guess my decision. He darted forward, striking at the arm that held the knife. The blade went sailing over the cliff. He grabbed me around the middle and lifted. I struggled violently, clawing at his eyes, his hair—whatever I could touch. He grunted and shifted me, trying to catch my flailing wrists. I twisted my body, attempting to dislodge his hold on me. Frantically, I reached for my gift. Naught was there.

I recalled Nulla—Bear had been one of the three to rescue me. Had he been in Kaesi's service, even then? Sharing bread with the very lord he had decided to betray? The fury that burned through me at that thought brought fresh energy to my limbs.

Even the smallest animal could harry a bear.

I kicked out at Bear's stomach, and my fingernails raked his face. He bellowed. Temporarily blinded, he stumbled, holding me in one large arm while he fought to regain his balance with the other. Rocks scuttled over the side of the cliff.

"Watch out!" Kaesi shouted. "Bring her back here!"

But Bear had strayed much too close to the cliff. His foot found empty air instead of packed earth. His free arm pinwheeled, but instead of dropping me, he clutched me tighter. With a rumbling scream, he tumbled over the cliff, taking me with him.

29

DORIAN

They were making good time, but it wasn't nearly good enough.

It had been light for many hours, and they were only just now scaling the rocky cliff at the rear of the island. It had taken more time than expected to get through the forest unseen with dozens of Memosinian soldiers patrolling the shore, then secure a boat and row to the island undetected. By that time, they had lost the cover of darkness.

The city of Calliope was situated on a rugged, mountainous island lodged in the very middle of the River Memosine. The arch-lord's castle had been built on the uppermost peak, surrounded by a vast stone wall for three-quarters of its girth. The remaining quarter on the windward side of the island was protected by a steep cliff. The city was mostly situated on the leeward side of the island, the cliff giving the impression of a stiffened spine holding the island upright and protecting it from the mouth of the river to the northeast.

A second wall, even taller and thicker than the first, had been built at the lowest point of the island, though it didn't wrap around the cliff. The Memosinians must have concluded that no one would ever be mad enough to attempt to climb it.

And no one was . . . except for them.

Dorian and his party had rowed around the island until they'd reached the sharp rocks poking up out of the frothing water. It was an effort just to keep the boat steady; every wave seemed determined to sweep them onto the rocks. But one of Regis's men, a Memosinian fellow called Tannis, knew the island currents well, and together, he and Cass had maneuvered the boat safely through. They dropped anchor at the base of an enormous cliff. They would need to swim a few yards until they reached a narrow ledge, and from there, they could climb upward.

Dorian eyed the vast stretches of nearly sheer rock. There were few handholds, and if one of their group fell, there was practically zero chance of survival. The memory of another cliff, another rockfall, hovered in his mind.

Cass, sitting across from him in the boat, guessed his thoughts. "No shield to catch us this time if we fall." He looked deliberately at Spartan. "The monk will need both hands on the rock."

The acolyte said naught in reply. Dorian remained silent as well, not wishing to summon the green ribbons of Cass's truth gift. It was always uncomfortable when the *lumen* was completely sober.

Light was beginning to gild the horizon to the east—timely for their ascent, since they couldn't climb in the dark, but it would make it easier for them to be seen. Xia's army would have moved out by now and would soon be approaching the shore. The outlanders would be here any moment, and hopefully, that would keep Kaesi's army distracted. As far as Dorian knew, none of her *alters* had wings. They wouldn't see the invaders coming.

One by one, they set about the monumental task of scaling the cliff. They needed to travel as light as possible, and fortunately, Dorian's staff and Xia's weapons weighed very little. Regis and Cass had their blades and their own amber shields, while Spartan had refused the offer of weapons. Aleria couldn't carry weapons in her eagle form, but her claws were deadly enough. Her wingspan was also larger than usual, since Dorian had learned that the *alter* could change sizes at will.

Not for the first time, Aleria's gift came in handy. As the day had brightened by approximations and they battled with the boat, she had assumed her eagle form and caught the updrafts, inspecting the cliff for possible hand and footholds. By the time the rest of them reached the ledge, wet and shivering, she had descended again, transformed back, and pointed out the best path to traverse the cliff. Not the quickest, but the easiest and safest.

Seven of them now occupied the ledge: Dorian, Cass, Spartan,

Regis, Aleria, Tannis, and a Lethean *alter* named Corsi, who was apparently good with unlocking doors. Dorian had wanted to bring more, but greater numbers would only attract attention, and as it was, they had only just escaped detection. Jewel's sense of danger would have been a welcome addition, but even a wolf could not scale the cliff that now loomed before them, full of shadows and crumbling, slick stone. Besides, she and Bear would keep Sephone safe.

As they wrung out their clothes, Dorian heard Magritte's voice in his head. *We have reached the bridge, Lord Adamo. It has been heavily fortified, but we will break through.*

Dorian looked at Regis inquiringly, and he nodded. "I heard the message."

"I admire your wife's optimism," Dorian told him.

"She's a brave woman." Despite the words, Dorian could see the fear in Regis's eyes. Magritte would remain close to Xia, but Kaesi was still out there. Would she spare a woman? An expectant mother? Dorian had no sense at all of the sister who had once been his closest friend.

At Regis's mention of bravery, Dorian reached for his *calor* gift. Even Cass seemed to appreciate the bolstering of his courage. Tannis and Corsi, who were unused to the gift, straightened considerably, their gazes hardening with determination. Corsi's skin—which was the faintest iridescent green—regained some of the color it had lost when they first beheld the cliff face.

Aleria assumed eagle form again, and she soared effortlessly into the sky. Dorian felt a prick of envy. With such a gift, she would never be afraid of falling. Cass watched her fly, and Dorian wondered if he was thinking the same. Then the *lumen* shook his head and started climbing.

Gritting his teeth, Dorian followed suit. His cold muscles gradually warmed with the exertion, though a chill breeze had arisen, and his fingers felt like chips of ice against the cool stone. He found himself wishing for his gloves.

Hours seemed to scrape past while they climbed—Cass, then Dorian, then the others. Dorian could see that Spartan was doing well, as were the other two men, but Regis was struggling, having grown up in Nulla, where hills were in short supply, let alone mountains. Cass and

Dorian called down instructions where they could, though the wind was always eager to snatch them away. Time and time again, Dorian drew on his gift.

Finally, they neared the top, or at least the highest part they could reach. The section of cliff supporting the arch-lord's castle was too steep to climb. They would need to skirt around it until they reached the base of the wall which protected the keep. Once they were over that, they would have a clear shot to the castle.

The more nimble Cass had climbed far more quickly than Dorian and was waiting for him on a rocky ledge, his breath once again smooth and even. As Dorian neared the ledge, the *lumen* shot him a grin.

"It would be so easy, you know," he mused, "to just push you off."

"You're forgetting our deal."

"I haven't forgotten." Cass extended a sun-browned hand—after a brief hesitation, Dorian took it and was hauled over the ledge. Dorian's empath gift registered Cass's fear, his simmering anger.

Dorian hunched over, trying to catch his breath. "Is that the only reason you didn't push me?"

Cass barked a laugh. "If I wanted to kill you, Thane, I would have done it months ago. But I'm not a killer."

"I know." Green light danced in the wake of Dorian's admission.

Twenty minutes later, they were all gathered on the ledge. Regis looked like he was going to be ill. Dorian let them catch their breath before telling them the next steps of the plan. "Aleria will scout ahead to see what's happening in the city. The rest of us will—"

He broke off as Aleria herself alighted on the far end of the ledge. When she was a woman again, she came to them. Corsi and Tannis looked vaguely unsettled by the transformation, but it was the stricken expression on Aleria's face which captured Dorian's attention.

"What did you see?"

Her topaz eyes were clouded. "I don't see how it is possible, Dorian—"

"What did you see?" he repeated, more firmly.

"Sephone. She's here in the city."

Dorian stared at her as Cass pressed forward. "What do you mean, she's here?"

"I saw her, just below us in the street. A man was carrying her with half a dozen more guards around her. She looked to be unconscious. They were heading to the great library."

Unconscious? The library? Comprehension dawned, banishing the fear. "Kaesi. She's a shapeshifter, remember? It must be her, pretending to be Sephone. They're trying to lure us into a trap."

"Are you willing to take that chance?" Cass challenged. "What if it really is her?"

Not for the first time, Dorian wished he could reply to Magritte. She would be able to give him Sephone's whereabouts almost immediately. He turned to Aleria. "Did you see Kaesi?"

She shook her head.

"Asa? Zaire?"

"Nay, but the gray is thick, and I couldn't risk getting too close. They could well be down there."

"Sephone was well guarded," put in Regis. "Lady Jewel was with her and Bear and several others. How could your sister and the others have captured her without first getting past Lady Xia's army?" He looked around at them. "As dear to us as Sephone is, we can't risk the mission on the off chance that she has been captured. She wouldn't want us to, and besides, the fate of Caldera depends on us."

Just as he said it, there was a clamor from the northeast. Dozens of hulking shapes glided out of the fog. Even at this distance, Dorian could see the bright sails of gold, deepest blue, and emerald green. Cheers and shouts skimmed across the water, distorted by the wind. Aleria stood a little straighter.

"The outlanders have arrived," breathed Tannis.

Regis caught Dorian's gaze. "Dorian, you mustn't—"

He focused on Aleria. "How sure are you that it was Sephone and not just a woman resembling her?"

"On that count, I am sure. Her hair is unmistakable. Whether it is her, or your sister pretending to be her, I cannot say."

Dorian turned to Regis. "Cass is right. Are you willing to take the chance? Trap or no trap, either Kaesi has Sephone, or she's waiting for us at the great library. There's no point infiltrating the castle if nobody's home. We're here for Kaesi."

"You're not thinking straight, Dorian. I know you care for—"

"She's your childhood friend, Symon. None of us think clearly where she is concerned." Dorian drew a deep breath. "Listen, we don't have to do anything rash. The library isn't far below us. All I'm suggesting is that we scout it out, maybe even see what's inside. Just a couple of us. Not enough to risk the mission."

Dorian glanced at Aleria, then continued, "Kaesi won't be expecting the outlanders' arrival. There's time, yet. While her army is distracted with the assault on the bridge and the gates, we can locate Sephone, Asa, and Zaire, and make our next move."

"And if they're surrounded by an army of *alters*?" asked Regis.

"Then we find a way in." Dorian surveyed the group. "We always knew this would be nearly impossible. But if anyone can find a way, it's us." He reached for his *calor* gift, wishing for the thousandth time that he could feel it himself.

"I'm in," said Cass immediately.

"Me too." Aleria scraped back a strand of feathery hair that had been loosened by the wind.

Spartan, Tannis, and Corsi all nodded.

"Regis?" Dorian asked.

A long silence and then, "Aye." Regis clapped Dorian's back. "Let's go see what's down there."

It was another difficult climb into the city. A short while later, they dropped into an empty street. To their backs was the rocky incline and the wall protecting the keep rising far above their heads. If they followed this road, it would eventually lead to the gates of the keep. How often Dorian had ridden past here in his early adulthood, never once dreaming that one day he would be walking it as a traitor.

On the other side of the street were houses. The windows were shuttered and lifeless, but at any moment, someone could look out and see them. And while the gray was thick, it wasn't thick enough to conceal their presence entirely.

"Come on," Dorian murmured. "Let's go."

"Don't drink any of the water," Cass added, reminding them that Draven had once tainted Calliope's water supply using Cutter's fear gift.

They made their way down the street, slipping into side streets and alleys when they heard footsteps or registered signs of movement. It was a slow and laborious process, but fortunately this part of the city was yet to be touched by the sunrise, and the streets were practically abandoned. Most likely, the majority of Calliope's people would either be barricaded inside their houses, or clustered down in the lower parts of the city, preparing for an invasion. No one was heading to the library, not on a day like this.

Despite Aleria's report of half a dozen guards, no one was about when they finally approached the enormous building that housed the library. On the rare sunny day, the great windows would be gleaming from within, the light radiating out across the city. But today, the library seemed as abandoned as the streets. The wrought iron gates were ajar; not a single window on any one of the three stories was aglow. Choked by fog, the great hall seemed to fade into the obsolescence of the very history it prized.

"Perhaps they didn't take Seph to the library," suggested Cass, pressed against the side of the narrow alley they sheltered in.

"Nay," said Aleria, who had been scouting ahead in her eagle form. "They brought her inside. I saw it."

Cass regarded her doubtfully, though his gift proved her honest.

"There's no point risking all of us," Dorian said, removing the staff from his belt and snapping it to full length. He twisted the ends to expose the sharp diamonds. "I'll check it out. The rest of you, remain here. If I don't return"—he glanced at Regis—"you're in command."

"I'm coming with you," declared Cass. "Don't look so horrified, Thane. I know you were hoping I'd volunteer."

Regis had nodded, but Spartan looked distinctly uneasy. "I volunteer as well, Dorian."

"Nay." Dorian glanced at the others. "You must keep them safe, my friend. If something happens to Cass and me, you're our best chance of completing this mission."

"You trust me so completely?"

The question checked Dorian. Why was it that young Spartan, with his loyalties so firmly devoted to the Mysterium and the warrior-monk he called Aedon, was the one who seemed most dependable? Regis had his Sons, Aleria had her outlanders, and even Xia had hidden agendas and plans of her own. But the one person who hadn't offered Dorian their allegiance had proved to be the only one he could really trust.

"With my life," Dorian answered him. Spartan smiled and extended his hand and Dorian gripped it, relishing the sense of peace that enfolded him as he did.

"Aedon be with you, Dorian," he murmured, so that only Dorian would hear. "Even now, he is close."

Spartan's *alter* was here, in Calliope? The boy was reserved at the best of times, and often he did not give information until he was pressed. But Dorian hadn't thought to press him on this.

Spartan's clear blue eyes looked into Dorian's. "Call to him, and he will come, Dorian. At the very hour—the very minute—you need him most."

"To a stranger who has never called on him before?" Dorian replied dubiously. Aedon was Spartan's friend, but Dorian had never known him. He doubted any man would be so obliging, especially if he risked his life.

"To any man, woman, or child who calls," Spartan replied with certainty.

Dorian slapped Spartan on the shoulder, then gripped his own staff and turned to Cass. "Come on."

Aedon of the Three might be nearby. But this task they had to do on their own.

Inside, the great library was shadowy and dim. Dorian and Cass crept along the hallway, pausing at every squeak of their boots on the waxed floorboards. The scholars' alcoves to either side of the hallway were empty and covered in dust.

"There's not a soul here," whispered Cass, readjusting his grip on one of his blades. "It's as if—"

Squeak.

Cass glanced at Dorian, his eyes brightening. Dorian nodded toward the alcove to their left. He held up his hand and counted: one, two, *three.*

Together, they rushed into the tiny space, Cass just behind Dorian. A low gasp, and someone shrank back into the corner. Dorian whipped his staff up, pressing it against a pale neck. A hood fell back, revealing white-and-black hair and wide brown eyes.

"Sephone!" Dorian pulled the staff away, and she faltered, clutching his forearms for support. "How did you get here?"

She shook her head. "It's a long story."

"How did you escape?"

"Also a long story."

A hiss sounded behind him. Sephone looked over Dorian's shoulder to Cass. Dorian was close enough to see the change in her when she glimpsed him. Her face softened, and she rushed to Cass. Eyes wide, he enfolded her in his embrace. She gave him a kiss on the cheek, and a broad smile filled his face.

Dorian looked away, feeling his heart shatter inside his chest.

"Seph." To Cass's credit, he didn't pause to gloat at Dorian. "Where's the bodyguard? Where's the wolf?"

"There's no time." She glanced between them. "Do you trust me?"

"Of course," said Cass.

Dorian nodded stiffly.

"The Reliquary is here, in the great hall," she said. "It's only guarded by a few soldiers, four at most. If we capture it, we can stop Kaesi from using it to hurt others."

"Kaesi? Have you seen her?"

Sephone shook her head. "She's not here yet. She probably doesn't know that I've escaped. But she will, soon. We have to move fast."

Dorian hesitated. His mission was first Kaesi, then the Reliquary. But what harm could there be in doing things the other way round? Especially if, as Sephone said, the Reliquary was relatively unprotected.

They might not get another chance to steal it back, especially if the battle for Calliope went badly.

Cass was looking at Dorian expectantly.

"All right, we'll do it. But Sephone, you must stay here where it's safe."

Her eyes flashed. "Not this time, Dorian. And besides, won't I be safer if I come with you?"

"She's right, you know," commented Cass.

"Thanks for that," Dorian retorted. "Come on, then. But stay behind us."

As they exited the alcove, Cass kept her behind him, holding her gloved hand. They stole along the hallway until it opened up to reveal a grand space, a full three stories high. Ornately carved staircases spiraled upward to the top mezzanine levels, where row after row of books and ancient relics gathered dust. The ceilings were covered in painted murals. Dorian's grandfather had once told him that they depicted the most beloved memories from the world-that-was. The great library was a sister building to Calliope's garden-museum, which housed real memories from the world-that-was that would allow Calliope's inhabitants to experience the past directly.

To their left was the tiny room where they'd once read old-world texts by lanternlight, and directly ahead loomed the great hall, filled with statues, armchairs, chaise lounges, desks, and other heavy furniture. Dorian even spied a large globe in a wooden frame, poised so that you could spin it and see where Caldera stood in relation to the rest of the known world. Every inch of wall space was covered with shelves, heavy wooden ladders leaning against some of the tallest. At the far end of the room were the enormous mullioned windows which looked out over Calliope. On sunny days, they would admit the light, spilling patterns and colors all over the polished timber floors.

Today, they were as lifeless as the rest of the city.

Sephone pointed to the center of the room where an object rested on a small table. Next to that table sat two other long tables, facing each other, positioned as if on the bottommost points of a triangle. The artifact resembled a flower unfolding gracefully, but seeing the hourglass in the center, Dorian knew better.

The Reliquary.

Despite what Sephone had said, no guards watched over the relic, and the hall was empty. Dorian was puzzled. Had they retreated into one of the dozen or more rooms that abutted the great hall? Were they watching Dorian, Cass, and Sephone even now, from the mezzanines?

It was far too easy.

Dorian whirled, clutching his staff. Cass seemed pierced by the same sense of unease, having stopped only a few paces away from the Reliquary. *If only Jewel were here.*

"What are you waiting for?" Sephone prompted. "The Reliquary is ours for the taking."

Dorian turned to study her, then looked past her to the windows, which should have been alive with liquid color.

Color. That's it.

Cass's *lumen* gift. No ribbons accompanied Sephone's words—neither black nor green.

"Cass," Dorian hissed, "this is a trap."

The *lumen* instantly drew Sephone closer to him, scanning the room.

"Nay!" Dorian lunged forward to jerk her away from him. "Cass, it isn't Seph!"

Sephone shoved at Cass, sending him sprawling backward. He crashed into a heavy desk and tumbled over it. He groaned as he hit the floor.

Sephone faced Dorian. Her features melted away; her black-streaked hair lengthened and turned a uniform blond; her brown eyes became blue. A blue he didn't remember on his sister, but he recognized it nonetheless.

"Kaesi."

His sister smiled. "Hello, brother."

30

DORIAN

Kaesi clicked her fingers, and a dozen or so guards appeared. They surrounded Dorian and Cass at once, two of them jerking Cass to his feet and pinning his arms behind his back. His weapons had scattered across the floor when Sephone—or rather, Kaesi—had pushed him.

"It was *you* who kissed me?" Cass looked angry and repulsed.

"Gag the *lumen*," Kaesi instructed. "But leave my brother."

They did as she ordered. At a wave of Kaesi's hand, the remaining guards surrounded Dorian, but they made no move to touch him.

"Your staff, brother." Kaesi motioned. "Or I kill the *lumen*."

Dorian handed it unwillingly to one of the guards, who looked like he was contemplating snapping it over his knee.

Good luck with that.

"And the other weapons."

"What weapons?"

She made an exasperated sound. "The Lethean weapons you're carrying. The sword and shield on your belt."

How did she know? Dorian handed them over to another guard, jaw clenched. Kaesi was already one step ahead.

"Don't bother trying to influence my guards. So long as I am in the room, it is pointless."

"Where's Sephone?" Dorian demanded.

Please, by all the old gods, let her be safe. Let her still be with Xia.

She chuckled. "Closer than you think." She clapped her hands, and three figures emerged from the long hallway.

Brinsley Winter, Asa Karthick, and Zaire, the latter in her human form. Seeing the scar over Zaire's eye and the heat in Asa's gaze, Dorian berated himself for handing over his staff.

Asa was carrying a woman, apparently unconscious. Her gloveless wrists were bound tightly together. Asa passed Dorian, casting a sardonic grin in his direction. Dorian caught a glimpse of the woman's face.

"Sephone!"

Asa carried her to one of the chaise lounges and laid her down. Oddly, her hair—and his—were damp. The water from their clothes soaked through the fabric of the lounge and dripped on the floor. A bloodied strip of cloth had been tied firmly around Sephone's upper thigh—was she injured?

Dorian rounded on his sister. "What did you do to her?"

"I did naught. She brought it on herself." To Asa, Kaesi said, "Rouse her."

Asa leaned over Sephone and tightened the bandage with a rough jerk. She gasped and came awake, instinctively clutching her leg. Asa removed his gloves and looked up at Kaesi. "You'll suppress her gift while I do this?"

Kaesi nodded.

He bent over Sephone again, placing his bare hands on her thigh. Dorian stiffened, and Sephone winced deeply, but the next moment, pale orange light bathed her leg in an unearthly glow. Dorian watched as she relaxed, color flooding back into her ashen cheeks.

Asa Karthick had a healing gift? They had scoured half of Caldera for a *healer* . . .

Asa leaned back, the faintest sheen of sweat lining his upper lip. "It is done."

"Good. She will need her strength for what comes next."

Sephone looked past Asa and saw Dorian. Her eyes grew frantic. "Don't trust her, Dorian! She's Jewel! And Bear is a trai—"

Asa backhanded her across the mouth, and she gasped.

Outraged, Dorian leaped forward, but two of Kaesi's guards grabbed his arms. Asa dragged Sephone off the chaise, keeping her in a near headlock with his elbow as he clapped his hands together. A tiny, glowing ball of vivid orange hovered above his palm. He brought it closer until it was barely a finger's width from Sephone's lips.

"Do you know what kind of damage fire can do to the tender interior of a woman's throat, Lord Adamo? Even magical fire?"

Dorian stilled, seeing the anger burning in the other man's eyes. Asa wanted revenge for what Spartan and Aleria had done to Zaire.

"Hush, Asa," said Kaesi, waving her hand. "Dorian is a clever man. He does not need your petty little threats to know we mean business."

Asa closed his fist, and the fireball winked out. He retained his grip on Sephone, his arm gripping her waist this time. Dorian heard Brinsley's low chuckle.

"What did Sephone mean?" Dorian glanced at his sister.

"Ah." Kaesi raised a brow. "Maybe not so clever. Maybe even a little blind at times."

As he watched her, his mouth went dry, his tongue sticking to the roof. As Kaesi's form dissolved, his heart splintered.

"Do you see now?" Asa smirked, and Zaire's laugh joined Brinsley's. A series of curses escaped from Cass's gag.

Before Dorian stood a wolf. Jewel. The magnificent, glossy head, the stunning blue eyes, the jagged scar from the night she'd tried to save his family.

And now the wolf was becoming a woman again. Becoming his sister.

Dorian met Sephone's frightened gaze, understanding everything in an instant. How the hooded man had evaded them for so long, though he was always so close. In the Grennor Mountains, they had frequently left Jewel to hunt, making it impossibly easy for Kaesi to slip away to visit Sephone. Piece after piece slid into place. Why Kaesi was always five steps ahead. How she had learned of Sephone's deal with Asa in Nyx. How she had known Sephone's location, *their* location.

She had learned, of course, that they would be coming from the cliffs, that Aleria would be watching from the skies. So Aleria would see Sephone with her captors, and Kaesi knew neither Cass nor Dorian would be able to resist going after her, even if they suspected it might be a trap.

Dorian had inadvertently left Sephone in the hands of the most dangerous of enemies. An enemy he had only ever considered a friend.

Kaesi was right. He had been blind.

We almost have the bridge, Magritte's voice said in his mind. *We will soon have the gate.*

His frustration at his helplessness mounted. *Go!* he wanted to shout back. *Kaesi knows everything! She knows you're coming!*

And then it struck him that someone else had known every detail of their plans.

"Bear," Dorian choked. "*Bear* was the traitor, not Bas."

Kaesi smiled thinly. "Aye, though he has died a traitor's death." She shot a glance at Sephone. "Your little *mem* made sure of that when she went over the cliff with him. Asa was generous enough to fish her from the water. But your bodyguard didn't survive the fall."

Bear was dead? Sephone had gone over a cliff? Tears streamed down Sephone's face, and she looked at Dorian pleadingly as if she wanted him to understand something. He recalled that Bear had been in charge of the Lethean weapons. Had he sabotaged any of them?

Grief, fear, and rage warred for dominance in Dorian. So much betrayal, so many lies. Anguish seared deep. He struggled against his captors as he raised his voice. "How could you do this, Kaesi?"

She looked at him earnestly. "I told you once before, Dorian. I did it for you. I will make amends for failing you if it is the last thing I do."

"Failing me? What are you talking about?"

"Do you remember the night I appeared at your door?" She began to pace like a wolf . . . like Jewel. "It was the same night your daughter was born, though that was merely coincidence, of course."

"Lida believed you were a sign. A blessing from the old gods."

Her lower lip trembled. "I like to think I was. If I'd revealed my true identity, you would have thrown me out. Tossed me back in the dungeons, most likely. But so long as I stayed in this form, I could be close to you and to your family. Sometimes I thought you loved me far better as a wolf than you ever loved me as a sister."

"That isn't true," Dorian responded instantly, though in that moment, he was grateful Cass's gift was suppressed.

Blue eyes pierced him. "Isn't it?" She went on, not waiting for an answer. "That night I came to you was the same night I left Silvertongue. I disliked his methods, and I didn't share his ultimate purposes. I came to you, thinking that I could hide from Silvertongue and Draven and nurture my gift at the same time. The longer I remained in wolf form, you see, the more it sharpened my natural instincts. I could sense better when I was in danger.

"But then, that terrible day, Draven found out you were my brother. He tracked me to Maera, and when he couldn't find me, he knew the best way to get at me was through you and your family. I arrived too late to save your wife and daughter. But I was in time to save you, though I was injured before I could do much more than chase your attackers away."

Dorian was taken aback. "I thought Draven left me alive so that I would be forced to watch Lida and Emmy die."

"Nay, Dorian. He left you because I drove him away. Why else would he have allowed such an important job to remain unfinished?" Kaesi shook her head. "I should have been there. I failed you."

"Nay, Kaesi."

"I almost failed you again in Idaea. That time, Silvertongue found out where I was, and he poisoned me. I would have died, if not for a *healer* who had expertise in poisons. I stole out to see him in the middle of the night, while you all slept. And then, as you left the city, I stopped Draven from killing you."

Dorian remembered the *alter* Sephone had visited. Jewel had been there that day. "That was why you were sick the night Cutter discovered us and we were forced to flee."

She nodded. "I renounced Silvertongue forever that day. I will never serve him again."

"You have started a war," Sephone rasped as she struggled in Asa's firm grip. "Thousands of innocent people are going to die. How can you be so sure you're not still in his service?"

Kaesi strode over to her, leaning close to sneer. "Last I checked, it was Lethe at Memosine's doorstep, and not the other way round."

We have the bridge. Dorian was startled by the suddenness of Magritte's intrusion. *The Memosinians are retreating into the city. The lower half of Calliope is burning, thanks to the efforts of the outlanders. Victory is in sight, Lord Adamo.*

Kaesi stood erect, the hem of her majestic blue gown sweeping the floor. "I will not fail you again, Dorian. What you have lost, I will restore to you ten times over. You will be king. You will be king, and I will be queen. Everything will be as it once was."

She was mad. She had to be. "I already told you," Dorian said clearly, "it cannot be. I will not be king."

"Because of her?" She thrust a finger at Sephone and made a disgusted noise. "I don't know what you see in her."

"Nay, Kaesi. Because the throne would destroy me. Just as it is destroying you."

But his sister seemed to have crossed over into a feverish madness. She dragged Sephone's head back by her hair, angling a knife Dorian hadn't been aware she'd drawn against Sephone's throat. "I was afraid you'd say that, brother."

Dorian's eyes narrowed. "Kaesi, if you hurt her—"

"How dare you pretend she was your sister," Kaesi hissed, "when you already had one."

Was that it? Kaesi was jealous of Sephone? How often had they been side by side, the very best of friends? It was Jewel who had saved Sephone's life. Was it simply to prolong the ruse?

"No matter," continued Kaesi, recovering her composure. "I have prepared for this possibility. You see, I have spared the *mem*'s life for one purpose, and one purpose only." She faced Dorian, her teeth sharper than a human's should be. "I could threaten to kill your friends unless you join me, but you know me, Dorian. I was never one for half-hearted efforts. You would only plot for freedom for all of you and seize it at the first opportunity, just as you did in Nulla. *Nay.* The change must be more permanent."

She glanced at the Reliquary and smiled. "I promised I would make everything as it was, and so I will. Miss Winter will selectively erase your memories—eight years or so should do it—and when she is done, you will love and accept me the way you did when we were children. You will care for me the way you did the lady wolf—as your faithful protector, your dearest friend and confidante in all the world."

Dorian gaped at her. She *was* insane.

"Of course, there is no point in telling you this, because very soon, you won't remember. But I wanted you to see the brilliance of the plan.

Isn't this what you wanted, brother? To forget your terrible past? When the *mem* finishes her work, it will be so. You won't remember Lida and Emmy. You won't remember what I did. You won't remember Sephone Winter. Or even Lady Jewel."

She laughed shrilly. "A fresh start, dear brother. Isn't that the most wonderful thing in the world?"

"It won't work," I said against the blade at my throat, my eyes still forced to the ceiling. I couldn't see Dorian's face.

"Oh?" Kaesi purred, circling me. "And why ever not, Miss Winter?"

"Because your brother will only love truly if it is of his own free will. It is impossible to love an illusion. To love a lie."

The knife pressed closer. A warm bead of blood ran down my neck.

"There is no illusion," Kaesi enunciated each word. "No lie. I am real. Dorian is *my* brother. It is only the past that comes between us. A past that will soon be done away with forever. It will become nothing more than a quickly forgotten dream."

My head snapped forward, dragged by Kaesi's hold on my hair, which had come loose from its braid. The knife remained. But now I could see Dorian. He was looking directly at me, something in his gaze I didn't quite recognize.

"One can love an illusion," I told Kaesi, though I didn't take my eyes from Dorian, "but eventually they will be forced to accept that it is naught more than that: an illusion. An illusion that cannot give them what they truly seek, no matter how dearly they crave that reality."

Dorian's face grew stark. Raw. He understood me.

Kaesi moved between us. "As I said, this *is* real. The Reliquary will make it so."

"Nay, Kaesi. Everything in this world"—I thought of the Garden—"is only a shadow of the things that were. And that includes the Reliquary."

Even now, I saw it in her face. Kaesi Ashwood was like me. More than anything, she craved a love without conditions. A love without end. Had she been drawn to Dorian's faithful character and *calor* gift also? Had she craved the certainty, the reassurance his love would bring her? My love for him was romantic in nature; hers was familial. Nonetheless, we both wanted from him what he could never give. We both wanted him to make us whole when he was just as broken as we were.

Jewel knows what it is to live with scars, Dorian had told me once. It was true in more ways than one.

I took a breath. "Your brother is the very best of men," I said to Kaesi. "But nothing he or anyone else could ever give you will make you feel complete."

For a long moment, I believed she had heard me. Then her face changed, and an indifferent mask replaced the flash of vulnerability.

"Enough." Retracting the knife, she gestured at Asa. "Bind her to the Reliquary. Then, my brother."

Asa picked me up easily, depositing me on the first table next to the Reliquary. I didn't struggle, knowing it was futile. Without my gift, he was far stronger than me.

"You don't have to do this," I told him in a low, urgent voice as he cut the ropes binding my wrists and secured me to the table. Leather straps restrained my torso, hips, and ankles. My right wrist was pinned beside me, while my left hand was dragged above my head. "You could be free of her. *Zaire* could be free."

He leaned close, murmuring into my ear under the guise of tightening the straps. "What are you suggesting, Miss Winter?"

"You healed the gash in my thigh," I whispered back. "You saved me from the river. I know there's good in you."

"What is freedom in light of a curse?"

He gave his head a slight shake and leaned back, the blue eyes so like Spartan's, though somber and lifeless. I remembered the prophecy that haunted his days, that he would die before his twenty-third birthday. "Aedon can help."

"Aedon?" His eyebrows rose. "My brother's upstart lordling?"

"Come away from there," Kaesi ordered, and Asa obediently left my side to join Zaire and Brinsley. My brother was still smirking, but

Zaire's face showed no expression. As Asa reached her side, he slipped his hand into hers, muttering something beneath his breath.

Dorian was fighting against the guards as fiercely as he could. One of the soldiers bled from his temple, and another was limping. Dorian's fist caught a third beneath his chin.

"Kaesi." Her name scraped between his teeth as four guards finally wrestled him onto the table. Three of them pinned him while the fourth tried to secure the straps. "Don't do this." Desperation marked his voice.

"I've made up my mind."

"If you do this, I will never forgive you."

She laughed. "In a few minutes, you won't even know there'd be a reason for such a thing. So I don't need it!" She leaned over me, staring into my eyes. "You know, Miss Winter, I could have used a substitute for this. Kept you alive a little longer. But seeing as you are no longer the only *mem* around here and you have one foot in the grave already, I think this is the last time I will have need of your services."

"I won't do what you ask."

"Oh, I think you will. For you must recall what happened when you tested me the last time." She snapped her fingers in Cass's direction, whose eyes were fuming over his gag. "Refuse, and I will kill your Marianthean friend. And the others, when they come out of hiding. The boy Spartan—Jerome. Your childhood friend, Regis, and his wife and unborn child. Whatever it takes for you to bow to my will."

She snatched up my hand and forced it into the metal glove. The wires constricted at once, and my arm went leaden. I couldn't move. My eyes closed of their own volition.

The subject of the procedure must always go last . . .

A moment later, I felt Dorian's presence. He was terrified. Desperate. His chest heaved as he wrenched his body from side to side, trying to dislodge the leather straps. The guards were still attempting to restrain him.

For once, my gift was under my complete control. The influence of the Reliquary? Or the rigid discipline of Dorian's mind?

Dorian, I said across the mental link, and felt him pause.

Sephone?

I'm here.

I sensed concern, for my wounds.

I fell off a cliff. I tried to sound amused, though the memory made me tremble. It flashed through my mind in an instant. Falling. Bear clutching me to him. Water, icy cold. Pain lancing my thigh from the sideways scrape of a sharp rock. Choking and spluttering, trying to reach the surface. Soon, Asa was in the water with me, dragging me sideways across the river current. When we reached the shallows, he hauled me upright, both of us dripping river water, and supported me to the beach.

Asa deposited me on the sand and went back for Bear's body. The giant had fallen directly onto the rocks and hadn't survived.

Had he reconsidered his allegiances at the last? Had he borne the brunt of those rocks for me? Because we had been falling together and I had been the one to survive. But I couldn't remember if he'd turned me midair. All I could remember was the frigid cold of the water rushing up my spine.

Persephone . . .

At the sound of my full name, I opened my eyes to Dorian's mental landscape. We were standing in a forest next to a small stream, birds chattering cheerfully overhead. The scene was oddly familiar. Here we could speak freely, and Kaesi wouldn't hear a word. "Is this the same—"

"Aye," he replied. "The very same place."

This was the stream where I'd first hinted at my love for him. Where he had pushed me away. Why did he return us to it now? For this was his doing, not mine. We were in *his* mind.

"Dorian," I said quickly, "Kaesi has to focus to use her gift. When this is all over, you may be able to distract her."

Would he even remember this conversation once I removed his memories of me? I would try to preserve this piece of knowledge, at least. It was his only chance against his ruthless sister.

Dorian stepped closer. "You can't do what she asks."

Tears pricked my eyes. "If I don't, she'll kill Cass, Spartan, Regis, Aleria . . . Everyone I love."

"She may well kill them anyway."

"Isn't this what you wanted, though? To become a new man? To forget the tragedy of the past few years?"

"*Nay*. Not this. Never this." He reached out and took my hands. His mental landscape shuddered and quaked. The wall in his mind crumbled, inch by inch, until it was nothing more than a pile of rubble. Memories flooded through the gap, one after another. All of them from his perspective, stained with his emotions and desires.

The night of the wolf attack . . . holding me closely as I struggled to resist the Nightmare's poison. I was unconscious, feverish, but he whispered words of encouragement. He pressed cool cloths against my forehead in turn, until the fever broke in the early morning. Then he went for a *healer*, tracking for miles in the snow.

Another memory. Watching me while I coughed into my bedroll in Orphne. Wishing he could take the sickness upon himself, even going so far as to pray to the old gods for a cure.

He opened his mind to me, hiding nothing. Revealing all.

"Brother!" Kaesi's voice intruded from the outside. "Stop struggling, and I promise you will have peace!" I was dimly aware that Dorian was still fighting his guards, delaying the inevitable moment when Kaesi would force me to erase his memories.

Dorian kept his attention fixed on me.

There was one more memory . . . but this one felt different. It wasn't a memory, but a dream. I turned away.

"Nay," he said gently. "Look."

The face of a woman and her child and a man who gathered them into his arms as if they were the most precious gift he'd ever been given. It was everything I'd craved before I met Dorian. Before I met Aedon and the Mysterium.

It was a family.

Mine. And Dorian's.

As the vision vanished, I looked into Dorian's eyes—and saw the heart within them. "Why didn't you tell me?"

"It wasn't something I could put into words. I've been more afraid than a *calor* should be. But I wanted you to know the truth, before the end. Before I forget. I'm not engaged to Siaki. I could never love another woman the way I love you, Persephone. Not even your gift can take that from me. The golden light, remember?"

"But you stayed away. Why?"

He seemed to beckon me closer, deeper. An image of the Reliquary flashed across our minds. Our bodies were positioned on either side of it. Though this time, our places were exchanged. I was last, not him.

And suddenly I knew.

"That's why you were seeking the Reliquary. And Cass was seeking an *altered healer.* You were going to use the Reliquary on yourself. To give your life for mine."

"Aye."

"Cass knew?"

He nodded, and my face felt numb.

I'm going to find a way to save you, I promise. That was what Dorian had told me, the night of the snow-blossom festival.

And he had found a way.

"How long have you been planning this?"

"Since Nyx. I wanted to tell you. But you must see why I couldn't."

"I would have forbidden it."

"I know. And for that reason, I had to push you away. If I had allowed you in my mind, you would have seen the truth."

Kaesi yelled, once again ordering her brother to be still. Threatening to hurt me, as if that mattered when she was about to kill me. The wires around my hand tightened, readying themselves for the inevitable. The forest around us shivered. The stream trickled on, but it was flowing less rapidly now. Any moment could be my—our—last.

"I'm sorry for deceiving you," he murmured. "But I won't let you die. Not if I am able to save you."

My tears nearly blinded me. This Dorian wasn't an illusion, a figment of mine or Kaesi's imagination. He was flawed, deeply so, but he was real. He had chosen to love me. No matter if it meant he could never be with me.

No matter if it cost him his own life.

Dare I open my heart to him, show him the truth?

In my mind, I dissembled a wall I hadn't known existed, brick by brick. I felt almost naked. Finally, I stood there, vulnerable, remembering Dorian's words from long ago.

Vulnerability and courage are brothers, Sephone. And they do not share a brotherhood of enmity, but of mutual dependence, the elder preceding the younger. Vulnerability comes first, emptying the ground of any obstacles, and in his wake, Courage comes . . .

Gathering my courage, I invited Dorian into my mind as I had invited no one else. Showing him my memories, just as he had done for me. The nights of sleeplessness, of doubt and fear, of wishing the boy from the ice loved me as I loved him. Showing him how I'd never forgotten him.

"There's something else you should know. I didn't always know the truth of what I possessed—the full measure of you—but I do now. I love you, Dorian Ashwood. I always have, and I always will. I would have chosen to remember you forever, no matter if you chose to forget."

His eyes softened. "And I love you, Persephone Winter. I should have said it months ago, the very day I realized. Forgive me. Forgive me for everything."

"I forgive you, my love."

I felt a sharp tug on my shoulder, and Dorian's mental landscape dissolved. I opened my eyes to see Kaesi looming over me, her pretty face mottled with rage.

"Now, Miss Winter, need I remind you—"

My left hand was still trapped by the metal glove. But the other . . . I worked at the leather strap pinning my right hand to my side. If I could just get it free—

A colossal crash behind Kaesi brought her head up. Her mouth fell open. I thought Zaire screamed.

"Step away, Jerome," came Asa's voice. "I'd hate to destroy all these beautiful books. All these precious relics."

And dazzling, blinding light illuminated the room.

32

DORIAN

Dorian could only watch the blur of activity. Regis, Spartan, and Aleria burst into the great hall at a run, Tannis and Corsi behind them. Seeing Asa, the latter two dove for cover, upending a heavy table as Regis tackled Brinsley to the ground, giving Sephone's brother no time to flick the switchblade usually hidden in his sleeve. Cass had somehow escaped his guards—possibly due to Spartan's interference—and had wrenched the gag from his mouth to join the fray.

In her eagle form, Aleria lashed out at Zaire, who quickly changed into her beastly self. The enormous lion-wolf swiped at Aleria, who dodged and whirled midair, striking at Zaire's head as she swooped, again and again. Zaire's iridescent black mane rippled, and she roared, rearing up on powerful hind legs, her massive jaws snapping. Aleria would have been killed if not for one of Spartan's shields, which appeared between her and Zaire.

"Step away, Jerome," warned Asa. "I'd hate to destroy all these beautiful books. All these precious relics." He waved a hand at the surrounding library and then flung it out.

A flash of green light, followed by a brighter burst of white. Asa's fireball melted against Spartan's shield like a snowball on a frying pan. Back and forth they battled, each colored projectile dissolving in the shimmering, crystal white. Spartan made no effort to advance on his brother.

Dorian looked to Kaesi, wondering why she had not used her gift. She had slumped against the table where Sephone was restrained.

Sephone's right hand had escaped its bonds and was clasping his sister's arm.

Kaesi has to focus to use her gift.

Had Kaesi been so easily distracted by the others' arrival?

I don't know how long she'll be out, Sephone said through their mental link. *We have to hurry.*

She was right, and the battle was far from over. Helplessly, Dorian watched it unfold, keenly aware of Sephone's presence. She was trying to escape the metal glove now, but it and the leather restraints still held her captive. He struggled against his own bonds, his panic mirroring hers. Magritte hadn't sent an update in a long time now, and he was uneasy about what that meant.

Brinsley lay on the ground, bleeding from his mouth. At a barked command from Asa, the remaining soldiers rushed Regis and Cass. Corsi joined their fight, while Tannis tried to harry Zaire. The Lethean weapons seemed to be working, perhaps because Kaesi was unconscious. But the amber-tinted shields were of little use against ordinary soldiers, and the lion-wolf didn't allow anyone close, scattering furniture and other objects in her crazed attempts to bring down the eagle.

Meanwhile, Asa and Spartan were still locked in their own deadly battle. It was taking all of the acolyte's focus to keep his brother at bay. He was ever defending, never attacking, absorbing each of Asa's fireballs with a fierce look of concentration on his young face.

Tannis's ankle hooked the leg of an armchair, and he tripped, dropping his shield. Zaire flung him across the room, and his body hit a large shelf, books and relics tumbling onto his head. He didn't stir. Regis bellowed a war cry and went after Zaire, who had finally succeeded in knocking Aleria from the air. Asa tossed a stray fireball in his direction, blocked at the last second by Spartan. Regis scrabbled for one of the Lethean shields, still clutching a long knife in his other hand, one of Cass's.

Zaire pinned the eagle with her heavy foreleg, and the eagle screeched and re-formed into a woman. But the situation was no less dire, since a woman's bones could break as well as an eagle's. Aleria uttered a cry as Zaire pressed more firmly against her chest. Blood ran in fine rivulets down Aleria's arms. Dorian felt Sephone's desperation, and the gift that suddenly began to stir without her permission. The metal glove encasing his hand warmed.

Fight it, he told her. *Fight it as long as you can.*

I am, she gasped. *I'm trying.*

"Enough," said Asa, wiping his mouth. Few of Kaesi's guards were still standing. Cass, panting, was holding a knife to Brinsley's throat. Regis and Corsi had produced what looked like the Lethean version of a bow, amber arrows nocked and aimed at Zaire's head. Aleria's face was pale beneath the bruising pressure.

"Let her go, Zaire," replied Spartan, meeting the lion-wolf's purple-blue eyes with considerable poise.

Asa's eyes narrowed. "It was that woman who injured Zaire."

Even in beast form, a scar distorted the flesh surrounding one of Zaire's eyes. Had she been blinded by Aleria's talons?

"To save Dorian Ashwood's life," Spartan returned.

At that, Asa clapped his hands, and a bright blue fireball appeared, aimed in Dorian's direction. Spartan immediately erected a crystal shield around the Reliquary, Sephone, and Dorian. Asa paused, then closed his fist around the glowing sphere, and the shields dissolved at once.

"A stalemate," said Spartan. "I will not let you kill them, brother."

"And I will not let them live."

"Asa, it doesn't have to be this way." Dorian projected his voice as he raised his head from the table. "Your father is dead. Spartan—Jerome—is your own brother. You have a chance for a new life." Dorian looked at Zaire, who merely snarled at him. "For you and Zaire together."

"You cannot win," Asa stated. "I have yet to summon my army of *alters.* And as soon as Queen Adamo wakes, she will render your gifts naught."

"Queen Adamo?" Dorian glanced over at Kaesi. "My sister is no more suited to be queen of Caldera than your father was to be king. You know that."

"My father," Asa growled back, "has naught to do with this."

"On the contrary, he established the throne. And he used your gift to impose his rule on every innocent man, woman, and child from Memosine to Lethe. You are more than a killer, Asa, more than a

Karthick. Follow your brother's example, and become the man you were born to be."

The prophecy, Sephone said in Dorian's mind. *More than anything, Asa is afraid.*

She was right. Even from this distance, Dorian could see the torment in Asa's eyes, the empty hollow of his soul. Press too hard, and he would flee. Delve too deep, and his outer shell would harden, keeping them out forever.

What did Dorian know about breaking curses or reversing prophecies? He looked helplessly at Spartan. This was *his* domain. Spartan nodded as if he understood and ventured closer to his brother. "There is still time, Asa. You can be free."

"Free?" Asa raised a brow.

"Aye," said Spartan, with certainty. "You are a slave to Kaesi, just as you were a slave to our father. But Aedon can free you. He can free you both." Green ribbons emanated from Cass, floating on an invisible current.

"Aedon, you say?"

Expecting mockery, Dorian was surprised to hear something different in Asa Karthick's voice. Was he so desperate to live that he was willing to believe in anything—even a dream?

"Aye," said Spartan. "The truth will unlock the cage you daily live in. I promise."

For a long moment, Asa looked at Zaire, and Dorian guessed that they were having a private conversation. Even though right now she was quite a contrast to the beauty she was in human form, it was easy to see the love Asa held for her. But for her, he might not have considered any of this.

Through the mental link, Dorian reached out to Sephone, but she shrank away from him. She was struggling now—struggling to keep from entering his mind. Her gift licked at the threshold of his memories like flames beneath a door. How long could she hold it at bay? He could feel her weakening. Any moment, her power would be unleashed in his mind, erasing his past forever.

There wasn't much time. If Dorian could only be free of these restraints, he could reverse the Reliquary . . .

But Zaire was becoming a woman again. As the pressure was removed, Aleria coughed, rolling onto her side. Regis lowered his bow and knelt beside her.

"I'm all right," Aleria said weakly. "I'll be fine."

Asa looked directly at Spartan. "Aye, we will do as you say."

Spartan's face flooded with relief. He looked as if he wanted nothing more than to cross the room to his brother and throw his arms around him. But Spartan's natural reserve and Asa's stiff posture ensured that, for the moment at least, they did little more than smile hesitantly at each other.

Brothers at last, after years of being enemies. It didn't seem like a trick. Asa's expression was too different, too unguarded.

Dorian needed help. "Cass," he called. "Get me out of this, would you?" Sephone's breathing was coming short. Was it Dorian's imagination, or was there a rattle in her chest again?

Cass hurried over and began working at Dorian's restraints, while Regis did the same for Sephone.

"Wait," Dorian warned Regis. "Don't touch her yet."

He obeyed, concern creasing his features.

As soon as Dorian was freed—the metal glove was the hardest of all to remove—he jumped off the table and came to Sephone's side, pulling on his gloves. Regis had carried Kaesi over to a chaise lounge and instructed Corsi to stand guard over her. Brinsley appeared to have passed out from blood loss. Dorian was relieved—he had no wish to face Sephone's brother again.

Cass joined him as he leaned over Sephone and eased the glove from her hand. The wires were warm to the touch, but they cooled rapidly the moment they were no longer in contact with her flesh.

"Dorian?" Sephone's eyes opened. She tried to sit up, but the leather straps held firm. "Won't you get me out of this?" She tugged at the restraint around her hips.

Dorian looked at Cass. "Your promise?"

A battle raged within Cass's blue-green eyes, but eventually he nodded. "Aye."

"I can't free you," Dorian told Sephone as Cass captured her hands in his gloved ones. "Not just yet."

"What do you mean, you can't . . ." She went still. "Nay, Dorian. *Nay.*" She looked at Cass. "Don't let him do this. Please."

"It's either him or you, Seph," the *lumen* said softly. "And that's hardly a difficult choice." Even so, anguish radiated from him.

"Dorian," interjected Spartan, who had appeared beside them. "There's another way."

But Dorian looked at Asa. "You have a healing gift, do you not?"

The *ignis* nodded.

"I would request your assistance—if you are willing." Dorian quickly told Asa about the poison and the plan to save Sephone. By the time he finished, Asa's eyes were wide.

"I don't know, Lord Adamo. If I do this, I would be party to another execution. Yours. Is my brother right? Is there another way?"

"Right now, the poison is only skin-deep. When it enters her bloodstream—her heart—she will have but a matter of hours."

"Aedon will be able to help her," insisted Spartan.

"Aedon and his Mountain are days away." Dorian ignored Spartan's beseeching gaze. "This is the only way. If we wait much longer, she'll die." The black in Sephone's hair had overtaken the white, and inky tendrils swarmed the base of her throat. If Magritte's last update was to be believed, Xia's forces were well on their way to capturing the city, and with Asa turned to their side, his *alters* would no longer be a threat. Calliope would surrender soon enough. Kaesi, when she awoke, would be Lethe's prisoner.

It was time.

"Then so be it." Asa's voice was grave as he slowly moved to the third petal of the Reliquary, picked up the wire glove, and slid it on.

"Regis, you must stop this," Sephone cried out. "This is madness!"

Regis glanced at Dorian. "She'll never forgive you for this."

An echo of a similar concern from Cass. Dorian pushed it aside. "I don't need her forgiveness. All I need is for her to live."

"Then let me take your place."

Dorian's mouth fell slightly open in surprise. "I thank you, Symon, but nay. This is my choice. And besides, you have a wife, and soon you will be a father. Live your life, and lead your people well. And be a good friend to Sephone when I am gone."

Thankfully, Regis didn't press the point. But his jaw was clenched tight, and his eyes were suspiciously bright.

Dorian turned to Sephone, who was still struggling against Cass, trying to pull her wrists from the *lumen*'s grip. When she met his eyes, she stilled. "Dorian, please, you must reconsider—"

"Look after her," Dorian said to Cass. "For me."

"As I promised . . . Dorian." Begrudging respect gleamed in eyes that were normally full of dislike.

Dorian was unable to say goodbye to Sephone. He braced himself, lay down on the table, and reached for the glove. It melded to his hand like a second skin.

"Dorian." Sephone's pleading was choked with tears. "Dorian!"

"Now, Cass," Dorian instructed—simultaneously locking gazes with Asa, who nodded. With considerable effort, Cass wrestled Sephone's hand into the glove, pinning her free arm to the table. Dorian could feel both Sephone and Asa through the mental link; Sephone battling to retain control of her gift, while Asa's power rose like a flood behind a dam wall. The metal wires tightened, biting into Dorian's flesh. The upper chamber of the Reliquary's hourglass was filled with inky black, waiting to drip down into the lower chamber.

Farewell, Lord Adamo, said Asa through the link. *I never knew a braver man.*

Then you have not met many noteworthy men, Dorian replied. *Look after your brother.*

A pause, and then, *I will.*

Dorian closed his eyes, waiting for Asa's gift to sweep through Sephone's body, relocating the poison to Dorian's. Instead, there was a series of shouts and cries of dismay, and sudden fear pulsed through the link. Another flash of blinding white, but this time it lingered.

Dorian's eyes flew open.

The largest light wall he'd ever seen shimmered in the middle of the room, reaching as high as the first mezzanine. Behind it stood Spartan, his bare hands extended in front of him. Dorian glimpsed Aleria's face, completely ashen as she peered through the barrier to the hallway beyond. Zaire had backed against the wall, and Regis swiftly drew his dagger.

On the other side of the nearly transparent shield stood a lone man—slightly stooped, slight of frame, with silvered hair. His face looked relatively youthful. Sharp, yellow-brown eyes swept the room. He looked familiar, but Dorian's mind had suddenly gone foggy, and he couldn't place the elderly man.

"Oh, there's no need for that, young Spartan," the old man purred. "I come as a friend."

"You are no friend of ours, Silas Silvertongue," Spartan retorted.

Silas Silvertongue. Why did that name seem so familiar? Why was the acolyte being so hostile to such a frail man?

"Nay, monk," said Zaire, the fear melting from her features. "Let him through. He is harmless."

Regis's knife clattered to the floor. "Aye, he's just an old man."

"Listen to them, boy," said Silvertongue. "Your friends are exceedingly wise."

Dorian watched as Kaesi roused from the armchair where Regis had placed her. Corsi blinked twice at her, as if there were something he was trying to remember, something he needed to do. Standing on wobbly feet, she faced the old man. "Silas?"

"Aye, my dear. You didn't think you could run away permanently, did you? Nobody ever leaves old Silas. But you are a queen now. And we are old friends, are we not? I have come to offer you my help."

Something tugged at the edges of Dorian's memory . . . something very important. Kaesi was awake—was that bad? She seemed as confused as the rest of them about Silvertongue's arrival. Just as slow-witted.

She mentioned one who was immune . . .

Who had said that? Who was *she*? Why did it matter if someone were immune from something?

"I could use your help," said Kaesi vaguely. "It is hard, you know, to keep a world in check . . ." She drifted off sleepily, and Dorian wondered if she was going to sink back onto the chaise lounge. He himself felt like closing his eyes to sleep.

Perspiration beaded Spartan's forehead, but he kept the shield in place. "You are not welcome here, Silvertongue," he stated. He glanced over his shoulder at Cass, the only other without a glazed expression. *"Lumen?"*

Cass quickly released Sephone and went over to Spartan's shield. Removing his glove, he pressed his right hand to the shimmering wall. Green spilled out from his fingers like droplets of ink until the entire wall was the color of jade.

It was as if water had been tossed into Dorian's face. He felt Asa and Sephone come back to themselves. The Reliquary . . . the poison . . .

Silvertongue's pleasant façade vanished. "You give me no choice."

The man morphed before their eyes. His lips knotted into a snarl, revealing the blistering, oozing interior of a red, fleshy mouth. His shoulders uncurled. The frail body was now muscular and impossibly tall. He extended his hands—wrinkled, liver-spotted, with long, yellow nails—and suddenly snakes were pooling on the other side of the wall, enormous beasts with copper backs and ruby undersides. Twisting, writhing, the infestation multiplied until they were numerous enough to begin climbing the wall, the uppermost ones supported by the bulk of their fellows beneath. Zaire screamed and stumbled back.

Spartan redoubled his efforts—extending the wall still higher—but he was deathly pale, and his knees were beginning to tremble.

Kaesi turned and saw Dorian, and his chest constricted. They had to move *now.*

"Do it!" Dorian called to Asa.

"Nay!" Kaesi screamed, lunging across the room. Of the three of them, Asa was closest to her.

Sephone was now frantic; the poison had entered her bloodstream. Asa gathered his power, opening the floodgate that held back his gift. Dorian braced himself, but Kaesi had reached the *ignis*. Before Dorian could react, she had torn Asa from the Reliquary and shoved him away. He hit his head on the corner of a heavy table and went down hard. As Dorian watched in horror, she slipped her hand into Asa's glove.

"Nay, Kaesi!" Dorian bellowed. "Don't!"

The subject of the procedure must always go last . . .

A wave of impossible, searing heat spilled over Dorian as Sephone unleashed her gift. His arm felt as if he had stuck it directly into a furnace. Then came a surge of white light, and he fell back against the table, blinded. Sephone's pain and Kaesi's fear exploded through his mind.

Was this the end?

Then the heat faltered—and somehow, he *knew*. Sephone was fighting for control of her gift again, drawing its effects back into herself, into her own body. The effort was killing her. Dorian could feel the poison racing through her blood, slowing her heart rate, strangling her lungs. She could barely breathe.

Nay! he said weakly into her mind. *You must not . . .*

Then someone was dragging the glove from Dorian's hand, heedless of the skin and hair that went with it. He could no longer feel Sephone or Kaesi. He blinked and opened his eyes to see Regis.

"Are you all right?"

Dorian nodded. Though he felt weakened, his body seemed intact, although his hand was reddened and covered in blisters, and throbbing painfully.

Levering an arm beneath Dorian's shoulders, Regis eased him into a sitting position. "That's it," he said. "Take your time."

Cass was crouched over Sephone. "She's alive," he said as he hurriedly removed the remaining restraints. "I pulled her out in time. But she's bad, Dorian. Very bad."

Zaire knelt beside the unconscious Asa. Cautiously, she edged over to Kaesi, who had collapsed on the floor, her hand still encased in the wire glove. She pressed a finger to the artery in Dorian's sister's neck. "She's alive, too. I think she's just passed out."

How much of his sister's memory would remain when she woke?

Behind them, Spartan was still maintaining the wall. The snakes, Dorian could see, had nearly reached the top. Each one was twice the length of a man and half his girth. The acolyte's clothes were drenched with sweat. On the other side, Silvertongue was laughing deliriously.

"You may as well give up," he said with glee. "A mere *boy* cannot defeat me."

Dorian stood, only to partially collapse. Regis caught him and half supported, half carried him to Sephone's side.

A second time, Dorian's knees nearly buckled—this time in shock. Sephone's hair was now as black as Cass's—there was no longer any white. Her shirt, partially unlaced at the front, showed a décolletage streaked with poison, extending up her neck and the sides of her face. She was conscious, but her chest convulsed as she struggled to breathe.

Dorian wrapped an arm around her. "We have to try it again," he insisted to the others. "We must perform the procedure." He didn't look behind them at Spartan and Silvertongue.

"How?" Regis asked. "Asa Karthick is unconscious."

"There's another complication." Cass indicated Dorian's chest, and he looked down to see streaks of black marking his heart. They weren't as extensive as the ones draining the life out of Sephone, but they would be soon.

Poison.

Regis's face suddenly grew taut. "We have to do something."

Dorian followed his gaze. The first of the serpents had crested the top of the wall and was slithering down the other side toward the ground. Screams ensued—from the scattering remaining guards; from Tannis, who had just awoken; and from Corsi, who was trying to stab the serpent with one of the Lethean weapons to no avail. Aleria morphed into an eagle and dove at Silvertongue. He only chuckled and flung out his hand, releasing a series of black sparks. The eagle sailed over the rails of the second mezzanine and did not reappear.

Dorian's stomach tightened. Was this how it would end? Sephone would die. They would all die. And he could do naught to save them. He would fail them, just as he had failed Lida and Emmy.

The snakes were coming closer now, twisting and veering toward them. Dorian looked at Cass, feeling his terror—a terror even a *calor* could not dissipate.

An anguished cry tore from Spartan's lips as the shield dissolved. "Dorian!" he shouted. "You know what to do!"

The staff? Dorian searched the hall for the weapon. Then, with perfect clarity, he heard the voice in his head—the voice from so long ago.

A time will come very soon, Dorian, when you will face an enemy you cannot defeat. You will hold the lives of those dearest to you in your hand, but you will not be able to save them. In that hour, you will be given a choice between life and death. That choice will come to define everything about you.

The ghost, Aedon, was also speaking. The voice of the man under the Mountain was like the clear peal of a bell.

A time will come, very soon, when you have nowhere left to turn, Dorian Ashwood. In that hour of need, call to me . . . and I will come to you.

Aye, he was right. Gift or no gift, they had nowhere left to turn. There was no more time. Dorian held onto Sephone's body. Despite all his best efforts, the nightmare had come true. He was going to lose her.

"Dorian!" Spartan bellowed as the snakes surrounded him, striking out with sharp fangs and flickering, forked tongues. "*Now!*"

All that was required was the death of pride, the admission that the Mountain was not as empty as he had first believed.

The death of himself.

He made his choice.

Please. Please help us.

Light flashed, even more brilliantly than one of Spartan's shields. Dorian was dazzled by a bolt of pure, sparkling energy. The man who stood in the lightning's place was about his age, or a little older. Every *alter* Dorian had ever met boasted a hint of iridescence at the very least—a few streaks in their hair, the unmistakable shimmer of their skin, the hidden gleam of color in their eyes. Cutter and Spartan had both had to shave their heads to hide their gifts.

But this man was completely, utterly ordinary, and no more dangerous looking than the old man had been.

"He's real," Sephone whispered, ink bubbling from between her lips. "Aedon is *real.*"

Wasn't she disappointed? Couldn't she see that this Aedon was just a man? Yet, at seeing him, Silvertongue's laughter died away. The snakes scattered, heading for the shadows. Spartan stood straighter, beaming at the man he had once called his true brother. His captain, his king.

Aedon turned to face Silvertongue, who plastered on a savage grin and began to polish his palms.

"So, you are here."

"I am here." The words were sure, even.

"And you are mine."

"For the present."

"Excellent." Silvertongue began to laugh again, a low, triumphant laugh that slowly grew in intensity as it rang through the great hall. His figure began to melt away.

The sound of his laughter resounded long after he disappeared.

33

SEPHONE

It had come true. Everything Aedon and Spartan had said had come true.

I mentally replayed his words from the night I'd first learned his name.

Before the end, everything you love will be threatened. But when that time has come, and you are in your hour of greatest need, you will call on me, and I will answer you. Everything I am and everything I have will be at your disposal. At the very moment death claims you, you will begin to live . . .

I had called, but it was too late. I could feel the Aeternum calling my name. A call I didn't want to answer but would need to nonetheless. The poison was working through my blood, leaving death in place of life.

"Wake up, love," Dorian said, shaking me gently.

I opened my eyes. Had I fallen asleep? "Stay with me, Dorian?"

Did he remember those words from long ago?

"Aye, I'll stay with you . . . until the end."

I reached out and touched his face with my bare fingers; my gift didn't awaken. There was probably not enough life left in me to sustain it. "Don't be afraid."

"I'm not afraid, love. More terrified." Cass's gift, eddying around our bodies, boldly pronounced the statement true. "Are you in pain?"

"Not anymore." The Reliquary had been agonizing, burning all the way to my soul. Every cell in my body must be singed. But then Cass had cut me from it—cut through the very wires themselves—and in a moment, I was free. It was good to die like this, in Dorian's arms, with my friends around me. It was good to be able to say goodbye.

"I would take this from you if I could," Dorian murmured.

"I know." My fingers slid to his chest, where black tendrils stained his skin beneath his shirt. "I think you already did."

Dorian caught my hand. "You are worth the ultimate sacrifice, Persephone. But I know now that I cannot save you."

Was I worth saving? I thought of the years of mind-bleedings and memory manipulations, the people of Nyx who had died when Kaesi circumvented my deal with Asa. The terrible things I'd done for Kaesi, how I'd vengefully attacked her guards. All the souls I'd helped to fade.

I was a thief, too. So many were dead or lost because of me. And now Dorian would die, too. *Nay, Dorian. I deserve exactly this.*

Aedon approached. "Can you save her?" Dorian asked him.

"Aye, my father can. But there must be a substitute."

"Then take me."

Aedon shook his head. "The one who does this must be free of poison. Not just on their outer layers of skin, but to the inner layers of their very soul."

A heavy silence grew in the great hall. We lived in a cursed world. None of us could lay claim to that.

Desolation filled Dorian's features. "Please . . . I love her."

Aedon regarded him closely. "It is because of love that I am here, Dorian Ashwood. My father's love for Caldera, and all it contains." He straightened. "Will you come with me to the Mountain?" He looked at Dorian, but the offer seemed to be directed at all of us.

"But the battle—" started Regis.

"You may stay behind if you wish."

Corsi was helping Tannis stand. Asa and Zaire held hands several paces away. Kaesi, Brinsley, and Aleria were presumably unconscious. If they were still alive.

"I will come," said Spartan.

"As will we," said Asa, with a glance at Zaire.

Regis, Cass, and Dorian all nodded.

I waited for Aedon to clap his hands, to snap his fingers, to summon a portal, like the one near the Mysterium. But instead, there was only another burst of bright white, and the great hall was gone.

We were standing on the side of the pool, Memoria. The cavern was filled with a sickly yellow light, and a foul stench arose from the sludgy water, which oozed and bubbled like a stew left too long on the stove. No longer did it bother with the façade of perfect clarity. The crooked trees surrounding the pool seemed to be leaning closer than ever, while the solitary tree which grew out of the water had lost its fine coat of leaves. The trunk was still scarred and pockmarked, and in the gashes welled red resin. A resin that looked uncomfortably like blood.

Dorian held me against him, but I could feel him weakening. A small turn of my head revealed the Reliquary, sitting on the ground only a few paces away. The hourglass was still full of poison.

Aedon knelt beside us and reached for my hand. Neither of us wore gloves, so I pulled away. "Nay, my lord. You can't."

"If I do not do it, you will die, Persephone."

Dorian's voice quavered. "Don't you require the Reliquary?"

Aedon shook his head. "All the Reliquary brings is death, Dorian. None of you are able to bear it."

"I don't understand. How do you plan to save her without the Reliquary?" Dorian glanced at Asa, who had approached. "And without a *healer*?"

I met Aedon's gentle gaze. He was so like Spartan, with his enigmatic ways and quiet reserve. Or perhaps Spartan was like him. I was beginning to suspect that one could spend an eternity with the *Infinitum* and never completely know the workings of his mind.

"This poison cannot be removed by an ordinary *healer*, Dorian. Not even the Reliquary can accomplish such a feat. This poison can only be erased through sacrifice, the ultimate sacrifice you referred to before. The poison must be returned to its source, and from there, the waters can be cleansed."

"Why would you do this?"

"Because of love," Aedon said simply. "Do you remember the golden current in your mind, Dorian? The love borne out of your desire to do anything to save your child, Emmeline? When Persephone saw it, she realized she could not take your memories—and she was right. Love is the greatest force in the universe, though the human version is but an echo of the divine. Because of love, my father has given you everything. Including me."

Once more, he extended his hand to me.

I studied his careworn face—his deeply lined eyes. No one who had ever gazed long into that ancient face could have doubted that Aedon was alive, that he was real. Kindness made its home there, and gentleness, and timeless compassion. Mingled with the incomparable power I had seen in Spartan's vial and my dreams.

The people of Caldera had thought they'd left their gods behind in the world-that-was. But the Three had never left, not even when they were rejected and forgotten. And now, at the very hour of Caldera's greatest need—*our* need—Aedon had come back to us. Offering a way through.

Offering himself.

"I can't let you do this." My lungs seized and I choked, coughing and spluttering. A hollow rattle grew in my chest, twin to the one that had crippled Cutter at the last. Dorian supported my head, but I could feel the poison dribbling down my chin. Tears appeared in Dorian's eyes, and he wiped them and the poison away with his sleeve.

"Why not, Persephone?" Aedon asked.

"Because you'll die."

"I have made my choice. But this is not the end. I will return. You have only to trust me."

I looked at the small circle which had gathered around us. Regis and Spartan—both stricken faced, though the latter was focused on Aedon. Cass had crossed his arms, his eyebrows knotted together. Asa looked hopeful, while Zaire's face was tight and impassive.

Trust me, a small voice said. *I have a plan for your sorrow.*

Was it truly so easy? I looked at Dorian. Sweat had broken out on his forehead, and I could feel his body shaking. He pulled me more closely against him, and I knew he was far sicker than he was letting on. Any moment, he might collapse.

I have heard rumors of a certain healer—*an* alter—*who can mend the impossible . . .*

The *healer* from Idaea's words flashed into my mind.

. . . I once knew a woman who'd been poisoned, and she was very close to death. After a passing encounter with this man, she was restored. To this day, she lives a street away from my house. But the healer *comes and goes . . .*

It must be Aedon. No other *alter* had come close to his powers, and Silvertongue was not inclined to altruism. Aedon had healed the woman, and both of them had lived.

They had lived.

I reached out and took Aedon's hand. My hand was weak and clammy; his was strong and warm. His fingers tightened around mine, and suddenly I felt strength flowing into my body, enlivening my throbbing muscles. The poison was retreating. I could lift my head from Dorian's shoulder. I could feel my legs. The harsh rattle of my breathing faded.

Aedon extended his other hand to Dorian, who took it hesitantly. But color immediately flooded back into Dorian's face; he stopped trembling; the black marks striping his chest and collarbones turned snow white, appearing stark against his deeply tanned skin. His posture straightened; his jaw firmed as he became the man I'd seen only in his memories. Strong, sure, whole.

But the joy as I watched Dorian's transformation turned to dismay as I looked upon Aedon. His face had turned sickly and pale. A vein throbbed thickly at his temple. His body shuddered as he bent over, as if to retch. The poison was coating every visible inch of skin, and the inky webbing grew thicker as it coursed through his bulging veins.

Nay . . .

The three of us stood, and Aedon nearly collapsed. Dorian and Spartan quickly came to either side of him, holding his arms. But he stumbled forward, out of their grip, heading for the pool. Black ink dribbled from the corner of his mouth.

A sinister, grating laugh echoed through the cavern, and the yellow light grew bolder, flickering upon the oily surface of the subterranean lake. Suddenly, shadows flitted along the cavern walls. Looming larger, coming closer.

We weren't alone.

"Wolves," gritted Cass. My ankle began to throb, remembering the sharpness of the teeth that had once punctured my flesh. I edged closer to Dorian and Spartan. These were far bigger than the Nightmares which had attacked us outside of Calliope. The same poison Aedon had drawn from our bodies dripped from their wickedly sharp teeth, soaking into the thirsty earth.

"Aedon!" shouted Dorian, beginning to go after him, but the *Infinitum* had reached the edge of the pool.

The seven of us watched as Aedon turned. "When I enter the water, you must leave this place. Do you understand?"

Dorian was frantic. "Don't you see? That is poison—"

"*Now* it is poison, Dorian Ashwood. Should I not enter, the poison will return to Persephone's body, and she will die. You will both die. But don't be afraid. All will be well. This is my choice."

Before Dorian could say anything else, Aedon waded into the pool. The water sucked at his clothes like mud. It almost seemed to be dissolving them. The pool turned an opaque black and then deepest red, as red as the resin now oozing from a gash in the tree's side. The water blistered Aedon's skin, making it raw and exposed. His agonized groans filled the cavern. But he continued on, never looking back at us, never once faltering.

I stood rooted to the ground, frozen and numb. He was an *Infinitum*, more powerful than the rest of us combined. How could he choose this?

Dorian tried to go after him, only for a wolf to launch itself from the shadows, snarling as it advanced. Several more wolves appeared, positioning themselves between Dorian and the shore of Memoria. Dorian felt for his staff. It wasn't there, but back in the great library, having been confiscated by one of Kaesi's guards. He drew his dagger instead, but it would be a pitiful defense against the pack.

"Get back!" Spartan exclaimed, and a shield appeared between Dorian and the wolves, encircling the seven of us. It wasn't anywhere near as bright as his usual shields—no more than a candle flame in intensity. Any moment, it could waver or collapse altogether.

I stumbled to Dorian's side. The wolves were closing in.

Dorian was staring agonizingly at the pool; the waters had risen to Aedon's neck. I heard the *Infinitum*'s hollow cry, mingled with the unholy chorus of the wolves, which had all but surrounded Memoria. Finally, without fanfare, Aedon's dark head slipped beneath the surface. Minutes passed as bubbles rose and burst . . . no one could survive that long underwater.

I should know.

"He's gone," said Spartan in an empty voice, and my heart sank to the depths.

Aedon was dead.

"It can't be. He said he would return," Dorian said stubbornly, seeming almost oblivious to the wolves that had surrounded Spartan's shield, waiting to spring.

Precious minutes slipped by, but Aedon did not resurface. The laughter echoing throughout the cavern became almost deafening. The wolves bayed, howling their triumph, and as we stood there, cracks formed in the roof overhead. A few rocks splashed into the water.

The cavern was coming apart.

Cass went to Dorian. "Come on, Thane. You heard the man. We must leave." He tried to tug Dorian away to no avail.

Cass uttered an exasperated oath.

"You might not care for your own life. But are you going to leave Sephone to the wolves?"

At that, Dorian came back to himself. Dragging his gaze from Memoria and sheathing his knife, he looked up as the roof continued to crumble. The wolves growled and tossed their shaggy heads but remained where they were. Spartan raised his shield until it formed a dome over us. It was too late to save the Reliquary, now behind the pack.

"Let's go," said Asa, grabbing Zaire's hand.

We hurried up the rim of the bowl and over the other side, heading for the river. No boat bobbed there like last time. We would have to swim.

I slowed to a stop, staring at the churning water. It looked impossibly deep, and the current was fast moving. "I can't do it." Even at the best of times, I was a poor swimmer.

"Aye, Sephone, you can," Dorian assured me. "I'll help you."

The others were stripping off their boots and outer layers, so I followed suit, trying to ignore the wolves that waited close by, and the cavern that disintegrated behind and above them. Several rocks bounced off the roof of Spartan's dome and slid down the side. One of the smaller stones struck a wolf, who merely yelped.

That same stone would have knocked a man unconscious.

Asa clapped his hands and a white-gray sphere appeared—almost exactly like a miniature moon. He flicked his wrist, and it glided upward until it was hovering above the water casting a long ray of light, like a ghostly staircase. Asa entered the river, followed by Regis and a carefully moving Spartan, who was still supporting the dome with upraised hands. Cass lingered, the water swirling around his ankles as he looked at Dorian and me.

Dorian had reached for my wrist when Zaire suddenly materialized between us. "Nay, Lord Adamo. There isn't time. Leave her to me." And then she became a beast, the beautiful form melting into one that was hideous and grotesque. She turned, presenting her back, and I swallowed as I comprehended.

She wanted me to ride her. Zaire. Who had nearly killed Dorian and Aleria . . .

But without hesitation, Dorian lifted me onto Zaire's back. I leaned forward, clutching the lion-wolf's glossy black mane as she plunged directly into the river. Icy water sucked at my legs as I gripped her middle tightly with my knees.

Easy, said a voice in my mind. *I won't let you fall.*

I loosened my grip and tried to relax. How different it was compared to riding the white stallion. With him, I had known for sure that I would not fall.

Zaire continued to offer the occasional instruction as we moved into the heart of the river. A glance over my shoulder confirmed that Dorian and Cass were following. Even with Regis's and Asa's help, Spartan was struggling to swim while keeping the dome aloft. The wolves had entered the water, their powerful bodies making easy work of the current, just as Zaire's did.

Let the monk ride with us, Zaire said to me, and I repeated her words to the others. A moment later, Spartan was sitting behind me, clutching my shirt with one hand as he held the other up high. But I could feel him weakening, feel the effort beginning to take a toll on his already exhausted body. A moment later, he slumped against me, and the shield winked out. I reached back for his arms and held them around my waist.

"Swim!" bellowed Dorian, but the warning was unnecessary. By the light of Asa's tiny moon, it was easy to see that the collapse of the river tunnel was imminent. Enormous fragments rained down on us from above, causing the water to froth and churn. I lost sight of Dorian and Cass as Zaire's powerful legs propelled us along the river. Spartan was a dead weight against my back. If I turned to look, I might dislodge him completely.

Dust from the falling debris choked the air. There was no sign of the bioluminescent glowworms that had lit the cavern the first time we'd visited. Even Asa's light disappeared in the flurry of rock. How could the others find their way out?

A few minutes later, we burst into the open. It was dark, the air fragrant and cool. The current slowed as the river widened. In no time, Zaire was making for a tiny beach, little more than a strip of pale white. If a moon shone, I couldn't see it through the gray.

All around us, the Garden was silent and still. A shiver danced up my spine as I recalled Spartan's warnings.

It is full of untold secrets and hidden dangers, and it can be treacherous, even deadly . . .

There was no sign of the wolves prowling the forest undergrowth, nor any other ominous-looking shadows. But, somehow, I sensed that we were not alone.

I had heard Silvertongue's laugh back in the cavern. Was he watching us even now?

As Zaire entered the shallows, I slid from her back, reaching up for Spartan. The acolyte was heavier than I expected, and we tottered backward into the water, soaking the half of me that had been nearly dry. Zaire, human once more, reached down to help us. Together, we carried Spartan to shore, where Regis and Asa were squeezing the moisture from their clothes.

Seeing us, Asa hurried over, giving Zaire a quick embrace before gingerly picking up his younger brother and carrying him over to a patch of grass. Regis's face filled with relief as he saw me, but then he frowned.

"Where are Dorian and Cass?"

I looked all around, barely registering the icy water lapping at my feet. Between the gray and the darkness, it was impossible to see more than a few feet ahead. The cavern could fall at any moment. My stomach knotted. They could be at the bottom of the river, pinned by heavy rocks.

"They were just behind me," I said as Regis reached my side, peering out into the gloom.

Please, let them be all right.

"I don't see anything," Regis said tersely.

A second later, there came the sound of splashing. My heart leapt. Two figures emerged from the darkness, one supporting the other with an arm around his waist.

The shorter man gave a low groan. "You should have left me behind, Dorian."

"And be plagued forever by your relentless ghost? Nay, I think I've chosen the better option."

I staggered forward and threw my arms around their necks. "I'm so glad you're all right." Green light wound between our bodies as I stepped away, exuberant with relief.

Cass grinned. "You know, I believe we feel the same way."

I returned his grin, then frowned—the side of Cass's shirt was bloodied. "You're injured!"

"Aye, I was hoping young Asa Karthick might patch me up. Or you, if you were willing." He winked at me, but the gesture was more solemn than flirtatious.

Dorian regained his hold on Cass's other arm. "Come on. We should get out of the water before we all freeze." I slipped beneath Cass's arm. Together, Dorian and I assisted him to the shore, Regis leading. The others had moved to a grassy clearing where Asa had a fire going—a magical fire that glowed gray.

"So we don't attract unwelcome visitors," Asa explained when he saw my questioning look. But none appeared to have survived the cavern's collapse to come after us. If they did, we had only Asa and Zaire to defend us, for Spartan was unconscious, and the rest of us were unarmed.

We must not linger here after dark . . .

I sat beside Cass as Asa healed the gash in his side, which was from an exposed tree root, apparently. He had been wounded, caught in a rainstorm of falling rocks and beginning to sink, when Dorian spotted him and went back, dragging him to safety.

"You know," Cass quietly observed when Asa went to tend to Spartan. "Once, I might have thought all lords the same—my brother, Lord Adamo—but as it turns out, Dorian is nothing like my brother. My brother would never have laid down his life for anyone. Let alone for his enemy."

I nodded, understanding.

Cass darted a look at Dorian, who was speaking with Regis a short distance away. If I weren't mistaken, resignation flitted across Cass's face. He turned back to me and lifted a hand, touching a lock of my hair. "You know, black suited you, Seph, but I prefer white."

The marks on my chest had faded, and what I could see of my hair had also returned to its usual color. There was no sign of the poison which had marked my body for nearly half a year.

Aedon had drawn it—all of it—into himself.

I left Cass to find Zaire and offer my thanks for her saving my life. She merely shrugged and rejoined Asa by the fire. It seemed we weren't to be friends, but maybe we wouldn't be enemies, either.

Regis returned to the fire. Dorian was walking away, heading for the trees. Wanting to be alone? Or unable to stay?

On a whim, I followed him. A fey breeze wove through the trees, stirring the grass. It was as if the entire forest collectively sighed. A quiver of expectation hung in the air, and once more, I had the feeling that the Garden was waiting for something.

My chest tightened. Aedon would never return to his vines.

Dorian stopped and pivoted to face me. His gaze was solemn, his shoulders weighted. Instinctively, I reached for my gift, thinking to share with Dorian my memories of Aedon. But in the place where my gift normally resided, there was something else. Something new. A well of warmth, of impossible depth. A gently humming current.

Gifts always come in pairs . . .

Inside my mind, I plunged my hands into the current, teasing out the energy. It bent almost immediately to my will, like a pair of gloves that was made just for me, or a ring designed specifically for my finger. I pulled it from my mind like taffy, watching as it obtained physical form in my bare hands.

I recalled the white-haired woman in the purple gown from Lord Faro's party.

Lady Cilla has the ability to capture the essence of something—a thought, a feeling, an image, or even an idea—in a jewel like the one you see there. She then uses her power to project it outwards. It is not so strange. You do something similar with your memories, do you not?

A heavy, round shape weighed down my palm. It was a perfect diamond, the dozen or so faces carefully cut and polished, scattering fractals of light, though no sun or moon hung in the sky. Rising to my feet, I raised my hand, and the jewel became a beacon, shooting shafts of pure, white light in every direction. Different than Lady Cilla's ruby, and yet similar. The light bathed the grass in rich, molten currents of silvery pearl, penetrating the gray.

I heard Dorian's exclamation of wonder. Shouts came from the direction of the others—they had seen the light. But the gift was drawing on my own strength, my greatly diminished strength. I lost my grip on the current and felt myself falling, falling weightlessly through a vast, cavernous space.

I opened my hand. The diamond was gone, along with the sense of hope that had filled me seconds before.

And the clearing was as dark as a starless sky.

34

DORIAN

He opened his eyes to a weak sunrise. Asa's fire hadn't burned low, as real fire would—even now, it gleamed sullenly in the circle of stones. The others were sprawled around the fire, fast asleep, except for Asa, who had taken the last watch. He sat on the edge of camp with his back to them, peering out into the gloomy day.

Sephone had a second gift. What it was, exactly, Dorian didn't know. He had seen it only once before, in Lady Cilla. He found himself craving the hopefulness he had briefly felt in the presence of the light—the memory she had somehow projected into the clearing, of Aedon's words.

Trust me.

Here they were stranded on an island without a boat or supplies or even proper clothes, days away from Calliope. Without Aedon, they couldn't return to the capital, to Lady Xia. She was on her own.

The others woke one by one, only to sit around the fire, trying to ignore the ache of hunger in their bellies. Spartan rushed into the clearing, though Dorian hadn't registered that he'd left. "You must come and see!" he exclaimed. "Quickly!"

They followed the acolyte through the forest, paralleling the river. What had Spartan found?

Dorian's stomach rumbled faintly. Breakfast, he hoped.

The ground rose gently upward as the trees thinned. They were approaching the Mountain. The gray was beginning to recede as Spartan sloshed through the river, which now only came up to his knees. Dorian followed, brow creasing. It had been dark last night, but surely this river was normally far deeper? And where was the great overhang—the river tunnel? The entrance had collapsed. Surely, they should be standing on a vast mound of rubble by now.

But instead of rubble, the gentle slope of the Mountain was covered with wildflowers and rich green grass, each emerald blade the width of Dorian's finger. He could see twenty paces ahead—then fifty, then a hundred. And then, suddenly, they stood in the open, in the fresh mountain air, with a vast blue sky overhead.

The gray was gone.

"Where's the cavern?" Sephone looked around. "Where's the Sacred Grove?"

Spartan pointed. "Over there."

They crested a tiny rise, and their mouths fell open.

They stood on the rim of a large mountain lake, gleaming like a freshly polished mirror in the early morning sunshine. Songbirds dipped and danced upon the surface, flashing tails of pale blue and gold, while larger waterbirds kept to the reeds, stalking their aquatic prey. Silver flashed here and there as gleaming, scaled bodies caught the sun, winking impishly. Larger schools of tiny fish moved almost as one; occasionally, they would disturb the surface, and it was as if the water shivered. A white-feathered bird with skinny legs and an impossibly long, slender neck stood in the shallows, waiting to strike.

Next to the lake squatted a grove of trees, their crowns full and green, their trunks tall and proud. But no tree was more magnificent than the one whose roots drank from the lake itself. That one was a mighty oak, whose canopy was large enough to shelter hundreds if not thousands of birds.

"Impossible," breathed Asa.

"He said there was no darkness before," Sephone said in an odd voice. "No cavern. The whole place was covered with lush forest. On a sunny day, you could see to the very bottom of the lake."

"Look," Zaire pointed. "Something is stirring in the center of the water."

She was right. It was more than the cheeky maneuvers of a large fish; a figure was coming up out of the lake. The sun fell blindingly upon him, illuminating a person who was both familiar and completely foreign. His clothes were whiter than Sephone's hair. The water he disturbed as he strode into the shallows appeared both clear and milky at the same time. Beside him trotted a white stallion, his coat dazzlingly white, with iridescent shades of green, blue, purple, and pink. The mane that graced his neck looked finer than spun silk.

But it was the man himself who drew Dorian's full attention, the man who had once seemed so utterly plain. *Alters* had iridescent hair, or eyes, or skin, and some, like Cass, possessed more than their fair share, though all were striking in their own way. But this man, coming toward them, was like seeing the whole after only knowing the part.

He *was* iridescence.

"Aedon." Spartan's voice was filled with joy. Sephone uttered a cry. Dorian stared, stunned.

"My friends," Aedon said, and if Dorian had doubted before, he could not now—there was no voice like his. Aedon opened his arms, and Spartan ran forward, laughing and weeping simultaneously, followed by Sephone. Both were embraced in turn, then nuzzled by the horse. Sephone threw her arms around the stallion's neck and buried her face in his mane.

It occurred to Dorian, belatedly, how similar they were. Both Spartan and Sephone had been betrayed by their siblings to some degree, and neither of them had truly known their parents. But all of that seemed to fade into insignificance in light of the bond he witnessed now. In Aedon and the white horse, they had found their family. They were like brother and sister.

Dorian hesitantly approached. "I watched you die."

There was no trace of the poison, though Aedon bore the same white marks on his collarbones, neck, and face—more numerous than Dorian's or Sephone's. Against his dark skin, they looked like scars.

"All those who desire to live must first forfeit their life," Aedon said. "If I did not do it, you would never be free, Dorian."

But he wasn't a slave. Not like Sephone, Cass, or even Spartan.

"Some chains are visible; others are not." Aedon's eyes looked deep into his. "Oftentimes, one may consider himself a master, only to find he is the slave. From all that, my brother, I have freed you. You need never be a slave again—to your past or to your future. You are free."

And suddenly Dorian understood. As he looked at Aedon, he could feel his sorrow and fears draining away.

"Won't you join me in the water?" Aedon beckoned him to the lake. "You need not fear Memoria now. There is no more poison. It is clean."

Sephone and Spartan were already splashing each other like little children. For the first time, the acolyte looked as young as he truly was. The white stallion managed to look noble, intimidating, and friendly at the same time.

"Aye, I will join you."

The water was cool at first, but it was warming with the growing heat of the day. It was hard to imagine that only last night, this same water had blistered and burned Aedon's skin. Dorian felt like a child again.

The four of them swam until the sun was high enough to indicate midmorning. Hunger brought them to the shore, dripping wet but impossibly joyful. It was as if they had left behind in the depths every shadow and memory that haunted, every dream of the future and regret of the past, every nightmare that had stalked them.

Cass, Regis, and Zaire were still sitting on the lake edge. Asa came forward to approach Aedon.

He bowed his head. "My lord, I would speak with you . . . alone."

Aedon's eyes twinkled. "Aye, Asa Karthick. Shall we?" He lifted his hand, indicating that they should stroll along the rim of the lake.

When they were gone, Dorian started toward the others, only to spy the Reliquary lying almost forlornly on the bank, at the base of the oak tree. It was unfurled, just as it had been the night before. Only this time, something was different.

Sephone saw his face. "What is it, Dorian?"

"The Reliquary."

She followed his gaze and gave a low gasp.

There were no more metal gloves. No more hourglass, with its green, cracked glass and silver filigree. No poison. No more curse.

The Reliquary was destroyed.

The day passed like a dream. The battle at Calliope had seemed so urgent, so important, but here, in the Garden, it faded into the background. It was as if they were in the eye of the storm, at peace while the war for their world raged on around them.

The gray had melted away, revealing the island in all its glory. Aedon showed them orchards of every fruit one could imagine, many of them fruits Dorian had heard about, but never tasted. Oranges, round and zesty; cherries, ruby red and deliciously tart; a sweet melon Spartan called a honeydew. Sephone gave an exclamation of pure delight when she spotted a patch of strawberries, their pitted, glossy fruit and white flowers peeking out from beneath dark green leaves.

"The strawberries," Aedon said with a smile at Sephone, "are particularly good."

All of them ate until they were full. Even Zaire and Cass, who had been uncommonly quiet, seemed different.

Asa had spoken at great length with Aedon. What they said, none would probably ever know, except perhaps for Zaire. But when he returned, Asa Karthick seemed a new man.

Aedon brought them to his vineyard, where the grapes were like enormous, glassy orbs, ripe for the picking. It was then that Dorian remembered the other member of the Three. But when he asked Aedon about his father, the *alter* only smiled.

"If you have seen me, Dorian, then you have seen him. And the more you look at me, the more you will see him. For we are one." And Aedon looked at the white horse who, from Sephone's recounting, had been a white raven.

Aedon was far more than just an *alter*. No *alter* could do what he had done. If Dorian wasn't mistaken, he possessed every one of their gifts—and then some.

Dorian had once described the old gods as having hearts of stone—"wily and capricious" he had called them. His ancestors had left them behind in the world-that-was and gone their own way, never once dreaming they were the root of their own troubles. But Aedon had come back to the very people who had sent him away.

"It was you," Dorian wondered, when it was just Aedon, Spartan, Sephone, Asa, and him. "You gave the gifts."

Aedon smiled. "Aye, it was my father. He is the source of everything good, you know, and not only the things that belong to *alters*. There are gifts of all kinds and sizes, each one given in the hour they are needed most."

He looked around at them. "But even the gifts are only a shadow of what is to come, my friends. Use them well, but know that they are only temporary."

Aedon led them past the vineyard to a sheltered pool, far smaller than the mountain lake. It was unnaturally quiet. The only sound that could be heard was the breeze, wending through the trees. The surface of the pool was so smooth, Dorian's first thought was that it had frozen over. Yet Sephone showed no fear as she beheld it. She was the closest to the white stallion, her bare fingers entwined in his mane.

"Do you have your bottles?" Aedon asked, and to Dorian's surprise, Spartan and Sephone produced tiny glass bottles from within the folds of their clothes. Aedon took them, bent, and though each one was already almost full, filled each one to brimming. With another smile, he handed them back to their owners. He did the same for a third and fourth bottle, which he presented to Dorian and Asa. "Taste and see."

Dorian took his wonderingly. The liquid inside was almost as iridescent as Aedon had first appeared. When he tasted it, a feeling of infinite satisfaction flowered inside his stomach as if he had eaten a meal so rich and filling that he would never be hungry again. Yet the desire to drink remained, though it didn't resemble any earthly craving.

He gazed at the bottle. It appeared no less full than it had been before. He drank of it again, more deeply this time, but the same thing occurred. Sephone and Spartan were both watching, beaming.

"What is this place?" Asa asked, looking at the pool.

"This is Vivus Aqua," replied Aedon. "Drink of this water every day, and like the oak tree, you will flourish. The more deeply you drink of it, the more deeply you will know me, and the more you will be changed. In time, it alone will satisfy your soul."

"It's an antidote," marveled Spartan. "To the poison."

"Aye. The only antidote."

"But I thought . . ." Sephone trailed off. "Isn't Memoria clean now?"

"Memoria is the source of all rivers, great and small," Aedon replied. "Eventually, its waters will filter to the furthest reaches of Caldera. But, for the time being, poison still remains in the world. The curse lingers. The second pool will protect you from this."

"What about our gifts?"

Aedon turned his knowing gaze upon her.

She fidgeted with her necklace and her voice sank. "Every time I draw on my gift, it nearly overwhelms me."

"Have you learned the lesson of the Reliquary, my daughter?"

"Aye," she said miserably. "I cannot save the world on my own strength."

"Nay," he replied kindly, "though it is possible to love its people—and love them, you will, after you have left this place. But this gift of yours was not given so that you would shoulder another's troubles alone. It was given so that you would realize there is only one who can. The moon only gives light because of the sun, Sephone. Let the sun lend you its strength, and you will shine with its radiance, its satisfying warmth, even in the densest darkness. First things first, and second things second, and all the gifts will work as they were intended."

Dorian thought of his *calor* gift and Cass's *lumen* gift. Was that why they had proven so unsatisfying and so burdensome in comparison to Spartan's peace gift? He had never tasted courage, just as Cass had never tasted truth. But Spartan—Spartan had peace in spades. His gift didn't just affect others. It transformed him.

He stared down at the vial. How could it be so simple?

"And the pain of memories? Will it be removed, too?" Sephone asked.

Was she thinking of Dorian or of herself? For both of them carried a lifetime of pain, and he could still remember Lida and Emmy. He could remember everything.

"Nay," said Aedon, with a small shake of his head. "At least, not yet. It is the pain and thirst of a soul which summons it to its source, my daughter. Just as it brought the four of you here, to seek the only draught in Caldera that truly satisfies."

He looked around the Garden. Part of it was tamed—the fruitful orchards, the neatly ordered and well-tended vines, the lush Grove beside the pool of Memoria. But the rest of it was still impossibly wild. Dorian remembered Spartan's warnings about the beasts that prowled the Garden at night.

"In this *altered* world, the real has imperfections. It is merely a memory of what once was, a glimpse of what will be. All things are an echo, a taste, of that future. Now, you see but a glimpse. Thereafter, you will have everything in full, and neither it nor anything it contains will ever be taken away from you. The pain of the past, in that place, will be nothing more than a distant memory."

"Can you not take us there now?" Sephone asked hopefully.

"I will . . . soon. But what you have seen here, my friends, you must show to the world. The love you have known here—the water that brought you back to life—you must bring to the rest of the world."

Dorian thought of Regis and Zaire and Cass. Each of them had, in their own way, refused to speak with Aedon, just as Dorian had in the beginning. But there was time, yet. They would come to see who Aedon truly was.

"But you're coming with us, right?" This came from Asa. "There is still a battle to be won."

"Aye, there will be a battle," said Aedon more solemnly. "But you will not go to Calliope alone." He looked at the white stallion, who tossed his glossy mane as if he understood, and then at Sephone. "You will never be alone again."

Dorian tucked the vial into the pocket over his heart, letting Aedon's words steal away his shame and guilt, soften the hard edges of his grief. All the while, he heard Spartan's voice in his head.

Shame does not share territory with joy . . .

Aedon brought them back to the others. Cass paced like a lion trapped in a cage, while Zaire bit her nails. She glared at Asa, who gazed earnestly back. Dorian had never seen the younger Karthick so altered.

The expression on Regis's face and its urgency threatened to steal away Dorian's newfound peace.

He hastened over to them. "Something's gone wrong with the

battle. I can barely understand Magritte, but I think there are problems between Lethe and the outlanders. We have to get back. Now."

Dorian looked toward Aedon and the white stallion, but the horse was gone. In his place fluttered a white raven, which alighted gently on Spartan's shoulder.

"Yes, you must go," said Aedon. "But first, I will give you everything you need."

Not for the first time, Dorian became aware that the Garden was not truly empty. Shapes moved through the trees, but they weren't wolves.

They were human.

Silently, Aedon's people came forward, carrying sacks and crates. Unlike the robed members of the Mysterium, they looked like warriors, except none of them were armed. At least, not visibly. Out of the sacks came clean clothes, softer and finer than anything they'd ever worn. Out of the crates came boots that fit like they were made for them, and weapons. Glee swept through Dorian as he found his staff. Cass pounced on his pair of knives. Except for Regis, the others wouldn't need weapons. Their gifts would suffice.

"Time passes differently on the island," said Aedon once they were dressed and ready. "To you, it is a full day since you left Calliope, but to your friends, you have only been gone an hour. I will bring you back to the library, and from there, you can find your way."

Dorian looked around at the others. Cass and Regis were restless, while Zaire seemed almost in a trance. Only the four who had drunk from the second pool were calm. Dorian tried not to think of what was waiting for them back in Calliope. What things Kaesi might have done in their absence.

"And Silvertongue?" Dorian belatedly thought to ask.

"You can leave Silvertongue to me."

Despite what Aedon said about us only having been gone an hour, back in the library it was unnaturally dark. After the peace and tranquility of the Garden, the state of the great hall was shocking. Books had tumbled out of shelves, along with ancient relics; armchairs and desks and other furniture had been overturned; glass crunched underfoot from the damaged chandelier. Several scorch marks remained from Spartan's battle with Asa. Many of the exquisitely carved banisters were snapped in half, and one of the spiral staircases looked as if it had been torn away and crumpled by a giant hand.

Seeing the rectangular tables with their leather straps, I shuddered and looked for Aedon. But he hadn't appeared in the library. The white raven was still perched on Spartan's shoulder, however. His clever, beady eyes swept the room, easily piercing the gloom.

Had Aedon gone in search of Silvertongue? Surely he wouldn't leave us alone.

You will never be alone again . . .

Dorian gave a low cry and fell to his knees, crouching next to a motionless body. Pale blond tresses spilled over his arm as he lifted Kaesi and, with effort, stood and carried her to one of the chaise lounges.

"Is she dead?" Regis asked.

Dorian began to feel for her pulse, but Kaesi stirred and sat up, blinking rapidly. "Dorian?" she said, touching his arm. "Is that you?"

He released a relieved sigh. She remembered him. "Aye, it's me."

"Good," said Cass, drawing one of his blades. "She's awake. The question is, does she remember enough to pay for her crimes?"

His rapid advance indicated that he, at least, intended for her to pay for them. Spartan and I darted forward to intercept him.

"Nay, Cass." I grabbed his sleeve. "You mustn't hurt her."

Kaesi blinked again, her eyes now more brown than blue. "Why would you want to hurt me?"

Cass shook off my hand. "Have you so easily forgotten that she tried to kill you, Seph?" he hissed.

"I haven't forgotten."

Cass glared and stalked to the other side of the hall and began sifting through the mess. Was he looking for Brinsley and Aleria?

Dorian knelt by Kaesi. "What's the last thing you remember?"

Kaesi's fair brows rose. "I was in Maera, riding in the mountains with you. We got back, and Father's soldiers arrested me." Her forehead furrowed. "I don't remember why."

"You don't recall Remon and the others? Your involvement with the—"

"I don't know what you're talking about, Dorian." Kaesi's panic rose visibly as her gaze swept the room. "Why am I here? This is the library in Calliope, is it not?" Her face paled. "Are we at war?"

"Aye, and of your doing," said Zaire unhelpfully, and somewhat untruthfully. For it was technically Lord Draven who had begun the war between Memosine and Lethe. Kaesi and Lady Xia had just continued it.

"That's enough," said Dorian curtly. He put his arm around his sister's shoulders. "She knows naught of that." Then his face went blank, as if he had retreated inside his head.

Magritte, giving another update about the battle?

A moment later, Regis confirmed it. "We must get to the lower part of the city. Xia needs us."

Asa exchanged a look with Zaire. "You can't take your sister with us, Lord Adamo. Not until Miss Winter has established just how much of her memory and gifts remain."

"Gifts?" repeated Kaesi blankly. "What gifts? I'm not an *alter*."

Indecision warred with uncertainty in Dorian's face. "I can't leave her here."

"There's no alternative," said Zaire firmly. "She's still dangerous."

"Hardly," Kaesi huffed. Despite her lack of memories, the word possessed a fiery edge. Was this the Kaesi that Dorian had once told me about?

Dorian turned to his sister. "I'm sorry, Kaesi, but they're right. I'll come back, I promise."

"What are you . . ." Her eyes widened as Cass returned from the other side of the hall and produced a coil of rope that one of Aedon's people had given him. Murmuring apologies, Dorian guided his sister to the metal post of one of the intact staircases, where he instructed her to sit at the base and wrap her arms around the pole at her back. Cass bound Kaesi's wrists together; at her low gasp of pain, Dorian glared at him.

"Not so tightly. You'll hurt her."

Kaesi looked up at Dorian, hurt and betrayal mingled in her teary eyes. "Dorian, I promise you I won't—"

"It's too late for that," snapped Cass, getting to his feet.

"What if someone tries to harm her?" Dorian asked in concern, his hand resting protectively on Kaesi's shoulder. "We can't just leave her alone, tied up and defenseless."

"I will guard her," came a weary voice from above.

The eight of us looked up as Aleria descended from the mezzanine via one of the spiral staircases, coming to stand next to Spartan. She was bloodied, and her clothes were badly torn, but she was upright, and her eyes were strong, clear.

"Where have you all been?" she asked, looking at Dorian.

"It's a long story," he replied. "We'll explain everything, but right now, we have to rejoin the others."

Aleria nodded. "I heard Magritte's update. Go. I will stay."

My stomach contracted painfully. Brinsley was nowhere in sight. Even without Kaesi to deal with, we could still lose this fight.

"Thank you," said Dorian gratefully, then turned to the rest of us. "Come on. Let's go settle this."

We ran through the streets in the near dark, Dorian giving hushed instructions as we went. Still pondering what he had meant by *settle this*, I was taken aback when he caught my sleeve and pulled me to a halt, pressing us both back into the shadows while the others continued on.

"Seph—"

"Don't you dare suggest I sit this one out."

His eyes smiled. "Of course not. I was only going to say, if we get separated, stay close to Spartan and Asa—"

I would rather stay close to him.

"—and remember what Aedon said. There are gifts of all shapes and sizes. And none of them are lesser, no matter what you might believe."

"I'm neither Spartan nor you."

Dorian reached for his staff and snapped it to full length. "I'm a *calor,* an empath, and a quick study of languages. None of those gifts are terribly useful in a fight. You're a *mem*, an *alter* far more powerful than me. I would offer you every last fiber of strength in my body, if I thought it would help you find yours. But I suspect it's not my strength you need. It never has been."

I recalled Aedon's words. *First things first, and second things second, and all the gifts will work as they were intended . . .*

"Hope is a gift, too, you know," Dorian added.

"You said that to me once before. The day after the Nightmare wolf bit me."

"Aye, I did," he replied. "I think, perhaps, that you were born not to help people forget the truth, but to help them remember."

"Why do you think that?"

"Because you helped me."

For a brief moment, we looked at each other. I nodded slowly, and he smiled at me. Then we were running again, sprinting until we caught up to the others.

The smoke found us first. And, seconds later, the flames. The lower sections of Calliope were burning, the thickening smoke trapped beneath the weight of the gray. I pressed my sleeve to my mouth, my eyes watering. From somewhere below echoed the sounds of metal crashing against metal and anguished howls of pain and tortured screams, fading away into nothingness.

Asa's *alters*? Or Silvertongue, wreaking havoc?

Asa and Zaire disappeared into the smoke. They were to find the Memosinian *alters* and get them to stand down, if they hadn't already. Regis had found himself a crossbow, while Cass drew his blades. Spartan produced a shield bright enough to light the way and protect us at the same time. The white raven remained on his shoulder, although I could have sworn that I'd seen a similar bird on Asa's before he departed.

"Magritte's this way," Regis told us, pointing down the street. "Lady Xia is with her now. I think . . ." His voice faltered. "I think they may be injured."

I whispered a silent prayer for the safety of his wife and unborn child.

We hadn't gone far when we came across the fighting. As houses, shops, and other buildings succumbed one by one to the growing inferno, Letheans battled Memosinians in tiny clusters, with a mix of crossbows, knives, pikes, Lethean weaponry, and magic. But just as frequently as Letheans fought Memosinians, Memosinians fought outlanders. And outlanders fought Letheans.

What had happened? Had the outlanders decided they wanted Calliope for themselves and turned on Xia's army? Or had Lady Xia joined forces with the Memosinians against them?

Aleria, I thought. Did she know? Had she betrayed us, too? And we had left her in charge of Kaesi . . .

"What's going on?" Cass growled as several warriors came at us, seeming not to care which side we fought for. "This is a bloodbath!"

"Magritte said it had turned ugly," said Regis through gritted teeth as he fired bolt after bolt. "But I didn't expect this."

Dorian pushed me behind him, whirling faster than a spinning top as he wielded his staff, this time without the blades. Spartan produced a series of shields, blocking attacks that came at us out of the smoky gray. Thinking of Asa's *alters,* I tried desperately to reach for my gift. I had no other weapon besides the dagger strapped to my thigh.

There was naught but the tiniest flicker of icy flames.

Somehow, we forced our way up the street without encountering any *alters*. The fighting grew more intense the further we went, the smoke lifting and descending almost at random, making it nearly impossible to see. If not for Spartan's shields, we would have been killed many times over.

At last, Regis led the way down a narrow, twisting side street. Two dozen or so smoke-stained figures gathered there, some of them leaning against the brick side of a building, while the others formed a barricade blocking the street.

"It's us!" Regis hollered as they raised their weapons. "Magritte, it's me!"

"Lower your weapons," ordered a female voice. Xia. She strode forward but held her sides as if she were struggling to catch her breath. Her eyes went straightaway to Dorian. "I thought you were dead," she said flatly.

"You weren't the only one," replied Dorian with a grin. He glanced at Spartan. "We bring good news, my lady."

Suddenly, Regis gave a cry and made a dive for the woman appearing on Xia's right, enfolding her in his arms. "Magritte," he said over and over, then held her at arm's length as he inspected her closely. "Are you all right?"

She mopped the perspiration from her brow, succeeding only in worsening the sooty, bloody smudges. "I'll be fine, Reg."

"Your voice sounds weak. Are you sure you're not injured?"

"Nay, I'm just weary. It's Lady Xia who's—"

"We could use some good news," interrupted Xia loudly, still looking at Dorian. The fingers of one hand were bloodied, but she stowed them behind her back.

"I'll bet," muttered Cass, "seeing the mess you've made of things."

"We've just come from the library," explained Dorian. "There's much to report, but most importantly, my sister is no longer a threat. Nor are Asa Karthick and Zaire. My sister has lost her memories, and the other two have joined our side. Even now, Asa and Zaire are trying to find the other *alters* to sway them from Kaesi."

"Lost her memories?" Xia raised her brow and sent me an appreciative look. My chest constricted. If only she knew how deeply I regretted the effects of my gift.

"Aye," said Regis. "She won't trouble us again."

"Good." But Xia was still frowning.

"This is the part where you tell us what went wrong for you," said Cass pleasantly, earning a sharp look from Xia.

"I do not answer to you, *lumen.*"

Her face had lost color, and she swayed slightly. Regis, who was closest, reached out to steady her, as did Magritte.

Dorian took a step forward. "Xia?"

After a moment, she straightened and addressed Dorian. "I don't understand it. We took the river with barely a challenge. Then, when the outlanders arrived, we attacked the bridge together. It was well defended, and there were numerous *alters* to contend with, but our weapons kept them at bay. Mostly. Some of the weapons were faulty."

I exchanged a look with Dorian. So, Bear had managed to sabotage some weapons, after all.

"After that, we stormed the gate. Victory was in sight. But then something happened, I don't know exactly what. The gray grew impossibly thick, making it difficult to breathe. The men became confused and restless. My people started arguing with the outlanders, and then, before I knew it, we were at each other's throats."

A shadow crossed her face. "It is a massacre out there. Lethean has turned against Lethean, friend against friend. My commanders are scattered." She gestured. "These men and women are the only ones who came upon my call. They alone are still loyal to our cause. All the rest . . . I do not know what they fight for now."

My stomach clenched. "Silvertongue is here."

"Silvertongue?" repeated Xia blankly.

"He will not want to make his presence known," I said. "But, if sighted, he will appear nothing more than a frail, harmless old man. He is the one turning our people against each other."

"Seph's right," said Regis. "I've seen him and heard him speak. He's a powerful *alter.* Perhaps even more powerful than—" He broke off abruptly, glancing shamefacedly at me.

After all he'd seen on the island, did Regis really think Silvertongue was more powerful than Aedon?

"Aedon is here, too," I declared, causing Xia's brows to hitch even higher.

"*Aedon*?" the lady of Thebe echoed.

How to explain the concept of an *Infinitum*? "He said he would deal with Silvertongue."

"Well, I will have to take your word for that, Miss Winter. But right now, we have other problems." Xia glanced past us. "How to reunite my scattered army, for one. How to win a fight against not one foe, but two, for another. And how to kill the upstart who calls himself General Winter."

My eyes widened. "Brinsley is here?"

"Unfortunately," said Xia sourly. "He appeared half an hour ago, declaring himself the new ruler of Calliope and rallying some of the Memosinians to him. He's surrounded by a circle of *alters* so dense we can't get close, not even with the Lethean weapons. Even if the outlanders were removed from the picture, we have no hope of taking Calliope so long as they remain unbeaten."

Dorian turned to Spartan. "Do you think we could get close to him with your shields?"

"Aye," replied the acolyte.

"Could you make the shield large enough to protect all of us?"

Spartan nodded.

Dorian's attention shifted. "Magritte, could you send a message to Asa Karthick? Tell him where we're headed?"

She pursed her lips. "I've never touched his mind before, my lord. It would be like diving into the ocean blindfolded and trying to spot a particular breed of fish. But I could try."

Xia was studying the raven on Spartan's shoulder with no small amount of curiosity. "What did you say you've been doing, Dorian?"

"I didn't."

"Trust me," Cass put in, "you wouldn't believe us if we told you."

Dorian looked at me, his dark eyes grave. "I would spare you this next part, Seph. Your brother—"

"Is a danger that must be removed," I finished for him. "You said you wouldn't leave me behind this time."

"Aye, and I won't. But still, stay close."

The side street became a hive of activity as Xia's warriors—many of them wounded, and all fatigued—prepared to re-enter the battle, and Spartan began to weave a shield large enough to cover more than fifty people. Dorian muttered something in a low voice to Cass, and both men glanced at me.

"Excuse me, miss," said a low voice in my ear as a hand cautiously touched my wrist. "But you mentioned a man called Aedon?"

I looked up, and a shockwave coursed through my body.

It was the advisor from the Grennor Mountains, the member of the Council of Eight whose memory I had wiped on Kaesi's orders months ago. He looked so altered, I would not have known him except for the brush of his skin against mine. In twenty-one years, I had never forgotten the imprint of a mind, and this one was seared onto my brain.

"You see," the man spoke humbly, "I can remember very little of my past. They tell me that I once lived in this city, but naught is familiar to me. A woman declares she is my wife of fifteen years, but I do not know her. And a young boy calls me his papa, but I would swear I've never laid eyes on him in my life."

Time ground to a halt as my blood curdled. I saw the man's wife as clearly as I saw the man now. The laughter of his young son still rang in my ears.

"I do not even know if I fight for Memosine or for Lethe, but one thing is clear in my mind. I have this memory of a man. A man with a plain face and smiling eyes, who tells me not to be afraid of my past. When you said that name just now—Aedon—his face came alive in my mind, as if the memory and the name belonged to each other. Might you tell me, young lady, who he is?"

I stared at him. He was meant to be a wraith, a no-being. Never in my life had I unleashed my power with such devastating effects. I had taken everything from him, just as Kaesi instructed. He shouldn't even remember his own name.

But he knew or at least recognized Aedon's. How was that possible?

I hadn't known his name myself when I took the advisor's memories. Had I somehow imprinted him with a memory of Aedon?

If I know him at all, he will arrange the meeting himself. Spartan had told me that about Aedon, the day he gave me the bottled water from the second pool.

"Miss?" The man's face changed. "I am sorry. I am being presumptuous. You don't know the man of whom I speak."

"Nay," I managed to say. "I do know him. I met him in the flesh just recently." I extended my bare hand. "I'm a *mem*, you see. Perhaps I could show you?"

He took my hand eagerly. He wouldn't have if he recognized me or remembered that one should only ever stay away from *mems*, not take their hands. I didn't know if what I was about to do was possible. But I had to try.

I think, perhaps, that you were born not to help people forget the truth, but to help them remember . . .

I closed my eyes and reached for my gift. Surprisingly, it awoke on my summons, stirring obediently to life. I felt the advisor's grimace. He was probably beholding the black tendrils. But he didn't let go.

Please forgive me, I said, letting my regret flood the space between our minds. *I have done you great wrong.*

I handed them over, one by one. All my memories of Aedon. All the things he'd said; everything he had shown me. Spartan, the Mysterium, the white stallion. Asa, finding redemption after only ever being the killing machine of monster after monster. Even some of the memories from the world-that-was.

And, finally, the memories that belonged to the advisor exclusively. The sight of his beloved wife's face, the first time he'd seen his son smile. Lord Ogdeth was his name—I gave him back that, too. He caressed them all wonderingly, but the greatest treasure seemed to be the memory of Aedon, going to his death.

Sinking to the poisonous depths of Memoria.

Why should he cling to that?

I opened my eyes and retrieved my hand, astonished to see that the tendrils of my gift were no longer black, but snow white. The advisor stared at me, his eyes as round and glassy as twin moons. A lone tear slipped down his cheek. He would recognize me now. He would know that I was the one who had taken his memories. Even now, what I gave him was only a shadow of what had been. Even knowing the truth, he would always feel like he was in possession of a history that was not his own.

"I'm so sorry," I said brokenly. "I would have spared you if I could. Forgive me if you will, but I will understand if you cannot."

I began to turn only to feel his hand on my sleeve. Tamping down my guilt, I looked up into his lined face and started at the compassion evident there.

"I am glad you did not spare me," he replied gently. "For if you hadn't, I would not have known the hope you offered."

"The hope?"

"Aye, hope. And it taught me not to be afraid."

"Seph." Cass suddenly appeared, taking my other arm. "We're leaving." He eyed the man but said nothing to him.

"With all my heart, I thank you," the advisor said to me, and then he was gone, melting away like smoke.

Still in a daze, I was dimly aware of Cass leading me down the alley. Lady Xia's men assumed a phalanx-type formation, with Xia, Magritte, and me at the center. Cass stood to my left, while Regis took up position on the other side of Magritte. Spartan was near the front of the procession, beside Dorian.

It taught me not to be afraid.

The phalanx moved forward, out from the side street and into the open. The warriors at the front brandished pikes, staffs, and even tridents—weapons made for a deadly assault. Though Spartan's gift provided ample protection, a number of our group carried the amber-tinted shields and weapons of the Letheans.

In the main street, men fell on every side. The phalanx was devastatingly effective, allowing Xia's warriors to strike out at their enemies, while being largely protected by Spartan's shield. The smoke cleared a little, revealing the marketplace where I had once helped Dorian look for Silvertongue. The hundreds of tiny stalls were gone now and, in their place, lay hundreds of bodies, stacked four or five high in places. My knees nearly buckled, and I stifled a cry. They weren't just warriors, either, but citizens. Innocent men, women, and children. Their blood ran freely into the gutters.

It was a massacre.

Beside me, Cass sucked in his breath.

Amidst the devastation stood an enormous, square-shaped building with a pair of heavy wooden doors, a white-columned façade, and a pyramidal roof. Dorian had pointed it out to me on our arrival in Calliope: it was a garden-museum, built to commemorate and celebrate the world-that-was. He had promised to one day take me inside. The roof was made entirely of colored glass, he'd said, more beautiful than Cutter's wall of liquid memories.

Right now, that same roof was almost completely obscured by the smoke and the gray. It was one of the few structures, however, that was not on fire, though flames had begun licking at adjacent structures. Even so, it was constructed largely of stone. It wouldn't burn easily.

As the phalanx disbanded to engage the surviving fighters, Xia gestured at the building. "Brinsley Winter has barricaded himself inside. As long as he stays there, he is practically invincible."

"Can't we smoke him out?" Asa emerged from the smoke. Behind him came Zaire and a handful of iridescent-featured people.

Alters. But they were only a few.

Spartan clasped his brother's shoulder. "You got Magritte's message."

"Aye, I did." Asa's gaze found Xia's. "So, we meet at last, Lady of Thebe."

Xia inclined her head, her expression as flinty as Asa's. "Lord Draven."

Asa's head lifted. "That is not my title. Not anymore."

Questions brimmed in Xia's eyes, but she didn't voice them. "We can't smoke him out. Our only option is to force our way inside."

"I think I can assist with that," Asa said to her. He clapped his hands, and a violet sphere materialized.

I suppressed a shiver, remembering how many times his fire had haunted my dreams. As Zaire assumed her beastly form—Xia did her best not to look disgusted—Asa hurled the fireball against the door, followed seconds later by another. Then another.

When he paused, Zaire charged forward. The colorful flames were still devouring the wood, but she paid no heed to them as she used her body like a battering ram. Again and again, she slammed into it; the door shuddered and groaned on its hinges. But it was no match for magical fire and brute strength, and finally she broke through, continuing onward.

I had to admire her courage.

The phalanx re-formed, and then we charged as one. Asa and his *alters* were with us now beneath Spartan's shield. Shouts and screams filled the air as Xia's soldiers encountered Brinsley's. A man sailed through the air over our heads, hit a wall, and became still. Up ahead, the lion-wolf tossed men like they were little more than ragdolls. Asa threw tiny fireballs faster than I could take note of the colors.

Well protected in the heart of the formation, I looked up and around. We stood in a vast, cavernous space, many times the size of the great library. The enormous square had been divided into four quarters, with a cross-shaped path elevated about six feet from the ground, wide enough for twenty men to stand shoulder to shoulder. The polished tiles led to a circular dais at the very center of the room, where a pale-haired man stood, surrounded by a dozen or so *alters*. Between them and us were hundreds of soldiers—Memosinians.

In each quadrant of the square was a garden, sunk into the floor so that visitors might view it easily from above. The first was green and lush, overflowing with wildflowers, as at the beginning of spring. I could even see a tiny stream trickling down a gently sloping hill to fill a fern-encrusted pool. The second was not as verdant, but nevertheless boasted an abundant array of flowering plants. In the third, the leaves on the trees were beginning to turn red and gold, and the ground was already covered with fall's crisp mantle. In the last quadrant, the trees were stripped bare, and a cold breeze came from that part of the chamber.

Spring, summer, autumn, and winter.

If I had seen it shortly after fleeing Nulla, I would have thought it beautiful. Real. Each garden was filled with hundreds of varieties of plants and dozens of trees, magically preserved for the people of Calliope to wonder at on any day of the year. But after Aedon's Garden, with its seemingly endless slopes, orchards filled with fruit, and rivers bursting with life, it seemed a dull recreation of the Garden-that-was, just as my transplanted memories of the world-that-was had proven to be different than the truth. Too often, the act of remembering changed the nature of the past, neglecting to show its ugly or mundane aspects.

The battle continued. The phalanx advanced along the path with Zaire, Asa, Spartan, and Dorian at its head. With the help of the *alters*, and Spartan's shield, Brinsley's men fell aside like chaff before a stiff breeze. The arc of Dorian's staff was nearly invisible.

"We're almost there," announced Cass as he slashed out with his blades. Xia stood not far away, firing flame-tipped arrows lit from a gleaming sphere at her feet. Beside her, Magritte was weaponless, but concentrating fiercely, her gaze fixed on Regis and the others. Giving warning of oncoming attacks? Conveying orders from Xia?

I looked up toward my brother. I was still a fair distance away, but not so far that I couldn't see the old man who suddenly materialized beside Brinsley and raised his hands. The yellow-brown irises lit with delight; the red lips curved in a slow smile.

Silvertongue.

Where was Aedon?

A veil fell over the entire hall. Zaire halted midlunge, looking like a puppet suspended without strings. Asa froze, the fireball he held hardening to a crusty, blackened shell which crumbled into dust. Spartan's shield dissolved like sugar in a deluge of warm rain. Xia and Regis lowered their bows.

Silvertongue began to laugh that maniacal laugh we had heard in the cavern. "Fools!" he bellowed. "I control this city, as I control all of Caldera! It has always been mine, and it always will be."

He snapped his fingers, and a woman appeared beside him. A woman with iridescent blue eyes and long, blond hair.

I gasped as Dorian stiffened. Kaesi.

My mind spun in confusion. Had Kaesi somehow regained her memories? How else was she here? I mentally replayed the events at the library, trying to remember if Cass's gift had been present when Kaesi spoke. How could we fall for that move a second time?

Aleria. Had the outlander woman betrayed us, or had Kaesi escaped her?

Silvertongue smirked and beckoned Brinsley and Kaesi forward until they were standing on either side of him. They wore the same feverish smiles as he did, but I thought I glimpsed fear in Kaesi's eyes.

That night I came to you was the same night I left Silvertongue. I disliked his methods, and I didn't share his ultimate purposes . . .

"Don't you see, my friends?" Silvertongue cajoled. "It is hopeless. I may not sit on Caldera's throne, but I rule you just the same. All that is left is for you to acknowledge me, your rightful high king."

Aedon, where are you?

"All your rebellion has come to naught. But I am gracious and forgiving. Swear your fealty to me, and I will give you everything your heart desires. I will protect you from the outlanders. I will make your world prosperous and great. All I ask is that you honor me as high king."

The words were tantalizing, tempting. Everything my heart desired . . . could it be so easy? Silvertongue was powerful . . . he could give us what we wanted most. Murmurs grew around me, building as the crowd considered Silvertongue's offer. Many on both sides moved forward and knelt before him, pledging their allegiance. My thoughts remained thick and sluggish.

Aedon. I couldn't forget Aedon! Couldn't forget a pool whose waters tasted like infinite satisfaction and a stallion whose very presence soothed and reassured. Couldn't forget the ink-streaked skin of a man as he drew the poison from my chest.

At a gentle fluttering of wings, I looked up. The bird had left Spartan's shoulder and was flying toward the dais. Light flashed, white and hot, and then another man stood before Silvertongue, with iridescent hair and eyes and clothes that nearly blinded. The raven perched on his shoulder.

Silvertongue's smile melted away, and his face became pale and waxy. He raised a liver-spotted hand to point at Aedon, but the finger trembled. "You came back."

"Aye, I did."

"You cannot have come for *them*."

"They are exactly why I have come."

In a swift moment, Aedon stepped forward and threw himself into

Silvertongue, and the men tumbled from the platform and disappeared in a puff of smoke.

Chaos erupted. Xia's warriors swarmed the soldiers protecting the dais, but confusion had overtaken them, and they fought the enemy as often as their friends. Zaire came at Asa, who yelped as one of her claws tore the sleeve of his shirt. Magritte pummeled Regis's chest with her fists. Spartan and Dorian stood helplessly in the middle of the fray, trying to protect others where they could, but how could they protect them from themselves?

Kaesi descended the dais and advanced through the crush of people, heading directly for Dorian. She was weaponless, but hate twisted her beautiful features. I cried out a warning to Dorian, but he couldn't hear me over the din.

Nay . . .

I forced my way through the crowd. Cass called my name, but I pushed on, blind to all else save Kaesi's location—and Dorian's. I stumbled over a fallen man but kept going, feeling the weight of my pendant against my heated skin.

Kaesi was now a mere eight feet from her brother. Her flesh melted away and was replaced with thick fur. Jewel's. Dorian's back was turned as he fought one of Brinsley's men, who was armed with an amber-tinted trident he must have stolen from one of the Letheans. Dorian twirled his staff, bringing it down on the man's shoulders with a disturbing *crack*. His opponent slumped to the ground. Dorian turned.

Too slow . . .

I felt a fluttering near my cheek, softer than a butterfly's wings. The raven? I put on a burst of speed, wheeling into Kaesi's path, throwing myself a few paces in front of her brother's exposed back just as the muscles in the wolf's hind legs tensed like springs.

Kaesi-Jewel pounced. Her sharp claws struck me in the center of my chest, her weight and momentum knocking me flat on my back. She snarled and struck. I screamed as her sharp teeth closed over the left side of my bare collarbone, severing tendons and splintering bone. Dorian bellowed my name and dived at Kaesi. Man and wolf rolled together, over and over, Dorian armed with nothing more than his hands. They rolled over the side of the elevated path into the winter garden, where a thick frost had turned the grass into a sea of silvery glass shards.

I staggered to my feet as blood gushed from the puncture wounds, making my head light and fuzzy. My left arm hung uselessly at my side. But adrenaline poured through my body, and I felt no pain.

Around me, the battle continued, with no obvious victors prevailing. Silvertongue didn't care who won this fight, he simply wanted Aedon to lose. Cass fought Brinsley not far away. Brinsley was no fighter—he was a merchant, after all—but he was accompanied by an *alter* whose sharp gestures were somehow making Cass yelp with pain. I could no longer see Dorian and Kaesi, but I could feel my gift again, weak as it was. Whatever was happening, Kaesi must be sufficiently distracted. Which meant that Dorian . . .

Where are you, Aedon? Won't you help us?

I felt it again: the featherlight caress of a bird's wings against my cheek. I turned my head to see the white raven; his intelligent eyes, as sharp and expressive as the stallion's, were soft and gentle.

A disheveled and bleeding Spartan stumbled to my side, and his eyes widened when he saw the raven. "Aedon's here. He hasn't left us." He turned to me. "Draw on your gift, Seph."

"What would you have me do?" Blood loss had already turned my knees to liquid. Any moment, I was going to pass out.

"Cutter tainted the water, remember? And Silvertongue has been wreaking havoc for years. Calliope is still under the curse of the ancestors. But you have the memories. Not just of what happened more than sixty years ago, but the pattern that has been repeating itself for centuries. Show them, Seph. Let them see the truth of Aedon."

Did he know about my second gift?

"I'm . . . I'm too weak."

"Aye," said Spartan with certainty. "But he is not. Draw on his strength."

I stared at him.

The moon only gives light because of the sun, Sephone. Let the sun lend you its strength, and you will shine with its radiance, its satisfying warmth, even in the densest darkness . . .

At the time when Aedon said those words, it had seemed so logical, so simple. Draw on his strength, aye. But now, with my strength failing, my blood seeping out of me to pool on the floor at my feet—it was impossible.

I would offer you every last fiber of strength in my body if I thought it would help you find yours. But I suspect it's not my strength you need. It never has been.

I glanced at the raven. How I wished he had assumed his stallion form, for then he could help me save my friends, and he could carry us far away from here. A stallion would be a formidable opponent for a wolf.

What was needed most was what was given . . .

Jewel's mournful howl rent the air in two, and I pictured Dorian's face.

I think, perhaps, that you were born not to help people forget the truth, but to help them remember.

"Seph?" Spartan said, with a little more desperation.

A deep voice sounded inside my head, impossible to mistake.

It is time.

Wincing, I raised my right arm, seeing the imprint of the burn and the slightly misshapen outline of my wrist. *If only Aedon were here . . .* I reached into my memories and found the one of our first meeting, the same night Dorian had stolen the Reliquary.

"The light illuminates many things . . ."

The light.

Instead of reaching for my gift, as I had done a thousand times before, I lifted my arm until my entire body shrieked with pain. I extended it as high as I could, opened my palm, closed my eyes, then called out for the Nightingale.

Aedon . . .

And his song came to me in the darkness. Pure and simple enough for a child to memorize, but rich and full of impossible, unfathomable depth. I heard the exquisite notes, the ethereal sequence of trills and whistles. All these years he had been silent, Calderans had believed him extinct. But now he sang to us across the ages, his voice heady and strong, his call unmistakable.

Come to me.

I was dimly aware that Spartan had taken my hand and raised his free one, just as I did. Light fell blindingly around us, dazzling in its brilliance. A jewel was forming in my empty palm, a diamond made of memories of a man. Of a single, impossible truth.

We were free.

A burst of light, this time from the jewel. Shafts of brilliant white shot upward, illuminating the stained glass roof with its scenes of the world-that-was. A rainbow of liquid color shone down from above, drenching the vast space with every hue imaginable. But at the heart of each one was molten gold, like the current I'd first seen in Dorian's mind. A current of enduring, unconditional love. It was a thousand times more vivid than the sun, and impossibly, deliciously warm. With it, I would never feel the cold again.

Slowly, the light died. I heard Spartan call my name, but I was fading, fading away. Even then, the darkness was no longer troubling, no longer filled with the lurking shadows of hidden nightmares. There was only Aedon's song and his kind, ancient face. The white stallion, with his powerful legs, his mane of silk, and his noble profile.

This was true peace.

36

DORIAN

Kaesi crouched on his chest in wolf form, so all Dorian could do was look up as a column of light illuminated the ceiling. Never in his life had he ever seen anything so beautiful. The stained glass roof, which was lovely in sunshine, was exquisite now. Scenes from the world-that-was came to life in the light, nearly forgotten corners bearing unexpected revelations. He had known, but now he truly saw. A hundred memories, a hundred conversations replayed in his head.

Kaesi whimpered and retreated, allowing Dorian to gain his feet. On the edge of the winter garden, in the middle of the fray, stood two figures, hand in hand. Sephone, her arm upraised with the white raven fluttering beside her. Light shone from the diamond in her hand. The jewel which, even now, filled the entire room with its warmth. Spartan stood beside her, his face suffused with golden radiance.

As Dorian watched, the light faded, and Sephone collapsed into a man's arms. His heart leapt. It wasn't Spartan who caught her, but Aedon. He was the source of the light—the gem which Sephone had held aloft. His clothes sparkled with iridescence; the very air around him seemed to glitter. Warmth radiated from him in waves. The bird once again adorned his shoulder.

Dorian hauled himself up onto the walkway, realizing that the room had gone totally silent. Most appeared subdued, some looked ashamed. For along with her memories of Aedon, Sephone had also projected into the sky the truth of the outlanders and Caldera's origins, the grievous sins of the ancestors. It would be impossible to deny now that Caldera was any different than the world-that-was. That Memosine's memories of their predecessors' valor, cleverness, and goodness were anything but distortions of the truth.

All eyes were now on Aedon, who cradled Sephone like a child.

Reaching them, Dorian knelt next to Spartan and felt the acolyte touch his shoulder. Dorian flinched. Given the state of his clothing, Spartan couldn't know that his skin had been raked by Kaesi's claws. Sephone's own shoulder was a mess of bloodied, shredded flesh. Her eyes were closed, her breathing reedy and shallow. Her shirt had been drenched with crimson.

"Can you heal her?" Dorian almost begged Aedon.

Aedon laid his bare hand over Sephone's torn shoulder. White light poured from his palm. When he removed his hand, her skin appeared unmarked and whole. The bones beneath looked to be in their proper place again. He whispered in her ear, and she came awake, her eyelids fluttering.

Whispers raced across the crowd, murmurings swelling in intensity. Aedon lifted his head and looked at Dorian. The raven studied him, too, with unnerving acuity. And Dorian had thought it difficult to maintain eye contact with Aleria at times.

"Thank you." Dorian dipped his head. "For saving her."

"You are welcome."

"What happened?" Sephone asked in wonder.

"You spoke the truth," replied Aedon. "You poured all your memories of me into a single jewel, which you projected outward. Truth always breaks a spell, as you have learned from your interactions with Silvertongue. This time, the truth broke the hold Silvertongue has had over this city for many years. It has set them free."

Aedon intercepted Dorian's glance at Sephone. Did the *alter* see the longing in his eyes? His distress that Kaesi had nearly killed her again?

Aedon's eyes reflected kindness and infinite compassion. "There will be time, Dorian, to find what you have long been seeking. But in the meantime, I have a task for you. Are you willing to take up your old duties, my friend? This time, for *my* sake?"

Dorian started. He couldn't be referring to . . . Surely not . . .

"Aye." Aedon's gaze encompassed Sephone, then Spartan and Asa, who had come up behind him. "This task I have is for all of you."

"What of Silvertongue?" Dorian asked, remembering how easily the old man had brought the entire room under his spell. Only the four of them had been immune from his puppetry—and only because Aedon had cut their strings.

Though Cass had been immune, too, with his truth gift.

"He is diminished," said Aedon quietly, "and his days are numbered. A time is coming when he will trouble you no more. But for now, he is in everything and behind everything. He is a villain in many guises, roaming the world, searching for those who would serve him in exchange for his twisted gifts. Until I return, he is in the gruff word and the unkind gesture, the sly knife in the back or the false hand of friendship. He will always be your enemy, and he will make villains of many of your friends."

"Your return?" Asa echoed. "Then you're going away?"

"Aye. But I won't leave you alone." As Aedon spoke, the white raven rose and came to perch on Sephone's leg. "He has the same gifts as me, you know. He urges people to act with courage"—Aedon looked at Dorian—"and he reads the truth of a person's soul." He focused on Sephone before his eyes swept to Asa. "He allows hurt so that he might heal." Lastly, he smiled at Spartan. "And he keeps the one who remembers me in perfect peace."

"I don't understand," said Sephone, gazing at the bird. "You say that we will not be alone, but I don't see how we can do this without you. Calliope has been torn apart. Caldera is in shambles."

"Do you remember the child you once held in your arms?" Aedon asked her. "The child of the Lethean woman, whose mind you peered into to set her mother's at rest?"

Sephone nodded uncertainly. Dorian had known how afraid she was that day, that the poison marking her chest would taint the child's mind. That she would corrupt her with the burden of her memories.

"You must become like that child, my daughter. For she knows her need and her mother's ability to provide, and that is sufficient. It is the same for you. Lean on me each day, and I will lend you the strength you need to go on. And you will never be alone. I promise."

Spartan spoke up. "What task would you ask of us, Aedon?"

Aedon smiled again, a warm, genuine smile that crinkled the skin at the edges of his eyes. "I would ask you to be my ambassadors. To this land, bring peace, truth, courage, remembrance, and healing. To this people, show the love that I showed you, and the truth that set you free from a deadly curse."

"But you're coming back again?" Asa asked hesitantly.

"Aye," said Aedon, his smile broader. "I am coming back."

A vision of a city filled Dorian's mind, built on an island as Calliope was, in the middle of a deep blue lake. Stately towers, covered with crawling ivy, numbered so many that it was impossible to count them. The uppermost rooms were so high up that they were crowned with clouds. There were no fortress walls, but dozens of gardens, green and lush. One could wander forever in such a place and never grow bored.

Where is this? he asked Aedon, somehow aware that the vision belonged to the *Infinitum.*

Dorian was surprised at the answer. Just a single word, but laden with longing, that carried a multitude of meanings. A single word that felt like it had been stamped on Dorian's very soul.

Home.

Just as easily as he had reappeared, Aedon vanished, leaving a room full of stunned people. Xia's worried face was streaked with dirt. Zaire's, openly hostile. Cass held a knife to Brinsley's throat. The *alter* who'd been protecting Sephone's brother lay dead at his feet. As Xia's men grabbed Brinsley and bound his hands, Cass rushed across the tiles to Sephone, whose tunic was still soaked with her blood.

The Memosinians, suddenly deprived of all their leaders, did naught. Was it too much to believe that the battle was finally over?

Kaesi wept on her knees on the frost-stricken grass. Leaving Sephone in Cass's care, Dorian went to his sister. She stood shakily as he approached. Seeing the blood on his shirt, she wept harder.

"I'm so sorry, Dorian," she said miserably. "I don't know what came over me. Silvertongue appeared in the library, and suddenly I could remember pieces. And then I was here, and Silvertongue spoke, and all I could think of was how you had betrayed me—"

He didn't care that she'd attacked him. "You nearly killed Sephone."

"I know." Her eyes flashed and her mouth twisted. She still hated Sephone.

"Did you kill Aleria Vega?"

She shook her head. "I only wounded her. She's alive, Dorian." She held up her arms for an embrace.

He backed away. "Fortunately for you, for the outlanders will not readily forgive you for murdering one of their own. And I—"

Dorian broke off. After everything she'd done, how could he forgive her? Even in her right mind, she would have killed Sephone, just as she had killed Draven. Rage and hatred mounted in Dorian's chest. She was a murderer.

And you are a thief, came the swift reminder. *And no less deserving of punishment.*

He thought of Aedon, going to his death for a stranger. And at that thought, Dorian's anger evaporated, and his bitterness melted away. Things between them might never be as either of them hoped—he doubted Kaesi would ever approve of Sephone—but he could right this one wrong.

He exhaled. "I forgive you."

Kaesi looked up at him through a sheen of tears. "Do you mean that, Dorian? As you say, I nearly killed the woman you love."

"Aye. I mean it."

Xia's soldiers came for Kaesi, and she didn't struggle as they bound her hands and led her away. Forgiveness or nay, his sister would still need to face her punishment. But her eyes—brown again, and as unremarkable as he remembered—remained locked on his, and he took hold of a new hope that, one day, a time would come when he could tell her about Aedon, who was powerful enough to set her free from Silvertongue forever.

Weary of the bloodshed, the Memosinians, Letheans, and outlanders declared a truce, spearheaded by Asa, Xia, and Aleria. As it turned out, the latter had suffered only a moderate concussion and several minor flesh wounds. Surprises abounded as Aleria also proved to be far more than the simple emissary they had believed. She was, in fact, the daughter of the outlander leader. Dorian hated to imagine what might have happened if she had died at Kaesi's hands.

Nevertheless, great joy ensued as Aleria and Sephone were reunited. Though doubts and suspicions had threatened to divide them for a time, hopefully their friendship would withstand everything the future could throw at them.

The Memosinians offered them rooms in the arch-lord's castle where their wounds were tended and they were given food and fresh clothes. Once they had snatched some rest, there was plenty of work to do. Many had died, and there were hundreds of bodies to bury. Fires needed to be extinguished and shelter found for those whose homes had burned. The robed members of the Mysterium moved among the wounded and the homeless, offering assistance where it was needed most.

In the meantime, dozens of meetings were held to negotiate the terms of the peace. Only one member of the old Council of Eight remained alive, Lord Ogdeth, who appeared to have no inclination to maintain the office. Kaesi and Brinsley were both imprisoned in Calliope's dungeon, awaiting trial, leaving Memosine leaderless and vulnerable.

Xia's intentions were obvious: she wanted Dorian to claim the throne. He had been Memosine's ambassador to Lethe and was one of the few with leadership experience, having been thane of Maera. The League wanted someone who would be friendly to their cause and, Dorian thought to himself, malleable to their influence.

Five days after the truce, he met with Xia alone in the arch-lord's hall, where the throne remained empty.

"Well?" his old friend asked hopefully. "Have you made a decision?"

"Yes, I have," he said. "I will not be king, Siaki. I have already told the others, so it is pointless trying to change my mind."

A line appeared between her pale brows. "Then who, Dorian? Who will lead Memosine? For if you do not claim the throne, someone else will."

He glanced at the ornately gilded throne Kaesi had ordered to be constructed, the throne she and Dorian had both found so tempting. The truce between Caldera's inhabitants was tense and uneasy. He knew some didn't believe the memories Sephone had projected into the sky. Silvertongue continued to sow seeds of doubt and discontent in his many guises. In time, many would contest what was, for the time being, widely accepted as true.

"Asa has nominated me for a position on the Council of Eight," Dorian told Xia. "And I have accepted. In turn, I have nominated Asa and Spartan for the position of joint arch-lord."

"Spartan?" Xia repeated, dismayed. "Jerome Karthick? And Asa was not so long ago the right-hand man of the very person who started all of this. Neither of them have even served as thanes, and you would make them arch-lords?"

"Asa and Jerome are nothing like their father, Siaki. And Jerome doubts his suitability even more than you do. But though they are young, they are wise and good-hearted men. They have already begun negotiating a compromise with the outlanders, returning lands that were stolen by our clans. I will mentor them as they require, but in the meantime, they have something far better than my help. They have Aedon."

Xia pursed her lips. "I have considered your account, as you requested. I'm still inclined to think you have had one glass of wine too many, my old friend. But if you will lend them your counsel, they may yet prove to be good leaders." She smiled. "Providing that Asa Karthick does not burn down the half of Calliope still in existence."

Dorian chuckled.

After leaving, he went in search of Brinsley. Calliope's dungeons were dark and filthy, like the dungeons of old, and Dorian adjusted his heavy mantle to keep out the chill as he descended the stairs. He had been down here several times already to ensure Kaesi had ample food, water, and clothing, and that her guards did not open her door, no matter who seemed to be on the other side. Not that Kaesi seemed to have any inclination for shapeshifting lately, with her memories still in disarray.

It was the first time he would see Sephone's brother.

At last, he stood facing Brinsley through the bars. Though Dorian knew he'd been given water for washing, along with the same luxuries Kaesi was afforded, Brinsley's face was streaked with grime, his white-blond hair lank and greasy. He was painfully thin. Dorian wondered how he was coping without his forgetfulness potions.

"Ah, Lord Adamo," he said, offering Dorian a mocking bow. "It is good to see you. Though I can't imagine how you have time for me, what with all the preparations for your coronation."

No wonder Cass had liked him. The two shared a similar sense of humor, though Cass's was a little more refined. "I'm not going to be king."

"Oh?" Brinsley raised his brow. "Then who is?"

"The throne will remain empty. Asa and Jerome Karthick will be joint arch-lords."

Brinsley's eyes widened. He hadn't expected that development. "And you?"

"I've taken a position on the Council of Eight."

"You won't return to Maera?"

Dorian thought of his parents and his other siblings. He'd been away far too long. "Aye, I will, though my duties will bring me often to this city. There is much to restore. Much to rebuild."

"And you will say I'm the man responsible for tearing it down," was the dry comment.

"Not the only one. But if you show remorse, I promise you that the Council will be merciful."

"Thanks for the tip."

A long silence stretched between them. Brinsley scraped out the dirt from under his nails, looking bored. How could he not ask about Sephone or even his parents? Did he care naught for them at all?

Dorian's patience grew thin. "Why did you do it?"

"Do what, my lord?"

346 J. J. FISCHER

"Betray your sister."

Bitterness curled Brinsley's lip. "Because after she was gone, I was never enough for them."

"For your parents?"

"For anyone."

Dorian understood. Hadn't it been the same for him? After Lida and Emmy had died, no one had been enough. Driven by despair and regret, he had travelled all over Caldera looking for a *mem* who could take away his past. He had left behind his family, friends, and servants who loved him, risking the lives of everyone in his service. Toria, Keon, Bear and Bas, Cass and Sephone. He had valued his happiness above them all.

You are forgiven, Dorian.

"Even after everything that's happened, she would forgive you," he said to Brinsley.

Brinsley scoffed. "Sephone *stabbed* me, you might recall."

"To save my life."

"Aye, my sister has rather poor taste in men." Brinsley's eyes raked over Dorian scornfully. "You know, you lied to me, that night in Nyx. You said you wanted naught from her but friendship. But I see the way you look at her."

Dorian said nothing. He didn't owe Brinsley an explanation.

"I betrayed her and broke her wrist. Can you forget that?" Beneath Brinsley's cavalier manner lurked vulnerability. He was waiting for Dorian's response, waiting for the moment Dorian would reject him, as his parents had rejected him . . . and he had rejected Sephone.

"Not forget, Brinsley, forgive. And it is because I care for Sephone that I offer you my goodwill. Because you are her brother and she will hope the best for you. Even if you forget her, she won't ever forget you."

Dorian left him standing beside the bars.

Tonight, the sky was almost clear enough to see the stars. Over the past few days, I had watched as the smoke dispersed and the gray began to recede. Every morning, I stood on the balcony of the room the Memosinians had given me and watched the sun straining through.

Five whole days had passed, and I had slept for most of them, though I'd had a steady stream of visitors during wakeful periods: Cass, Regis and Magritte, Aleria, Spartan, Lady Xia, Asa, and even Zaire. The only person I hadn't seen was Dorian, though the woman who had been assigned to me had said he'd visited every day, but always while I was sleeping. If I had been stronger, I would have gone in search of him myself, but I was still too weak to leave my room.

A tantalizing current of warm summer air rushed in via the balcony's open double doors, and I swept aside the sheer, gossamer curtains and moved outside. From this vantage point, I could see all of Calliope laid out before me, down to the lower walls and the bridge with its six mighty arches. I leaned on the stone railing. The night breezes were cool, and my skin broke out in hundreds of tiny goosebumps, but I remained where I was. I was sick of being in bed.

"You know," said an amused voice behind me, "your room is much nicer than mine. I always knew you were the thane's favorite employee."

Gripping the railing, I whirled. "Cass, don't sneak up on me like that. I could have tumbled over the edge."

"My balcony is just below yours. If you fell, I could catch you again." He winked as he moved past the curtains and stood there looking at me.

I smiled. "Not if you're here."

He only grinned, and I knew he was waiting for something. He had visited me every day, but this was the first time he had come at night, when I was alone. Cass looked like he was on his way to a ball. His tailored clothes fit him to perfection; his knee-high boots were freshly polished; waves of iridescent black hair came to his ears, carefully tousled in a dashing but undeniably boyish way.

Even without starlight, his green-blue eyes gleamed. The first time we had met, I had compared them to a sea grotto: beautiful on the surface, but with surprising depths. He was an attractive man. But far more than that, he had proved to be a loyal friend and a devoted protector.

Of course, I had known this conversation was coming. I just hadn't expected to have it so soon. At least there weren't any green or black ribbons . . . Cass's truth gift would not make an appearance tonight. But the truth would need to be voiced nonetheless.

"Why have you come, Cass?" I murmured in a last-ditch attempt to delay the inevitable.

"Because it's over," he said simply. "You're free of your obligations to the thane, to Xia, to Memosine and Lethe." His eyes lit like one of Asa's flaming spheres. "Come with me to Marianthe, Seph. I will show you the sea. It's so beautiful. Impossible to put into words, really. We can build a life together, free of everything but the things we decide to include in it."

"Free of Aedon, too?"

His black eyebrows knotted. "You are free to follow whoever you like. I've always been an open-minded man. A tolerant man. I won't stop you building a shrine to him, or any other ancient relic that captures your imagination."

So long as that commitment didn't touch my heart. So long as my devotion to Aedon didn't affect my devotion to Cass. But was that all Cass thought Aedon was? An ancient being or relic—a mere leftover from the world-that-was?

I thought of the bottle from the second pool nestled against my skin in one of my pockets, which grew more precious to me every day. The liquid which brought the past, the present, and the future to life. It was so much more than a memory or a relic.

It was freedom. Freedom from a curse, which had long held Caldera and our ancestors in bondage.

"Cass, if you only knew what Aedon could give you—"

"Don't." He abruptly held up his hand. "Don't try and fix me."

"I'm not trying to fix you. I can't, remember?" I recalled Aedon's words on the subject. "But you could be free, too."

"Maybe I don't require liberation." He stole closer; his lips quirked, but his eyes remained solemn. "The thane is finally at peace with his past. Perhaps I can make peace with mine, too."

"Dorian only made peace with his past because of Aedon, Cass. Because of his sacrifice. Because of love." I stepped back. "Cass, I am sorry. But I've made my choice. I can't come with you." I had said as much in the letter I'd written him in Nyx, but now the words were heavy with finality.

"Are you sure you're not still affected by his gift? The man is almost as persuasive as Silvertongue when it suits him—"

I looked at him, aghast. "Cass, how you could accuse him of that is beyond me."

"I could free you from his spell. I could take you from here. Spirit you away to a place where you can come to your senses."

Was he serious? "You wouldn't."

Cass's lips curved ruefully as he grasped my wrist in his gloved hands. "It would be impossibly simple, you know. The thane would believe you came with me of your own volition, as would everyone else. I could throw you over my shoulder and smuggle you out of here."

Just as Cutter had, and Kaesi. But when he saw my fear, he sighed heavily. And I knew he had finally accepted my choice.

"You were right, Seph. A caged bird cannot love truly. If I were to take you, it would be against your will."

Compassion replaced the fear. "What you want from me, Cass, I am not able to give."

"Your love?" He snorted. "You already said that."

"Nay." I thought of the Garden, lovely in its impermanence, but only a shadow of what was to come, what the Three had promised for those freed from the curse. "You are looking for forever, but I am only temporary."

He cocked his head, eyes on me.

"Do you remember the day we met?" I asked.

"How could I forget?"

"You told me that strawberries were one of your favorite memories." And I relayed the encounter with the old veteran and his dog, Felix. How I had given up one of Cutter's strawberry potions to comfort him in his poverty, only to be shown a glimpse of what strawberries really tasted like. And how, in Aedon's Garden, I had finally consumed the real thing. It was better than any memory. Any fleeting substitute.

"The love you seek," I told him, "is not for any woman to give, Cass. You want to be loved just as everyone does—unconditionally, without limits, no matter what you have done or ever will do. That is Aedon's love. That is the love of the Three. Even if Dorian never chose me, I was already chosen by them. My life is already complete."

"You would be content to live your entire life alone?"

"I'm not alone," I said, thinking of the white raven Aedon had promised would always be with us. "And you're not alone, either."

He frowned. "This is real to you?"

"Aye. More real than anything in the world." I looked at him squarely. "If you called to him . . . he would come."

For a long moment, I thought he was going to agree. That he would call on Aedon's name and embrace the man he was meant to be. But instead he shook his head. "The only reason I would call on him now is to ask him to remove my feelings for you."

The words stung. "I'm sorry to cause you pain. I wish . . ."

He gave me a weak smile. "Don't trouble yourself. I'm not going to try and remove them. Love is rather good at keeping a man focused— the thane is proof of that. These feelings for you, perhaps they'll keep me from returning to my old ways." His smile turned devilish and charming.

I didn't voice what he must suspect was true: that kind of love wasn't strong enough to sustain a man's willpower in any area of his life.

There is time, daughter. His story is not over yet.

"I'm still going to Marianthe, Seph. Since the Reliquary is no more, and I was still a *lumen* the last time I checked, I'm going to find another cure for my gift. So this must be goodbye."

"You're leaving tonight?"

"First thing in the morning." A shadow of pain crossed Cass's face. "I think it best we only farewell each other once."

I moved forward and hugged him. If he held me a little more tightly or longer than he should, I didn't begrudge him the contact. For something told me that, after tonight, I might never see Cassius Vera again.

"I will miss you," I told him honestly. "You have been the very best of friends. And I wish that you would stay."

He said nothing, but I realized that he was looking at my hair. I glanced at the sky. Above us flickered a dozen or so pinpricks of celestial light. Was Cass remembering the bridge where he had first noticed the iridescence in my hair?

If only he would look for the iridescence that would never fade, even in the darkness.

"How am I going to live without you, Seph?" The words were playful, though I knew he was serious.

I smiled. "You're looking at my hair, when you should be seeking the moon, which does the shining. It's just as you're always reminding me, Cass. All you need to do is look up."

I kept imagining Cass setting out alone on his journey to Marianthe. The Memosinian attendant, Sara, must have sensed my restless mood, for in the early afternoon she brought me to the castle gardens to wander the paths at my own pace. It was the first time in six days that I had worn real clothes, and this was a lovely, ankle-length dress whose rich red fabric brought out the golden tones in my hair and the snowy-white freshness of the blossoms in my necklace.

The arch-lord's garden was secluded and private, with large hedges that concealed vast sections from view and a number of unexpected pleasures. A large fountain stocked with orange-white fish, a stone bench soaking in the sun, and an archway bursting with honeysuckle and roses. I turned a corner to find a stretch of wildflowers, noting a narrow rectangle at the edge of the miniature meadow had recently been disturbed. A fresh bouquet of wildflowers had been carefully placed atop the mound of earth.

It must be a grave. But whose and why here?

A wooden stake had been driven into the ground; I bent to read it. I didn't understand the words, which must be Memosinian. But the name carved into the wood was clear.

Berin Mardell.

"Berin," I murmured.

"You knew him as Bear, of course."

I turned to see Dorian standing behind me.

"He always preferred Bear, just as Sebastian preferred Bas." He looked at the grave. "The stake is only temporary, of course. Soon, I will have a proper gravestone carved—one which lists Bas, too. I only wish I knew where he was buried, so I could bring his body back here to rest. He would have wanted to be near his brother, regardless of what happened between them at the end."

I straightened, wondering how Dorian had retrieved Bear's body. He had gone to such effort, and all for a man who had betrayed him. But then again, he had held a funeral for Bas when he had believed Bas to be the traitor.

"Why would you do this for him, Dorian?"

"Because no matter what he did in life, I want him to have peace in the Aeternum."

"Kaesi didn't tell you why he betrayed you?"

"Nay, though I'm aware Kaesi and Bear knew each other, back in Maera. There was a time when the twins were sympathetic to her revolutionary ideas. She may have come to Bear with her plans to overthrow Draven and claim the throne. Bear might not have seen it as betrayal, at least not until Bas made him choose a side.

"But I have something for you." Dorian took something from his shoulder that I recognized as my satchel. Had he had it with him this whole time? "Can we sit down?"

"Of course."

He led the way to the stone seat I'd seen earlier, which was now blissfully sun warmed. After we were both seated, Dorian reached inside the satchel and drew out a sheaf of papers, along with two identical copper bracelets. My throat tightened when I saw them. Dorian placed the bracelets into my hands, along with the papers.

"These are official documents of Calliope," he said. "You're a free woman now, Seph. You no longer belong to me or to anyone. I am sorry it took so long." He smiled slightly. "Bureaucracy makes everything move very slowly, and wars don't help."

For some reason, tears filled my eyes.

"I brought them as soon as they were ready. The Memosinian woman, Sara, said you would be here. I should have guessed, though, that the first thing you'd visit when you were strong enough would be a garden."

He watched me try to decipher the first line of text. "It's in Memosinian, of course. But I can read it to you, if you'd like. Or I can teach you the language so you can read it yourself. Whatever you prefer."

I raised shining eyes to him. Did he know how much time that would involve? "Thank you for all your efforts," I said. "But I'm afraid I have to decline these papers."

"Decline?" Shock suffused his face.

"Aye. If you are willing, Dorian"—I gathered every shred of my courage—"I would still like to belong to you."

He stilled, his brown eyes solemn. "Cass left early this morning for Marianthe. I could say naught to change his mind."

"I know."

"I offered him a position here, as an advisor to the arch-lords—my equal on the Council—but he refused. He said the sea was calling him home."

"He told me much the same."

Dorian reached out and took my hands. His accent had thickened. "Despite what we'd said to one another, I have to admit I feared you might go with him."

I laughed. "Oh, Dorian. I told him I had definitely decided to stay."

His dark eyes bored into mine. "You are free, Seph. No man will ever enslave you again. But you should know that I would like you to belong to me, too. Just as I would like to belong to you, if you are willing."

Planting my hands on either side of his bearded face, I kissed him. The serpentine cuffs on my lap tumbled to the ground, and the papers scattered in the dirt as our kiss blossomed and grew. His mind was open to me, but I didn't enter it, nor did my gift compel me to do so.

After the kiss ended, we sat together for a very long time, me nestled in Dorian's arms.

Eventually, Dorian spoke. "I met a man a few days ago. A Lord Ogdeth."

"Ogdeth?"

"Aye. He had an interesting tale to tell, of a young woman who gave him back his memories, and some of her own, too." Dorian's eyes twinkled. "They are calling you a *luminare,* you know."

"A what?"

"A *luminare.* Like Lady Cilla, the woman you observed at Faro's party."

"*Luminare,*" I tasted the word, then laughed. "It certainly sounds better than *mem.*"

"Aye, perhaps it does. But I have another word in mind for you, Seph." He stroked my cheek. "I have accepted a position as a member of the Council of Eight. It is only for a year, until things are settled. But I will be returning to Maera soon, to see my family and set everything to rights, and I wondered if you might come with me. If you might come home . . . to me."

Home. The word brought tears to my eyes.

"Ah, I'm doing this all wrong," he said, lowering himself to the ground amidst the scattered papers, then propping himself up on one knee. He took my hands. "A few months ago, Seph, I believed the best thing I had to offer you was a blank mind. Well, my mind will never be empty—the curse of a politician—and my thoughts are still rather broken. But if you are willing, I would form new memories with you—a whole lifetime of them with you as my wife."

My heart skipped several beats, and I smiled through my tears.

He smiled sheepishly. "What I'm asking is, will you marry me, Persephone Winter?"

I threw myself off the bench and into his arms. "Of course I will."

There were more kisses, whispered promises, and Dorian clutched me to him like he held a precious artifact. Joy swept through me, filling the hollow places with a warmth not unlike the touch of his gift. Only this was far better.

Finally, I drew back. "I accept," I told him, "but you must give me a year." He opened his mouth to speak, but I swiftly went on, "Your sister is still in prison, awaiting her trial and sentencing. Your new role will have responsibilities, and Spartan and Asa will need your guidance more than ever. And I . . ."

I thought of Brinsley, in Calliope's dungeons, and my parents, back in Thebe. Much needed restoring. Before I built a new family with Dorian, I wanted to try and repair my original one. "There are things I must put in order before I come home."

"Home," Dorian echoed, with considerable pleasure at my use of the word. But he appeared to have guessed my reasons. "Then when you come, Seph, bring them with you. Your family will always be welcome in Maera."

"Truly?"

"Truly." His eyes sparkled again. "It will be a long year, you know," he mused, fingering the locks that now reached past my shoulders. "And you should know by now that I'm not a patient man."

"I promise I will be yours as soon as my hair is the length of a freewoman's." I grinned.

"It is long enough now." He grinned back.

A stirring came from the corner of the garden, and we both turned to look. A nightingale balanced on the rim of the fountain, flashing brown, buff, red, and white as his eyes darted from side to side. A rather plain bird, when one considered the other birds in the world, but when he opened his mouth to sing, we were enthralled. For no other songbird sang with such purity, such beauty . . . such power.

"Exquisite," Dorian breathed, and I couldn't help but agree.

A sudden breeze sent the papers flying across the garden, and we ran to retrieve them, laughing. A dusty boot print had marked the middle of one page, while some of the others were crumpled or torn. One page went further than most, threatening to leave the garden altogether.

A tall man trapped it with his boot, then leaned down to pluck it from the ground. Dorian and I stopped in our tracks to look at him, our mouths falling open as we observed the man's weighted shoulders, his travel-worn clothes, and his weary-but-sincere smile. My hand flew to my mouth as I gasped.

"Am I very late?" he asked mildly. "I seem to have missed a large battle."

"Bas!" Dorian's voice was overjoyed, and he ran to enfold his bodyguard in a tight embrace.

Tears tracked down Bas's dusty cheeks. As they stepped apart, Dorian clasped Bas's shoulder. Bas did the same to Dorian. "I once said I was willing to die for you, you know. And as it turned out, I was. But"—Bas winked—"I never said I wouldn't come back."

He turned to me with that smile and extended his arms, one hand holding the paper he'd trapped.

I stepped into his embrace. "Bas."

In the wind, I heard Aedon's voice, rich and warm as it enfolded us in a peace that would never fade, a song of unending joy as deep as Memoria itself.

It was good to be back.

Dorian stood on the stone balcony, tilting his face to the warm breeze, inhaling lungful after lungful of the clear mountain air. It smelled faintly of pine, gently bruised mint, and the jasmine that grew in abundance in Maera. But the longer he stood there, basking in the beauty he had once so readily called his home, the more a yearning built in his chest. A yearning for a meadow whose grass would never wither or succumb to heavy frost, a summer that would not give way to autumn and winter, a Garden which would endure forever.

The Aeternum. Their real home.

Aedon had been true to his word. The white raven—or stallion, as he sometimes appeared—had not abandoned them. All those months, he had been there, overseeing every meeting, listening to every exchange, and Sephone, Asa, and Spartan all swore that it was the same for them. Dorian had yet to determine how the bird could be in so many places at once.

They hadn't returned to the island; Dorian wasn't sure if they still could. But each of them still carried their bottles, full of a liquid that never ran dry, no matter how deeply it was drunk or how extensively it was emptied. It was Spartan who had discovered that the vials could be used to fill others, and as word of Aedon spread from Calliope to the Mysterium, from the Mysterium to the rest of Memosine, from Memosine to Lethe, and Lethe to Marianthe, it was not just the four of them who drank daily from the second pool.

"Dorian? You're up early."

A pair of slender arms twined around his waist, causing his heart to put on a burst of speed. He turned in Sephone's embrace to face her. Her hair had grown nearly to her waist and now tumbled about her shoulders in disarray.

"Good morning, Lady Adamo," said Dorian, planting a featherlight kiss on her lips. "Or is it Lady Nightingale?"

"Lady Adamo," she murmured, her eyes sparking. "Shouldn't you know that, given it was you who gave me the ring last month?" She held up her hand; the white gem in her silver band winked in the pre-dawn light.

"Aye, so I did." He held her closer, and they turned together to watch the sunrise.

Sunrises in this part of the world had always been beautiful, but Dorian had begun to notice changes. The sun appeared stronger, and the days seemed longer, even in winter. At sunset, the sky boasted a palette of colors more vivid than any *alter*. It was the same in Calliope and the other places Dorian had travelled. The gray had begun to recede from the world, allowing light—real, constant light—to filter in for the first time in years.

"Have you given any more thought to Spartan and Asa's request?" Sephone asked.

It had been a busy year. Asa and Spartan had proved to be wise leaders despite their relative youth, and it was largely thanks to their guidance that the fractures between Memosine, Lethe, and Marianthe had begun to mend. The new peace had been welcomed by most, especially the slaves who gained their freedom under the brothers' rule.

And though Dorian had thought his influence minimal, especially after the other positions on the Council were filled, he had been taken aback when Spartan had requested to be known not as Jerome Karthick, but Jerome Ashwood. Having long seen the young man as nearly a son, Dorian had heartily agreed. And, with Sephone's blessing, Dorian had formally adopted him.

The term of their rule was now up, and the two brothers had come to Dorian in Maera, the day before he and Sephone were wed. Dorian had been a thane, so he was eligible for the arch-lordship. They had offered Dorian their personal nominations and heartfelt support. Would he claim the position?

"Aye," Dorian said to Sephone. "I have given it more thought, and I think it is time to begin the quest Aedon gave us."

She nodded, smiling. "I've been studying the maps in the library at Calliope. There are worlds beyond Caldera, you know. Many worlds, with many languages. Worlds where a *calor* and a *luminare* may share what they have learned beneath the gray."

He stroked her hair back from her face. "And what of you?"

"What of me, Dorian?"

"You came to me, bringing your family with you. How can I take you away from them again?"

While Dorian had travelled extensively throughout Caldera as the personal emissary of the arch-lords, Sephone had been busy. Since Brinsley was a Lethean, Lady Xia had brought him back to Thebe to stand trial, and Sephone had gone with her brother. She was a *luminare*, so she would fill her parents' and brother's hearts with the truth of her love for them.

Though Dorian knew they would never be the family she had wanted them to be, much of the bond between them had been restored. Faint recollections emerged, such as Damae holding Sephone as a baby and Odiseas teaching her as a little girl to spell his rather troublesome name. And after Lady Xia pardoned Brinsley on Sephone's request, Sephone had brought them back to Maera for her and Dorian's wedding, hoping they would find a home in the mountain city so similar to their beloved Nyx.

Kaesi had also been pardoned, though she hadn't returned to Maera. Dorian had spoken with her as much as he could before she left Calliope, but still she pushed Dorian and their family away. Rumors abounded of a shapeshifting wolf who patrolled the mountains surrounding Maera, keeping its people safe from animals more dangerous than she. Dorian still hoped for the day when she would return as the sister he had once known.

And he knew Sephone hoped so, too.

In the meantime, fresh joys abounded. A short while after Regis returned from Marianthe with his newly freed brothers, Magritte had given birth to a daughter, who she and Regis named Persephone, in honor of their friend. And, at the end of that year, the past was laid to rest, and a new future embraced. Dorian had buried his chain with its rings beside Lida's and Emmy's graves, and he'd been touched when Sephone asked to visit them the day of the wedding. He had watched, love swelling in his heart, as she laid her bouquet and pendant on top of their graves.

He had thought he knew her, understood her. But every day, she surprised him with some hidden quality he hadn't yet observed, a lovely depth he was still to plumb. Like light itself, it was impossible to view one of its many faces and conclude you had seen them all.

Was that what the Aeternum was like? And the Three?

Sephone simply smiled. "I am home with you, Dorian. We are family. And we have both come home to Aedon. Life will be fuller and brighter from now on. Not easy, nay, but we have a richer home in Aedon. We will never be alone."

Aye, they wouldn't be alone. Dorian would make his apologies to Spartan and Asa, but they would do well to rule for a second term. Meanwhile, ambassadorial duties awaited. The world beyond Caldera—beyond the outlands, even—was still in shadow. Wherever the gray had infiltrated, they would go.

Once, Dorian had thought his life was over. And it had been; he could still see the marks on his skin where the poison had infiltrated his body. But now, thanks to Aedon, he was alive. They were alive. Fully alive.

And at long last, Dorian Ashwood, Lord Adamo, former thane of Maera, and Persephone Winter, *luminare* of Nulla, were truly free.

"For now we see only a reflection as in a mirror;
then we shall see face to face. Now I know in part;
then I shall know fully, even as I am fully known.
And now these three remain: faith, hope and love.
But the greatest of these is love."

1 Corinthians 13:12-13 (NIV)

AUTHOR'S NOTE

Avid fans of ancient languages such as Greek and Latin may notice that the word "Aedon," while meaning "nightingale," carries a feminine association. Please note it is not my intention to suggest in any way that the Persons of the Trinity are feminine in nature—the name "Aedon" was chosen purely for creative reasons, and I personally adhere to the Bible's use of masculine pronouns to characterize God.

ACKNOWLEDGMENTS

Of the three books in this trilogy, *Memoria* was by far the hardest to write. In 2021, when I was halfway through the first draft, my husband was unexpectedly diagnosed with lymphoma (cancer of the lymph nodes). We'd gone through hard seasons before with my chronic illness and several acute illnesses, but Dave's cancer completely blindsided us. We were in the middle of a worldwide pandemic, in one of the harshest lockdowns our state of New South Wales (Australia) had yet seen, largely isolated from family and friends. And while I'd just received a diagnosis for my chronic condition some months prior, recurring migraines made it difficult for me to reliably drive Dave to and from chemotherapy sessions.

But God provides, and He is always at his strongest when we are weakest. My husband came through the cancer treatment into remission, I was able to drive him to almost all of his chemo sessions, and eventually, I picked up the threads of *Memoria* again. This story, which first took root amidst working through the trauma of my work as a psychologist and the impending deaths of two of my grandparents, was concluded against the backdrop of other types of hardships.

I share all this to say that the dark, soul-sucking, clingy ickiness of the pool of Memoria is not just an abstract idea for me, but a creative, storied representation of the pain (and also sinfulness) of my own life. I imagine you have your own version of Memoria, filled with things you've done and awful things that have been done to you. You might not even have shared these things with anyone before.

But, dear friend, I want you to know that Jesus sees you, and loves you. He will not leave you gasping on the shores of Memoria, spluttering for breath as the poison works its way through your veins. Instead, He wades into Memoria to draw out the poison from your chest and give you a new life, a life beyond the darkness of a subterranean grave filled with sparkling sunshine, vibrant love, and soul-transforming hope. In this life, at least, the scars of poisonous Memoria may remain. But beneath the light of eternity, they will fade.

As Psalm 56:8 says: "You keep track of all my sorrows. You have collected all my tears in your bottle. You have recorded each one in your book" (NLT). Not one drop of pain in your Memoria has gone unseen, my friend. It is lovingly counted by a God who promises to one day wipe every tear from your eyes (Revelation 21:4).

As always, it's impossible to make mention of all the people who have shaped this trilogy to be what it is and who have invested in me as an author, but I'll take a stab . . .

To Kirk DouPonce—thank you for an utterly magical, transporting series of covers that still make me sigh dreamily even after all this time. *Pinches self for assurance this is still real*

To Stacey Glemboski, whose narration brought the world of Caldera and its characters to life. Readers endlessly tell me how much they love your narration!

To those wonderful authors who took the time to endorse each of this trilogy's installments, and to all those who've read and reviewed the books and raved about them on social media etc.

To my amazing cover reveal and street teams for each book, who've gone above and beyond to spread the word—you guys rock!

To the team at Enclave and Oasis Family Media (Steve Laube, Lisa Laube, Sarah Grimm, Megan Gerig, Trissina Kear, Jamie Foley, Lindsay Franklin, Charmagne Kaushal, and others) . . . there is no publisher quite like Enclave, and you guys are quite simply out of this world. Thanks for taking a chance on not one but *three* books of mine!

To my special author friends who champion each book as it comes out, and send me many messages of encouragement and support that keep my head above the proverbial raging waters: Cathy McCrumb, Misi Troutman, Marian Jacobs, Sara Davison . . . and more.

To my amazing family, who have supported me through what will soon be the release of *eight* books (!). This book is dedicated to my Mum and Dad (Guido and Lucy) in particular, who have shown immense support for my writing, and who faithfully read every book I write. From childhood, you've nurtured in me a love of stories and literature, and I thank you so much for always having my back (and never telling me to get a "real job").

To my husband Dave, my personal hero. Thanks for fighting by my side and subconsciously influencing all my heroes to reflect little (okay, fairly sizable) pieces of you.

And finally, to my great God, who has carried my husband and me through all our trials, and sent His Son to brave Memoria so we could live. Thanks for being the very best of Authors . . . and the true Nightingale of our hearts.

Soli Deo Gloria,

Jasmine

P.S. Dear readers: if you've borne with me through all this rambling, I have a surprise treat for you. Cass's story is . . . not over yet. ;) Look out for a follow-up sequel/companion novel to the trilogy releasing in 2025, finishing off Cass's, Spartan's, and Kaesi's stories. Cass does a wonderful job as the leading man (okay, he takes over the story completely and I was simply holding on for dear life throughout), and I think you're going to enjoy his adventure very much. Also, if you're still grieving about Cass not ending up with Sephone, I can reassure you that Cass's love interest is *perfect* for him!

ABOUT THE AUTHOR

Jasmine's writing dream began with the anthology of zoo animals she painstakingly wrote and illustrated at age five, to rather limited acclaim. Thankfully, her writing (but not her drawing) has improved since then. Jasmine began writing her first proper novel at age fourteen, which eventually became her debut fantasy series, The Darcentaria Duology, which was published in 2021.

Jasmine completed her Bachelor's in English Literature and Creative Writing in 2012. Also a qualified psychologist with undergraduate and postgraduate degrees in clinical psychology, Jasmine's dream is to write stories that weave together her love for Jesus, her passion for mental health, and her struggles with chronic illness.

When she isn't killing defenseless houseplants, Jasmine enjoys devouring books, dabbling in floristry, playing the piano, eating peanut butter out of the jar, and wishing it rained more often. Jasmine is married to David, and together they make their home a couple of hours' north of Sydney, Australia, where they live to satisfy the every whim of their ginger overlord cat, Simba.

You can stalk Jasmine on social media or visit her official website at www.jjfischer.com, where she's always open to swapping good memes, talking about chickens, or complaining about Luke Skywalker.